# HEAVEN HELP ME . . .

I froze. The ground began to throb below the great feet as the tyrant approached, growing larger with a terrifying swiftness, coming straight for us. From the corner of my eye I saw the fearsome silver head against the sky when it passed behind the mast of the chariot. A rank animal stench stung my nostrils.

The angel raised his club to his shoulder, but backward—the wooden part against his shoulder, the long metal handle pointing up at the monster's head. *Thunder!* Startled, I lost my balance. A moment after I hit the ground, so did the tyrant, and the whole world seemed to bounce.

By Dave Duncan
*Published by Ballantine Books:*

A ROSE-RED CITY

SHADOW

*The Seventh Sword*
THE RELUCTANT SWORDSMAN
THE COMING OF WISDOM
THE DESTINY OF THE SWORD

WEST OF JANUARY

# WEST OF JANUARY

## Dave Duncan

A Del Rey Book

BALLANTINE BOOKS • NEW YORK

Library of Congress Catalog Card Number: 89-90748

ISBN 0-345-35836-8

Manufactured in the United States of America

First Edition: August 1989

# Table of Contents

The probe telemetry was wrong! Close, but not close enough—the damned thing's not locked on the star as we thought. Revolution—264.6 days; rotation—263.6. Not much of a difference, is it?

But do you realize what that does to all our plans?

*Mike Angeli, Planetologist,*
*Colonization Expedition*

We named the ship well, didn't we—the *Mayflower*? With a hundred years of daylight, we're all going to be mayflies!

*Celeste Gabriel, Sociologist,*
*Colonization Expedition*

For a thousand years in thy sight are but as yesterday when it is past, and as a watch in the night. Thou carriest them away as with a flood; they are as a sleep: in the morning they are like grass which groweth up. In the morning it flourisheth, and groweth up; in the evening it is cut down, and withereth. . . .

So teach us to number our days that we may apply our hearts unto wisdom.

*Psalms 90*

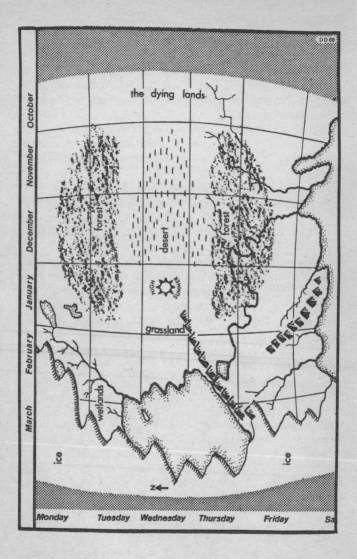

# 1

## The Herdfolk

I was still very young when I first saw an angel, yet so great was the impression made upon me by his visit that it remains as my earliest memory, like a most distant tree at the limit of vision on an empty plain. Or so it seems, for all I truly remember are a few vague images enclosed in mist, recalled in later times. Inevitably the details have smeared and become entangled with details of other visits by other angels, when I was older and better able to understand. Even that first time, though, tiny as I must have been, I was disturbed and troubled. What I recall most clearly is a small child's sense of injustice and betrayal.

The herdfolk divide a man's life into five stages, and then I barely could have reached the second, the toddler stage. I can retrieve no other specific event from those far-off times, only a general blur of memory, the soil that nurtured my infant roots. All the landscapes have merged into the endless rolling grassland of my youth, and all weather has become the constant golden sunshine of childhood.

Certainly that sunshine was spotted by showers. Certainly among the little hills lay innumerable sloughs and watering holes, set in their guardian clutters of cotton trees. It was by those that we camped. But again all those are merged, one into another. I remember sitting in my mother's tent, listening to

3

rain and the thump of cloth beating in the wind, spraying me with a fine mist. I remember playing on the edges of wide stretches of blue water, immeasurably vast to a toddler. And yet all storms are now one storm in my mind, all rainbows one rainbow, all lakes one lake. In truth those little ponds were larger then, for they did dwindle as I grew, but to the small eyes of a small child they seemed most terrifyingly huge and clear and shiny.

Angels were the only visitors the herdfolk trusted or made welcome. They honored angels, admiring their lonely courage and self-reliance, valuing the information and counsel that an angel could bring, his advice and his warnings. In return, they freely offered their humble hospitality—food and shelter and safe rest.

I do not recall the angel's arrival. I do not know who first noticed him coming. Most likely it was my father, for little escaped his notice by land or sky. We may have been camped, or we may have been on the move, but if that was the case, then the tents would have been pitched again at once.

The earliest of all my memories is of that angel sitting at my father's side, cross-legged on cushions on a rug. Behind them were the tents—four of them, for at that time my father owned four women. Later he had six, and when I was a herdboy I was proud of his wealth, but when the angel came he had but four. The rug, the tents, and the cushions were all made of wool from our own herd, all striped and checkered in saffron and scarlet and vermilion, eye-nipping bright in the harsh white sunshine, squatting on small puddles of black shadow.

The visitor must have alarmed me already to have made such an impression. He was a great contrast to my father, for like all herdmen my father was enormous. He outweighed any two of his women, and even sitting he towered over the angel. In fine weather he wore only riding boots and leather breeches. He had little need for a shirt to protect him from the sun, for his thick black hair flowed down to mingle with the dense fur on his shoulders and back. His great beard merged into the pelt on his chest and belly. In only a few places, such as the sides of his ribs and the undersides of his forearms, was any of my father's walnut skin ever visible.

The angel, in contrast, was blond and slight. His face was

clean-shaven and ruddy. His boots and even his breeches may have seemed unexceptional to my childish gaze, but his upper half was enclosed in a leather shirt, open down the front because of the heat, and decorated with very alarming fringes. He had fringes on his trousers, also, and he carried a broad-brimmed hat. Horrified, I clung to my mother's gown and peered around her as if she were a tree.

Doubtless the crowd of older children had streamed in from the herd to sit wide-eyed, observing the visitor. I do not recall. Doubtless the women had blushed and simpered as they prepared and served the best feast they could assemble. And doubtless, also, each had donned the finest, brightest gown she owned to honor the angel. My father would have expected these things of them.

The meal ended. I recall the four women lining up and my father leading the angel forward to look them over. The tents were at hand. My father would have made the customary offer.

Vividly I recall my terror when the angel's eyes met mine. They were a brilliant blue, and I had never seen blue eyes before. I buried my face in my mother's dress.

Of course this monster did not want me. My mother was the youngest. I expect she had already recovered her figure after bearing my sister Rilana. My brother Uldinth may well have been conceived by then, but not showing yet. Obediently she set off toward her tent, and the stranger followed.

My aunt Amby scooped me up and held me. I screamed at my mightiest pitch. I do not need memory to tell me that, for a herdfolk toddler was never separated from his mother, even when his father came to her tent. Older children were banned at those times, lest they snigger or be tempted to copy the games their elders played, but among themselves the herdfolk were not prudish about mere toddlers. An angel, though, was an honored guest, who would normally have been granted privacy to enjoy his rest and recreation.

Yet in this case, I was released. The angel stood aside, and I rushed for the tent flap as fast as my stumpy legs would take me. That was unusual, and the angel himself must have interceded on my behalf.

And the image that follows is the clearest of all—of my small self sitting on the rug in a corner of my mother's tent, sucking my thumb, watching the angel take his pleasure with her. Certainly I must have seen my father do that many times, yet I have no recollection of doing so. I have only a vague memory of the details. I assume that the angel's methods were quite orthodox. I doubt that the actions bothered me, the urgent movements, the moans and gasps of pleasure. I must have known that those were normal. The tent was hot and dim. The lovers' bodies moved in spangles of color as the sun shone through the cloth. I remember the setting clearly, for it was my home.

What remains most strongly in my memory is the sense of wrongness. This was not my huge and dark-furred father. This smaller, smooth, pink person did not belong there on my mother, and somehow my young mind resented him. When he had done, when they were at peace again together, soaked and panting, my mother stretched out an arm for me. I remember that. Probably it was her custom at such times to reassure her child that he was loved also, to cuddle him in between my father and herself. I have vague half memories of warmth and closeness, of soft breast on one side, of hard and shaggy chest on the other, of sweat and thumping hearts.

This time, I know, I refused her summons and shrank away. I remember the stranger raising his head to smile at me—and again his brilliant, terrifying, blue-blue eyes.

He slept, then—being an angel is a tiring business. My mother lay and held him, and I stayed in the corner. Perhaps I slept also. I think that he made love to her again when he awoke, and that again I refused their offer of comfort afterward. Then he dressed and departed. Quite likely he was fed a second time before he raised sail. That also was the custom.

He never returned, that blue-eyed, golden-haired angel. It would have been astonishing if he had. But I am sure that that was not his first visit to my father's tents. I remember his smooth-skinned pinkness, his smallness, his smile, and his uncanny bright-blue eyes, but I cannot recall his face.

I have a clear memory of the way he lifted his head from my mother's breast to speak to me. I do remember his smile. But the face that memory insists on putting there is the face I would see when I was older, in a mirror. My hair was golden once. My eyes, also, are a brilliant blue.

\* \* \*

I was born somewhere in the west of January, probably near the middle of Wednesday. I cannot locate the spot more closely. Even if I knew it exactly—even if there was a bronze tablet there to record the event—I could not name it for you. In Heaven they tell of other worlds than Vernier; they tell how the people on some of those worlds give names to places. I found that idea almost as incomprehensible as the measurement of time. People or even animals could have names, I thought, but not places, and on Vernier place names would be a useless exercise anyway. Until the saints taught me otherwise, I had little concept of time or space. "Now" and "here" were all I knew.

The angels define the world by strips—twelve strips running north and south, seven east and west. The names of these are very old, given by the firstfolk. It is a sensible arrangement, with only nineteen words to be learned. Any place can be located by reference to this grid. The west of January is but one example. Geographical features can be named also, like the March Ocean or the Wednesday Desert. This is much easier than remembering an endless arbitrary list, and much more practical when a forest may soon become a desert, or a desert ocean.

There are a few exceptions. There is the Great River, which flowed in one direction in my youth, in the other later, and now flows not at all. The larger mountain ranges have names—Urals, Alps, and Andes. The saints in Heaven tell of greater yet, the Himalayas, which will not reappear until after I am gone. There is the South Ocean, which is at times little more than a sea, and the North Icecap, which is always an icecap, although it waxes and wanes. Even Heaven moves.

It is of the angels that I would speak, yet here I am rambling along in old man's style about geography and my childhood. I promised to tell you of Heaven and the angels, of how they failed me and I deceived them . . . Well, I shall, but the way there leads through tales of my youth, of hatred earned and love betrayed. I have little to boast of and much that would be better left not said, but I shall tell it all. What cause would I have to lie to you now?

The world is a hard place, and I have done my share to make it so.

I have told of my birth and toddlerhood. Toddlers in turn became herders, and herders . . . herders became loners. I remember when I saw this happen to Kanoran. It must have been a common enough event while I was still too small to realize what was happening. Now I understood better, either because I was older or because I was especially fond of Kanoran. He was kind to me, often stopping the others when they mocked my sun-bleached hair and azure eyes. Like my earlier vision of the angel, Kanoran's departure stands out in my memories like a single stormcloud in a clear sky.

We had just completed a move. Wednesday-in-January is an icefield now, but in my youth it was all rolling grassland—baking hot, mostly, and growing hotter. In fact it was insufferably hot, but we were used to it and knew no better. The low hills were frequently stony and rough, all heaped and jumbled without pattern; many of the hollows held swamps or ponds.

The herd was always grazed in a spiral outward from the camp. When the distance became too great, four out of the two hundred or so would be routed back to serve as baggage animals, and the rest dispatched in whatever direction my father dictated. Each of his women would gather up her few possessions and her tent, put them on a travois and the travois on a woollie, and set off with her toddlers and her current baby.

As always my father had chosen our next campsite in a small hollow where there was standing water. Woollies need no water, but people do, and so did his precious horses—herdfolk have no dogs, because roos eat them. The slough would give us drink, the trees shade and firewood. There would be birds to net, birds' nests to raid, and sharp-eyed herder slingmen would soon locate the nearest miniroo warren.

This, I think, had been an unusually long trek, or else I was a very young herder still, for I had been allowed to ride part of the way on one of the baggage woollies. But we had arrived at last. My father had ridden in also, having satisfied himself that no dangers lurked in the vicinity. I was jumping up and down in my eagerness to rush over to the new pond and fall in, for we youngsters lived more in the water than out of it, but before anything else happened, the whole family had to give thanks to the Almighty for leading us safely to this haven. That meant that we had to wait for the older children, who were bringing up the herd. Woollies cannot be hurried.

Native to the hot lands of Wednesday, woollies seldom stray

even into the southern edges of Tuesday. For all their enormous size, they are very primitive. Their dense siliceous coats maintain the high body temperature they need and also protect them from predators. Woollies never move faster than a walk, but they never stop moving—rounded stacks of gray wool, eating constantly, crawling endlessly over the landscape, with only a short pink snout protruding at the front. They have three small eyes in the snout, although they see poorly. Turn the snout with a stick, and the woollie will change direction.

The woollies loomed as large in my childhood as the unbounded land itself, or the burning-metal sky. I took them all equally for granted, essential components of a world.

At last the herd crept into view over a distant ridge. The herders came running in to join us, and my father called for the first hymn. After that he led us in prayer, then a second hymn. We children sang almost all the time, but his strong bass voice inevitably reminded me of thunder. Our faith was simple, a Heavenly Father who must be obeyed. If we were good we would go to Paradise, else to Hell. I grew up believing that Paradise must be very much like the grasslands, with a plentiful supply of dashers for food and miniroos for sport. Hell, I had been informed, was cold and dark. As I had never met either cold or dark, my ideas of Hell were vague. It mattered little, for we had few opportunities to be bad.

As soon as the service was ended, we small ones raced off to enjoy our bath. Some older children were sent to guide the herd again, for woollies are too stupid to be natural herd animals and would scatter like seeds if left unattended. Several boys headed for a nearby miniroo warren to launch a massacre—looking back, I am sure that they benefited more from the exercise than from any meat they caught, although a miniroo is a tasty treat when spitted, charred over hot coals, and eaten whole —and the women had a fire to build, tents to pitch, and screaming children to feed. Babies were always raised on woollie milk, so that their mothers could conceive again as soon as possible.

When I came dripping back to report on the pond, I found Aunt Amby and my mother just about to milk one of the baggage woollies before it was returned to the herd. They had enlisted the aid of Kanoran, largest of the boys. Each took a travois pole, thrust it under the beast, and heaved. It always seemed like a miracle that human muscles could move such a mass, but the woollie slowly toppled over on its side. As long as its snout was then held off the ground, it was helpless and could be milked—unless it contained a dasher. This one did.

Pink and hairless and incredibly fast over short distances, the dashers are the woollies' males. They live on milk from the rear teat—the front teat is for the young—and they have no teeth. They do, however, have truly vicious claws. A dasher roasted is the finest feast in all Vernier, and catching them was the greatest sport in our childhood. Like all herdmen, I still bear its scars. The wounds can easily go bad, and I lost several brothers to the game; my sisters always seemed to have more sense.

Of course, the dasher did what dashers always do—streaked to the nearest woollie to take cover. As often happens, there was already another in residence. One or the other—they cannot be told apart until they start wounding each other—emerged at once and headed for another woollie. The procedure was due to be repeated until the refugee found a vacancy or was killed, but in this case Kanoran made a wild leap and threw himself on the second dasher—or on the first dasher at its second appearance, perhaps—and expertly snapped its neck before it clawed him to shreds.

To kill a dasher single-handed was a noble feat. He delivered his prey proudly to the cooks and then went strutting around, letting us lesser folks admire his gashes while they were still bleeding. And admire we did, secretly wishing we had some like them. The girls started singing a hero's song.

Milk and woollie meat were our staple diet. Roast dasher was our delicacy. Soon everyone not herding had drawn close, tugged by that seductive odor. Even my father, who had been grooming his horses, came striding over, the currycomb still in his hand.

We all rose, of course, even the toddlers. One of the women said timorously that the feast was not quite ready yet, but my father ignored her. He was staring hard at Kanoran, as if he had been overlooking him recently. Proud hero shrank into cowering boy beneath that fearsome gaze.

"Raise your arms, lad."

Kanoran obeyed in silence, a guilty pallor seeping into his face. One of the women—his mother, I suppose—choked back a sob at what was then revealed, and I think it was that more than anything else that imprinted the scene on my memory. I was certainly too young to understand what terrible sin had been committed. The meal was forgotten. My father glanced at Aunt Ulith, and the distress in her face disturbed me even more.

"Olliana, sir?" she whispered.

He thought for a moment, then nodded. He led the trembling Kanoran aside. They walked together up a nearby hillock. They sat down and talked. My father talked, and his son listened.

He was a good man. Some herdmen take the word "loner" at its literal meaning. I saw this done later, but my father was not so cruel. Indeed he was generous. I do not know what facts of life were imparted in those talks, for I never received one, but I suppose only the obvious—sex and how it worked; custom and dangers; angels, perhaps, and traders; and certainly the incest taboo, for the herdfolk take that rule very seriously.

When the long talk was ended, Olliana was waiting, dressed in a fine new wool robe of many colors. On her back she carried a bundle that the women had made up for her—food, I expect, a knife, and a pot maybe, and tinder. Eyes downcast, she walked at her brother's heel as he left the camp.

However much his inner self may have quaked, Kanoran bore his head up bravely as he walked away into the world. He did not look back at us sobbing children. He wore only his calf-length woolen pagne. He carried only a sling. But he was allowed to take four woollies, and two people could live easily on the milk from four woollies. Some fathers gave more than four then, but few gave a woman, as well. In those times a woman was worth ten or a dozen woollies. Later, the price dropped to one or two.

Woollies move slowly, and the tiny herd was visible for a long time, trailing slowly away over the ridges. The boy and girl beside them were smaller, and vanished sooner.

I saw this happen again many times, as my brothers and half-brothers grew older—footprints on my trek through childhood. My father, I suppose, was aging, and thus his family also. Puberty rites came more frequently as I grew to be a herder—helping the older children at first, then teaching youngsters in my turn. Never did we think of herding as work. It was what life was. Children herded woollies. Women cooked and made babies. They also spun wool, they wove and dyed and sewed cloth. Men . . . but we had only one man to study.

He was never idle, never at peace. Mostly he rode his horses, each in turn, tiring them long before he tired himself, and end-lessly scouting the countryside for signs of strangers—strangers were dangers. Of course we children did not know that. I re-member him returning once with blood on him. The women told us that he had fallen, but probably he had taken an arrow.

He wore boots and leather breeches. In wet weather he would add a poncho and a broad-brimmed hat. A knife hung at his belt, a sword and bow by his saddle. He practiced his archery often, letting us boys watch him and run to retrieve his shafts, but never allowing us to try for ourselves. Slingshots we were permitted—indeed, we were encouraged to become proficient with them. A sling is a good weapon against small game and predators, but only at close range. Arrows carry farther. Thus he taught us the principle of archery, but withheld the skill. He never explained the reason for that, and we should not have believed him if he had.

His face I can still see clearly, but always outlined against the roof of a tent or against the sky. His hair and beard were dark and flowing, and the glitter of his black eyes was the terror of my dreams. More imposing than anything else in my existence, even the landscape itself, my father ruled his family without raising voice or hand. No one ever hesitated or questioned. He was impassive and rarely spoke, but by the standards of the herdfolk he was a good man. He must have had a name, but I don't know what it was.

He spent much of his life on horseback, scouting the land in all directions. A horse is a four-legged, two-eyed mammal, much smaller than a woollie, but much faster. Horses are another symbol of wealth, and eventually my father had three of them.

So we knew that children grew larger, and we knew what women did, and we boys respectfully studied my father. As I said before, he was a good man by his own standards. He was kind to me, without cause. Disposing of unwanted babies is an ancient and widespread human custom, but he had let me be, although he must have known I was not his. I was always small for a boy. I had gold hair and blue eyes, unlike everyone else in the family.

No, he was not my father, but I can think of him in no other way. I used to think his name was "Sir," until I heard him use that word himself to a trader.

Traders were rare, although more common than angels. We saw their caravans only from afar, and their womenfolk not at all. Likewise, whenever traders were around, my father would order his older daughters and his women into the tents. Trading was done on neutral ground, with us boys trotting to and fro, carrying out the cloth or yarn my father sold, bringing in the wares he bought. I remember it as being hard work, for woollie wool is heavy. I envied those wealthy traders with their many horses.

Traders seemed very small men to us herders, but very grandly dressed. Their shirts were exploding rainbows of color, their trousers garishly decorated with beadwork and piping. They wore short, pointed beards, and hats with curled brims, and jeweled swords dangling at their sides.

Small or not, they frightened me—I was scared my father would trade me off for something. That is not so foolish as it sounds, for the traders often had girls to offer. He bought his fifth woman, Rantarath, from traders. I was old enough to notice how much cloth she cost, and young enough to think she could not possibly be worth it. But my father never sold off his surplus daughters—he gave them away to his sons, which in a herdman was true generosity. What he did trade was cloth and wool. In exchange he acquired pots and tools, dyestuffs and medicines . . . a new sword once, I recall . . . a better horse. Our needs were simple.

The sun always shone. Rain became scarce as I grew older. Life continued with few interruptions to mark its passing. We ate when we were hungry and slept when we were sleepy—outdoors, curled up on the sun-warmed grass by the tents. Except on a move, there would always be some of us asleep and some awake, but the life of the camp continued regardless—children singing, pots clattering, the click of looms, the crack of wood chopping, the laughter of the toddlers.

Only when my father was sleeping were we told to keep quiet. He never slept alone. He honored each tent in turn, playing no favorite—unless, of course, a woman was due to conceive again and needed special attention. It might seem like a very fine life for a man, if the risks were not considered.

He knew the risks and he took precautions. He scouted far, studying the grass to see where other herds might have passed recently. He watched, too, for roo packs, although once in a while roos would slip by him and come bounding through the camp, hoping to catch an undefended toddler. Woollies were armored against roos, but we were not. Often my father would return with a dead roo dangling by his saddle and a bloodstained arrow in his quiver. Roo meat was second only to dasher in flavor, and their leather is the finest of all.

Those roo attacks were landmarks in an otherwise uniform existence. There were few others—visits by angels or traders, other herds passing in the far distance. And puberty.

My older brothers and sisters disappeared, two by two. Imperceptibly I became one of the oldest. Traders became rarer and angels more common. Trouble is angels' business. They knew what was happening. They must have told my father, but he may not have believed.

We children certainly knew nothing of that. I had been born in January, when the sun had been over the January–December line, roughly. Now we were into February, and the sun stood high to the east, apparently motionless and unchanging. Yet the winds grew lighter, ponds rarer, rain less frequent. The grass was sparser, more grazed by other herds; dungheaps were more numerous. My father must have been finding greater and greater difficulty in directing our progress.

On the face of it, he was prospering. He had more woollies for milk and meat. More food would support more women to breed more children to herd more woollies. The other herdfolk prospered also.

But the sun does move, and ahead of us lay the March Ocean— and inevitable disaster.

## 2

We had no way to measure time except by eating and sleeping. What clock could be less reliable than a growing boy's stomach? Yet four landmarks defined the end of my childhood, and they seem in retrospect to have stood very close together.

My oldest brother, Aloxth, had gone. The next, Indarth, would soon follow him out into the great world. Being one of the older lads now, I was aware of what must happen, but it worried me as little as death, for it seemed as remote. Yet the time came when I discovered Indarth cowering behind a woollie, sobbing in terror. He showed me the damning evidence he had just discovered, and I swore not to tell. Yet I spared him little sympathy, for we two had never been close. Indeed I obtained some amusement from noting how thereafter he avoided my father's presence, and how he held his elbows close to his sides, trying at the same time to disguise the increasing breadth of his shoulders. His sense of guilt must have been obvious to the adults, and probably all the other loners in their turn had done the same. As I have said, our father was a kindly man, and he always gave his sons as much time to grow up as decency permitted. Indarth's terror was the first of my four landmarks.

Having no sense of time, I could not comprehend the difference between growing older and growing bigger. I was small and did not appreciate my danger. Talana's son Arrint was larger than I was, so I assumed that he must go next, after Indarth. Then, once, while bathing in the pond, I glanced down at my groin. There have been few events in my long life that frightened me more than seeing that sheen of golden fuzz. Hastily I checked my armpits. So far they were innocent, but I had enough sense of time to know that they must soon follow. Now terror stalked me also, and thereafter I was much less interested in childish behavior such as splashing around in water. That was the second landmark.

The third was the arrival of my father's sixth woman, and this was important to me because I was conscripted to play a part. It gave me a glimpse into men's affairs and a hint of what seemingly lay in store for myself.

My father rode into camp and dismounted, but he did not unsaddle his horse, merely dropping the reins and striding across to the weaving place. The women scrambled hastily to their feet.

"Hanthar?" he said.

"She is sleeping, sir."

"Wake her. Get her ready." He was not a man to waste words. The family buzzed with excitement and bewilderment.

I was eating—small as I was, I had an appetite second to none.

My father glanced around, and his eyes settled on me, who was suddenly no longer hungry. I remember wondering if my pagne was decently in place and doing its job.

"Knobil!"

"Yes, sir?"

"You will come also. And help me." Then he added an unusually long speech: "You will be coming back, so don't worry."

Help him? That was unprecedented. I suppose I swelled with pride and flashed arrogant glances at the others. I can see now that he had chosen me because I seemed younger than my true age, and therefore relatively harmless. Fortunately for my self-esteem, I did not know that then.

There were no emotional farewells—or, if there were, they were made within the tents. My father rode. Hanthar walked on one side of him in her new gown, bearing a bundle on her back. I strutted proudly on the other, full of contempt for her foolish silent tears.

It was a long outing and seemed very pointless, for we were retracing our last move. Our own woollies' dung lay everywhere. But when my father unslung his bow and strung it, and thereafter kept it to hand, my self-assurance wavered. Then, after a wearisome trek below the merciless sun, we crested a ridge and saw our objective on the next hill—two woollies and two people.

My father reined in his horse. "Go to him, Knobil. Tell him: If he wishes to trade, he is welcome. Else he must depart."

I did not fully understand, but I ran.

The newcomers waited for me, turning their woollies so that they did not approach closer. I ran so hard that I had almost no breath to speak when I came up to them, but by then I had realized that I was facing a boy little older than myself and a girl very much like Hanthar. Probably I then knew what was going to happen, but I would not have understood why, for no one had ever lectured me on the incest taboo.

I gasped out my message. The boy seemed as nervous as I was, but he nodded. "I come to trade," he said.

There was a moment's pause, for neither of us knew what should happen next, then I turned and started running back. I saw my father and his daughter start down the slope toward me.

He had left his horse and weapons on the ridgetop. The boy and girl came behind me, and all five of us met in the marshy hollow.

My father must have seemed like a very terrible hairy giant to the lad, who was quivering like the grass dancing in the wind. He quickly gabbled out a speech, obviously well rehearsed and probably taken word for word from that father-to-son lecture that I was never to hear.

"I offer my sister Jalinan, a woman unspoiled, well trained, and of good stock, suitably furnished."

My father waited, and then prompted, "Show me."

The boy nudged his sister angrily and pointed at her bundle, lying now at her feet. She knelt to unfasten it.

I had never heard my father's voice softer. "Not that. Her."

Blushing furiously at his error, the boy ordered his sister to strip, trying to help her with inexpert hands. Solemnly my father inspected the trade goods. I suppose he was establishing that the girl was a virgin and had not been a victim of incest. I do not recall what emotions she was showing. I probably did not care, and I was certainly not looking at her face.

He rose. "She is as you state." That sounded like a set speech also. "In trade I offer my daughter Hanthar, who is likewise unspoiled, well trained, and of good stock, suitably furnished."

I had forgotten how to breathe while this was taking place in that little hollow. Marsh worms could have eaten off my toes and I would not have noticed. Now my sister had to remove her clothing also. The boy inspected her briefly, but even then I doubted that he knew what he was looking for. He straightened up, redder than ever, and obviously at a loss. Probably his instruction had not gone as far as this.

A small smile escaped from within my father's beard at that point, one of very few that I can ever remember seeing there. He offered a hand. The boy flinched, and then shook it as if he had never shaken hands before. The girls were hastily dressing.

"Go with this man and serve him well," my father said, giving Hanthar a gentle push. He beckoned to Jalinan. When she stooped to raise her bundle, he told her softly to leave it. "Two woollies are not enough," he said. "I shall send out two more."

"Sir . . . you are most generous." The lad seemed thunderstruck.

"I should not want my daughter to starve," my father said, almost as if that were an admission of weakness.

Hanthar carried the two bundles off, following the boy. My father watched until they were halfway up the hill before turning away himself. He may have been taking a last, sentimental look at his departing chick, or perhaps he was guarding against treachery.

By the time we reached the camp, the women had already erected a sixth tent. My father said only, "This is Jalinan," and handed her over to Amby.

He sent Indarth off with two woollies, then attended to his horse, ignoring the large band of curious onlookers. We boys all wanted to know what would happen next.

What happened next was not very informative. The women had prepared a large and steaming dish of food. I expect Amby had also prepared and instructed Jalinan, who was waiting within the new tent. My father took the dish and entered. The flap closed, shutting out our eyes, if not our imaginations. A couple of my half-brothers claimed to have caught a glimpse of the new woman with no clothes on. I, of course, could brag about my earlier comprehensive overview.

Eventually we lost interest and wandered away to bathe, as boys will, for whatever was happening seemed to be taking a very long time. I expect it was done gently. He was a kindly man, and patient.

That, then, was the third of my four landmarks. Now I knew the ending of the ceremony that began when a boy was ordered to raise his arms. How much time elapsed before the fourth landmark, I cannot say. Not a long time, I think, but long enough for little Jalinan to be accepted as just one more of the women and start to swell into a woman's normal shape.

It happened with no warning. Once again I was by the fire and eating—I have already confessed the appetite I had in my youth. I think I was the first to notice the stranger walking boldly into camp. He was young, with only a shadow of beard; tall, but slender as a dead tree. I remember my astonishment at the thinness and length of his legs. His ragged pagne reached barely to his knees. He had a bulky bundle under one arm and a bow on his shoulder, a much longer bow than my father used. And he carried a sword in his free hand.

The women shrilled in terror and then fell silent as the stranger approached the fire. They rose hesitantly to their feet. We children followed. I remember staring around wildly for my father to defend us, while at the same time wondering if this armed intruder could possibly be an angel.

The youth stopped and looked us over. "Who is senior?" he demanded.

Aunt Amby stumbled forward and sank to her knees.

The newcomer threw down his bundle before her and it fell open. The wrapping was my father's breeches, and the bloody, hairy thing inside it was his head.

# 3

The stranger was very nervous and therefore dangerous, although at the time I understood only the danger.

The rest of the women followed Amby to the ground, prostrating themselves, and of course we children copied them at once. The babes and toddlers did not understand, and the rest of us were too shocked to make a sound. Thus there was silence in the sunlight, broken only by a crackle from the smoky fire and a listless flapping of wind in a loose awning somewhere. I crouched on the grass, staring at my shadow before my nose, trembling uncontrollably. A pair of large, bare, dirty feet walked by me as the newcomer inspected his catch. Eventually I risked an upward glance, and other heads were rising also.

He was very tall and very thin, but his feet and hands were large, his shoulders broad. I was never to learn where he had come from, or how. He had apparently been sent out as a true loner, without woman or woollie, for he did not send any of us to retrieve a herd. Perhaps he had lost them to another; he never saw a need to tell us his history. He must have survived for some time on his own—time enough to grow that haze of beard around his mouth, time for his hair to reach down to his shoulders. Unless his father had taught him more archery than mine ever taught me, this loner would have needed time to learn that also. He must have lived off the land—which explained those conspicuous ribs and the crazy, sunken eyes.

"You!" he snapped. "What's your name?"

I shriveled small with terror. "Knobil, sir."

"Go and fetch the herders. All of them."

I was running before I was fully upright, racing over the dusty grass between the tents, off toward the distant woollies, making the horses shy and jerk at their tethers as I passed them, hearing my own heart thud and soon my own gasping breath.

By the time I led the herders in, small ones at the rear, larger and faster at the front, the newcomer had ordered each woman to sit before her tent, with her brood around her. Sleepers had been wakened, and the entire family assembled for the scrutiny of its new owner.

He studied us with a fierce smile on his thin face, his ribs heaving periodically with deep breaths of satisfaction. He still had his bow and quiver on his shoulder, and he held my father's sword, naked and caked with dry blood. Now he could see that his coup was not going to be contested, so his nervousness was fading. He must have been savoring a great sense of achievement, for at one stroke he had transformed himself from impoverished waif to man of wealth.

I huddled as close to my mother as I could, but her smaller children were thick around her. I probably looked—and certainly felt—as terrified as Indarth, on her other side. It was then that I first wondered how our father had come by his start in life, and if he also had murdered for it. Amby must have known, but I never had the courage to ask her.

"I am Anubyl," the stranger said. "You belong to me now."

Heads nodded.

He stepped first to Aunt Amby and demanded her name. He looked over her children, then moved to Aunt Ulith. When he reached us, his eyes narrowed. He told Indarth to stand, then to lift his arms.

"You," he said, "will leave." He pointed across the empty ridges. "That way."

Indarth licked his lips, nodded, and started to move. After a few steps he stopped. "Who goes with me?"

"No one."

White showed all around my brother's eyes, but somewhere he found the courage to argue. "How many woollies can I take?"

"None. Go!"

Indarth's face seemed to crumple. "That's not fair!" he shouted.

The giant skeletal youth thrust the point of his sword in the ground, so that it stood close to hand. He pulled the bow from his shoulder. He took an arrow from the quiver. Indarth fled, and the rest of us watched in silence. Anubyl notched the arrow, drew the bow, and waited.

Some way beyond the camp, Indarth stopped and turned. At once Anubyl lobbed the arrow at him. Had my brother not been running again before it reached him, he would have been squarely hit. But Anubyl could have killed him easily, had he wanted. As I said, our new owner was a good archer.

I was small. He did not pay me much heed. He frowned at Arrint but let him stay, probably because two loners in the neighborhood might combine against him. I could guess that Arrint would follow as soon as Indarth had vanished into the wilderness, or was known to be dead. Arrint's face showed that he believed this also.

The rest of the changeover went smoothly. Anubyl inspected all of his people and his two remaining horses—the mare my father had been riding had bolted and never returned. He sent herders back out to tend the woollies, then settled down in the eating place without a word. The women rushed to bring food, which he crammed into his mouth as if he were famished. He ate everything they had ready. They prepared more, and he ate that also. I had never seen a man so gorge himself, and I don't think I ever have since. We others huddled where we were, shocked and silent.

Finally our new master rose and stretched and belched loudly. He glanced over the women and selected Jalinan with a nod. She headed for her tent.

Amby fell to her knees again before this lanky, terrible boy. "Sir . . . may we hold the rites?"

Anubyl agreed, reluctantly—carrion in the neighborhood would attract predators. He pointed. "That way." Then he followed Jalinan.

Some of us larger herders accompanied Amby and Ulith when they went in search of my father's body. It lay surprisingly close to camp, so Anubyl was a good stalker, as well as a good archer. The evidence was clear. He had lain in wait behind a boulder. My father had not had time to string his bow. He had charged on horseback, drawing his sword, and there were marks to show where he had been dragged until his boot had come off in a stirrup. One arrow had sufficed, and it still protruded from his chest. We lifted the huge, headless corpse onto a rug. We dragged it back to the tents, wailing as herdfolk do at funerals.

But the horrors were not over yet.

Anubyl stormed out of Jalinan's tent, still fastening his belt. "Quiet!" he bellowed. "Bury him quietly, with no . . . *You!* Woman! Come here!"

He was glaring over at my mother, who was some distance from the tents, heading the way Indarth had gone and carrying a bundle wrapped in a blanket. She jumped nervously, then came scurrying back.

Once—as in my ancient memory of her with the angel—she had seemed tall and slender, smooth of skin and merry of spirit. Now she was plump and shorter even than I, a squat figure in a patterned wool dress, her youth and beauty eroded away by the bearing of eleven children. A lifetime of constant sun had crumbled her face, and the hair below her kerchief was silvered.

Anubyl strode forward and waited for her by the dying fire, folding his arms. She stopped in front of him with eyes downcast.

"Tip it out and let's see!"

She shook the blanket. A cascade of smoked meat and a few roots fell at her master's feet—a knife, also, a water bag, and tinder.

He reached out with both hands and ripped the gown from her. He threw her to the ground. Then he took a long stick from the firewood pile and laid it across her back. He struck her again before the blood had started to ooze from the first welt.

I took one step forward.

Anubyl paused and looked at me inquiringly.

I stopped.

I have done many things in my life that shamed me at the time, and many that shame me yet. But none ever caused me larger and more immediate pain than that revelation of my own cowardice. From then on, I knew that I was a coward, worthless and despicable. No act of mine ever hurt me more than that failure to act. Still in my worst nightmares I stand and watch with the rest while my mother is battered half senseless. I taste again the blood from my bitten lip and feel my nails cut into my palms.

Finally he stopped and tossed away the stick. "Get up!" he

ordered, panting and wiping sweat from his brow. There was a long pause, then she levered herself to her knees and reached for her gown. He put a foot on it. "Go to him like that. Let him see. And tell him that he must leave, or I will kill you."

He had to help her to rise. She swayed, then began to move.

"What is the message?"

She stopped. "He must go, or you will kill me."

"And your other children."

"And my other children."

He nodded. "And hurry back."

Naked and bleeding, my mother hobbled away into the grasslands. The monster looked over the rest of us and evidently concluded that he would have no more trouble. Smiling, he order Rantarath to her tent so that he might try out another of his prizes.

Indarth had gone north. The herd was to the south. Westward lay my father's death place, I went east, sunward.

I had never heard of suicide, but had any obvious means presented themselves, I might have reinvented it. How long I wandered I cannot tell—long enough to discard as impossible every means of revenge, long enough to reduce a boy to staggering exhaustion, long enough for gnawing hunger to dull his shame and send him creeping miserably home again.

That was the fourth landmark, and the end of my childhood.

The ranchers who live in Friday maintain that bad bloodlines make bad foals. They blame a man's faults on his breeding.

The hunters of the forests say that everyone chooses his own paths through life, that he must himself accept the blame for his own mistakes.

The gentle seafolk raise neither voice nor hand to a child. They claim that we are all molded by our upbringing, and that defects of character are due to poor rearing.

I do not choose between these opinions.

I pass no judgment. I make no excuses.

But that was my childhood.

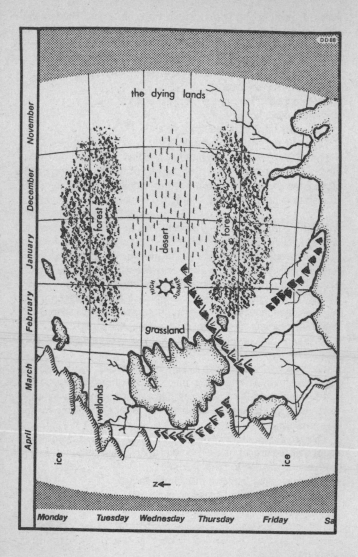

# 2

## The Tyrant

When I returned to camp, Anubyl was visible in the distance, having trouble staying on a horse. Probably, like me, he had watched riding done but had never been allowed to try. I hoped he would fall off and break his neck.

My mother had been bandaged by the other women. She was lying facedown, covered by a thin blanket. The flaps of her tent were open, and a soothing breeze floated through. To save her having to raise her head, I stretched out flat on the rug at her side, horrified by her pallor.

She smiled and moved her hand closer. I took it. It was cold.

"I am glad," she whispered. "I was frightened you would not come back."

"I will kill him!"

She tried to shake her head. "No. I am glad, too, that you did not try to interfere."

"I am a coward!"

"No," she said again. "I was wrong. He was within his rights. You were not a coward. You did right."

I was almost sobbing. "He is a tyrant!" Of course I had never seen a tyrant, but I knew the stories. It was the worst thing I could think of to call him.

Speaking was obviously difficult for her, but she insisted on trying. In broken phrases she explained things I did not know. Anubyl could have done worse. He might have killed off the babies. He might have slain Indarth out of hand, and perhaps others, like myself, or even the older women. He was herdmaster and could do what he liked with any of us. Rantarath and Jalinan were pregnant, and he had ordered them to contrive miscarriages right away, but that was to be expected, for of course he would want the women to start producing his own young as soon as possible. Anubyl, my mother told me, had done nothing outrageous.

I was too innocent to think of it then, but I have often wondered since: Had she guessed that our new master would soon contrive to establish his authority by making an example of someone? Had it not been she, it would likely have been another of us, woman or child. She may well have taken the risk she did not merely in the faint hope of aiding her banished son Indarth, but also by way of volunteering to be the scapegoat if she was discovered. That would have been like her. Certainly she must have known the danger.

She even made excuses for Anubyl. "He has traveled far alone, Knobil. Being alone can make a man mad. He will heal now, with women to tend him."

Then she whispered, "Is he near?"

No—the monster was far off, still fighting with his horse. When I said so, my mother told me to close the flaps. Now I realized that the other women must be staying away, and keeping the children away, for some reason. So I did as I was bid and returned to her side.

"Look in my brown pack," she said. "Be quick."

After some prompting, I discovered what I was supposed to be searching for, wrapped in a cloth at the bottom of her tiny collection of belongings. I sat down and opened the package. All I found was a triangular piece of leather, small enough to fit on the palm of my hand. The back was rough and still its natural tan shade, except for a few curious black squiggles. The smooth side had been painted pale blue, with a strip of green along one edge. I stared in bewilderment at this inexplicable object.

"Come close," my mother whispered, so I lay down again, nearer than before, still holding this meaningless, and yet apparently important, token. "It is yours, Knobil, and precious. So he said."

"Who said?"

"Your father. You must keep it in the dark. No sunlight. The color will fade."

I knew that properly fixed dyes would not fade. I knew a lot about dyeing and weaving. Those things were women's work, but my father had supervised them, so I had watched, and learned also.

I heard my mother's scratchy voice again: "He said you must take it to Heaven."

Probably she did not realize how little I understood, for she was in great pain, and very weak. Probably I did not catch everything she said in that thin, gasping whisper. I did not know anyone called Heaven, and although she may have thought she was making clear to me which father she meant, I did not catch that important distinction.

"Does everyone get one of these?" I asked.

"Only you."

I saw that she was too exhausted to say more, and I must leave my questions for later. So I rose and put away her pack. Fortunately, I did have a place where I could keep a small valuable, although until then I had never owned anything more precious than a sling. Slings need shot, so we boys all carried pouches on our belts to hold any suitable pebbles that we happened to see. I wrapped my green and blue treasure back in its cloth and placed it carefully in the bottom of my pouch.

My mother seemed to be sleeping. I threw open the flaps and went off in search of food. When I returned, she was dead.

"Would you help me, Knobil?" Aunt Amby asked. "Please?"

She was kneeling in the door of her tent, braiding something, and I had been going past. A woman could give orders—or even punishment—to a herder, but certainly not to a loner. Now I was one of the oldest herders, and the women's attitude toward me was changing. I found that "please" more alarming than flattering.

I condescended to help, and knelt to hold one end of the string she was making. Her callused brown hands fluttered like butterflies as she combined the thin woolen yarns. My assistance did not seem necessary—she could have used her foot as easily.

"I am making him new breeches," she said, not looking up. Of course I knew who "him" was. Only a herdmaster wore breeches. Anubyl was growing out of them as fast as the women could sew them, and they were proud of him. He could still eat half a dasher at a sitting.

I did not know what use this cord would be for breeches, but I said nothing. Amby flashed me a worried glance and bent to her task again.

"He let Arrint take food and water," she said defensively.

But no woollies, no woman.

"Who's next?" I asked bitterly. "Todish?"

"He is growing fast." Then she added quietly, "You were born before Arrint."

I had already come to suspect that. I was learning the difference between growing up and growing bigger, coming to realize that I was never going to be big. My fair complexion disguised my increasing maturity, but now I had to keep my elbows close to my ribs, and this talk reminded me that I had not been doing so. Fortunately Amby seemed to be concentrating entirely on her braiding and had not noticed.

Always I stayed as far away from Anubyl as I could, but at the moment he was out riding—he had mastered the horses—so I could be brave. "It is shameful to make you and Ulith and Talana share a tent!"

She shook her head. "Oh, no! Old wives do not need a tent each. It is customary. A man does not want too many tents showing. We do not mind sharing. We do not all sleep at the same time! We are grateful for being allowed to stay at all, Knobil."

"Then it is shameful about Oapia and Salaga!" Two of my half-sisters had been promoted to their own tents. Anubyl was spending much time with them.

Amby glanced up briefly at me. Her wrinkled cheeks blushed very bright. She dropped her eyes again. "No." Then this white-haired mother of many children started to stammer as she told me things that a woman should not discuss with a man, only with other women. She explained the incest problem. She explained why my father had been required to trade daughters to obtain new women. Anubyl need not do so—he had an unlimited supply ripening to hand.

Once I understood that, she added more truths. "Of course a loner can circle round and kill his own father, Knobil. But it is a foolish thing to do. He is better to find another man's herd, so he gains more women for his own use. Do you see?"

I saw. I saw also that these were things my father should have lived to tell me. I was much more interested in vengeance than in this legendary sex thing. I said nothing.

Amby muttered quietly. "You will tell the others, Knobil?"

Were the women afraid that we boys would mutiny? They were overestimating us, I thought. I was the oldest, apparently, and I was a craven nothing. Did they think I might lead a revolution? I turned my head away so she would not see my tears and shame. I detested Anubyl with every breath I drew. I dreamed constantly of vengeance and justice, but I was a yellow-haired runt, a blue-eyed freak. And a coward also! Revolution? I was not capable of talking back to a woollie.

Amby sighed. "There! That's done! Pass me that knife, please, Knobil."

Reluctantly I rose and went where she pointed.

"Be careful!" she called. "It is very sharp."

I took the knife to her, preparing a snappy retort about being old enough to know about knives. Then the odd quality in her voice registered. She held out the knots, and in silence I cut off the loose ends for her. I was puzzled, but she was avoiding my eye.

"I have a good sharpening stone," she said. "Makes a knife so sharp you can split hairs with it."

Then she rose and walked away, out of the tent.

I was left holding the knife. It was a very tiny knife, the smallest in camp. At my feet lay the cord she had braided. It would make an excellent bowstring.

I had aimed my line of woollies so that it would pass by a very large boulder and give me double cover. I was sitting behind the boulder, biting my tongue with concentration and getting cramps in my fingers. I had never heard of shaving, so it had not occurred to me that a very sharp knife could be used in razor fashion. It is not easy to grip hairs in your own armpit to cut them, and blood running down my ribs would certainly attract attention. But this was why Amby had given me the knife. It might buy me more time to grow a little more, and I understood time just enough to appreciate that. I had the bowstring wrapped around my thigh, under my pagne.

Armpits or not, I would not be sent away soon. I was terrified at the prospect. Anubyl had gone out into the grasslands and survived, learned his archery and other skills. He had grown to manhood, and then proved it by winning women and fortune. But he was big, and I was a midget, or so I thought.

Yet the waiting was torture also. I dreaded my coming ordeal and simultaneously could almost hope for it, for then I would be free to go off alone to a tree-filled hollow somewhere and make a bow and learn to use it. I would shadow the family's progress from water hole to water hole until I was ready. Then I would gain my revenge!

Somebody laughed, and I almost cut myself. It was my sister Rilana, watching my antics.

"Come and help me, then, if you think it is so funny."

She shook her head and knelt down at a safe distance. "What you are doing is not proper," she said smugly.

"Easy for you to say! How are you going to feel when he drags you into a tent and pushes bits of himself inside you?" I was still weak on the theory of intercourse.

She smirked. "Rantarath says it feels wonderful. She always asks him for more, she says. Jalinan says he does it better that Father did."

"Dungpiles!"

"What do you know? Perhaps you should cut something else off with that knife? You obviously have no other plans for it."

I felt sudden terror. "You won't tell him I have a knife?"

She considered. "Maybe. Maybe not."

"I'll—I'll cut your breasts off! Except you haven't got any!"

"Yes, I do." She smoothed her woolen dress to show the bumps. "Anubyl says they are growing nicely. He felt them. He says I am going to be next after Thola, as soon as he gets the others all bearing."

"He killed our father! He beat our mother to death! And you want him lying on you, kissing you, rubbing on you?" I felt sick at the thought.

Rilana tossed her hair. "Yes. I shall please him greatly and make lots of daughters for him and be the best of all his women."

Where this argument might have led, I cannot guess. It ended there, though. The wind changed. We heard the noise simultaneously, and I suppose my eyes widened at the same moment as hers did—a distant squealing and rattling, the sound of an angel's chariot.

Rilana was about to run, but I jumped and caught her arm. She was taller than I, but I was stronger.

"You stay here and herd!" I said.

"Why? It's your turn. I want to go and see the angel."

"I am going to the angel!" Hope blazed within me. Here was a solution that I had not thought of, and certainly had not expected. "You stay here!"

"Will not!"

I punched her and she yelped. "I am going to the angel!" I insisted. "Angels stop violence! So I am going to tell him what Anubyl did to Father, and what he did to Mother. The angel will punish him!"

# 2

I raced between the woollies like a dispossessed dasher, not even waiting to conceal my illegal knife. When I reached the other side of the herd, I stopped, balked already. Below me was the camp and beyond that the pond. It was a poor one, a slimy puddle in a wide expanse of white dried mud, flanked by a tangle of crisp brown undergrowth and the stark silver skeletons of trees. Against that drab decay, our five tents shimmered in the sun's glare, a line of brilliantly colored prisms. The angel's chariot stood on the far ridge, dark against the sky.

It was a strange, dirty violet color, with one red sail and one dark blue. Even as I watched, the red sail vanished, then the blue did the same, more slowly.

But already Anubyl was almost there, thumping along the skyline on his horse. I was too late.

Smoke was billowing up from the campfire. The women flustered around, preparing to serve the honored guest, and children romped in wild excitement. Herders were streaming in from all directions.

I sank down behind a small boulder, stuffing the knife into my pouch and pondering. Confrontation would have to wait, obviously.

Anubyl slid expertly from his saddle and led the horse forward. He shook hands with the angel. The two of them started down the slope, angling to avoid the prickly thicket and the pond, heading for the camp. This would be an exciting moment for the usurper, his first chance to play host to an angel, and he would be hard on his women if they did not provide good hospitality. Unlike my father, Anubyl was not above hitting them when they displeased him, although now he used fists or belt, not a club.

Angel and herdmaster reached the camp. Amby was fussing around with cushions and rugs. The mare was given into the care of Todish, who strutted off proudly with her. Talana was spitting dasher steaks by the fire.

Alongside the visitor, Anubyl seemed enormous. His beard was thicker now, and he had meat over his bones. Already his fourth set of breeches strained to contain him. He had discarded all weapons, even his knife, as a courtesy to the angel.

The newcomer was elderly, red-faced, and portly, with sparse white hair plastered to his scalp by sweat. His fringed leather shirt hung outside his belt and protruded far out in front of him. He was fanning himself with a leather hat. I stared at him in dismay. His trousers were tattered. He had *jowls*. How could this shabby old man distribute punishment to the lean young herdman towering over him?

But everyone had always spoken with awe of angels' powers—although those had never really been explained to me—and I managed to convince myself that he was no older than Aunt Amby. She was still boss among the women although Anubyl thought he had appointed Jalinan the senior. Moreover I could see that Anubyl was being very respectful to the pudgy little visitor. With the wisdom of true age to guide me now, I know that my youthful inexperience had been deceived by his baldness and large belly. He was not old, barely middle-aged.

The two men settled on the cushions before the center tent, Jalinan's, and were hidden from my view. Rantarath came forward, kneeling to offer a bowl of water, towels, and the crude soap we made from woollie fat and wood ash. The unoccupied members of the family, the herders and toddlers, formed themselves into a wide half circle beyond the fire, to sit and stare unblinkingly.

I crouched behind my cover, with my heart thumping furiously. I had to plan my move carefully, for I was in clear view of the children. If they gave me away to Anubyl, he would certainly intercept me. What was needed was good stalking technique, but stalking was something I had always been good at and lately had been practicing assiduously. I dropped to my belly and began to wriggle.

It was not a pleasant journey. The grass was patchy, and any bare rock or even pebble would blister. There were also cacti. I did not recall noticing such problems when I was small, and of course I did not understand why things should be different now. By the time I reached the cover of the old wives' tent at the near end of the line, the angel had almost completed his meal. With few exceptions, the whole family was facing in roughly my direction. I eased across the gap between the first tent and the next as slowly as grass grows. There was no outcry, so no one saw me. The women were still busy, and probably nervous about the coming moment of decision.

"I find your advice strange, sir," Anubyl was saying. "Why not continue westward to this ocean before turning north?"

"Because there are a thousand herds between you and the ocean." That had to be the angel's voice, of course. It was higher pitched, and it had a curious soft lilt to it. My skin shivered with excitement at being close enough to hear an angel speak.

"And they are going north?"

"I hope so." The angel sounded exaggeratedly patient, as if he was repeating something he had said before. "We have been telling them for long enough. They certainly can't go west. Any who go south will be trapped. There is no way out to the south."

"How far north?" Anubyl was angry.

"The beaches extend into the fringes of Tuesday—about as far north as woollies like to go. The problem is that you have all these others ahead of you, and they will have cropped the grass. You may have to go very far north to find good grazing. I admit that you will have trouble. The woollies will become very sluggish—but that is better than having them starve."

There was a silence and then Anubyl's harsher voice said petulantly, "I have scouted good water holes to the south, several of them."

There was more silence before the angel spoke again, still patient. "You have many fine women, I see. How many are with child?"

"Two, at least, the old wives say. My first crop!"

"I congratulate you. But if you go south, Herdmaster, the babes will die before they walk."

"You croak a hard call, sir."

"And all your woollies, also."

Anubyl grunted. He did not want to hear that hard call. "More tripes, sir? Some curd? You will not try the roo-brain mash?"

"I am so full I could not eat a flea's earlobe, Herdmaster. Your women are most outstanding cooks, even among the herdfolk, whose food is spoken of with awe throughout all Vernier."

"You are kind. They have other abilities, sir, also." I heard a handclap and guessed that Anubyl was gesturing to his women to line up for inspection. "I offer you rest from your travels and the enjoyment of whichever companion may please you."

"Your hospitality has already put me more in your debt . . ."

The speeches became formal, the angel complimenting his host and politely declining, the herdman insisting. This must be a ritual, I thought, like the speech Jalinan's brother had made when he offered her to my father. But the second of the voices had changed, meaning that the two men had moved. Hoping my heart would not jump right out of my throat—where it had no right to be—I rose to my feet. Then I dashed through between tents to deliver my accusation.

I almost ran into Anubyl, but he had his back to me. I dodged around him, and past the angel also, seeking safety on his far side. The two of them were standing and had been studying the four younger women, who were likewise standing—in a line, blushing, excited, all greatly hoping to be chosen for this honor. The three old wives stood behind them, watching with interest. Nine sets of eyes turned to stare at me in shock or horror.

"That man killed my father!" I shouted. My voice came out much shriller than I had expected, and at the same moment I registered with astonishment that this pudgy angel-man beside me was barely taller than myself.

Anubyl roared and began to move.

The angel stopped him with a gesture, and everyone froze.

The pink, baggy, sweaty face studied me without expression. "What's your name, lad?"

I blurted out my name as Anubyl began to move again.

"Truce, Herdmaster!" the angel snapped, and Anubyl stopped once more, quivering with fury.

"And who was your father?"

"Er . . ." I did not know my father's name. I croaked and fell silent, choked by conflicting rage, and terror, and embarrassment.

The angel's white eyebrows dropped in a frown. "Was he herdmaster? Is that who you mean?"

"Yes, sir." Certainly! Who else?

The angel glanced toward Anubyl. "I just had to be sure, you understand? The coloring?"

"Of course, sir! Now, you will permit me to teach a few manners?" The young man's eyes had blood in them—my blood.

"Also he beat my mother to death!" I squealed.

The angel looked back to me and shrugged. "That is not my business either, young Knobil. Did you think it would be?"

"Sir . . . Angels prevent violence—don't they?"

"Not that sort of violence. And if Herdmaster Anubyl wants to beat you also . . . did you think an angel truce would save you from that?"

I had no words left. My plan had failed utterly, and I had not considered that possibility. I began to tremble more violently even than Anubyl, although for other reasons.

The angel turned back to him. "Perhaps it does. I have never heard of the truce being carried that far, I admit, but I suppose violence is violence . . ."

"With respect, I disagree! This is a family matter." Anubyl showed his teeth and began to edge around the angel to get his hands on me. Violence he wanted.

The little man moved slightly, blocking him. "He expected to be safe while I was here, Herdmaster. It was ignorance, but perhaps we should not disappoint his ideals?" He shrugged, seeing that his audience was not supportive. "Oh, well . . . These so beautiful damsels? You were about to introduce me to that one."

Anubyl shot me a murderous glare and then turned to describe Oapia's virtues and skills. The angel glanced at me briefly. I was not too stupid to read the message in his eye—I had been given a reprieve, but not for long.

With a sob, I turned and ran between the tents, and began racing up the hill. At the crest I paused for a moment to look back. I was just in time to see the angel following Oapia to her tent. The rest of my family had not moved—women standing, children sitting, all staring up at me. Anubyl was already running, not toward me, but in the direction of the horses. His bow and his sword were there, also.

Ahead of me, empty ridges marched outward to meet the sky. On my right was the herd, with very few herders tending it.

About three woollies out of five owned a dasher, so the odds were against me. I was lucky, else this tale would have ended right here. I would have been ripped to fragments.

The underside of a woollie, I discovered, was cramped, smelly, and unbearably hot. The great shaggy feet shuffled on either side of me, and I had barely room to move, my back pressed against the monstrous belly, which rumbled and bubbled continuously. A calf-length pagne was not designed for crawling on hands and knees. The heat and the stench made my head spin.

In theory, I could remain there as long as I could stay awake. I had food, for the rear nipple dangled in my face. In practice, of course, the heat was deadly, and I quickly rubbed my knees raw, for I had no way of avoiding rocks and cactus as the woollie blundered ahead, continuously grinding grass. I had not known that woollies avoided eating cactus, but that one did. It was a humiliating refuge, a mobile torture chamber, and a very fitting prison for a coward.

What could I hope to accomplish? Anubyl had only to wait until I became exhausted, and the woollie would crawl away, leaving me lying in full view. He would certainly stay awake long enough for that to happen, and I did not think his murderous rage would cool very much in the meantime. I should have run while I had the chance and died with a little more dignity.

And eventually I managed to convince my craven body of that, or else the pain in my knees did so. I spread myself flat and let the rear canopy of hard wool scrape over me. Sunlight and blessed fresh air returned. I prepared to breathe my last . . .

Somebody sniggered.

I sat up with a wail.

It was Rilana, regarding me with much amusement. "What's it like in there?"

"Where is he?" I looked around at the humped shapes of woollies.

She smirked. "He's gone to get the women and poles."

Of course—I should have thought of that. Work parties could evict dashers, and they would race around until they found unoccupied woollies, or the one with me under it.

"Here!" Rilana said, and held out a canteen. "It's only half full, but it'll have to do. There's a gully over that way."

She shook her head and was suddenly serious. "Good luck, Knobil!"

I grabbed the water bottle, spotted a quick kiss on her forehead, and ran.

So my cowardice did save me in the end. Anubyl had first looked for me in the open, and then guessed—or been told— that I had hidden in the herd. Later, while he was looking for me under the woollies, I was fleeing away over the grasslands. Obviously Rilana kept her word and did not tell him I had gone.

My luck held again—I was able to stay down in gullies for a long way. One small herder does not show up very far on a landscape so huge. He did not come after me on his horse—or, if he did, he did not find me. Probably he preferred to stay close to the camp while the angel was there.

By chance, or because my luck still held, I was heading south. Anubyl had said that there were water holes that way. Even after the angel left, he would probably want to scout to the north, if he believed what the angel had told him. South was my safest road.

I settled into a long-distance lope, a loner at last.

# 3

The lope fell to a walk, the walk at last to a stagger.

The sun burned without mercy above my left shoulder. Desiccated ridges and hollows rolled on without end. Boulders and sand, scabby grass between patches of gravel and shattered dry clay—an empty land below a vacant sky.

"You can't go on forever, you know," said a whisper in my ear.

"Who are you?"

"I am Loneliness. I am your companion now."

"Go away."

"Not until you die. I shall be with you always, until then. It won't be long."

"I have a knife, and a bow string, and a water bottle."

Loneliness laughed at my side. "An empty water bottle, and no sling. Even Indarth had a sling."

"What need I fear? Thirst? I shall find a pond. Food? I can eat miniroos. Poisonthorn? I am not a child!"

"Eagles. Rocs. Roo packs. People."

"They are rare," I insisted. "Anubyl survived. I shall find a pond with trees and make a bow."

There was no shade, but I sat on some thicker grass to fashion a sling from my pagne. It had been tattered before, and I was left with little to cover my nakedness. That hardly seemed to matter very much.

"Or even traders!" I said loudly. "I may meet some traders."

Loneliness laughed again. "You have nothing to trade. Traders would not be interested in you."

He was wrong, of course. He did not know—because he was me, and I did not know. Traders would have been very glad to see me, but I met no traders, not then. Those canny, nervy folk would have fled the grasslands long since.

I was surprised at the effort needed to force myself back on my feet again. Loneliness fell into step beside me once more. His voice was the sound of the wind on the hills. It was the crunch of grass below my feet, and sometimes it was my voice.

"What if you see another herd?" he asked. "People? You will want to go to them, won't you? You have never been away from people before."

"And the man will kill me. No, I must be alone. Until I can go back and kill Anubyl."

"He is a man. You are a boy."

"I am a man now."

"Are you?" Loneliness inquired. "Your body hair is coming

in gold, like the stuff on your head. Your eyes are blue, like a
newborn's. They never turned brown, as eyes should. There is
something wrong with you. You will never be a proper man,
freak.''

The grass was withered to its roots, littered everywhere with
dry dung. The hollows held the corpses of ponds, and the only
trees I saw had been long since cut down, or shriveled to useless,
brittle tinder.

My heart burned with contempt for the angel. So my mother's
death was not his business? What use were angels, then? Nasty
little man, I thought; old and fat and useless.

"You can't go on much longer," Loneliness remarked. "If
you lie down, you will never rise. The sun will cook you while
you sleep."

He was right. Without water I must die soon. Even my eyeballs were dried out—I fancied my eyelids squeaked when I
blinked, and I laughed long and loud at the thought. Todish
would have found that funny, too, and Rilana . . .

I stopped in a hollow and tried digging in the clay with a
stick. I found no water and almost fried my feet. I scouted for
miniroo pellets, and even those seemed to have vanished from
the great lonely world.

"There is a hill," my invisible companion remarked help-
fully. "It is a little higher than the others. Climb that, and if you
do not see water there, then give up."

"That's a good idea," I said. "Thank you."

I was almost ready to drop to hands and knees when I reached
the top, and it was so wide and flat that I could not see the land
beyond. Behind me, to the north, there was no sign of the
family's woollies; no sign of anything except endless gray rum-
pled landscape, shimmering and writhing in heat haze below a
cloudless sky. I must not stray east or west, or I would lose my
sense of location. I wanted to keep that, so that I would be able
to find Anubyl when I was ready to kill him.

"His danger does not seem very great," Loneliness said, but
I did not reply.

If Anubyl had truly found water holes in this direction, then
I had missed them. Scouting was much easier on horseback than
on foot.

For a while I sat on a rock and gave way to despair. Never

had I been alone like this, out of sight of my family. Even our herder hunting parties had been communal affairs. The thirst and hunger were bad, but the solitude was worse. I was the only boy in the world.

Finally I managed to overcome my frightening torpor, climb on my aching feet, and trail wearily over the flat summit. The country to the south came into view. I stood and stared blankly. It seemed just the same as the country to the north . . . except . . .

Fatigue had slowed my thinking, I suppose, and at first I thought it was only a roo. A single, solitary roo would be no great threat—and edible, if I could somehow catch it. Then a terrible recognition began. Roos traveled in packs, and this creature was alone. Roos bounded, and this one was walking. It was very far off to the southeast, two or three ridges over, and a roo would not be visible so far away. Therefore it was very big. It had to be a tyrant.

At that distance it seemed white, and the tiny forelimbs were invisible. The massive tail balanced the forward-sloping torso above the enormous hind legs, the gigantic, melon-shaped head. The pointed ears stuck up like horns.

My mind began to race, rummaging through memory for all the stories I had heard. Tyrants were so huge that they could overturn and eat woollies. They were implacable and could outrun a horse. No arrow could penetrate them far enough to kill. They had one weakness, their eyesight. All they could see was movement, and a man who stayed still was invisible to them.

I dropped to a crouch.

It saw me. Even at a distance, even so small a motion, it had seen. The massive head swung around, and the monster came to a halt, peering across the landscape, seeking the source of that movement. I stayed as still as a boulder, only my heart moving.

That may have been the first time in my life that I truly appreciated what time was . . . it crawled. Then the great jaws opened. And closed. And a faint roar came drifting over the ridges to me. I shivered, feeling a strange prickling down my back.

At last the tyrant decided that it had been mistaken. It started moving again, resuming its original progress, going north.

I was enormously, intoxicatingly, relieved. All I needed to do was stay where I was, and it would go away.

Go away north. I thought of Anubyl, riding out with bow and sword to defend his ill-gotten riches. The tyrant would swallow him whole and his horse, also, and my soul rejoiced at the vision. Then I thought of the others: my brothers and sisters, my aunts, the woollies. The tyrant would have a great feast. Once it came in sight of the woollies, my family would be lost, for there was no way to make woollies keep still. There would be no way to keep the toddlers still, either—not for the length of time it would take a tyrant to eat all that herd.

My sense of relief died. It dried up and blew away, and horror replaced it. I must try to turn the tyrant. We had been traveling southwest for the last few camps, so the monster was merely prowling, not following our tracks. I tried to convince myself that it would change direction of its own accord, as if by mere wishing I could create a wisdom about tyrants. But I watched, and it did not deviate at all from its course. It vanished briefly in a small dip and then reappeared, still striding northward.

Duty? I doubt that I had ever heard the word, but it was only Anubyl I hated. Aunt Amby, Aunt Ulith . . . young Todish, who had been my closest friend since Arrint left . . . even Rilana, nasty little snit though she was . . . Their faces floated before me in unexpected tears, and I knew that I must try. Better one than all.

When? Trembling, I rose.

Again it saw me. This time the motionless inspection lasted longer, the roaring was repeated several times. But it was still farther south than I was. I saw that I must wait until it had progressed more to the north. Then I would be turning it away from my family, roughly to the southwest. I must hope that it would pursue me for long enough to fix that southwest direction in its mind, so that, when I had escaped, it would continue to the southwest. If I escaped . . . but all I would have to do was freeze and it would lose me.

So I thought. The only animals I really knew were woollies and horses. Woollies were as stupid as cactus, but I should have remembered that a horse was not. I should have know that tyrants must have some means of catching prey and hence could not possibly be evaded as easily as that. I should have known that any predator in the grasslands would die of starvation, were it so brainless. But had I known, then I could not have done what I did.

I waited until I dared wait no longer. My terror seemed to be growing to fill the whole world, and I thought my courage would fail. I poured sweat. My teeth chattered. I dribbled where I stood, not even daring a hand movement to lift my pagne—fear is an agony, and we cowards pay dearly for our defect. The tyrant vanished, reappeared, vanished . . . now it was moving away from me, and I thought I might do nothing if I waited longer. I jumped in the air and waved my arms. I think I even yelled, although it was so distant that my voice could never have carried to it.

In instant reaction, the tyrant spun on one foot and headed toward me. Thirst and hunger and weariness were all forgotten now. A basic human instinct for survival took over, and I began to run in earnest. I fled.

Had I been smarter I would never have started that race. Had I had any sense at all, I would have planned my route and conserved my strength for a final spurt. Instead, I plunged headlong down the slope into the next hollow and then straight up the opposite side. Not having eyes in the back of my head, I paused at the top and turned, panting for breath and watching for my pursuer. But this crest was lower, and I could not see beyond the ridge I had left.

As the moments passed and it did not appear, I began to appreciate my stupidity. I did not know which way to run, and I was not sure I had any strength left to run with, anyway.

Then it came into view, rising enormous over the skyline like the thunderclouds I could remember from my youth. And it was already on the hill I had just left. Far faster and far more huge that I had realized, it seemed to grow up and up, white against the sky—ears and wicked eyes and then the enormous, fang-filled jaws. Petrified, I could only stand and gasp for breath, and feel sick.

Then the whole monster was visible, striding across the mesa toward me. The great legs did not seem to be hurrying, but they ate distance relentlessly. Now I could see the tiny forelimbs, curled close to the chest, each bearing a single, gleaming curved claw. But mostly I saw the endless array of ivory daggers around the ghastly black maw.

*Panic!* My paralysis vanished. I turned again with a squeal of terror and raced down the next slope.

Why I did not break my neck is a great mystery, for the hill was steep. I traversed it in bounds almost as long as the tyrant's strides, and I was looking over my shoulder most of the time. The ground thumped against my battered feet, every blow rattling me to my teeth—cactus and rocks and slithery patches of gravel—but I ignored the pain. I knew I must get out of sight for a moment and change direction, but I seemed to have left it too late. The slope was steep, but not steep enough. The tyrant's eyes were high enough to keep me in view, and it was still moving faster than I was, even though it was on the flat plateau.

Then, mercifully, it reached the gully and dropped swiftly out of sight. And I had reached the base of the main hill. A long, gentle slope stretched down to a tangle of dead, silvery trees in the center of the valley. Water gleamed there. How I needed that water! The trees provided cover . . .

Fortunately I retained just enough wit to remember my strategy. I was not going to reach that cover before the killer came over the ridge behind me. Water must wait, and I must change direction. I veered hard to the right, leaping and staggering and bounding over rough grass and low scrub, still twisting my head around to watch for my pursuer—and running right into a boulder. I cracked my knees with an excruciating blaze of pain. I toppled over, hit the ground, rolled, and stopped. The tyrant's head appeared against the sky.

That rock had saved me, for I had not been expecting the monster so soon. Had I still been running, it would have seen me and been able to hold me in view. I lay flat, with blood running from my shins and tears of pain or terror running from my eyes. I tried not to breathe. The tyrant reached the top of the slope, leaned back, and slid all the way down in a landslide of gravel and dirt, balanced on its great spread feet and massive tail. The impact of its landing shook the world.

It stopped and peered around the hollow: where is lunch?

Its size was unbelievable, four or five times what I had expected. At close range—much too close now—it was an iridescent silver, the short fur gleaming with rainbow lights. I recalled a vague memory of a trader once showing my father a length of tyrant fur, and my father's derision at the price being asked.

The head stopped moving, the eyes and ears did not. They flickered this way and that, together or separately. I wished I could turn off my heart—for if the tyrant could not hear it, I could hear nothing else. Then the monster roared, filling the whole valley with bone-breaking noise and rolling echoes. I very nearly jumped to my feet and fled in terror at that unexpected explosion of sound. Which was the why of it, obviously.

More roars followed, but now I was ready for them. My neck trembled with the effort of holding my head in the awkward position it had happened to be in when the tyrant came over the skyline. I did not even blink. Give up! I thought. I have beaten you! Go away!

But I did not say that, and the tyrant did not believe that. It lurched into motion, heading down to the copse of withered trees, and the ground trembled with the impacts: Boom . . . boom . . .

Yet still I dared not move, for I could see that a tyrant, like a roo, had a third eye in the back of its head. Every animal or bird I had ever seen had three eyes, except people and horses, and I had always felt cheated by having only two. So I remained in my awkward sprawl, with gravel digging into my elbows and a steady agony of cramp spreading through my neck and shoulders from the twisted angle of my head. Black flames danced over my vision as I forced my eyelids not to blink.

The tyrant reached the little grove and swiftly demolished it. Stamping its huge feet and lashing its tail, it wheeled and trampled in a frenzy of destruction, pausing once in a while to bend and snuffle and inspect something suspicious. Tree trunks splintered and toppled, mud splashed, until in short order what had once seemed like a safe hiding place had been leveled. Nothing remained but a puddle of splinters. Then the monster paused, baffled, glaring around and roaring.

Could it not hear my heart? Would it give up?

No! Now it began circling outward, the thunder of its tread shaking the valley floor, the massive tail sweeping wide arcs over the grass. The tail caught a boulder larger than me and hurled it sideways. In a flash the monster spun around and slammed a foot down on it. It bent and sniffed, then turned back to its systematic quartering of the ground. My heart sank into black despair.

I blinked. Nothing happened. Very slowly I began easing my head into a bearable position. If death was imminent, then there was no point in enduring more pain. The tyrant froze. Two evil eyes peered across the valley in my direction. I stopped breathing again.

At that moment came salvation. The monster's ears swiveled, then its head, and it stared hard at one of the flanking hills. Without more warning, it turned and went striding off, faster than ever, clods of mud flying from its taloned feet. With a whimper of disbelief, I watched as the tyrant flowed up the hill and vanished over the skyline. I collapsed with sobs of relief, my heart thudding against the ground, my gut fluttering with nervous reaction.

Then I heard what it had heard—a distant rattling and squeaking, faint hints borne by the wind. But there was nothing I could do to warn the angel, and I did not care what happened to him anyway. Sounds of monster footsteps and angel's chariot died away together. I was left in peace, alive.

Soon I rolled over and sat up to inspect my injuries. I had badly scraped both my shins, and a few other places, but the worst damage was to my knees, and especially the right one. It was already puffed and stiff. The left was painful, but not so bad. Only with great difficulty was I able to rise. Yet I needed water desperately, and I would willingly drink whatever foul muck the tyrant had left in the water hole.

I tried a step and almost fell. The valley danced black about me, and then slowly cleared. For a moment I considered crawling instead of walking, but that seemed likely to be more painful, and slower. So I lurched another step . . . then another . . .

The hollow was a wide place between three mesas. Three valleys led into it. I had not progressed very far when I heard the rattling of the chariot again, coming from the gap on my left. My terror surged anew. I had been hoping that the tyrant was now engaged in eating angel, but somehow the angel had escaped and was now leading it straight back to me.

Sure enough, in a moment the red and blue sails came into sight, and the violet body of the chariot below them. It was bouncing along at a leisurely pace, zigzagging around between the rocks and hummocks, certainly not moving fast enough to escape from the tyrant. The angel had seen me—he waved. Perhaps he had escaped the monster by accident and did not even know it was after him?

I stood, helpless and almost immobile, watching the chariot veer across the valley floor, growing steadily larger. I had never been close to one before, for chariots were strictly out of bounds for us children. It was bigger than I had expected; I should hardly have needed to duck to walk underneath it. It rocked and swayed, and I was surprised to see that the four great wheels were in some way flexible, as if made of something springy, like cartilage, and they absorbed the worst of the shocks from the uneven terrain. Two of the wheels were alongside the main body, just in front of the mast. The other two stuck out behind on a sort of flat tail.

Inasmuch as the chariot was like anything else I had ever known, it resembled the baskets in which my mother and aunts had gathered roots—wide and flat-bottomed, with sides sloping outward. But those baskets had been rectangular, and while the chariot was squared off at the back, in front it was pointed and had a long pole protruding there, the *bowsprit*. The sharp front is of no great advantage on land, but it does help when the chariot floats on water. These were all things I was to learn much later, like *mast* as the name of the vertical pole in the middle.

The chariot swung suddenly up the slope on which I stood, slowed, and then turned aside before it reached me, stopping with a final squeal and sway. Silence returned. The angel was sitting by the mast, peering at me from under his wide-brimmed hat.

He bent from sight and then straightened up. "Catch!" he shouted. His throw was a poor effort, and the missile landed several steps short of me, but it was a leather water bottle. I almost forgot my pain as I lurched over to grab it. Nothing in the entire world could have been more welcome. Few things in my life have matched the joy of that drink. I spilled water over my chest in my eagerness. I almost choked. In that climate there was no such thing as *cool* water, of course, but I could feel the wet relief running down inside me, all the way to my stomach.

By the time I lowered the half-empty bottle, suddenly nauseated, the chariot's sails had disappeared, and the angel was climbing down clumsily at the back. Then he waddled over to me with a flat-footed, rolling gait, wiping his red face with a grubby cloth. In his other hand he held a club, a wooden blade on a long, thin metal handle.

"Thank you, sir," I croaked.

He scowled, looking me up and down. "You did that deliberately, didn't you?"

"Did what, sir?"

"I was watching. I saw it notice you and then lose you. I thought you were safe. Then you started to run."

"I thought it would find my family. I hoped to turn it."

"You're a brainless little bastard!"

"Yes, sir."

He grunted and turned to look back the way he had come. "Your cute little pet will be along shortly. Keep still again, and let's hope it goes right by us."

And if it didn't? Would he hit it with his club? He seemed strangely unworried.

"You can't outrun it, sir? In your chariot?"

"Shut up!"

As he spoke, the tyrant came into view around a distant bend in the valley. I froze. The ground began to throb below the great feet as the monster approached, growing larger with a terrifying swiftness. It came straight for us, as if it would pass between us and the chariot. From the corner of my eye I saw the fearsome silver head against the sky when it passed behind the mast. This was its closest approach yet. A rank, animal stench stung my nostrils. It moved beyond my sight, and I dared not turn my head to follow.

I remember watching the set of three colored ribbons streaming in the wind at the top of the mast and wondering why that sort of movement did not attract the monster. Either it could ignore wind motion somehow, or else it saw moving objects well enough to know that ribbons were of no interest to it. Once again I was not even daring to blink. The angel was motionless also, near me but out of my view. I stared at mast and distant sky, and trembled.

The death tread stopped.

Silence. Only the wind . . .

*Roar!* The noise was so close that I jumped.

"Oh, for Heaven's sake!" my companion snarled. That broke the spell. The tyrant and I moved at the same time. I turned, and it was so close that I had to bend my head and look upward. It was spinning around, its beady eyes glaring down at us in triumph, the great jaws opening. I clearly remember the wet ropes of spittle hanging from them.

The angel raised his club to his shoulder, but backward—the wooden part against his shoulder, the long metal handle pointing up at the monster's head. *Thunder!* Startled, I lost my balance on my bad knee and fell in a sprawl of agony. More thunder.

A moment after I hit the ground, so did the tyrant, and the whole world seemed to bounce.

The angel said, "Fornicating vermin!"

In great agonizing spasms, I threw up all the water I had just drunk.

# 4

"What in the name of Heaven am I going to do with you?" the angel demanded.

He was holding a bloody ax over one shoulder. Under his other arm he clutched the tyrant's two foreclaws—curved, pointed murder, like shearing sickles . . . trophies. The rest of the vast carcass lay as the death throes had left it, so close that I could watch the insects settling on its eyes.

I was sitting on the earth, still close to my damp patch of vomit, barely mobile at all. The angel had laid a wet compress on each of my knees, had washed the worst of my scrapes and given me a rag to make bandages. He had produced smoked woollie meat for me to eat, and I had drained the water bottle.

I was feeling shaky and light-headed, more like a small herder, or even a toddler, than a bold and predatory loner. The world was turning out to be a much tougher place than I had expected.

To the angel I was obviously an unwelcome complication. All the time he had ministered to me, he had muttered angrily under his breath. It was very foul breath—he stank. Everyone did, of course, but his sweat smelled different. Now his fat face bore a ferocious scowl.

"You have been very kind, sir."

He spat. "You insult a herdmaster in front of his women. You provoke tyrants. Now you have mashed your knee. Your life expectancy is not very high, stupid."

"Sir?"

"Oh, shut up!" He stumped back over to the chariot and tossed the foreclaws up into it. He wiped the ax on the grass and threw it up also. Then he turned around and glared back at me, spreading his feet, folding fringed sleeves over the round, white-haired belly that bulged from the front of his unbuttoned jerkin.

"I was going to make sure you found a water hole, that was all. Not for your sake, you understand!"

"No, sir?"

"Shut up!"

"Yes, sir."

"For your father's sake . . . Then I saw the tyrant and decided to let it have you. It would have been a mercy. But you had the sense to keep still. And then you deliberately provoked it!" He glared in angry silence for a while. "Do you know how slim your chances are?"

I shook my head, not understanding any of that.

"About one loner in thirty lives long enough to make his kill. You have no herd, no bow . . ." He bared very yellow teeth. "And it's hopeless anyway . . . the sun is coming."

"Sir?" I glanced up uneasily at the sun.

"You're almost into High Summer! Dry water holes . . . no grass . . . cactus . . . tyrants . . . A herd wouldn't save you." He shook his head in exasperation. "Stupid little herdboy doesn't understand."

"Sir? What did you do to kill the tyrant?"

Again that yellow-toothed snarl. "That's a *gun*. Only angels have them. That's why people are nice to us."

I had thought it was because angels helped people.

He was a strange man. I had very little experience with men, yet I could sense a deep rage in him. He was venting it on me, but I had done nothing to anger him.

"I suppose I could take you with me until we find a decent slough. Except there aren't any left around here."

"No, sir?"

"No, sir! And I'm heading west. Every pee hole from here to the ocean has a herd around it—packed in like flies on a dead roo. You'll die for certain, anyway. Why should I bother with you?"

He was talking more to himself than me, but I said, "No reason."

The fat face scowled even more furiously, but for the first time he spoke to me as if what I thought might matter. "What do you want?"

"To kill Anubyl."

He snorted with disgust. "That's all?"

"That's all."

"Why?"

"He killed my father and my mother."

"Your mother, maybe. But I've never see a herdman with fair hair and blue eyes. Those come from the wetlanders, mostly. Did any of your older brothers or sisters have your coloring?"

"No, sir." I had thought I was the only one in the world. Yet an ancient memory stirred . . . an angel with gold hair . . .

"Probably your real father was an angel. A herdmaster won't let any other males near his women. Only angel sperm can cuckold a herdman. I'm surprised he kept you when he saw what had happened."

I had never even considered that possibility, for I knew nothing about inheritance and precious little about sex.

The angel cursed under his breath. "But if he did, I suppose I can do no less. Get in." He pointed.

Astonished, I never thought to question or disobey. He did not help me to rise and he frowned impatiently at my snail progress. With every twitch of my right knee a red flame, I lurched over to the back of the chariot, trying not to sob with the agony, dreading that one little cry might reveal to the angel what a contemptible wastrel I really was. I scrambled up as fast as I could. He stood and scowled, and made no move at all to assist me.

"I'm out of my mind," he muttered. "Brainless, ignorant, murderous little herdbrat!" He clambered heavily up behind me. "But spunky . . . crazy like an angel . . ."

# 3

## Violet-indigo-red

I suspect that what I did next saved my life: I went to sleep.

An angel chariot is an incredibly versatile vehicle, able to go anywhere, but the price of that versatility is clutter. Even when neatly packed, the interior is a tight jam of spare sails and wheels and axles, of tools and supplies, of skis and yokes and horse collars and harness and ropes. Usually there are chests at the rear for medicines and weapons and personal effects. At one side of the mast is a winch for emergencies, and on the other a slung seat, of elastic weave to absorb some of the bumps and vibration.

An angel takes his name from the color code of his chariot, so my new guardian angel was Violet-indigo-red. Even after he had mentioned that, much later, I never called him anything but "Sir," but other angels would have addressed him as "Violet" or "Violet-indigo," and he might have refused to acknowledge his original name. He bore his colors on his sleeve, and they flew also at the masthead.

Violet's chariot was not neatly packed. It was a midden pit, a jumbled confusion of wood carvings, sets of antlers, fur robes, and other souvenirs lying amid the normal equipment. I had little experience with material possessions, but I recognized that there were more of them here than my whole family owned, and

I also sensed the shabbiness, a worn-out, spent look that some-how suited my fat and balding host.

"You go there!" he ordered, pointing to a heap of cloth and fur near the front. "And if you're going to throw up, be sure you do it over the side."

I clambered painfully forward and sat there where I had been told.

The angel unrolled his mainsail and raised the foresail. They both billowed satisfactorily, but nothing else happened. I guessed then why angels always stopped their chariots on hilltops, but this slope was too gentle, and the wind too light. I know now that he would have tried to find a spot where the wind eddied off the valley wall. If he had, it was not enough.

He cursed continuously to himself, trying various settings of the boom and the foresail. He heaved on ropes, and the back wheels swiveled obediently. He tried jumping up and down, rocking the whole chariot. His cursing grew louder. Then he took hold of one of the front wheels, whose upper edges pro-truded above the sides. He heaved—and that did it. Reluctantly the chariot began to roll down the slope, and then the wind could keep it moving—wind and a great deal of skill.

Soon we were bouncing and veering along in surges and hes-itations, past the muddy shambles that had once been a water hole and a stand of trees. The axles squeaked. The load rattled and jostled. Chariot wheels are made of cross-laminated boards from the rubber trees that grow in Dusk, and they will absorb some of the buffeting, but not all. Violet's concern about the steadiness of my stomach was understandable, but I proved to be immune to motion sickness—an inheritance, I suppose, from my true father.

I did not then appreciate the fact, but Violet was a superb charioteer. Much later, when I tried to do the same job myself, I came to understand the feat his expertise had made seem so easy. To travel by wind power over rough country is the greatest test of an angel's skills. We were close to the doldrums of High Summer. The sun was in the west of January, and we could have been no more than halfway across February. The sickly, fitful breezes would have immobilized nine out of ten drivers totally, and he was traveling away from the sun and hence upwind. That required an instinct for wind bordering on the uncanny, plus a fine ability to estimate slope and an eagle eye to avoid the boulders and gullies that infest the grasslands. I took it all for granted—I had been much more impressed by what he had done to the tyrant.

Sitting on the angel's bedding, with my throbbing legs stretched straight out, I could just see over the side. But I was physically and emotionally spent, so I lay down and turned my face away from the sun. I was accustomed to sleeping whenever I wanted, on hard ground, in the midst of a noisy camp. Despite the noise, the shaking, and the strangeness of my new surroundings, I was too exhausted to stay awake. Youth is wonderful.

When I awoke, we were stationary, parked on the crest of a hill. The angel was standing up, holding a long tube to his eye, pointed at the horizon. Then he lowered it and saw me watching him.

"If you need to pee, do it over the side, herdbrat. Downwind!"

"Yes, sir." Did he think I was not tent-trained?

I sat down again in silence. Somehow he had driven his chariot back to high ground, but the country looked the same in all directions. Where was Anubyl now? How was I ever going to find him? I puzzled over that, and fantasized how wonderful it would be to have one of the angels' guns to kill him with.

Violet now hung a small board on the mast beside him, spread something on his face, and then scraped it off again with a knife, while studying the board closely . . . a procedure I found most curious.

Finally he wiped his face with the familiar filthy cloth. "There's a herd ahead," he said. "Going south."

Woollies smear one another's dung, so it is not difficult to tell which way a herd has been moving. I did not know about telescopes.

"So I'm going visiting. More leathery, burned meat. More broiling my brains in the sun. Another stupid herdmaster who won't listen to reason. Another bony, stinking woman."

"Yes, sir."

"If the herdmaster sees you, you're dead."

I glanced around at the dry landscape. There was a very small tangle of shrubbery at the bottom of the hill. It looked quite withered, unlikely to contain water. My right knee was as big as my head, and the left one little better. "Shall I get out, sir?"

He was tempted, regarding me with his usual sourness, but I had slept in his chariot. I suppose that had seemed like a great display of trust, and to turn me out there to die would have felt like betrayal of that trust. I can only guess, but I think that it was my act of sleeping that saved me then. He must have known that my sleep had been brought on by exhaustion, not trust, but emotions are not always controlled by knowledge.

He growled. "No. Are you hungry?"

"Yes, sir." I was always hungry.

"Then eat now. Drink. Then keep down while we're in their camp. No one will know you're here."

"Thank you, sir!" Soon I was gulping down handfuls of delicious smoked woollie. The angel watched me with nauseated disbelief.

The chariot came to a halt again, and children were shouting in the distance. I had vacated the pile of furs and was now stretched out at a lower level on a much less comfortable collection of spars and oars and other hard things. The angel lowered his sails.

"Remember: Keep down!" he warned. He began moving toward the rear, and now I heard and felt the sound of hooves approaching.

Then the angel paused, turned back to rummage among the loose junk near his seat, and straightened up with one of the tyrant's claws in his hand. Scraps of bloodstained fur showed at one end of it. He sent me a cryptic and disagreeable smile, and then resumed making his way to the back. As he climbed out, a deeply masculine voice hailed him. I shivered nervously and tried to wriggle lower in my bone-breaking wooden nest.

I assume that Violet was feasted and that he tried to explain to the herdmaster about the catastrophe building in the grasslands. He would have had to accept the hospitality of a tent and the woman who came with it. I soon decided that I could safely move back to the more comfortable bedding if I lay flat there. I arranged a sun screen and slept some more. I ate again, having decided that my angel would not grudge a few more strips of woollie flesh. I had the sense not to drink, but long before Violet at last returned, I was frantic to relieve myself, a deprivation I had never before experienced.

I heard voices. Violet came into my view as he clambered to the little platform at the back of the chariot. Someone handed up a bundle, which he tossed in. Then he was passed a bow and quiver, and he placed those more carefully. Farewells were spoken.

Sails went up, brake came off, and the chariot began to pick up speed down the slope. The bouncing was torture. It was impossible to speak over the squealing of the axles and the rattling, but I put agony on my face and pointed at my groin. The angel scowled angrily—having just made a good start, he would now have to find another leeward slope to stop on again. He probably did so as soon as he could, but it seemed a long torment to me.

"I traded your claw," he announced as I gratefully raised my pagne over the side.

"Sir?"

"I was going to let you have one of the claws. I traded it for this bow, instead. The herdmaster is very puzzled as to why I should want one, but he dared not ask. And he is very cocky about the claw."

A bow was a wonderful gift. I thanked him sincerely. He looked even more disgusted than ever.

More bouncing . . .

As I was now well rested, I sat up and watched the country go by, enjoying the experience, savoring the sensation of being an angel. This marvelous chariot was faster than a horse, I concluded, and it did not tire. An angel was not bound to a herd; he could go anywhere. Had I a chariot like this, I could soon track down my enemy, Anubyl. I probably assumed that two or three tries with that bow would make me an expert archer.

Then, unexpectedly, Violet spilled wind from the sails and the chariot rolled to a halt at the top of a long slope. I saw what he had seen—open water.

It was only a small puddle in the middle of a wide dry flat, but there were trees around the edges and no woollies in sight. I turned to look at him, and he was snarling in silence.

For a healthy man to survive alone was a feat, for a cripple

an impossibility. How could I even learn archery if I could not
retrieve my arrows? Memory of terrible loneliness crept back,
and my dreams scattered in the wind. Yet somehow I knew that
pleading with this surly old man would be worse than useless,
and I suppose I had pride. "Do you want me to get out, sir?" I
asked.

"I don't owe you anything, do I?"

"No, sir."

"Then . . . Good-bye and good luck, herdbrat!"

I struggled to my feet and began to make my stiff-legged way
to the back, clutching the mast or anything else handy to keep
my balance. Getting down to the ground was a torture, for my
left knee hurt badly, and even to put weight on my other leg sent
spasms of agony through my whole body. Sweat seemed to explode from my skin. But I made it, and he passed down the bow,
the quiver full of arrows, and then the other bundle.

"That's more of your filthy burned woollie."

"Thank you, sir. You have been very kind." I meant that.
Yet, as he had said earlier, it might have been a greater kindness
to have let the tyrant eat me than to abandon me here in the
grasslands as he was doing now, even with a bow.

"Can you walk?"

I loaded myself up with my new gear and tried. The answer,
in truth, was "no," but I managed a couple of limps and said,
"Yes, sir."

"Wait!"

He pouted at me, hesitating. "Come here." He fumbled in a
pocket and brought out a leather packet. As I retraced my two
lurching steps, he opened this and took out a small triangle.
"I'll give you one of these," he said, "just in case."

He poked at it briefly with a short stick that had also come
from his pocket, and then dropped it to my hand. The rough
side was marked by more of the black squiggles, the smooth
dyed in three colors—a violet strip along one edge, a dark-blue
triangle, a smaller red one . . . the colors of his chariot.

"Keep it in the dark," he said, "or the dyes will fade away.
Then it's useless. They're not supposed to outlive you. You know
what it is?"

I shook my head.

"It's an angel token. Take it to Heaven and they'll let you in."

He laughed. "Or you can show it to another angel if you need help. It's a mark of approval. I liked the way you tried to draw off the tyrant, herdbrat. We give these out, sometimes."

"I already have one, sir."

I laid down my burdens and fumbled in my pouch. By the time I had produced the triangle my mother had given me, Violet had clambered down and was regarding me with a very angry expression. It grew even more furious when he saw what I had.

"So I was right? Green-two-blue?" He inspected the rough side. "West of January, Wednesday? Of course! Well . . . tell me?"

So I told him.

He shook his head. His pink jowls quivered when he did that. "You have a strange effect on angels, herdbrat."

"Sir?"

"It's against the rules to give you a ride in my chariot . . . although that one gets broken often enough. It's much more against the rules to go back to a woman. Did you know that?"

"No, sir."

"You don't know nothing, do you? An angel is supposed to enjoy a woman once and never go back to her. If he visits the same tribe, he should choose another. Your father must have gone back to your camp, or he could not have known about you . . . and he certainly could not have passed her this unless they were alone in her tent again."

Now I was recalling a vague image of a yellow-haired man with no clothes on, playing romp with my mother. I could just remember it, I thought. Or remember being able to remember it once. Or was I making it up? I said nothing.

"It's supposed to be a mark of approval!" The angel's face was turning redder than ever. "How old . . . big . . . could you have been when he met you?"

"I don't know, sir."

"Green-two-blue?" he repeated. Violet spoke to himself a lot. He was a bitter, sour, old man, and more than a little crazy— which is not uncommon among angels.

"Do you know . . . my father . . . sir?"

"I'm not sure. There were a couple of blond cherubim . . . younger than me. I think that one of them may have looked rather like you. He might have won his wheels just after I left the first time.'' He stared at my face as though he had not seen it before. "An angel baby! A real angel baby!'' Then he snorted and handed me back my token. "Well, now you have two of them. Get back in the chariot, angelbrat.''

Again a reprieve . . . I did not understand. I hesitated. He pushed me and I staggered, with a yelp of pain.

He shouted. "We're not supposed to know! Of course angels make bastards! I must have some, too, here and there . . . but I don't have blue eyes.''

I looked at his eyes. They were brown, and bloodshot with the dust of travel. They were also strangely moist-looking eyes, a point I had not noticed before.

"Get in! And stay downwind from me. You herdfolk all stink . . . it's that woollie meat that does it.''

He could have been eating little else himself lately, I thought, but I made haste to obey.

Yet when he followed me up into the chariot, he did not immediately set sail again. He threw open a chest and began rummaging through the contents, all the way to the bottom.

"Here!'' he snapped at last. "If you're going to travel as an angel, you'd better look like one.''

He wadded a bundle and threw it at me—leather breeches and a fringed leather shirt. They were badly worn, with holes in the knees and elbows. They smelled of rot, like a bad water hole, but I hastened to discard my pagne and don these unexpected gifts. They must have been his before he swelled around the middle so much. They were still huge on my stringy frame, but I was not about to complain.

Yet even a very flexible youngster will have trouble pulling on breeches if he has never done so before and cannot bend his legs. With difficulty, with much straining and puffing, I at last succeeded.

Greatly pleased with myself, I looked to the angel for approval. He was watching me with an unpleasant, yellow-toothed leer.

"You're older than I thought,'' he said. "Well, perhaps you can be of some use to me after all, angelspawn.''

"Sir?''

He cackled at some private joke. "You'll see.''

As I said, he was more than a little crazy.

## 2

We traveled mostly without speaking, for the chariot was noisy. The country gradually became more rugged, but the wind less fitful, and my angel was a master navigator. Breeches or not, when he stopped at camps he left me in the chariot as before, and of course we had little time for conversation at those stops.

Between the camps, he would halt once in a while for a brief break—to eat, for respite from the constant bouncing and noise, or rarely to sleep. For sleeping he had a leather cover he could fasten over the chariot, making it into a low, uncomfortable tent. It grew incredibly hot and smelly in the hot sun. We both sweated lakefuls, we felt limp and dizzy when we awoke, but he told me that roos might attack a chariot, so he needed the protection. Here was one way that a companion could have been of assistance, and I offered to stay awake, as guard. He refused my offer. I think he did not trust me to control my own eyelids, and probably he was wise, for I had never needed to stay awake at will, and so had never learned how.

When we camped in this fashion, he slept on the pile of cloth and furs. I had to make do with a rug over the oars, spars, and spare axles.

When we did see roo packs, Violet would give chase if the wind was favorable. Twice he managed to draw close, and then our ride became wilder than ever as he tried to run down the bouncing, fleeing roos and at the same time fire his gun over the side. He felled a few with the gun, and I watched carefully how that marvelous weapon was used, but he never managed to crush any with the chariot. He almost wrecked it on boulders, instead. Violet did not like roos, and he left the bodies where they lay. To me that seemed like a shocking waste of good leather.

We did have a few conversations during halts. I discovered what shaving did, and what the strange board was that he hung on the mast. I asked to try that, and so I viewed my own face clearly for the first time in my life. Until then, I had seen my reflection only in water, usually muddy. The near-white eyebrows were a shock, as were the unwholesome blue eyes. They brought back my hazy image of the angel with my mother . . . or did they lead me to invent that flimsy scrap of memory?

He had other miracles, too—his telescope, which he let me try, and a jug of rough red pottery, all marbled with white lime. That was the greatest wonder of all, for water left awhile in it would emerge cool, the only cool water I had ever tasted.

Violet had accepted me as passenger. He made no more threats to evict me, but his contemptuous attitude did not mellow. Herd-folk, he said, were the most ignorant, stupid, barbarous people on all Vernier. I could not argue, not having known that there were other types to compare. I was more than willing to put up with his jeers if they were the price of the ride. My knees were healing, and I would need those knees in good shape when he did at last turn me out.

Once I dared to ask where we were going, for I had noticed that he avoided herds and camps whenever he could do so un-observed, and so he must have some other objective.

"I'm going back to Heaven," he said. "You . . . well, we'll see when your leg is healed."

"Sir? Who is Heaven?"

"Not who, stupid. It's a camp . . . where the angels live."

I tried to imagine a camp with more than one man in it. "And if I take that token you gave me . . ."

He spat, his sign of special disapproval. "If a young man wants to be an angel, then he has to go to Heaven with a token. He's called a pilgrim. If they think he's any good they'll let him be a cherub, and teach him what an angel needs to know. If they still think he'll do, then they'll make him an angel—give him a chariot and send him out to help people."

A chariot! With a chariot I could find my way back to Anubyl. With an angel's gun I could kill him, as the angel had killed the tyrant. He did not wait for me to speak.

"Forget it, herdbrat! You don't know enough. Herdmen never make angels. They're too ignorant. And stupid."

But at another stop I brought up the subject again. "Where is Heaven, sir?"

He pointed east. "Under the stars."

I had never heard of stars, and we were going almost due west.

He read my face. "The sun is that way, dummy. High Summer . . . it would boil your lungs. No man can live in High Summer, and not much else can, either.''

I must have still looked doubtful.

"I'm going to the March Ocean,'' he said grumpily. "It's faster. Think of a very big water hole. Then I shall sail along the Great River . . . Oh, forget it!''

"I should like to be an angel like you, sir, and help people.''

He laughed derisively, showing his yellow teeth. "A herd-man help other men?''

"I should have died without your help, sir.''

"You damned well would.''

"Will you not take me back to Heaven with you?''

"No! That's very much against the rules. Every man has to find Heaven for himself. It's a test. They'd ask you if an angel had given you a ride. We're going the wrong way now, so this wouldn't count.''

Well, I had to go back east to settle with Anubyl. I decided I would find Heaven first and make my main task easier by getting a chariot. I had no conception of the size of the world.

Gradually my knees healed. Gradually the country changed. Sixteen or twenty camps had gone by, and now we were seeing woollie corpses rotting on the grasslands, and solitary, wandering woollies, abandoned as the grass became too scarce to support the herds. We passed human skeletons, perhaps loners. Some of them looked old, some not.

The herds were becoming enormous as they packed in closer against the ocean, for when two herds meet one herdmaster will inevitably kill the other and own both. My angel came back from his visits looking grimmer every time. Eight women he'd been offered, he would say, or even ten.

Then he decided that I could walk well enough for his purposes.

# 3

"I have never known angels to travel in pairs,'' Herdmaster Agomish rumbled in the deepest voice I had ever heard.

I could not see his face, for I had been told to keep my eyes lowered. I could see the end of his black beard, however, and it hung below his belt. I could see his boots and breeches, and two giant, hairy hands, either of which could have snapped my neck without calling for help from the other. I had not known that most herdfolk males were made on the same scale as my father. That rock-smasher voice seemed to fall from the sky.

Violet had ordered me not to speak, for he had said that I spoke like a herdman, not like an angel. I doubt that my dry throat would have put out intelligent sound, anyway. I stood at his side with my eyes down and my mouth shut. I stared at the herdmaster's enormous boots and fervently wished I was safely hidden in the chariot as usual.

But this time Violet had decreed that I would accompany him, without saying why. He had also told me not to believe anything he said about me. Herdfolk were too dumb to see through a few lies, he had said.

"Even angels have to be trained, Herdmaster," he now replied cheerfully. "He is merely here to learn, though, and will remain silent in the presence of his elders, as children should."

The hint was taken. My fair complexion deceived the herdman, as it had earlier deceived both Anubyl and Violet.

"The *boy* is welcome as you are, sir," Agomish retorted. "I offer you whatever hospitality I have to give. Come, then!"

I limped painfully behind my guardian angel as he accompanied the giant herdman down the slope toward camp. I had observed the tents earlier, nine of them. The colors and designs looked wrong to me, and there were many more than nine women fussing around the fire, so Agomish had several old wives in his family. There were strangely few children, yet woollies without number swarmed everywhere, in all directions. Perhaps the children were out herding, yet the herd was straggling badly. I disapproved.

As we drew near, though, the familiar bustle and the familiar smells of a herdfolk camp sang softly to me of my lost childhood, and a lump grew hard in my throat. A girl laughed like Rilana. I saw a boy so like Todish that I almost called out to him.

Cushions had been spread on rugs before the tents. Angel and herdmaster sat down together. Still favoring my right knee, I lowered myself to the ground behind Violet, keeping my face turned as far away from Agomish as I thought I decently could.

I was no angel, but a herdman, within sight of his women. If he as much as suspected that, how long would the truce last? As long as one breath—my last.

The unexpected appearance of a second visitor had caused some confusion among the women. There was a brief delay. Agomish clapped his hands angrily, with impacts like ax blows, and then two bowls of water were rushed over to us. One of them was held before my downcast eyes. A woman . . . *a woman* . . . was kneeling on the other side of it. I admired the pattern of her skirt furiously, to avoid seeing anything above her waist. Copying the angel's actions, I splashed water over my face, laved my hands, and accepted a towel.

But the savory scent of cooking was making my young mouth water. Dried and smoked meat had been my diet for too long. Now I could smell hot fresh meat and juicy delicacies . . . roo brains . . . roast dasher! Another dress appeared before me. Two slim hands laid a piled dish alongside my outstretched legs. The woman vanished and I set to work to make the feast do the same.

"Think of a tall tree, Herdmaster," Violet was saying with his mouth full. "If you stand close, you have to bend your head back very far to see the top of it . . . Is this not so? While, if you are far away, then you can look straight at it? Well, the sun is very high, but the same is true of the sun. Is it not higher—closer—than you remember it as a child?"

The herdman growled. "I had not noticed, sir."

"Think back to when you were a herder. Remember your shadow?"

I paid little attention as Violet went patiently on, trying to persuade his host that the sun did move, although so slowly that a man would not notice. Woollies did not like to be too far from the sun, he said—they became sluggish. But they could not live too close to it, either, for the heat dried up all the grass, and also the water holes that the herders needed. So the herdfolk always lived about the same distance from the sun, moving slowly westward as it advanced . . . in a crescent shape . . .

Agomish insisted that he had been a herdmaster long enough to sire twenty-eight live daughters and he had not moved westward more than in any other direction. Always he had gone to the best water and grazing.

As the conversation dragged on, as my appetite died of its own success, I began to gain an inkling of Violet's repeated insistence that herdfolk were stupid. It was obvious, if what the angel said was true, that the moving sun would gradually push the herdfolk ahead of it. It was obvious to me, but not to the mighty, thunder-voiced Agomish. I felt rather smug when I understood that, but of course I had been given this explanation before and had had much time to think about it. And I had enjoyed an angel's eye overview on a long journey through a grossly overgrazed, overstocked countryside.

Then I realized that the other two had finished eating. I quickly dropped the dasher bone I was gnawing. I licked my fingers.

"You will need rest, sir." The doubts had crept back into our host's voice. "I shall be honored if you will accept the use of one of my tents, and a companion to ease your cares. And your . . . boy?"

He wanted to know how many tents, how many women . . . and suddenly I wanted to know, also. What did Violet have planned now? A mingled rush of renewed nervousness and incredulous hope began to interfere with my hard-working digestion. My groin tingled strangely. He couldn't expect . . .

Could he?

"I shall be most honored to accept your kind offer, Herdmaster. The lad can curl up in a corner of the tent. He will not interfere with my rest, I assure you."

"I do have an ample supply of females now," Agomish muttered, torn between greed and pride. "I have been extending my herds, also, as you may have guessed."

"One will be more than generous. He is only a child, as you can see."

I was greatly relieved. And yet, just for a moment, I had almost hoped . . .

I stood behind my angel as the herdman showed off his women—eight of them, with a cluster of five old wives in the background in case the guest wished to choose experience over agility. I could not help sneaking glances, for I was safely behind Agomish also. Three were obviously pregnant, and hence out of bounds.

". . . and this is Ullinila," he boomed. "Not quite the youngest, yet unusually sprightly. The old wives are not certain, but it is possible that she is with child . . . but do not let that possibility worry you if she pleases you . . ."

The catalog continued, but even I had caught the extra enthusiasm over Ullinila. Agomish believed that she had already conceived and therefore he would prefer that she be chosen.

She was. I followed Violet as he followed Ullinila to her tent. I was not looking forward to the experience, and yet I was naturally curious to see how this intriguing activity was performed. Would the angel actually couple with her in my presence?

I waited outside briefly, as old wives bustled in with a second set of bedding. Then they departed. I entered. I made sure the flap was securely closed. I turned around.

The second pallet had not been placed in a corner. It lay next the other in the center of the stuffy dimness. Ullinila was little older than myself, or perhaps even younger, for women blossom sooner than men. She was wearing nothing but a sheen of multicolored light, and she sat with outstretched legs, leaning back on straight arms, smiling up nervously at Violet as he lowered himself to his knees beside her. My throat tightened at the sight of her youthful grace, the play of color over her skin as she leaned forward to put her arms around his neck.

"No, just stay as you were, my dear," he said. He still wore all his clothes, which must have been surprising to her—even if he had no plans for intimacy, the tent was chokingly hot. "Come here, Knobil, and look at this."

I limped across the rugs toward them. The camp outside was falling silent, giving the honored guest peace for his rest.

"Sit, lad. Closer! Let me show you."

Awkwardly, I seated myself on Ullinila's other side.

"Closer!"

I heaved myself nearer.

Ullinila, finding herself between two fully clothed men, glanced from one to other of us apprehensively, not understanding.

I feasted my eyes on her as greedily as I had eaten her master's food. I had seen Jalinan naked, of course, but at a distance, and I had been younger then. Ullinila was no older than Jalinan had been, and more deliciously rounded, a miracle in smooth brown skin. One long braid hung behind her slim feminine shoulders, the other trailed down between . . .

"These breasts, Knobil," the angel said. "Are they not magnificent? Observe the generous proportions, the bold angle and graceful curve, the roseate perfection of the nipples and aureoles. In a hundred camps, I have never seen a woman with finer adornments. Feel them!"

They were indeed superb. I remember them distinctly—exquisite, just starting to swell in the early stages of pregnancy. Violet cupped one breast in his hand. Sweating mightily, I obeyed orders and fondled the other. I wished I was able to pull my knees up. I laid my unoccupied arm in my lap instead.

"And the soft, luxurious firmness of these thighs . . ." Violet sighed and stroked. "Statements of strength and promises of indulgence. Feel them, lad! These hips—the ideal of feminine physique expressed to perfection, do you not agree?"

I may have croaked an answer. I do not recall. My heartbeat had risen dramatically, and not only my heartbeat.

Now the poor girl was thoroughly alarmed. "You will take pleasure with me now, sir?" she whispered to Violet.

He sighed. He sat back and crossed his legs. "Perhaps later. First try that young fellow with the big eyes and the bulge in his breeches. He has a stiff leg, also, so he will need some help."

I could only gasp, wondering if I had heard correctly, but Ullinila did not doubt and did not hesitate. She swung around to me with a big smile, white teeth in heart-shaped child's face. Still so innocent, I had not dreamed that my slim youthfulness might hold more appeal for her than the balding obesity of my companion. Probably I had never considered that a female could have any preference in such matters.

It is very alarming for a virgin to have his pants pulled off him by a naked woman, and then to be straddled by her as she tugs his shirt up over his head, but she had sensed that my need was already urgent, and she expertly did what was required. I discovered that the procedure could be completed in only a fraction of the time I had expected . . . indeed I did almost nothing except fall backward, drowning in torrents of unendurable joy. And among those heaving spasms of pleasure, I vaguely decided that if this was what herdmen killed for, then their murders were forgivable.

All too soon it was over, and I was lying naked and unashamed, sweaty and panting, but secretly exulting in the knowledge that my fears had been unfounded. I was a real man after all! No more need I worry that my strangely pallid coloring indicated some lack of virility. Apparently all my equipment was satisfactory, and operating as it was supposed to.

Ullinila was lying, half beside me and half on top, soft yet firm, solid but delicate, smooth and desirable still. I had my arms around her. I reveled in the sweet scent of a herdfolk woman, a distinctive muskiness remembered from my childhood, forgotten once, now recovered and imbued with a new and deeper excitement. She turned her head toward my companion.

"And now you, sir?"

I heard another, longer sigh. "Not yet. Try him again. He obviously needs a lot more practice."

She looked at me with an inquiring and mischievous smile. I smiled back.

Ullinila! How sweet she was!
How insatiable, how rewarding!
No man ever forgets the first time.

I awoke when Violet nudged me in the ribs with his foot. I blinked around in alarm at the unfamiliar tent, remembering where I was and what I had been doing.

"Get dressed, *herdman*!"

I winced—too loud! The camp was still quiet beyond the tent walls. "Yes, sir." I sat up and fumbled awkwardly with my breeches, seeing now that Ullinila had vanished, and her garments, also. Even the memory of her was an excitement.

The angel grunted. "Don't tell me you wanted more? She's gone to warn the others—so they can fry up another batch of vomit to feed us."

"Yes, sir. Did you . . . I mean, she was good, wasn't she?"

He growled angrily and turned away.

"Are they always as good as that, sir?"

"No, probably not . . . Get dressed!"

I was going as fast as I could. "Sir, did I do something wrong?"

"You were no damned help at all!"

"Sir?" I did not understand, but I was suddenly heartbroken

and ashamed at having somehow failed him, who had done so much for me. What more was I supposed to have done?

Violet ducked out under the flap, without explaining.

The chariot squeaked to a halt. Violet cursed. We had not long left Agomish and the unforgettable Ullinila. I was stretched out on the bedding, face downward and bare to the sky. He had noticed in the tent that my fair skin was losing its pigmentation inside the angel clothes I wore. He was teaching me to sunbathe.

I knew that oaths at a halt meant that he had made a misjudgment. He would have to turn the chariot and run back downhill to try again. "May I do it for you, sir?" I asked.

"No." He had risen and was scowling off to the north. I peered and saw woollies.

"You hungry?" he asked.

"Not very, sir."

"Amazing! Sleepy?"

"No."

"Even more astonishing! We'll have to visit them, though—they've seen us."

His expression was foul, but his tone so unusually pleasant that I daringly said, "Why?"

He shook his head at me. "They're all terrified, Knobil. Didn't you notice? Next time look at their eyes. An angel going by without stopping . . . that would be a great cruelty." Then his usual acerbity returned. "If you're not hungry or sleepy, then you'd rather stay in the chariot?"

My face must have been answer enough.

He sneered. "Herdboy glutton fancies another little woollie, does he?" He headed for the rear, to dismount and turn the chariot. "Very well . . . At least they can't try to talk to me while you're fornicating them."

My second visit to a herdfolk camp went much like the first. I was less nervous of the herdmaster, and much less interested in the food. I eyed the women openly, wondering which one the angel would choose. When the tent flap closed behind us, Violet wasted no time in teasing. He merely said, "You go first."

I wasted no time, either. The first-time magic was missing, but I could tell that this was not a procedure that would soon pall on a man. She was taller and slimmer than Ullinila. I forget her name.

Again I awoke to find Violet and myself alone. I struggled into my pants and scrambled to my feet. I had just pulled on my tattered coat when I remembered his curious remark on the previous occasion.

"Was I more help this time, sir?"

I cringed, expected a blow—his face flamed redder than I had ever seen it. He grabbed me with one hand and balled the other into a fist. Then he saw my bewilderment, and with an obvious effort he released me and patted my shoulder instead.

"You did fine, lad . . . a great performance! Very manly."

Delighted, I puffed out my chest. "Thank you, sir."

"But it won't hurt if you speak to the girls in the future. They won't tell their masters that you sound like a herdman."

"What should I say, sir?"

He rolled his eyes and seemed to go even redder. "For Heaven's sake! Tell her you're glad I chose her . . . how much you want her . . . that she has mouthwatering tits . . . you can't say you love her, but don't treat her like an animal! I know you're a beginner, but you're humping like a herdman. Make love—like an angel!"

"Sir? Teach me?"

He snorted incredulously and led the way outside to eat again.

But at the next camp he took me at my word. He chose a woman who was slightly older, yet still well worthy of a man's attention, Kininia. Then he proceeded to instruct me—stroke here, kiss there . . . try this . . . try that. Kininia was at first astonished and then much amused. She soon joined in the game, with hints, criticism, and suggestions. She made demonstrations of her own—coyness leading to enthusiasm, turning without warning to fierce resistance and then sudden wild collaboration. The two of them coached me, coaxed me, and teased me. They had a riotous time at my expense . . . but I was the one who journeyed in Paradise.

## 4

The country was changing again, the slope becoming perceptible even to my uneducated eye. We journeyed now in a wide valley, flanked in the distance by ever-rising hills, but a dry riverbed careened back and forth across our path, making a straight route no more possible than before. By way of compensation, the winds were growing stronger and more dependable. Rarely we saw clouds in the sky ahead, faint and remote and tantalizing.

Tributary valleys joined at intervals, bringing in stony gullies to bar our road, and also bringing in more herds. Slimy little pools still held water among the rocks, and the camps were so numerous that it was almost possible to see from one to the other . . . not quite, though, for no herdmaster can ever tolerate a rival within his sight.

The valley grew wider as our descent continued, the hills more remote—higher, fainter. The many springs in this country were keeping the people alive, but the great corpses of starved woollies lay everywhere. Roos and vultures and lesser scavengers went openly about their work. Death and despair patrolled the grasslands.

Again and again I listened as Violet tried to explain. Rarely a herdmaster seemed to understand, a younger one, usually. Again and again the angel tried to offer advice. It varied, because he knew he had no answer and was willing to try anything. He would try anything to make them try anything.

There were too many woollies—if the herds were to be culled, then a few might survive and buy time . . . but the herdmen would not hear of it.

If several herdmasters in an area were to cooperate . . . that was even less thinkable.

Take the women and horses and abandon herd and children . . . not that, either.

I was no longer afraid of the herdmasters, for they hardly seemed to care now, and the angel's prestige protected me. I saw what Violet had meant about their eyes; they had a strange flat look to them, a hopeless deadness. All their lives these men had wandered empty plains without sign of other human life.

Now, inexplicably, other herds were crowding in from all directions. The grass was dying, and there was no road out.

Old wives became rare, and even I could guess what was happening. Soon children became rare, also, especially boys.

Our routine was established now. Violet chose the youngest girl, insisting that I would sleep "in a corner of the tent." Then he told me to go ahead, and I did. Sometimes he watched me, sometimes he just lay down and slept.

I learned not to look in their eyes. Since the lesson with Kininia I had developed some finesse, and very rarely I managed to rouse some excitement in my partner, also; but that was only in the first few camps. Later the women's eyes took on the same dead flatness as their menfolk's and they were incapable of anything except willing submission. I did not care.

Yet, on two or three occasions, when I had done with her, a woman tried to speak to Violet, denouncing the herdmaster for killing off her mother, or her children by a previous owner—just as I had tried to denounce Anubyl to him. His answer was always very much the same: "That is not my business, woman. He is herdmaster and may do what he thinks fit. Now attend to your duties—the boy is being lazy again. See what your skills can do to perk him up."

Madness hung over the grasslands like the stench of rotting meat.

I lost count. I remember my seventh, because my father had owned only six women. Of course they had been his for repeated enjoyment, and I was merely sipping on the wing, but I impressed myself when I reached seven. Soon the names and faces blurred. Our journey was long, the stops many. Two dozen women . . . fifty . . . perhaps even more than that. What more could a growing boy want?

Poor Violet! His plan had failed abjectly. He had looked to me for inspiration, and found instead only mocking confirmation of his own inadequacy. Of course I did not understand. I was merely very puzzled that he would not indulge in such a superlatively enjoyable activity when it was freely available. Perhaps he did so, once or twice, after I had fallen into a satiated slumber, but I don't believe he ever even tried.

He was aging. He was grossly overweight in a murderously hot climate. Doubtless those things were the main cause of his trouble. But much later, in Heaven, I once overheard a discussion between a couple of learned saints. Great mental strain, one of them maintained, can depress not only a man's mind but his body also. It seems a strange idea, but it might explain Violet. The herdfolk were looking to him for aid, and he was impotent to help them. Perhaps that failure gnawed at his brain and thus sapped his physical health. He put me forward in his place, he encouraged my efforts in the hope of encouraging himself . . . or perhaps he thereby sought to punish himself. Perhaps my callous indifference held some sort of morbid fascination for him . . . I don't know. He was more than a little crazy.

I knew none of this at the time. I took each woman as she came, and with no thought that she was doomed to die with the rest, when the last woollie corpse had rotted away. Heedless of the darkening horror, of the very real danger that even we might not escape before famine and disease closed the trap, I ate, and slept, and pleasured to mad excess, relentlessly strengthening my resolve to become an angel.

Then, without warning, our long descent through the grasslands was ended. Vegetation vanished. The chariot hissed smoothly over hard sand. The hills became rocky and barren and the rivers shrank into the ground. I know now that we had reached the farthest former extent of the March Ocean, already retreating before the hot caress of the approaching sun. At the time I was shocked. I had never seen terrain without vegetation. Violet must have guessed that it was coming, for he had been begging gifts of water bottles in the last few camps. Now he put on all the speed he could, in a desperate race to reach the water's edge before we died of thirst.

The heat in the lowlands was incredible, even to me who had never known cold. Light flared up from the sand in unkindly waves and silvery shimmers of mirage, roasting a man's eyeballs. The wind alone could flay him. Teasing, useless clouds still hung far ahead of us, seaward, while the hills we had left were now elevated to the sky, transformed into pale-blue ghosts of mountains—so far had we descended.

Far off on either hand, great spurs of highland flanked the sand. Our course lay toward the ocean, but also toward one of these barriers, the more southerly. That was our fastest route, Violet said, in that wind, and also a better chance for water. He spoke little, and the silence was broken only by the hiss of our wheels and a keening of the wind in the rigging.

How long . . . but I have no way of knowing how long we took to cross that desert. I slept three times, I think, but my sleep was fitful in the heat, and thirst tortured my dreams, so perhaps my sleeps were short. Violet sat grimly by the mast, working the sails, steering with every speck of his great skill, losing not a moment. Red and bloated still, he somehow could yet look haggard, his face caked with dirt and a silvery growth of whiskers, his eyes almost hidden below the brim of his hat, screwed up against the glare. Our tongues felt huge and callused in our mouths.

As the ordeal continued, I began to worry about him—I, who had cared nothing while a whole people died around me. I wondered if he would hand over the controls to me and give me my first lesson in driving a chariot. He might have done so had the way been flat, but the sand rolled in ridges. There were fields of deadly soft dunes and outcroppings of rock. A broken axle would have doomed us. So I remained on the bedding in the front, and he stayed by the mast, and the chariot hurtled endlessly over the limitless plain like a frantic ant.

Then came a strange tang in the air, and an inexplicable sound. I looked to Violet and found there a smile for the first time in longer than I could recall, perhaps the first I had ever seen on his face.

"Breakers!" he said.

I watched breakers in amazement. He had told me to imagine a big water hole, but my mind had never conceived an ocean. I wanted to drink all of it, until he explained about salt, and soon I could taste the salt on my lips. Breakers and unfamiliar white birds, and interesting things being washed up in places—all these I could not tarry to investigate.

Now we must follow the shore, still southward, looking for fresh water. We were down to our last canteen when we found it. Where the sand ended and the hills sank gratefully into the sea, a tiny stream trickled from the rocks to die away into the back of a beach ridge. It was barely more than a lagoon—acrid, dead-tasting, brackish stuff—but it was life for us. We plunged in bodily, soaking and drinking at the same time as if we could absorb moisture through our skins. Yes, it was life to us, but it also meant death for the herdfolk, the steady draining of the last groundwater from the grasslands, emerging here to die in the ocean. We splashed and drank and laughed.

Then Violet went squelching back to the chariot, stretched out below it in the shade, and went to sleep.

When I saw him sitting up, leaning against a wheel, I went marching over and knelt down to speak. During his long absence I had napped, eaten, napped again, tried archery, bathed many times, and discovered the fun of rollicking in surf. I had almost drowned in learning about undertow. I had killed a bird with my sling. I had even dug out the mirror and confirmed what my fingers had been telling me about a moustache, although it had a disappointingly accidental appearance.

"I thought you'd died," I said. I had checked three times to make sure he had not, but I tried to sound as if I were joking.

He took a moment to reply. "No." It was a sigh of regret.

"Can I bring you some food, sir?"

He shook his head and continued to stare at the faint smudge of hills that we had left behind us. He looked very old and spent—and limp, as if he had been blown against that wheel by the wind like a litter of leaves.

"Can you live by that now?"

I was holding my bow. Archery was not as simple as I had hoped. "Not yet, sir."

"I'll show you how to fish. There are lots of fish."

That sounded as if he might be planning to abandon me. I was alarmed, but I did not question. When he spoke again, it was of other things. For the only time in our acquaintance, in this moment of defeat, he revealed a glimpse of his soul.

"They knew," he said. "Heaven has known for a long time. The texts warned them. It always happens."

"Sir?"

"Happens every cycle. But not so bad. Never as bad as this."

"No, sir?" But he was not really talking to me.

"Trouble was, not enough angels. Not enough men, not enough equipment . . . too many herdfolk. You got any idea how many descendants one woman can have in the ninth or tenth generation?''

"No, sir."

"About a million—and that's not counting sons."

He wiped his face with the usual rag and let his hand fall back to the sand with it. "They've been sending us out for . . . for a month. Your father must have been one of the first."

A month is one of the twelve north–south strips that the angels use to define the world, but they also use the term to denote time, the time taken for the sun to cross one month. I was about a month old, more or less. But I did not understand all that then.

"Doesn't work with herdfolk," he went on. "They won't spread the word around, like other peoples . . . won't cooperate." The wind lifted the rag from his hand and rolled it out into sunlight, and away across the sand. I jumped to retrieve it. When I returned, he was still talking.

". . . at the north end. Let just enough woollies by to feed them. Kill off the rest and spare the grass . . . narrow, it is. And the rest of us were to send them up there, stop them going south. Should have stayed."

"You did what you could, sir?"

He looked up at me blearily. "I went to save the herdfolk. Looks like I saved one. No, you're half angel. So I saved half a herdman. Should have stayed."

He fell silent, staring again at the distant hills where the people were dying. Suddenly I knew what was alarming me most— his eyes. They had the same flat hopelessness that had haunted the eyes of the herdfolk . . . yet we had escaped, had we not?

Probably he had guessed what I only learned much later, from the saints. Heaven lost more angels on that herdfolk mission than it had ever lost before. Too many waited around too long and died alongside those they had come to save, snared by the doldrums of High Summer.

Then I asked the one question that I had been carefully trying not to consider. "My family, sir?"

His unwinking eyes crawled around to study mine. "What do you think?"

I nursed my agony for a while in silence. Violet had been running away, even then. He wouldn't have been running if he'd thought he could do any good by staying. I shook my head.

"Not quite hopeless," Violet said, but he didn't fool me. He didn't mean to—he was just being gentle. I wanted Anubyl to have saved my family. I wanted him to have escaped, so I could find him and kill him myself. But I knew he could not have reached the sea before he starved.

Vengeance was denied me.

"What do we do now, sir?"

"You go south. Eat fish. Lots of fish in the surf. There will be springs, along the edge of the sea."

I looked over the barren, windswept sand, the rocky hills and misty islands. I shivered.

"Go south, lad. Then west. The ocean will be shrinking. By the time you've got your growth, you'll be on the west shore. The herds will be coming in from the north. You can make your kill then . . . little woollies of your own, little blue-eyed herd-babies."

"Sir, I want to be an angel."

He sighed and reached for the canteen that I had laid beside him when he first went to sleep. The drink seemed to revive him slightly, and he sat up, wiping his mouth.

"No. They'd never take a herdman."

"I shall go and ask, anyway."

"Then you still go south . . . turn east at the Great River."

I was already on my knees. For the first time I begged. "Sir—take me with you! Please?"

He stared at me glassily and said, "Not where I'm going."

So he knew.

He unloaded his chariot and caulked the seams where planks had dried out. Then he repacked it in seaworthy fashion, as he had been taught when he was a cherub.

He showed me surf fishing and clam digging, and there are few easier ways of gaining a living than those. He told me how to approach strangers, and he explained about doing work to earn charity, and how to behave toward women. He talked of Heaven, but he still advised me to go west.

I helped him, and practiced archery. I cooked our meals, doing what I could to be useful. We ate and slept and worked more, while the sun glared murder from the sky, while the wind blew sand, and the whitecaps rolled unceasing. In a sense, he gave me a lecture as my father would have done, although he told of other things, and it went on much longer.

Then he left me standing on the shore, wearing a pagne, as I had when he snatched me from the teeth of the tyrant. He had given me what I needed to survive—a rod and much line, bow and arrows, and a hat, and two water bottles. And a purpose. He turned his dead eyes away from me as he said, "Good luck, son!" I was the taller now.

"I'll see you in Heaven!" I said, hoping my lip was not trembling too much. "That's a promise."

He nodded and shook my hand, and sailed away.

I watched until I could not be sure of his sails among the waves. Then I turned to the south and began to walk, already beginning to hear the mocking whispers of Loneliness in the rush of waves and the sighing of the wind.

But in his last words to me, Violet had not called me "herdbrat."

From the joyful moment of joining until the final tears of farewell, most men have only one father to give them life and show them their place in the world.

I had three.

# 4

## The Seafolk

The great ones saw me first, an emaciated wild man, burned almost black by the sun. My long hair was bleached white, my beard hung halfway down my chest. I was without bow, or rod, or clothes, and must have been very close to death.

The great ones told the seafolk. Pebble and some of the other men came ashore, and I fled in terror into the rocks. The men went and fetched the women, and Sparkle came after me alone, bearing food and water. Sparkle always had courage.

I do not recall that meeting, nor how she calmed my wild-beast soul. I do not even remember the subsequent journey, when the women had coaxed me at last into their coracle—which I called a chariot, to their great amusement. I should certainly never have entered it, or stayed in it, had I observed how it was powered.

They took me out to the grove and put me in a bower, a dim wickerwork nest, fragrant and bright with trailing blossom.

At first my only companion was ancient Behold, gnarled and scraggy, the first truly old person I had ever met. Her dangling dugs made me think of tent flaps, but she was a gentle nurse and a resolute protector against those who would have pestered me.

A few meals, a few sleeps, and I began to take notice of my

surroundings—an egg-shaped green shade, more spacious than a tent and much higher. The walls and floor were spongy with seamoss. Next to the watervines, seamoss is the most useful of the many plants that colonize a seatree grove. There was no furniture, but the floor was more comfortable than any bed I had ever known, rocking as waves ran through below it. The walls blazed with blossom—chains and bells and sunbursts of pure color—soaring to meet a roof where blue sky sparkled through leaves. Had I died? Could this be the Paradise that the Heavenly Father promised?

The seatree is a curious vegetable. Far below the surface it trails a single long root—for balance, and to act as anchor if the plant drifts into shallows. It also spreads a shallow canopy of floating tendrils that lock with those of other trees to build a grove. Upward sprout a multitude of thin trunks, barely thicker than canes. Wherever two come into contact, their continuous shiftings rub off the bark, and they grow together, merging into a solid joint. Left to itself, a copse of seatrees would soon become an impenetrable jungle, twice the height of a man. The seawomen cultivate passageways, weaving walls and floors, and forming a single communal dwelling of enormous extent. Basketwork becomes solid grid, the leaves keep out the sun, and the whole network flexes and squeaks as the waves run below it and through it. It is cool and secure and comfortable.

The grove creaked and rustled all the time, and over that steady melody I could hear voices, both near and far, in song and talk and laughter. Sometimes I heard voices raised, but never in argument or quarrel, only in conversation—it was usually easier just to shout through walls than go visiting.

Eventually I sat up, shakily. At once a man's deep bass burst out near at hand, and I flinched with a wail of alarm.

"Are better, then?" said a voice.

With another start, I saw that I was not alone. Toothless old Behold was sitting cross-legged at the far end of the bower, braiding leather.

"Some," I said nervously.

She grinned at me, her face a restless seascape of wrinkles.

"Feel strong now?"

"Oh, very strong!" I said. "Like a horse." I was joking, but Behold misunderstood. Chuckling, she rolled up her work, tucked it under one arm, and crawled across the billowy floor to a hole not much larger than a tusker burrow. I watched her depart with some apprehension. Had I somehow insulted her?

Still weak, I lay down again and tried not to tremble when those male voices sounded too close. If I couldn't eat or drink, I could always take another nap, I thought. Then the light was blocked, and my eyes snapped open again. A woman was kneeling over me. Like Behold, she wore only a pagne. She was much younger, and very close, and I did not think of tent flaps. Cool fingers brushed my cheek.

"Says are feeling strong now?"

I gulped. "A little stronger."

She smiled, and lowered her lips to mine.

I turned out to be stronger than I had thought—strong enough to accept what was offered, at least. I also decided that my suspicions were correct. I must certainly have died.

When I awoke the next time, there was another woman altogether lying at my side, just as inspiringly desirable as the first. Much of my recovery is a blur in my mind, but food, sleep, and loving care of that magnitude work miracles on a man. The dream girls appeared and ministered to me and then vanished, to be replaced by others no less lovely. With the third I was capable of asking her name. With the fifth I began to make conversation.

While I was still dallying gently with the sixth, a man thrust his head through the doorway and leaned giant fists on the moss. His arms and shoulders were as massive as a herdmaster's, but smooth instead of furry. His hair was tightly curled, and his brown woolly beard encircled a huge toothy grin.

"Am Pebble!" he said.

I managed a timorous smile, clutching tight to my companion, whose name was Flashing, and who seemed quite unconcerned at being discovered in such revealing intimacy.

"I'm Knobil."

The newcomer grinned more widely yet and extended a hand that looked as large as a small saddle.

With my heart thumping madly, I released Flashing and crawled over to him. His hand swallowed mine whole and my wrist as well.

"Like sunfish, Knobil?"

"I don't know."

"Will have good surprise, then! Are feasting. Caught very big sunfish! Come!" He chuckled and disappeared.

Flashing was tying on her pagne, and I suddenly realized that I should do the same. I scrambled back to her to get it, while congratulating myself on having actually shaken hands with a man. I had seen Violet do that, and my father.

The seafolk garments were much briefer than any I had known in my youth, merely a scrap of sealskin with two thongs attached, wrapped around and knotted. Flashing laughed. We were both kneeling on the moss; she reached out and grabbed my pagne, and for one inspiring moment I thought she wanted a rematch, but all she did was give it a twist around. "Tied on wrong side!" she explained, her eyes twinkling perceptively. The knot went on the left side, apparently.

Pebble was waiting for me in the corridor, and I was astonished to discover that he was no taller than myself. He wore the same scanty pagne of golden sealskin, and above it he had the chest and shoulders of a herdman, but from the waist down he was as slim and short as a trader. The seafolk, I was soon to discover, are all that shape—not truly large, but seeming so because of their enormous chests. I had already noticed the women.

"Come!" he said again, and set off along the passage at a trot.

The floor was springy with moss, moving rhythmically as waves ran below it. I took two steps and pitched flat on my face. I scrambled up and repeated the process.

Chortling loudly, Pebble returned to help me. There was no sympathy in his grin, but there was no mockery, either. He just found my clumsiness very funny, and evidently expected me to do the same. Flashing had either tarried behind or gone another way.

Steadied by Pebble's giant hand, I staggered along the passage, feeling like a stupid child. The corridor twisted and branched until my head spun. The grove was not solid, though. From time to time we passed water-filled clearings. The small ones were dark and shaded, the large ones sun-bright. The seafolk call them "doors."

As we walked, Pebble was continually catching protruding sprigs and tucking them back into the wicker walls. He was probably not even aware he was doing it, but it is only thus that the seatrees can be kept from filling every cranny of the copse.

"Will like sunfish!" he proclaimed. "Is very hard to catch. Am best hunter in the tribe! Have big feast now."

The thought of a big feast was unnerving. Already I regretted my rash decision to come. I knew so little about these folk! They seemed to be friendly, and I was deeply grateful, but I was now remembering Violet's sternest warning—that with strangers one must always try to discover their mating habits as soon as possible, because sexual customs vary greatly. A mistake with those is the fastest road to trouble, he had said. I wondered what trouble I might have stumbled into already.

"Sir . . ."

Pebble's teeth shone. " 'Sir' me and feed you to fish!"

"Pebble, then?"

"Mm?" Without breaking stride, he pulled a blossom from the wall and proceeded to eat it.

"Friend Pebble? This . . . making waves . . . with Flashing . . ."

"And Wave? And Sea Wind! Is good one, yes?" His twinkling eye said that my activities had been no secret. "And Silver? Mmmm!"

"It's all right, then? No one minds? I don't understand your customs, you see."

"Is not customs, is just way of life." He looked puzzled, chewing vigorously. He plucked another flower and handed it to me. "Eat that—is good. Did enjoy Flashing?"

"Very much!" I was sure that such open generosity did not fit any of Violet's teachings—it also deeply offended my herdman sense of right and wrong, although that had not stopped me from accepting it. "What happens if . . . what happens if the woman becomes . . . if she learns she is going to bear a child?"

Pebble stopped dead and stared at me wide-eyed. "Have big feast for her! Are very happy! Love babies very much!"

"Oh!" I said warily. "That's nice."

I did not dare inquire what responsibilities the child's father had, but in fact the answer would have been outside my wildest guesses—none at all. Unique among all the peoples of Vernier, the seafolk need never worry about food, because they have the great ones to help them. Moreover, any adult would die of starvation before seeing a child go hungry. The whole tribe nurtured the children.

"Is my feasting place!" Pebble exclaimed proudly, leading me into one of the larger clearings. The central pool shone bright in the steep rays of the sun, while the broad shelf of soft green moss surrounding it was shaded by the overhang of the trees. Water and moss flexed together as the sea's gentle swell ran through the glade. A fire crackled and steamed at the far side. Many people were already there, standing or lounging around on the platform—mostly women, but a few children of assorted ages. From the smallest to ancient old Behold, who was tending the fire, every one showed the thick chest and shoulders of seafolk, and every one of them had woolly brown curls. At the sight of me, they fell silent in surprise.

I was paralyzed to be facing such a crowd, and yet at once I sensed that something looked wrong. There were at least four times as many women as men there—that seemed perfectly natural to me—but very few children. I had opened my mouth to ask about that, but fortunately I didn't have a chance to hurt my hosts' feelings.

For at that moment a roar of welcome filled the feasting place. I might have turned and fled, had Pebble not still been gripping my arm. Before I could even try, I was enveloped in a breaking surf of people, all riotously attempting to hug and kiss me—men, women, and children. The mossy shelf on which we stood could not bear the weight; it bent, and the giant ball of seafolk with its terrified herdman center tipped gently off into the water.

To everyone but me, this was hilariously funny, and became even funnier when they realized that their visitor could not swim and had not returned to the surface. I was hauled up from the depths, set on the moss, and thumped until I stopped coughing. The smaller kids were rolling in helpless mirth, and some of the adults openly weeping at such unexpected merriment. The inside of my nose hurt even more than my dignity, and my breathing was not helped by the number of people still trying to kiss me.

But then a voice began calling for some consideration for the guest. It was not Pebble, though. As a herdman, I was shocked to discover that a woman was shouting orders and hauling people back to give me air. Much more surprising was that even the men were obeying her with good-humored grins.

Pebble beamed proudly. "Is wife, Sparkle."

Violet had told me about wives. In cultures where marriage was practiced, he had said, a woman was allowed to choose the man who would own her, or at least she might protest if she did not approve of her father's choice. Usually, but not always, a man was limited to owning one wife, and therefore might display dangerous jealousy.

Violet would very likely have approved of Sparkle. I certainly did. She was older than Pebble, smallish and rather slender for the women of that tribe. Some races might have preferred wider hips in a woman, but the seafolk are a beautiful people, and although the men of the tribe did not rate Sparkle as the loveliest, I considered her just perfect. She had a dignity and purpose that others did not, and yet she lacked none of the childlike gaiety that they had. Her face was round and happy—dark eyes, brown curls, and a fascinating dimple that came and went unpredictably. Even if she did not curve as voluptuously as some, true beauty flows also from within, from a brightness of spirit, and none could match Sparkle in that.

She sat herself on one side of me and put an older man, Eyes, on the other, all our legs dangling in the water. Then she directed the flow of people, so that I could meet the company one at a time. First the children climbed all over me, giggling, fingering my straight gold hair and beard, gazing close into my blue eyes as though they were peepholes to my soul, hugging, and kissing.

Behind them came the women. Their greetings were just as innocently intimate and exuberant as the children's.

Then even the men, in their turn, enveloped me in tight embraces that I found strange and frightening. But I was delighted to discover that none of the men was larger than I. Either I had grown enormously in my time on the sands or I was not a midget, as I had always believed.

Pebble was now running around, greeting his guests and putting flowers in their hair. My hair was too straight to hold a blossom, so he tucked one behind my ear and the laughter started all over again.

More visitors entered the clearing from underwater, including a woman holding a tiny baby, who seemed undisturbed by the experience. There was more kissing and fondling. An elderly couple came in through one of other doorways.

Behold's fire sizzled and hissed on a floating pad of moss. The seafolk made fires rarely—at least in that climate—and always put them on such a floating hearth. Probably the surrounding jungle was much too damp to burn, but it was their home and on this they took no chances.

The steamy odor of sunfish was making my mouth ache. Pebble came around with a basket full of tasty morsels, urging everyone to fill both hands. They were delicious, although I did not know what they were, and I was shocked speechless at the sight of a man serving food.

By then I had met everyone, and the hugging had ended. By then, too, the mossy shelf had sunk so that we were all sitting in the sea, with the warm swell rising to our waists.

I noticed that all the men tied their pagnes at the right, except one. His name was Sand, and he was a fuzz-faced adolescent, Pebble's brother. Apparently Sand lived within a permanent cloud of girls, having rarely less than four clustered close around him. All of them, and almost all the older women, tied their belts on the left hip, like Sand himself, and Flashing, and me. Having been able to catch my breath, I asked Sparkle.

She half-turned to smile at me in disbelief. "Not know? Is sign of being married, Knobil. Am Pebble's wife. Is my husband. Have our pagnes tied at right. Sand not married. Nor you."

I nodded in understanding. "There were some girls who came . . . I mean, I dreamed that girls came to visit me . . ."

"Were making waves?"

I nodded uneasily.

Sparkle was well named. Her eyes gleamed brighter than anyone else's and her laugh was pure sunshine. "Not wives, Knobil! Don't dream of wives. Make waves with others—no waves for wives!"

"I promise," I said. "It may not be an easy promise to keep, though."

"Must be very strong!" she said warningly. Under the water,

her hand was stroking my thigh. Sparkle had been the very first of those dream girls to come to my bed.

Pebble had slid into the sea and begun bringing the fire around the clearing. He was effortlessly treading water, only his head above the surface. As he reached each guest, he would spear a slice of the sunfish on a big bone fork and hold it up, laughing and talking all the time. I would not have thought that forty or so people could have produced so much noise. Even the singing continued while they ate.

I accepted a slab of sunfish so large I had to hold it in both hands. I tore at it joyfully. Everyone else was doing the same.

"Herdmen have many wives?" Sparkle inquired innocently, so at some time in my illness I must have told them that I was a herdman.

One thing I had not learned from Violet was tact. "Not wives. A herdmaster owns his women."

Sparkle wrinkled her gorgeous nose in disapproval.

"I . . . I don't disapprove of wives!" I said hastily.

She half-choked on a mouthful of sunfish and sniggered.

"I mean . . ." I said, and then lapsed into uneasy silence.

Pebble finished serving the sunfish and emerged onto the shelf with the rest of us to begin gorging, talking all the time like everyone else. Unwanted scraps went into the water and ominously vanished.

"Friend . . . Knobil?" Pebble said with his mouth full. "Is foolish name!"

"Why so?" I asked politely.

"Doesn't mean anything!"

"It means me."

Pebble pulled a face, wiping dribbles of fat from his beard with the back of a paddle-sized hand. "Need a song!"

The audience broke into cheers of agreement.

"What sort of song?" I asked.

When a child is born to the seafolk, I was told, the parents compose a song and sing it to the tribe and to the great ones, and that song is the child's name, although usually only the first word is used. His song is almost the first thing a child learns to say . . . or sing, rather.

I demanded some examples, and several youngsters eagerly sang their names for me. As a herder I had whiled away much of my youth in composing impromptu jingles—singing was about the only entertainment possible for children herding woollies, and I had always had a knack for inventing verses. I scratched my beard for a moment, then sang how the golden sand was warm and soft, but mourned because the sea was brighter; then a lucky wave washed over it and thereafter the sand was happy because it could also sparkle.

This faint effort earned tremendous applause, probably more because of the tune than the words—I had used a fine grassland melody that was obviously new to my audience. I had to repeat the performance several times, and from then on I was not Knobil but Golden.

Then Pebble called for silence.

"Being better makes us all glad!" he proclaimed. "Will now tell us his story. How did come to be on the beach, Golden?"

"I am a pilgrim," I said. "I am on my way to Heaven."

Cold disapproval fell over the clearing. Black glances were exchanged. There was no sound except chewing.

"What's wrong?" I asked nervously. "You don't approve of pilgrims?"

"Is waste of good man!" Sparkle said. "Need you here, Golden." She had finished her meal and was now surreptitiously fondling my thigh again—the underside this time.

"Must stay!" Pebble agreed.

"I need to recover my health. I shall be very grateful if you let me stay until then, until I've recovered my strength."

Sparkle pinched me.

The seafolk could not remain disapproving for long, and soon Pebble asked which way I needed to go. I mentioned the Great River, and explained that I had only a vague idea of where it might be. There were many thoughtful glances around, and then everyone turned to the three old folk.

"Is long," Behold said. "But going downstream. Help Golden with raft, maybe?"

Sparkle saw my surprise. "Remembers journey here," she explained. "Before was born."

"Before she was born?"

She laughed. "Me! Came from South Ocean."

"Talk to great ones!" Pebble shouted, jumping to his feet.

"Time met them, anyway. Can hold breath, Golden? Will take you!"

I was not sure what was involved, but already I felt I could trust Pebble. Ever since Anubyl had beaten my mother, I had known that I was a despicable coward, yet I hoped to hide that fact from my hosts. I was overwhelmed by the hospitality of these kindly seafolk, and I would certainly lose their friendship if they learned the truth about me, so I rashly said that of course I could hold my breath. Pebble was in the water at once, waiting for me. I joined him, nervously supporting myself by clutching at the tangle of roots below the moss.

"Deep breaths!" he commanded. "More! Now hold my belt."

I took hold of his pagne and was yanked under as he sounded—down into darkness and utter silence. It was the first complete darkness I had ever known. I could feel the water surging past and the power of his strokes below me. Tentatively I opened my eyes, and saw nothing at all. Fortunately I did not panic—I just froze, too terrified even to struggle. Roots stroked along my back like hard fingers.

How long? I did not think I could hold my breath much longer.

Then we passed under another clearing. I saw a glimmer of light and vague shapes as our smaller or older companions surfaced for air, for the whole company had come along, but Pebble did not think to stop to let me breathe. He was hardly less at home underwater than on the surface, and any journey was a race to him. Now I was learning what those massive seaman chests were for. Although I was not exerting myself and he was swimming for two, I ran out of air long before he did, while the brightness of our destination was still far, far away.

That time I came very close to drowning. They laid me in the sunshine on the moss apron that bordered the grove, and they worked me like a bellows to empty my lungs of half the March Ocean. Pebble thought it was hilarious.

"Must teach you swimming, Golden," he said, scratching the woolly beard around his grin. "And soon, think."

By the time I had recovered enough to take part in events again, everyone who had been present at the feast had arrived. A wide moss platform fringed the outside of the copse, and despite many small seatrees sprouting in it, there was easily enough space for fifty or sixty people. I noticed with surprise that Sparkle was holding the baby I had seen earlier, and again the little mite had not objected to being submerged. More men and women were popping up out of the water, attracted by the noise, clambering up on the spongy green beach. Other seafolk emerged from corridors and walked along to join us in the blinding sunshine. Pebble began making introductions, and I was hauled to my feet to be hugged and kissed by these newcomers. Soon we were ankle deep again, and the wave crests ran past our knees. Again I noticed the strange scarcity of children.

I was between Pebble and Sparkle, with my back to the sea. Fortunately Sparkle had just handed the baby to another enthusiastic admirer. I had been embraced by Blossoms, a hugely fat man, jovial and grizzled, and was now being kissed by his wife Cloudy, who was equally large, and whose way of greeting a young man came perilously near to rape. Then an explosion of whistling and chirping close behind me made me tear loose and whirl around.

I panicked. Cloudy and two others went over in a giant splash as I plunged screaming into the mob. Unable to run in the water, I overbalanced and went down myself, taking two more people. I tried to rise and was struck by a returning wave, and submerged again.

Arms gripped me tightly. I was blinded and spluttering and shaking with terror, but someone was holding me, clutching my head firmly against something soft, soothing and comforting me. Everyone else was bellowing with laughter and, I suppose, helping my victims to rise. I blinked my eyes clear and found myself sprawling on Sparkle's lap. She was kneeling in the foam, clasping my head to her breast and also yelling furiously. "Is not funny! Pebble! Eyes! Must not make fun of a guest . . ."

The mirth faded awkwardly away. I became aware that my face was positioned on Pebble's wife in a way that he might not appreciate. My arms, by merest chance, were around her. I looked up and our eyes met for a moment. Then I tried to struggle loose.

"Tell," she said, not releasing me.

"I thought it was a tyrant . . ." I twisted my head around to take a better look at what had so alarmed me.

Of course the great ones do not look at all like tyrants. They

are fish-shaped, black above and white below, with a big triangular fin on their backs, with two paddle-shaped arms, and wide,
flat tails. They are four or five times the length of a man, some
of the males even larger. This one had surfaced by the edge of
the platform, holding his head out of the water to discover why
the humans were making so much noise. I had seen only the
white underside, the eye, and the slightly gaping mouth, full of
teeth, grinning ominously. The eye was close to the corner of
that mouth and seemed tiny in the huge head, but it was larger
than my hand. No, it did not look like a tyrant, but it was very
near and unthinkably enormous. The head alone stood as high
as a man.

I recoiled with a whimper, and Sparkle clutched me to her
even more tightly. "Is Gorf," she said gently. "Great one. Will
not harm you."

I had made a fool of myself yet again. Worse, I had exposed
my timidity, my lack of manhood. No wonder they had all
laughed at me—a pilgrim, and a coward? Yet I saw that Sparkle
held some sort of authority over them, for again they had obeyed
her commands. But a pilgrim should not need to be held like a
frightened child, and I should not be in this close contact with
a wife. Again I tried to pry free.

"Tell me what is a tyrant?" Sparkle asked, seemingly unaware of the intimacy. Concern filled her dark eyes—her large,
deep, so beautiful eyes.

"It's a people eater. They live in High Summer. But they don't
really look like . . . like Gorf."

"Help you up?" Pebble reached down and helped, firmly.
He was smiling, but perhaps not quite so widely as usual.

"I was startled," I muttered as I regained my balance. "I've
never met a great one before." A weak excuse.

"But have met tyrant?" Sparkle asked, rising also.

I nodded, and stupidly jumped as Gorf piped his ear-
shattering, high-pitched queries again. Pebble wheeled around
and waded over to the edge of the platform, tugging me along
behind him as if about to feed me into that tooth-lined chasm.
I tried vainly to resist until I discovered that Sparkle was coming
also.

Pebble reached out to pat the monster. Gorf snorted and gently
sounded, the vast head going forward and down, the great fin

and back rising, slowly curving over to follow, then the tail for a moment darkening the sky. The crowd rose and fell unevenly as the grove surged.

"Will tell us about tyrant, Golden," Sparkle said, "at next meal. Frighten all the children, and grownups also?"

"Must meet great ones," Pebble insisted. "Stand here! Sing them your song, so know who you are. Then shall ask about Great River." He took Sparkle away and left me to my fate.

So I found myself alone at the edge of the shelf, while everyone else stood back, smiling broadly. My voice was not at its best as I first sang my name to the great ones. I was trying not to wonder if I had been put forward as a human sacrifice. Half a dozen great heads rose from the shiny sea to listen, remaining motionless while the beady eyes studied me carefully.

Then the closest of the great ones turned slightly and hurled a whole ocean of water, taking me completely by surprise and washing me over backward. I sat up to find the human audience howling with laughter, the great ones responding in ear-splitting whistles and deep boomings.

"Like you!" Pebble announced as he ran forward and once more pulled me to my feet. "Only do that for people are liking. Now again!"

I saw amusement in his eyes, and challenge. I set my teeth. The first group of great ones sank out of sight and a dozen others replaced them. This time I kept my voice from quavering, and I was ready for the soaking, as three or four squirted at me.

There were about fifty of the great ones in attendance then, and I had to sing my song four times before I was allowed to rejoin the crowd at the edge of the trees. I wiped my eyes and wrung water from my hair.

Sparkle patted my arm. "All right?" she asked, her smile reassuring.

I nodded and smiled as best I could. Apparently great ones were harmless, but I was still quivering.

Now Pebbles and young Sand and grizzled old Blossoms had taken my place at the water's edge, and were having an argument.

"Speak to the great ones," Sparkle explained.

"They can do that? Really talk?"

She shrugged. "Sometimes works, sometimes not. Is dif-

ficult because don't have real words. Also often don't want
to talk . . ."

Then a head rose from the sea. It was Wheen, a female,
Sparkle said. Apparently Pebble had won the argument, and it
was to be done the way he wanted. He waved his hands to beat
time. Then Blossoms began a string of deep booms, Sand made
clicking notes in the midrange, and Pebble himself shrilled
squeaks in a painfully high falsetto. It was melody, not speech.

I could see fins and dark surges farther out, where other great
ones flowed up to the surface to steal glimpses of the activity
and blow plumes of spray.

The recital ended, Pebble rubbing his throat as if it hurt.
Wheen snorted and responded with a roll of deep thunder below
high clickings. The men tried again, and were drenched for their
pains. Wheen vanished, as if in contempt. Another great one
put his head up—Gorf again, Sparkle said—larger and closer.
The singers tried their harmony once more. Gorf's reply was
longer and more complicated. The audience began muttering
querulously.

Sparkle was frowning. "Think says no river flowing out of
this sea. Is one running in."

Old Behold shouted from somewhere, "Flows out! Think not
remember? Was long, hard, upstream." A couple of the older
folk agreed loudly.

"I'm not sure," I said. "My angel did not say which way it
ran."

Pebble and Sand and Blossoms, intently conferring about their
next message, were suddenly catapulted into the air as a great
one jostled the platform below their feet. All three disappeared
into the sea with ungainly splashes. The human audience yelled
with laughter, and a few of the great ones raised their heads to
make rude chattering noises. Then one of the largest of the
males reared up with Pebble in his mouth. I cried out in horror.

"Is all right!" Sparkle insisted beside me. "Will not eat him."

Up . . . up . . . rose the monster, only the upper half of
Pebble visible. He was yelling and laughing and beating his fists
on the huge snout. At the top of the leap he was released with a
motion halfway between tossing and spitting. He went spinning
through the air, cartwheeling and still shouting. At the last moment he straightened and slid into the water without a splash.

The great one balanced on his tail for a moment, then toppled backward to vanish in an explosion of spray. The seatree grove heaved and swayed.

Two more of the great beasts had emerged, bearing riders. Clutching the giant dorsal fins, Sand and Blossoms were being carried off into the distance in great bounding arcs, faster than a horse could gallop. I thought it must feel like riding a roo.

Then Pebble reappeared, this time upside down, head and arms and chest inside the great one's mouth, legs kicking. Again he was lifted high and flipped even farther into the sky. Again he straightened before he hit the water. I was horrified by the danger—if he fell badly he could break his back. It was a ridiculous game.

Then everyone was playing it. Men and women, youths and girls, all streamed off the platform to sport with the great ones, until only a few old folk and mothers with babies remained. The mossy shelf reemerged as the load decreased. I watched this mass insanity in rank disbelief. Any one of the great ones probably outweighed half the tribe of seafolk, and yet they were all mixed in there together in one mad watery roughhouse, sea and sky full of people and leaping sea monsters.

Then Pebble and another man were thrown skyward simultaneously, narrowly missing each other, and arching over a group of swimmers. I shuddered and averted my eyes. An arm slid around me.

"Is foolish, yes?" said a tallish, young, close lady.

"Oh, yes," I agreed. "I've, ah, I didn't catch your name?"

She moved even closer, smiling dazzling teeth and moist red lips. "Am Misty."

"Am Raindrops," said another voice, and another arm came around from the other side. Shorter and slightly plumper.

"Was first!" Misty said crossly. "Need rest now, Golden."

I put my arms around both of them while I pondered. The mad romp was still proceeding with no sign of end or caution. Now that Misty had mentioned it, I realized that I was indeed staggering with fatigue.

"I do need rest," I agreed.

"My bower!" Misty said.

Raindrops would likely have argued, but I spotted a kiss on

her mouth before she could speak. "Yours next time?" I promised.

"Oh, yes," she said breathlessly, and I went off with my arm around Misty.

Apparently I had a real knack for making friends.

Later I came to know the great ones better, although I could never join in their play as enthusiastically as the seafolk did, and I never quite understood the relationship between them. Many other peoples train animals and use them, as my father rode his horses. Some beasts, like woollies, are used but never trained. But no other people claim to talk with their livestock, as the seafolk do.

The great ones were not confined or tethered. They seemed to gain little from their association with humans except grooming, for the seamen cleaned parasites from their hides. Yet in return they carried the seamen on their backs to hunt fish, they towed boats, they caught seals and retrieved them—and they indulged in those wild watery romps. Indeed, the great ones usually seemed to initiate the play, so I had to assume that they enjoyed the sport as much as the human participants. That raised a question that worried me greatly—who was master and who was pet?

In Heaven I discussed the great ones many times with Saint Kettle. He had been born a seaman, and looked it—a massive, jocular tub of a man, with a tonsure of snowy curls. He was also wise and learned, and I pressed him often to tell me how well he thought the seafolk could truly converse with the great ones. He would never quite commit himself.

"Are they intelligent, then?" I asked him once.

"The great ones? Of course they're intelligent!" Then he sighed and added quietly, "But I'm none too sure about the seafolk."

# 2

The grove floated in the mouth of a wide bay between two ranges of hills that ran down into the sea to become islands. At about the time I arrived, the trees rooted themselves to avoid being washed ashore. There was some discussion among the seafolk over this, for they felt happier when their home was mobile. They could have cut the longest roots and then asked the great ones to tow the grove back into deeper water, but nothing was decided, and soon there were too many tethers in place to bother with. It was a pleasant location, all agreed, with a good stream of fresh water nearby. The watervines were not quite adequate and even seafolk like to wash off the salt sometimes.

As he had promised, Pebble taught me to swim, although almost any child was better at it than I ever became. Then he took me hunting and taught me that also, riding on the backs of the great ones.

The procedure was simple. The hunter took net or spear to the water's edge and sang his name. Only rarely was there not a quick response. It was also possible to sing the name of a particular great one, but they would not always come to such a summons, even if they were in the neighborhood. Usually Pebble rode Gorf. I was never sure whether Gorf was his favorite or he was Gorf's—probably the latter, for I was adopted by a young male named Frith, who came to my voice more often than any of the others did. He was very patient with my beginner's shortcomings, but I soon learned the clicking sound that represented laughter.

Eventually the great ones persuaded us that the river I sought lay not far off to the south, and it flowed into the ocean, not out of it as the old folk had expected. A raft or a boat was what I needed, everyone agreed. A raft was easier, so a raft it must be. Driftwood tree trunks were not uncommon, and I began gathering them, with Frith's assistance, and laying them on the beach to dry out.

I learned to hunt, which was a male occupation, although some men did nothing more than trawl a net. With the great ones' help, one man could easily have fed the whole tribe.

Pebble's idea of hunting was nothing like that. The harder the chase the better the taste in his view. He even claimed to be fond of oysters, which contain nothing but bland slime. Collecting those was a terrifying business involving diving very deep while tied to rocks; therefore oysters were mostly a test of manhood. I hated diving for oysters. I hated being battered black and blue in a mad pursuit of sunfish, or crawling through underwater caves that might contain all sorts of stabbing, munching monsters.

Pebble himself seemed to be totally without fear. He must have known of my innate cowardice, but he never mentioned it. He would tell me in vivid detail what horror he had planned for me next, then demonstrate how an expert like him could survive it, and then just grin, daring me to try. I'm sure my teeth were visibly chattering with terror many times, my knees knocking, but I would always try to bluff my way through somehow, and Pebble would then pretend to look impressed. It was very childish, really.

Worst of all, perhaps, were the snarks. A snark looks something like a water-dwelling woollie, paddling madly around on the surface. It is indifferent eating, and comes armed with deadly pincers and stinging tentacles by the hundred. Given the choice, I would not have gone into the same ocean as a snark, but whenever the great ones reported a snark in the neighborhood, Pebble would insist on organizing a snark hunt.

Spears go right though snarks without effect. The only way to catch them is to put a rope around them and tow them to shore. The only way to put a rope around them is to jump over them on a great one. And the only way to survive getting that close to a snark is to run the monster to exhaustion first. This needed every rider we could enlist. The great ones seemed to enjoy the romp also—why not? The stings did not affect them! Vigorous splashing alarmed the quarry, so the great ones drove it with their roolike bounding gait, which was terrifying for a beginner who could not swim much. But I must admit that a snark hunt did have a certain exhilaration to it—a dozen or more great ones, all with riders, arching and leaping over the sea—herding the foaming patch of water where the snark thrashed around—plunging in close when it began to tire—seeing who would be the first to dare try the jump and place the rope. That man was the hero of the hunt, of course. Yes, it was insanity, and the stings hurt like hell, but I admit I never turned down an invitation to hunt snark.

And all this I owed to Pebble. Endlessly joyful and willing, brave and gentle without limit, he was the first friend I had ever known. The very idea of friendship was alien to a herdman, and Pebble had to start by teaching me that. He never knew a mean thought in his life, Pebble. He was my first friend and the best I would ever have. And in the end I killed him.

Fortunately Violet had warned me that not everyone venerated the Father God of the herdfolk. The seafolk's deity is the Sea Mother. She is generous and undemanding, asking little of her people. I learned her joyful hymns and tossed small offerings into the water as the seafolk did, and no thunderbolt came to roast my bones. Yet when I was out of earshot of the others, I sang to the Heavenly Father also . . . quietly, just to be sure.

Mathematics was not one of my greater talents, yet I could see that the tribe had fewer children than my father had sired on a mere four women. At first I wondered if the sea was prowled by some marine equivalent of roos, a predator that could carry off youngsters, but then I noticed the absence of pregnancies. The birth rate was at fault, therefore. I assumed that this was due to the fish diet. Certainly I yearned often for red meat.

Company I never had to yearn for. I had only to smile and I would be invited into a bower to rest. Seawomen had very energetic ideas of what resting involved. Even some of the knot-on-the-right-side wives were not above fluttering eyelashes in my direction. Having unlimited choice available elsewhere, I politely ignored such improper suggestions.

I had innumerable friends, both male and female; I had food and comfort without limit; I had the thrill of hunting and the satisfaction of mastering new skills. What more could a man want?

Well, Sparkle for one thing.
And Heaven for another.
How foolish is youth! In the midst of every comfort and satisfaction a man could possibly desire, my ambition to be an angel still niggled at me like an unreachable itch. I had promised Violet I would meet him in Heaven. I had promised myself! I was still young enough to believe I could make the world a better place, and my conscience scolded me for tarrying when I should be hurrying. Of course I didn't know it was my conscience speaking; I thought it was the Father God.

I was a welcome guest at all the feasting places, rewarding my host with a gift of my catch, when I had one, and with my herdfolk songs. The best melodies I knew were hymns that might have offended the Sea Mother, but my knack for inventing doggerel let me put new words to the old tunes. Young and old, the seafolk loved to laugh, and they liked nothing better than hearing some trivial incident of their commonplace lives turned into a satirical ballad, especially if the victim was known to be within earshot. Often the end of my song would be greeted by laughter and applause pouring in through the walls all around. Then I would have to repeat it, again and again, until the whole tribe had memorized it and was chorusing in complex harmony. The victim usually sang along as heartily as any.

And eventually I would be lured away to a bower to rest.

I have never thought of myself as clever, yet I cannot imagine why I was so stupid as to miss what those young ladies really wanted. My enlightenment came suddenly, at a *big* feast.

Feasts were commonplace. A *big* feast was a special event, involving the whole tribe. No normal eating place could hold everyone at the same time, but the copse happened to have a large natural clearing in the middle that served very well, although it was an odd shape. A *big* feast was held in someone's honor—and if there was no one who deserved honoring, then apparently an excuse could always be found to honor someone anyway. The first I attended had been dedicated to Surge, to celebrate a proposal of marriage from young Sand. All the other unwed maidens were looking very long-faced, for no other boys seemed about to start developing moustaches and related qualifications.

I had congratulated Sand when I heard the news, of course, and asked him jocularly what factors contributed to his decision. He had produced a leer astonishingly like his brother's, and whispered that Surge was going to bear his child—a fact that everyone but me would have already guessed. I just added more congratulations and complimented him on his taste, carefully not mentioning that I had enjoyed surging with Surge a couple of times myself.

Then we had a *big* feast honoring Wave, and then one for Misty. They were both widows—Misty's husband Darkly had broken his neck romping with the great ones. That was why she had not wanted to stay and watch the roughhousing, that time she had snatched me away from Raindrops and led me off to rest. I had heard all about it later, while she wept all over my chest, in great need of more comforting.

Nobody had told me why Wave and Misty were being honored. Or Spiral, or Sea Wind, two other widows whose feasts followed. They were just great people, I was informed, and of course I agreed. Especially Misty.

As least by this time I had managed to account for the missing men. They had not been sent out like herdmen loners, as I had at first suspected. With very few exceptions, they had been victims of accidents. Fin had drowned collecting oysters. Watery had been stung by a lilbugger, and Sing eaten by darts. Such news did nothing to encourage a novice swimmer and sea-hunter. When I thought about all those deaths, I saw that a great many of them could have been prevented had there been help at hand. Having much more wisdom than courage, I never went hunting alone; nor did I let my romps with Frith get out of hand.

And then—long, long overdue—I solved the mystery of the missing children. I was attending yet another *big* feast, and I was in a sulk. We had been hunting snark. Pebble had tried to jump it too soon, and been brutally stung. Pebble, in consequence, was not present. He was in no danger, everyone had assured me cheerfully. The oozing red welts that covered him and the screams he was not entirely able to suppress . . . they would pass. So Pebble had been left to suffer alone, writhing in lonely agony, and everyone else had gone off to the *big* feast, dragging me along also, insisting that Pebble did not need me.

I had assumed then that the *big* feast was going to be in my honor. I had made the next jump, very shortly after Pebble. That was an unheard-of display of recklessness for me—I must have given Frith the wrong signal in my excitement. But I had made the jump and I had not been stung, and so I could reasonably expect to be honored. Why else would I have been dragged bodily to the feast?

But the feast was to honor yet another widow, Thunder. I liked Thunder—we had made oceanfuls of waves together—and yet I did not feel much like singing her praises. I was, perhaps, worried about poor Pebble. I was probably miffed because I thought I deserved the feast more than Thunder did. And I was certainly disturbed by Sparkle.

There I was, sitting on moss in the shade, leaning back against a wall of cane, chewing an insipid chunk of snark, while Pebble's wife snuggled closer and closer. Her shoulder was against my shoulder, her thigh against my thigh. She did this every chance she got. Lately her invitations had become quite blatant. Pebble was my best friend, my first friend . . . I was not going to bed his wife!

The problem was to stop her bedding me. There are limits beyond which a man's self-control should not be tested.

Her authority over the others had not faded—no one else would come near me while Sparkle was flirting. She was my friend's wife. Worst of all, though, I had been already half crazy with desire before she even started.

She had rescued me from the rocks, although I could recall little of that. She had been the first one to visit me in Behold's bower. That experience also was fuzzy in my mind, but it had been glorious therapy for me. I had recovered very rapidly after that. She had comforted me when I was frightened by the great ones. I wanted her desperately.

Crazy!—so many gorgeous women available, and I was hankering most after one I must not take. Other wives did not affect me like that. Some of them dropped hints, but I found them easy to refuse. But Sparkle . . . she roused me like storms raise waves.

And she knew it, damn her!

Then cool fingers found their way through the seatree canes and stroked my kidneys.

"Sparkle!"

She sighed. "Yes, Golden?"

"You should not be doing this to me."

"Want to do much more to you."

"It is not fair to Pebble."

"Is sick! Cannot love poor Sparkle. Won't know!"

"Sparkle! This is wrong! Why are you behaving like this?"

"Am trying to get baby."

I choked on a hunk of snark, and it was a moment before I was able to speak again. But by then I had located young father-to-be Sand putting on airs at the far side of the clearing. Surge was by his side. She bulged visibly now.

So did Wave. So did Misty. *Almighty Father!*

"That's what this feast is for? Because Thunder thinks I've . . . because she's expecting?"

"Thinks is expecting," Sparkle said complacently, while the scratch of her fingernail on my backbone was shooting muscle spasms all the way to my toes.

That was why they had all insisted I come to the feast—typical seafolk humor! I was appalled. How stupid could a herdman be? Not one woman in the grove had been visibly pregnant when I had first come, and now there were . . . I started to count, and my mind was instantly boggled. No one was close enough to overhear, yet my voice shrank almost to a whisper. "But what's going to happen if Surge's baby has blue eyes?"

Sparkle sniggered. "Is still Surge's baby. Is still Sand's baby."

"Oh, is it? Is it really? And whose baby is Misty going to produce?"

"Darkly's," Sparkle said airily.

"But he was dead before I came. Long before!"

Sparkle raised delicate eyebrows almost to tight brown curls. "So?" Patiently she explained—any baby born to a widow was naturally regarded as her late husband's. Only if she remarried would the real father be recognized. So strongly did the seafolk accept that fiction that Sparkle had no doubt at all that Darkly would be the father of Misty's baby. Blue eyes and gold hair would not change her mind if she did not wish to have it changed.

The seafolk doted on babies. They adored babies—and their womenfolk were not producing them. Hence the promiscuity that I both despised and enjoyed. Apparently every woman was willing to try every man in the hope that the right combination would work the magic.

And into this desperate but unspeakable situation blunders a virile young herdman, raised on a diet of red meat. *Impact!*

My explanation was all wrong, of course, but it was to take another angel to correct me.

Sparkle leaned crushingly against me and gazed soulfully into my eyes. "Need help, Golden!"

"No!" I insisted, while sweat trickled down my temples and my heart tried to smash itself to pieces on my ribs. "Pebble is my friend."

"Wants a son very much, Golden."

Big black eyes, had Sparkle—eyes to melt a man like butter in sunlight. "Then let him make it himself!" I scrambled to my feet and ran from her before my resolution rotted away completely.

I went straight to Sparkle's bower, but I went alone. I stayed there, laying cool compresses on Pebble to ease his pain. He was very grateful, but I suspected he had been surprised to see me.

The seafolk had been right, though—a couple of sleeps made Pebble as good as new, completely unrepentant. I knew he would be wise to take things easy, and very unlikely to, so I cornered him and begged his help for my raft.

I had a plentiful supply of wood gathered—the problem had been finding spare rope. Rope was made from vines or sealskin, and everyone in the grove had promised to braid me some. Nobody ever finished any, of course, except old Behold. From her, from odd corners, and with what I had made myself, I had enough to start.

So Pebble and I headed for the margin of the copse, each bearing a weighty bundle. I found a certain irony in thinking how glad he should be to help me leave, for I knew that Sparkle would wear down my resistance eventually—I burned whenever I thought of her. And I was determined to be gone before all those golden-haired babies started to appear. Surely the other men would tie a boulder to my genitals and drop it in deep water?

And my ambition to be an angel? I could feel it seeping away. If I didn't leave soon, I never would.

We loaded my supplies into one of the coracles. I sang for Frith, but Gorf came instead, having noticed Pebble. I tossed him the towing hoop and sat down quickly, knowing how fast a boat would leap forward when a great one began pulling.

It leapt, but seaward. I gestured toward the shore. We continued to plunge in the wrong direction, bouncing violently over the swell, with Pebble leaning back and grinning at my annoyance. I knew the procedure, though. I cast off the towing line and we came to a stop, rocking gently. In a moment Gorf tossed the hoop back at me and raised his head over us to gibber angrily.

So we began again. This time we raced twice all around the grove at high speed, until I thought my teeth would be shaken from my head or the boat would fall apart. Once more I had to release the line. All this was typical of the great ones' idea of fun, but at the third attempt Pebble held up my bale of rope so Gorf could see it. His curiosity aroused, Gorf then took us where we wanted to go.

We beached the boat and indulged ourselves by bathing in the creek, removing the salt that always encrusted us, luxuriously drinking our fill. Then we set out along the shore to my treasure of driftwood. We waded through the edge of the waves, for the dry sand would have roasted our feet. The sun's reflected glare made my head swim. After the shady grove, the beach was a murderous white crucible, the wind rough as raspshell.

Pebble scratched his woolly pate and studied my collection of tree trunks with a puzzled expression. They were arrayed like the rungs of a ladder, the latest addition already a few steps from the water and the earliest a long way off. "Why did move them so far, Golden?"

"I didn't," I said. "I think the wind must roll them. It usually blows shoreward, doesn't it?"

"Perhaps is why called 'driftwood'?" he suggested seriously. "Keeps on drifting?"

"I should have thought of that!"

So, in our innocence, we decided that the wood itself must be at fault. Not having thought to bring any sort of foot covering, we could not reach it. Pebble yawned, stretched, and lay down in the lacy edges of the ripples. "Too hot! Need rest."

Not surprised, I sat down beside him to survey the waves breaking and the great ones lolling offshore, spouting and watching what we were doing.

"Sorry are leaving," Pebble said, his eyes closed against the glare of the sky. "Want you to stay."

"I made myself a promise. My family all died, Pebble, because there weren't enough angels. I promised myself I would go to Heaven so I could learn to help people."

"Can have a new family. Lots of girls! Thump them all the way through moss! Make big, big waves! Make babies."

"A man is more than just a baby-making machine!" I protested—and that was a surprising insight for a herdman.

"Are best hunter after me." Of course he was joking, but I had never heard Pebble sound so close to serious before.

"If I wrapped our two pagnes around my feet," I said hastily, "I could roll the logs. How many do you think I'll need?"

Pebble sighed and sat up. "None."

"What?"

For once there was no smile in that curly mat of beard. "Can ride great ones now, Golden. Suggested raft before that learning. If have to go against flow of river, much easier to carry you than pull raft!"

For a while I sat with my chin on my arms. Then I said, "You all knew that, didn't you? That's why the rope never got made?"

He nodded and for once looked quite solemn. "Want you to stay, Golden. Women all like you. Need you! Are not enough men."

"The women like me," I admitted. "How about the men?"

"Men like you!" His voice went softer. "Need you also, think."

Startled, I glanced at him and then quickly away. Did he suspect what Sparkle had been proposing?

"I think I should leave," I said, weakening.

"Sand will have child soon. Want son, Golden!"

I wanted to scream. I knew my face must be burning hotter than the blistering beach behind us. I racked my brain for something to say.

"Merry-son-of-Pebble!" Pebble said sadly. "Have song all ready." And then he sang a little name song. It was as banal a jingle as could be, but it brought tears to my eyes.

He did know about Sparkle's invitations! He might even have suggested the idea to her, and in another moment he was going to suggest it to me.

"No!" I shouted. "To black hell with the raft, then! I'm not going to stay here and . . . and . . . Oh, damn!"

I jumped to my feet and ran into the surf. I dived through the first breaker and started to swim. Soon Frith surfaced below me, and my legs found his back. I headed for the grove.

I collected two water bottles, a spear, and a hat as fast as I could, but in one of the leafy corridors, Pebble blocked my path.

He spread his feet and put his hands on his hips. In that stance, Pebble was very wide. "Going to collect oysters!" he announced. Even in the dim green shadow, his smile would not have convinced a blind shark.

"Good!" I said, and my smile probably rang no truer than his. "Make sure someone goes with you, though!"

"Very good for manhood."

Oysters had that reputation. "Maybe," I said. "But it would be easier to save the shells and fill them with seawater. They'd taste just the same."

Pebble regarded me sadly. Then he threw his arms around me and hugged me until my ribs creaked.

"Go in care of Great Mother, Golden."

"And you," I mumbled. "Give my love to everybody. Kiss all the girls for me."

He let me by, and I ran for the open sea.

I sang for Frith and he came at once. I mounted his back, singing the notes for *far journey*.

We headed south. Ironically, I could also have gone west, for a ride across the whole width of the March Ocean might have been physically possible, although I never heard tell of anyone trying it. Had I done so and survived, then I should have found the west shore well watered at that time, and the herdfolk reestablishing their way of life after the great dying. The future of Vernier might have been changed . . . but I went south.

I waited for Loneliness to find me and start his maniacal laughing and jeering, but he did not come. Perhaps Frith was keeping him away—or he may have known that I was not going far.

I felt Frith's great body tense. Then he issued the brief squawk that meant he was going to submerge. Startled, I sucked in a quick breath and grabbed tight to his fin. Down we went, into silent blueness, with me peering anxiously around, wondering what unexpected threat had provoked this. I saw nothing except the vague shapes of the two companions he had invited along, or who had perhaps chosen to come with us. I heard nothing, either—but the great ones did, for they can talk across great distances underwater.

Frith spun around so fast that I was very nearly torn loose. Then he surfaced and went surging back toward the grove at all the speed he dared expose me to, while his comrades bounded around us impatiently. They were singing.

Trying to tell me.

I had very little skill at understanding the great ones, and this was a very strange song, a single line of melody instead of their usual complex harmonies. It was maddeningly familiar, and so simple a refrain must be a human message.

Then I knew it. It was a name, a human name, transposed into haunting minor keys.

I kicked Frith savagely, for more speed. I gripped his fin with all my strength and wept into my shoulder from mingled fear and pain. My arms were almost wrenched from their sockets as he dragged me through the water, streaming behind him like trailing weed. I gasped for breath whenever I had the chance, but the lower he sank in the water, the faster he could travel. Once or twice he slowed slightly, rising so that I could settle onto his back again. It was a form of question: can you take this? Each time I answered with harder kicks: more speed!

But human hands and shoulders had their limits, and I was being slowly drowned. My grip failed, and I was gone. Frith spun on his tail with a surge of power that seemed to churn the whole ocean; he took me in his mouth. It was neither comfortable nor dignified, but it was faster. Sitting on his tongue, with my legs jammed hard against his palate, I was forced steadily backward through the sea at a pace I had never experienced before. Buffeted by the torrent, crushed by the pressure, I needed all the strength in my ill-used shoulders just to hold my head up and force my chest away from his snout far enough to breathe. I could see nothing but Frith's great fin and the white wake we were leaving behind us, and I felt every savage beat of his massive tail.

When he spat me out on the moss, I was so battered that Sand and Breakers had to lift me, and hold me up. I looked at their faces. I looked around the platform and dread became stark reality. The seafolk in assembly were waiting only for me, and Pebble's body lay by the water's edge.

"How?" I screamed. "What happened?"

He had gone to collect oysters, they said. No one would go with him, so he had gone alone, and still weak from the snark stings.

He had told me, asked me. I could have done that for him, at least—I had refused to impregnate his wife for him, but I could have helped him gather oysters. One sleep's delay would not have hurt. I could have helped him gather oysters.

Quietly wailing a sad hymn to the Great Mother, the seafolk stood in head-hung dejection, loosely grouped by families . . . a hunter and those who usually ate at his feasting place. I stumbled through the wash to join Sparkle, for I belonged nowhere else. With her were Jewel and Sun, who had never been married and never would be, but who had been eating at Pebble's feasting place lately.

The hymn ended, and heads rose to watch the sea, speckled now with fins as the great ones surfaced. I had never seen so many, nor known that the pod was so large. From time to time one would spout, but otherwise they just seemed to be floating, unmoving and still. I had seen funerals on the grasslands, when a boy was mauled by a dasher or a babe sickened, but I had never imagined anything like this.

For Gorf rose silently from the depths, close by the grove, his great triangular fin like a chariot sail, and one shrewd, cold eye watching us, barely above the water. A great one speaks through a spiracle on top of his head, just in front of the third eye. Now Gorf began to sing Pebble's name. I had heard that often, a summons to come hunt or play, but now it was transformed, a wordless melody converted to a dirge. Gradually the other great ones joined in, harmonizing and embellishing, migrating through strange minor keys in a manner too complex for the human ear to follow, rising to triumph and joy without losing the basic theme or the underpinnings of grief, mourning and yet celebrating, dying away at least through desolate fragments of sorrow and pain until only the song of the ocean itself remained.

Then Gorf drifted in right to the platform edge, and Pebble answered the call from the sea, his body laid across his steed's wide back for his last journey.

We watched without a sound as Gorf moved slowly away toward the horizon, the rest of the pod closing in around him as escort. When fins and waves were barely distinguishable in the glare and tears, Sparkle began to sing, calling Pebble back again. One by one the rest of the tribe joined in, echoing the harmonies of the great ones . . . but that call was not answered. Slowly the lament faded away into stillness and quiet weeping. Pebble had gone.

Why, when the gods created friendship, did they leave us mortal?

The funeral was over, yet I sensed that there was more to come. All eyes were turning in my direction, but it was the women beside me who were the source of interest. Widows and spinsters must eat somewhere, so now Sparkle and the other two must choose a feasting place. I knew what rights they would be granting in return . . . and only a married man could have a feasting place.

I had been moved to tears by the singing, like everyone else, but now my fury came howling back, my rage over an unnecessary death. I had killed him. I had accepted appointment as tribal stud, so I should have agreed to service his wife, and then he would not have gone looking for the stupid oysters. Or I could have postponed my departure and assisted him.

But any of those brainless, thoughtless seamen there could have gone with him, too. It was as much their fault as mine—more, in fact! Pebble would have asked them, or at least some of them. He might not have thought of danger, but he loved company. Eyes, Sand, Blossoms, Breakers . . . one by one I glared at the men, and each dropped his gaze before the silent accusation.

I glanced down at Sparkle, and her red-rimmed eyes were fixed on me.

"Stay now, Golden?" she whispered. "Need you."

"Need babies, you mean."

She flinched, and then nodded. "And need wise hunter."

I looked bitterly around the groups again. Young as I was, in a sense I was older than anyone there. Loneliness had done that for me—hunger and thirst and unending screaming loneliness. Not one of those seamen had ever endured anything like my long solitary wandering on the beaches. If they needed me it was not for babies—not to father the babies. They needed me to mother the adults. The seamen were killing themselves off through thoughtless stupidity. Even among the herdfolk, a boy never left camp alone—not even to visit the nearest miniroo warren. Why should I struggle all the way to Heaven in the hope of helping people, when here I had a whole tribe in desperate need of a little common sense and discipline? I could do more good here than in Heaven.

I turned back to Sparkle.

She was no longer off limits, and I began to shiver as my desire flamed up to white heat at the thought.

"Marry me!" I said.

She gasped and shook her head. "Would be wrong!"

"Why? Tell me why!" I stepped closer and gripped her arms.

She stared down at the water. "Must make babies for Pebble. If marry you, then make babies for you." She looked up at me in despair, then she winced, and I realized I was squeezing too hard.

"Marry me anyway."

"Marry Thunder?" she said. "Sun? Or Jewel? Can make waves with me, too, then, Golden! Promise."

"No. I am a herdman—I will not share you." I did not ask if she loved me. I don't think the question ever entered my mind. I don't think I even wondered if I loved her. I craved her fiercely, and I must have her for my own.

I could resist all the others, but for Sparkle I would give up even Heaven.

If she was merely one more of the widows, she would be free to leave my feasting place and transfer to another man's. I wanted Sparkle more than anyone or anything else I could imagine, but she must be mine alone.

"I will marry you and no one else!" I said, hearing mutters of disapproval. A crowd was gathering around us as the unmarried women moved in. The platform sank lower.

"But Pebble?" Sparkle wailed.

"Pebble is dead. Say you will be my wife, or I am going— and going now!"

She glanced around the angry throng. The whole world seemed to stop, hanging breathless on her decision. But I knew. Only Sparkle among all of them would risk the tribe's censure— that was why Sparkle was special to me. And suddenly a small smile of triumph escaped at the corner of that seductive mouth . . . she had known what I would say, had foreseen every word. She raised her chin in defiance and nodded agreement at me.

"Will be my husband, Golden?"

Without a word I kissed her until I was giddy with arousal,

then hustled her off to her bower to quench my lust. I did not even wait for all the good wishes and congratulations being showered on us. Cheers and wedding songs had broken out. Seafolk cannot mourn for long.

So I killed my best friend through selfishness. Before my tears were dry I stole his wife and her future children and thereby dishonored his memory. I betrayed my promise to Violet. I discarded forever my ambition to become an angel.

From then on my affairs with the other women were no longer merely mutual fun, they were deliberate baby-making.

I laid down rules for the hunters to reduce the dying. They smiled and obeyed—until the next time I wasn't looking.

As well try to regiment the great ones.

I became a seaman.

Forgotten and unwanted, my collection of driftwood crawled away across the plain until it disappeared in the heat haze.

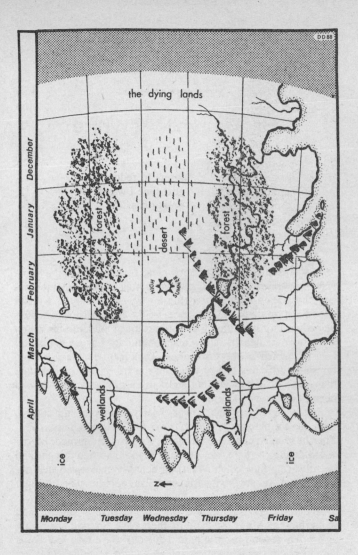

# 5

## Brown-yellow-white

With salt still drying on my skin, I crept through the doorway of Sparkle's bower and paused to make sure I had not wakened her. Then I started picking my way as quietly as I could over the sprinkle of yellow leaves on the floor. The grove itself helped me, its creakings and rustlings much louder in the rough water near the beach. Below that continuing chorus I could still hear the jabber of the great ones. They had been very excited for some time now, but no one in the tribe could understand their distress. I had just cut short my swim because they had been pestering me so much.

At the far end of the bower, Merry muttered and stirred, crinkling the blanket of bronze leaves that had settled upon him. Then he seemed to go back to sleep, and silence returned. Merry was Merry-son-of-Pebble, because Sparkle claimed that she had been bearing him when I married her. I had accepted that obvious falsehood and so the tribe had also, but Merry had straight hair.

So did Sea Wave's boy, and Wave's, and Silver's daughter and many others. Many of their mothers, like Sparkle, were big again. My second crop, a herdman would have said, but I was careful not to use that expression among the seafolk.

I reached my wife and settled down beside her as quietly as

I could. I don't know why I bothered—I doubt that any husband in the history of Vernier ever managed to be quiet enough under those circumstances.

"Who was it this time?" she inquired drowsily.

She had been asleep when I departed. She needed much sleep now, for her time was near.

"Don't remember."

With a great heaving, as if a storm had struck the grove, she rolled over to face me. We adjusted position, but it was hard to cuddle her present bulk satisfactorily.

"Not funny."

"Whoever it was," I said, "she wasn't pretty like you. Not as lovable. Couldn't be."

She frowned and spoke very quietly, in case there might be listeners beyond the wicker walls. "Must not go to wives, Golden."

How do women know such things? Still, Sparkle was jealous of my other duties, and I loved it. "You know I would make waves only with you if I could, love," I assured her. "You're always my favorite."

She bit her lip, so I tried to kiss it better. She wouldn't let me.

"Never mind worrying, my dearest Sparkle," I said. "You concentrate on that baby of yours. She's going to be my first, remember!"

"He!" she insisted automatically. "And who shouting at?"

I must have been louder than I thought. "Sand. Young weed-brain!" I had caught Sand hunting alone again—I told them and told them . . . Since Pebble died, though, we'd only lost one more man. A shark had bitten off Clamshell's foot and he had bled to death. Great ones alone could outrun sharks, but they could not apply tourniquets. We had lost one man, but many others had been just plain lucky. They promised, and they forgot again, and I screamed again . . .

"And the great ones are getting worse," I muttered, hearing the constant clicking and booming.

Then the old cracked voice of Icegleam rose in triumph from some nearby bower.

"Visitor!" he yelled with sudden comprehension. "Is what have been trying to tell us! Visitor coming!"

Sparkle's big eyes widened. "Visitor? What sort of visitor?"
I could guess what sort of visitor.

His chariot was brown, streaked with salt; mainsail yellow,
foresail white. It approached very slowly in the fitful wind,
flanked by a leaping escort of great ones almost to the place
where its wheels grounded on shingle. Momentarily it bounced
and twisted in the surf, then dozens of willing hands grabbed it
and rushed it up to dry land.

The angel stood tall and lean against the sky as he furled his
sails, quickly and efficiently. Then he vaulted nimbly over the
side of his chariot, landing with a crunch of boots on shingle.

His hair was a chestnut plume, hanging thick behind his ears
and held by a beaded headband. Sun and wind had burned his
face almost the same umber shade as his fringed buckskins, and
its bony planes projected endurance and authority and a wry
good humor. He was as unlike Violet as man could be.

We spent more time on shore now, and I made sure there was
a supply of shoes there, but there were not enough for everyone.
Thus the tribe had spread itself in a long line along the water's
edge to wait for the angel's greetings. The women came first,
each speaking her name and embracing him with fervor. He
responded conscientiously, obviously wise to the amorous ways
of seafolk, and aware that any response less than ardor would
be a slight.

He was flushed and grinning as he embraced the last, who
happened to be the youthfully alluring and enthusiastic Surge.
She prolonged the encounter, squirming against him erotically.
Sand grinned proudly nearby.

The angel broke free from her. He rolled his eyes and took a
deep breath, and the men smiled. Then each of them also offered
a hug and spoke welcome. When he arrived at me, I was tempted
to shake his hand and say "Knobil," but I embraced him in
seafolk fashion and gave my seaman name. Nevertheless, he held
my shoulder for a moment, studying me with shrewd gray eyes.

Finally, of course, he had to meet all the children. He knelt
on the shingle to hug and kiss as was expected of him. Then he
rose and glanced around as if counting. His gaze lingered again
on me, the obvious fair-haired misfit.

The grove lay close to shore now, more gold than green. We

no longer dared light fires, even on the floating hearths, so I had set some of the men to building a bonfire on the beach—a hellish task, with the heat of the flames adding to the sun's crippling glare. I was worried, although no one else seemed to be.

The creek trickled listlessly through the shingle, its flow a dismal mockery of what it once had been. Offshore the great ones lingered, spouting and watching. They could no longer leap and sport close to the grove, for the water was almost too shallow there for them to approach it at all.

Now there was an awkward pause, as the seafolk shuffled feet and exchanged bashful glances, uncertain who should speak, or say what. I hung back, amused. As I would have guessed, it was Sparkle who took charge. She handed Merry to me, having enough trouble balancing without any additional burden. He wrapped arms around my neck and squealed, "Golden!" in my ear. Being Pebble's son, he did not call me *Daddy*, and that was one faint rankle that I could never quite suppress.

"Shall all be honored if will feast with us, Angel," Sparkle said.

He nodded graciously. "Your hospitality will be welcome, lady. But if the feast may be delayed briefly, I would first speak with your elders. My stay with you must be short. My mission is urgent."

Sparkle called over the senior members of the tribe—Behold and Icegleam and Tusk, the surviving members of the original settlers, and introduced them again. I was surprised to learn that Tusk was Behold's brother. These three were certainly the elders in the literal sense of the word, but they held no special authority in the tribe. No one did, unless it was perhaps Sparkle herself, for she had a natural grace and a most uncommon common sense . . . and me, of course, but I was more of a *younger* than an *elder*.

The elders settled in the ripples and Sparkle sat behind them. I crouched at her side, to hear what the angel had to say. I have always had more than my share of stupidity, but I was not stupid enough to be unconcerned. I knew already that the seatree copse was ailing and the sea itself retreating. White sand had become shingle, the creek had dwindled, my ancient, half-forgotten driftwood collection now lay far inland, out of sight across the plain. I had seen angels come to warn herdfolk, and I could guess that this new one brought no good tidings.

Some of the other adults clustered around also, but most went off to play languid games with their children, for it was a rarity to have everyone gathered onshore at the same time. The angel remained standing, tucking thumbs in his belt and looking us over for a moment before starting to speak.

"Your home is dying," he began. "You must know that it will soon be out of the water altogether?"

"Time yet," Behold said complacently.

"Soon it will lie in the surf zone and be ripped to pieces. You do not have long . . . before that babe you carry learns to crawl, lady." He meant Sparkle.

"Great ones will find us another."

He shook his head. "It is not the shallow water that is killing the seatrees. There are other groves. I have passed many, and they are all dying."

No one else spoke, so I said, "Why?"

"Salt. The ocean is shrinking—evaporating—and the water is becoming too salty."

"The watervines!" I said. "They all—"

The angel flashed me an odd glance and I stopped, puzzled.

Old Tusk cackled. "Was born on land, in much colder place than this. Will show them how to make tents. Is always changing—the sea. Are able to change also."

There was a mutter of agreement, and some of the audience wandered away. The angel's eyes scanned the rest of us carefully and fixed themselves on Sparkle. "And what will you drink?"

"He is right," I told the silence. "The stream is much smaller than—"

Again the angel caught my eye, and this time he plainly shook his head. He wanted me to stay out.

"Rain," Tusk said, less confidently.

"When did you last see rain?"

He got no answer. I looked at Sparkle, who was frowning. There had been no rain since I had come to the grove.

"Will find another stream, then. Great ones will know."

The angel shook his head sadly. "Even if you do, it will dry up soon. The sun is coming . . . do you know that the sun moves?"

I did, of course, and I had seen the grasslands die, but my seafolk hosts had never cared much for that morbid tale. Now the angel began to tell a terrifyingly similar story. The springs would dry up, the ocean would dry up, the fish would die. When High Summer arrived, the sea itself might boil. The prospect horrified me, but I was even more horrified when I looked around my companions and saw no alarm on their faces. The seafolk were going to be as disbelieving as the herdfolk.

"What must do?" Sparkle asked. More of the other listeners were scrambling up and going off to join in the play.

"You must leave! Load your boats, mount your great ones, and travel the Great River, back to the South Ocean."

The three elders scowled and muttered, "Cold!"

"You must go soon!" the angel said. "The Great River is flowing very swiftly. Soon it will be too fast even for the great ones and they will be trapped here. They cannot leave on foot, as people can."

Already people were leaving on foot—leaving the meeting. Only Sparkle and the three elders remained, in sullen silence. And me. Sparkle blushed and said, "Have many women with child . . ."

The angel's bright eyes flickered toward me and then away again. "You must not delay, even for that. Pregnant women can travel in boats."

The listeners glanced at one another. "Are grateful, sir," Sparkle said. "Will talk it over soon. Now have feast, and singing?"

The angel smiled. "I shall enjoy that. First I must attend to a few things in my chariot . . . Then I shall join your feast."

With sighs of relief, the gathering dispersed. The angel caught my eye again and jerked his head. I handed Merry back to Sparkle and strode off alongside him.

He was a handsbreadth taller than I, that lanky angel, and he looked down at me with his needle-sharp gray eyes as we paced along the strand toward his chariot.

"Your name was not always Golden."

"Knobil, sir . . . once."

"Wetlander?"

"Herdman."

That surprised him. We reached our destination, but obviously his only purpose had been to take me aside for a private chat. He leaned back against one of the big wheels, folded his arms, and studied the scene on the beach for a few moments.

"What do you think of seafolk?" he asked quietly.

"They are very kind. Very happy people. Very hospitable."

He nodded, and a small grin crinkled the sun-browned skin around his eyes. "They have obviously been hospitable to you, Knobil . . . or should I call you 'Herdmaster'?"

I felt my face grow hot. "What can you mean, sir?"

"Very few toddlers, but a great many babies? Many women pregnant? I see a lot of youngsters with straight hair."

I shrugged. Fortunately there had been no scandalously blond or blue-eyed babies.

"How many are yours?"

"None of them—according to the tribe."

"How many according to you?"

I contrived what I hoped was an innocent boyish grin. "Thirty-nine, sir."

He shook his head in what might have been admiration. "You have cause to be proud of your manhood."

I shrugged modestly. "Any herdmen can outbreed a seaman."

"It isn't only that." He hesitated and then said, "I don't question your prowess—you're obviously a fabulous stud, and they're very fortunate to have you available—but their trouble is mostly inbreeding."

"It is?" I was taken aback. The incest taboo?

"How many founders?"

"Sir?"

"How many came from the South Ocean?"

"Six . . . four women, two men."

The angel nodded sadly. "And they were probably highly inbred to start with. You can tell just by looking at them, Knobil, right? They're all as look-alike as a clutch of eggs. When relationships get that close, the fertility drops. The women don't conceive, and when they do, they usually abort. They won't lose yours, of course. How do they dispose of the freaks?"

*Freaks?* "I . . . I don't know, sir." I had not even known about miscarriages. No one ever mentioned such things. Freaks? I shuddered.

"And the intelligence goes down," Brown added. "They're like kids, aren't they?" He eyed me thoughtfully.

"I try to be patient with them."

He nodded. "This is the fourth group I've talked with, and they're all the same. It's very serious! There isn't much time."

I had little understanding of time, but I nodded profoundly.

"The woman . . . your wife? . . . said they would talk it over. Will they?"

"Probably not. They prefer to ignore unpleasant things, sir." They would forget the angel's bad news as soon as possible.

"But I think you can help me . . . Herdmaster."

"I'm a seaman now, sir."

"But you deserve the title. Very few men of your age have sired so many—and fine, strong babies! I'm really impressed. You won't mind if I call you 'Herdmaster' while we're alone?"

"Of course not."

"And you may be able to save your family and friends— perhaps even many other tribes also. Now, tell me your story."

"Once I was a pilgrim." I fumbled at my neck for a leather amulet that Sparkle had made for me long ago, and which I had dug out now in the angel's honor. It closed very tightly around a small packet, well waterproofed with grease. I opened this and showed my two tokens.

"Two!" The angel whistled. "I've never heard of anyone collecting two! And if you will help me, of course I shall give you one of mine . . . You'll have three then, Herdmaster! That's never been done before, I'm sure."

"Of course I shall help, sir. Not for a token—I am a pilgrim no longer. But in a sense I feel they are all my children."

"Of course you do," he said. "But three angel tokens! I'm sure Heaven has never heard of such a feat. Let's get up in the chariot, where we won't be disturbed. I want to hear this!"

So we clambered up and sat down opposite each other on the two chests near the rear. This chariot was a great deal tidier and smarter-seeming than Violet's had been.

I told him my history, and all about my escape from the grass-lands, and of my former ambition to become an angel. I confessed that I now just wished to remain with my family, and he assured me that he understood. Once or twice some of the sea-folk sauntered over. The angel ignored them and they wandered away again without speaking. He listened carefully, nodding, solemnly attentive.

When I had done, he sighed. "I knew Violet. He taught me how to drive a chariot. A plump, stocky man?"

"*Knew?* He didn't arrive?"

Sadly the angel shook his head. Of course Violet was an ancient memory to me now, but I had not forgotten that I owed him my life and that in his way he had cared for me. I had promised to meet him in Heaven. I had often wondered if he even remembered the gawky blond herdbrat, but I had always assumed that he had driven safely home. And yet I had spared no thought for Violet in a long time.

After a moment's silence Brown said, "We . . . I mean Heaven . . . we lost many, many angels in the grasslands tragedy, Herdmaster. They are being replaced, but it takes so long . . . We are late in getting the message to the March Ocean—here, to the seafolk. Now, I'll try to explain properly. Did Violet show you any maps?"

I shook my head blankly.

He shrugged and settled back, although I had thought he was going to open the chest he was sitting on.

"Well, I'll show you later. The March Ocean was born before you and I were, when the sun melted the ice . . . you know that the Dawn area is all covered with ice, of course? The water is salt, because there is salt left behind when it dries out . . ."

I had no notion what ice was, but I nodded solemnly and did not interrupt as he continued speaking in a very man-to-man sort of way. I paid much more heed to the way he was addressing me than to what he actually said.

Later, when I reached Heaven, I was given the explanation again, and listened better. Every cycle is the same. Meltwater fills the basin, eventually overflowing to create the Great River. All the folk of Vernier must travel westward during their lives, but seafolk try also to find northerly bays or small seas, for those are warmer than the main ocean. Behold and her family—and many other families—had fought their way up the salty torrent of the Great River. They had found a paradise of calm, warm water.

Eventually drainage is diverted and the influx from the wetlands ends. As the water level falls, the Great River stops running. The approaching sun begins to evaporate the March Ocean. Partly because of the increased rainfall that this produces elsewhere, partly by accident of geography, the next part of the cycle is marked by a rise in the South Ocean, which finally floods along the Great River in the opposite direction. So the door was now open again. The seafolk could escape from the trap.

But only if they went soon. The flow was increasing as the relative level of the two oceans changed. Rapids and waterfalls would multiply until even the great ones would not be able to swim against the current. People could still leave overland—if they wanted to and were shown the road—but the great ones would certainly be trapped. Like a true seaman, I was almost more horrified by the danger to them than by the risk for humans. Ultimately input from the Great River would not be able to keep pace with evaporation. The March Ocean would become a desolate salt flat.

The angel stopped talking then and stared along at the seafolk, who were beginning to collect near the bonfire. The feast was almost ready. "They are indeed your children, Knobil. Your tribe. Your herd. They do not know that, but you do. It is your duty to save them."

"What must . . . what can I do?"

His steel-bright eyes came back to mine. The bony planes of his face shone with sweat like mirrors, but I sensed again that strange intensity.

"This happens every cycle. Usually there is a disaster. When there is not, it is because the great ones have been told. The records say that the great ones can speak to each other across the whole width of the ocean. You must warn them, and they will round up the seafolk."

I stared at him in dismay. "I cannot speak to the great ones!"

He was surprised, and skeptical. "But you ride them? How can you hunt with them if you can't speak their language?"

"Hunting is easy. Oh, I know some signals and a few words. I can understand a very little of their song, but anything complicated, like what you want—that needs three people."

"Why three?"

"To make the harmonies."

He frowned, as if he should have remembered that. "Well, you could ask two others to help you, surely?"

As a callow youth I had cared nothing when I saw the herdfolk die, and there had been no way I could have helped them anyway; but these were my friends—and my children. I wanted to save the tribe, and I also wanted to please the angel. I watched the seafolk as they laughed and frolicked in the surf, then I turned away. I avoided the angel's eyes, and stared down instead at the bony shins protruding from his boots.

"I don't think so, sir," I whispered.

"Why not?"

"I can tell my mount to dive, or turn, or find seals or sunfish . . . but I don't know any of the words you want. Not that they really have words . . . they speak in chords and in rhythm."

"But can you not then ask three to speak for you?"

"I could ask . . ."

"So?"

"I wouldn't know what they said," I mumbled, still glumly studying his feet. I could guess what sort of message would be passed—squirt Golden, dunk him, swim him around in circles . . . If the seafolk did not want to admit the truth of the angel's warning even to themselves, they would certainly not tell the great ones.

"There must be some you can trust, Knobil? The women?"

I did not reply.

Brown turned again and studied the crowd on the beach. "Widows I can understand—I know their ways. But I see at least six pregnant wives over there. Obviously you've talked yourself into enough beds—"

"Not so! They talk me! I won't go to a wife unless her husband asks me outright."

Brown said nothing until I looked up. Not liking what I saw, I dropped my eyes again quickly.

"You are not exactly brimming over with tact, are you, herdman? You make them beg?"

"Ask! Just ask."

He grunted. "I expect it feels like begging. Name of Heaven! 'Please breed my wife because I'm not man enough!'? Couldn't you have just settled for a hint or two? You don't leave them much pride, do you? You think they can't tell straight hair from curls as well as you can? Do you gloat much?"

He did not expect a reply, and I squirmed in silence. Then he sighed. "Well, I shall keep trying. There must be many other tribes, and perhaps I can convince one of them to tell the great ones in time. The records insist that it is the only way."

I did not know who the records were, but obviously he listened to them and thought them wise.

"There is another possibility," the angel said. "It is a faint chance. The Great River is not far from here—I think you could almost make it in one long ride, without a sleep, because the great ones travel much faster than my chariot does. If you were to go upstream as far as the worst rapids, in the mountains, and then come down again . . . I think your mount might understand. They are very smart, you know. They could taste the better seawater coming in. You might have to do it twice—to show them that the flow was getting faster. It might work."

"My wife is going to have a child . . ."

"Your wife is going to *die*. And all your children. Or don't you care about them? Is hot groin all you're interested in?"

I clenched my teeth till they hurt. Someone shouted my name from the fireside and others called for the angel. I forced myself to look at him again.

"There might be another way."

He regarded me warily. "Go on."

"There is no one in the grove at the moment . . . no one at all."

"You can't be certain of that."

"I am. I counted. I'm always counting . . . they stray worse than woollies—"

"What are you thinking?"

"If they lost their home right away, while you were still here to lecture them again—then they might listen? I could run down for a swim." It was so hot that everyone was taking quick dips to cool off. "No one would notice if I slipped out to the grove. I have tinder and flint at my feasting place . . ."

"Did you ever see grassfires in your youth?"

"Of course!"

He nodded. "And you fought them with backfires? Woollies themselves are fireproof, so I'm told . . ."

"I could be back here before anyone noticed. Then we could organize a rescue, to save the tools and clothes and things . . ."

"No!" His voice cracked with the finality of a club hitting a seal's skull. Again I averted my eyes from the expression on his face.

"Why not, sir?"

"First—it would be violence, so I will not condone it. People must be able to trust angels. In fact, I shall stop you if you try . . . you know that I have that power?" I remembered Violet slaying the tyrant; I shivered and nodded. Again there were shouts for us from the feast.

"Secondly—you're judging by grassfires, which are relatively harmless. That grove is a dry trelliswork, packed with dead leaves. It would explode in one big roar of flame. You would save nothing. You would leave the tribe not merely homeless but destitute, with no possessions at all. Forget that, Knobil!"

Sparkle was heading toward the chariot, plodding heavily along the shiny shingle.

"My wife is coming to tell us the meal is ready, sir."

"What will you say to her?"

"That we are coming?"

"And what will you say to her when she comes to tell you that the stream has stopped flowing? Well? *Look at me*, dammit!"

This time his gray eyes held me as if he had nailed me to the side of the chariot. No water? The children could die of thirst while we searched for another stream. The tribe kept no emergency supply, and of course we ought to be doing that, but the seafolk never would do anything so strenuous, not even after this warning.

His stare was a challenge—to my courage, to my manhood, to every stitch of the self-respect he had just rubbed threadbare.

I licked my lips, and surrendered. "I'll try, sir."

He smiled in triumph and held out a hand. There was a small triangle of leather lying on his palm: brown, yellow, and white.

"Your third!"

I took it, and was committed, and wanted to weep.

I wiped my mouth and tossed the remains of my blackfish into the surf. The whole tribe was sitting in one long line in the fingertips of the sea, listlessly debating the problem of ferrying the children back to the grove for the singing. A dozen girls flocked around the angel.

"I am going away," I said.

Sparkle was cracking a crawler leg for Merry. Her head twisted round to me. "No!"

"Just to look at the Great River. A few sleeps, is all."

"No! Not leave me!"

"It's very important, dearest. The angel is right. We are all in danger."

She patted my knee. "Stay till after baby. Then go."

"That might be too late."

Alarm flickered in her eyes. "After angel leaves, then."

"No. Now." I did not think the angel would go before I did.

Suddenly she looked angry, as if I were being a foolish child. "Must wait at least for singing!"

I had meant to wait for the singing, and had she reacted differently, I think my resolution would have collapsed altogether. Instead her sharp tone made my own terror flare up in petty rage.

"Dark hell the singing! Now! You can eat at Sand's place while I'm gone." I trusted Sparkle to be faithful to me—and she was much too pregnant not to be.

Sparkle glared. "Taking who with you?"

"No one. If I wait for anyone else, I'll never get away."

"Stupid to go alone!" she shouted, and pushed Merry aside as he tried to climb on her lap. Unaccustomed to such rebuffs, he burst into tears. We were attracting attention. "Is your rule—not to go alone!"

"I've asked them!" I had asked at least a dozen, and heard a dozen different excuses. Even a herdman can take a hint if he's thumped hard enough.

Suspicion settled over Sparkle's face. "Did give you token?"

I nodded.

"So going to Heaven?" She was starting to shout. "Pilgrim again? Again want to be angel? Visit camps and tribes and meet lots of nice girls? Tired of being father and husband?"

She was hugely pregnant, and miserably uncomfortable in the heat. I should have made more allowances, but I was on edge, too, and I was still under the spell of the angel's flattery.

"Not that. I told you I'm coming back as soon as I can."

"Don't! Stay away!"

"What?" I howled, as she heaved herself unsteadily to her feet. "Sparkle! You love me. You said so!"

And I truly believed that I loved Sparkle.

"And you? If loved me, would not go! First Pebble, now Golden? Soon have married all the men. Think Whistler is old enough for next one?"

I rose also, trying to explain the angel's plan, but she would not listen. Soon we had a shouting competition going, while the rest of the tribe watched in horror. I could send another in my place, she said. I was a herdman, who did not like his possessions talking back to him. If I really loved her, I would not make waves with all those other women. I must not forget to kiss Surge goodbye . . . How did she know about Surge?

"And big kiss for Salty, also." She turned her back on me.

I was supposed to put my arms around her at that point.

I didn't. Of course she was frightened, and seafolk did not know how to handle fear. Now I see that. Then I did not.

I also was afraid, and now ashamed. I pushed past sobbing children. I strode away into the surf, without a word and without looking back. I should have been more understanding. I should have explained better, but I did nothing that I should. Like a petulant child I just walked away. It would have made no difference, but it is another of the great regrets of my life.

# 2

Frith was a full-grown male now, almost as large as Gorf. He had a mate, Pfapff, who came with us, and three or four other great ones kept us company for a while. I carried two water bottles, a knife, and a net. I wore hat and pagne, and my amulet contained three angel tokens. In my throbbing, angry head was a muddled account of the geography, given me by that raw-boned, steel-eyed angel.

I hated him.

The great ones were still excited, and I am sure that their discussions were booming to and fro across the ocean. Having to stay near the surface, Frith would not have been able to hear properly, but the others listened to the long-range talk and repeated it to him in their local chatter—or so I believe. I may be wrong, for neither saint nor seaman fully understands the great ones.

I was weary and sun-baked when members of another pod came leaping and spouting to meet me and lead me to one of the other tribes that Brown had mentioned. Their grove had long since vanished, and they camped in cheerfully ramshackle tents on steaming sand by a stream that I noted glumly to be even smaller than ours. There would be no refuge here for us if our water failed.

I was given food and a place to rest. I was not told whose home it was, and I slept alone. I awoke screaming. For the first time since my marriage to Sparkle, I had dreamed of Anubyl beating my mother. I had felt my nails cut into my palms and tasted the blood from my bitten lip.

I refused my hosts' entreaties to tarry longer. Frith had waited, as I had asked him to, and we continued our journey south, with Pfapff at our side. Our other escorts had departed. I did not feel the same lonely terror that I had known before. I was a seaman, Frith was with me, and he would take care of me.

The Great River was easy to find. Even I could smell the difference in the water, and the tussocks of vegetation floating in it were not yet yellowed by excess salt. Most rivers are narrow, short-lived, and drinkable. This one was a moving sea, too wide for both banks to be visible at the same time. Frith and Pfapff seemed excited at the chance to explore a new environment, and they plunged eagerly ahead.

Eventually I grew so tired and hungry that I had to call for a halt. The sun was near to being overhead and there were few shadows, but I asked to be put ashore on some high rocks, and I found a shaded ledge. Soon thereafter, Frith put up his head, made his chuckling sound, and threw me a fish that would have fed half the tribe. I ate. I slept. This time I dreamed of Loneliness, and nearly wept with relief when I awoke and saw that Frith was still there. Had he left me, I should have died very quickly on that barren little island.

Two more sleeps brought me to the mountains and to faster currents. By then my skin was peeling in sheets from the continuous salt and the sun, yet I had no alternative but to continue, and I was excited by the sight of the huge hills and the vaster, hazy blue giants raked along the horizon behind them.

With no warning, Frith and Pfapff balked. They swam in circles, chattering furiously, and no signal or word from me would persuade them to go farther. Of course the words I knew were little closer to their true speech than "Whoa!" is to horse talk. I could tell what I wanted, but in no way could I explain why it was important.

Important or not, my journey seemed to have ended. I even tried dismounting and swimming in the direction I wanted to go. They let me do so, clattering with amusement as the current swept me backward toward the March Ocean. Only when I was exhausted and sinking did Frith stop laughing and retrieve me.

I asked again, and was refused again. Then, just as I was ready to admit defeat, a strange thing happened. A tremor of excitement ran through the great muscular back I straddled. At the same instant Pfapff sounded. I knew from the angle of her tail that she was going deep. Frith sank as low in the water as he could without drowning me and then just drifted, listening.

Of course I remembered how I had learned of Pebble's death, and I was filled with dread that something bad had happened back at the grove. I felt deep booming sounds from Pfapff. Those I knew to be long-distance talk. Some important message was being passed.

Both great ones surfaced simultaneously, spouting and gibbering. They held a long conversation, but if they were trying to tell the news to me, they failed utterly. To my astonishment, however, they then set off against the current at high speed, with me hanging grimly to Frith's fin and Pfapff leaping exuberantly alongside. Showing no further hesitation, they carried me up the Great River and through the mountains.

Of course I was perplexed beyond measure at their change of heart. It was much, much later that I received a plausible explanation, and it came from Kettle, a former seaman, and by then a saint, great scholar, and senior aide to Gabriel himself. My companions' initial reluctance to go farther, he suggested, was probably due to the increasing noise of the river. It would have been cutting them off from the sounds of the ocean and from the chatter of the other great ones. Then, just as I had concluded that I must abandon my mission, they had learned of the impending disaster.

Brown-yellow-white, the angel who had bewitched me into

this folly, was one of two who had survived the journey down the Great River to the March Ocean. They had then split up. Brown had gone north. The other, Two-pink-green, had followed the southern shore, and his efforts had met with success. He had been able to convince one tribe of the imminent danger. They informed their great ones, who immediately passed the news to all the others. Then Frith and Pfapff knew what I was trying to do, more or less. Perhaps they were excited at being pathfinders for the great migration. Perhaps they were even ordered by some central great-one leader to go ahead and explore. Who can say?

The canyon through the Andes Mountains is one of the wonders of the world, and traveling up it on Frith's back was the most awe-inspiring journey I was to know on all my wanderings. In many places it churned and roared, with waves standing like hills and great whirlpool mouths howling at us impudent wayfarers, seeking to suck us down to our destruction. Repeatedly I was swept off, helpless as froth, and rescued by Pfapff, who was keeping close behind Frith to guard me. The two great ones reveled in the tumult, at times leaping like roos up the cataracts, although at other times even they needed to seek out calmer pools and rest. As for me, I could only hope that they would take my screams of terror to be shouts of joy, or that those went unheard in the violence of the waves.

This was the route that Violet had intended to sail. We can never know how far he went after leaving me, but a few angels did return to Heaven at about that time, and by that road. Their accomplishment shows how greatly the respective levels of the two oceans had changed while I wandered alone on the sands and then dallied among the seafolk.

Yet also there were wide, calm places, where the river wound through chasms among barren hills, scoured to sterile rock by the higher floods of the past, or cauterized by the heat of summer. Sometimes it narrowed, with rocky sides rising sheer until the sky was a ragged slit of light shining far above me, reflected on the black stillness as if it were also far below. At those times I seemed to float in air, rather than on water. Plumes of cataracts graced the walls, some dropping from heights so great that only mist reached down to dimple the mirrored surface. For long stretches I traveled on dark glass, leaving a narrow, vee-shaped wake behind me.

Earlier—at about the time of my birth—the river had been much higher, but I have been assured by the saints that I saw only a part of the canyon. They estimate that it was still about half full when I went through, and at other times the gorge is that much deeper. I have never had any desire to go back and see.

The only more terrible journey I can imagine would be to descend that hellish torrent in an angel chariot. It had never been done so late in the cycle, but it was the fastest route from Heaven to the March Ocean, and with time running out for the seafolk, the archangel had sent his six best sailors. Brown and Pink survived. The names of the others are recorded on the Scroll of Honor.

We emerged at last from a rift in the mountains onto calm water stretching out of sight in three directions. I thought it must be another ocean, but it was only an inland sea lying to the east of the Andes. On Heaven's maps it looks very small.

Here I was greeted by a gentle rain, an experience I had almost forgotten, the first shower I had seen since my childhood. It cleared almost at once, to show a nearby hillside clothed in rich grass and bearing real trees.

I was battered and spent, much too weary to think of food. Frith took me to this idyllic shore. I drank deeply at a stream of crystal water, found a dry spot under a bush, and lay like a dead man.

I awoke stiff, bruised, and famished. By then, the surface of the sea was already dotted with fins and spoutings. Even as I watched, more great ones were emerging from the mouth of the canyon. Of course I did not know about Two-pink-green. I did not know that my mission had been completely unnecessary. I assumed that the honor was mine, and I congratulated myself on being a hero. All Brown need do now was watch as the seafolk were rounded up by the great ones and borne away to safety. That was, indeed, what happened. Unlike the tragic dying in the grasslands, there was no disaster on the March Ocean in this cycle. Not everyone made it—many bodies floated back down the Great River—but most did, and Heaven recorded a success.

Battered and naked and starving, though, the self-hailed hero wanted breakfast. In the tumult of the canyon I had lost everything except my knife and my amulet. Hopefully I mounted a rock at the water's edge and sang Frith's name. The shore sloped steeply. In a miraculously short time he thrust his head up almost at my feet and tossed me a fish, clicking welcome and amusement. I called out my thanks, greatly relieved that he had not deserted me.

Yet raw fish is a dull diet. After I had taken the edge off my hunger, I began collecting dry leaves from below the densest shrubs and soon worked up a sweat twirling a stick, while I pondered my immediate future.

The passage of the canyon had been a torment for even a strong mount and a relatively skilled rider. Towing coracles of terrified children and pregnant women would be a feat I just could not imagine the tribe achieving without my help. There was not a man I would trust to keep his head. My obvious duty was to return to the March Ocean and take charge.

If Frith refused to go through that hell again—and of course my craven heart hoped that he would refuse—then I could camp quite happily on this hospitable shore. Or so I thought. I could wait for the tribe—great ones and people both. So I thought. Even if I was asleep when they passed through the gates of the mountain, Frith and Pfapff would tell them where I was. They would almost certainly head for this stream anyway, the first fresh water. Whether I went back or stayed, we should be reunited. I would ask Frith, and he would decide. I saw no other possibility.

But I was fairly certain Frith would take me.

By the time I had worked all that out, I had roasted a piece of my fish on the rocks of my hearth. I skewered it on a stick. With my mouth watering, I rose to my feet to find a comfortable spot, away from the heat.

I had earned this feast, I thought, and a rest in this so-serene campsite. I had earned the joy of smelling grass again, and the soothing shade of real trees, the inspiring view of mountains and shore. This was Paradise, and I longed to share it with Sparkle and my friends.

Above me, the smoke from my fire climbed slowly up the azure sky, visible to half the world.

I think of that moment as the end of my innocence.

# 6

---

# The Ants

Something hurled me down, spun me over with sharp agony in my shoulder, and then crushed me into the ground. It dug claws in my shoulders and belly. It pushed a black-furred muzzle close to my face. Too dazed and horrified even to scream, I stared up at huge yellow eyes with vertical slits for pupils, at pointed ears, at white teeth as long as my toes. It snarled and spat, and the reek of its breath was nauseating.

"Stay very still," said a nearby voice, "or it will rip out your guts."

I rolled up my eyes and pretended to faint. I felt my knife being taken, then the weight moving off me. A boot slammed into my ribs. "Now get up!" Obviously my deception had failed.

I clambered dizzily to my feet. My captor was short and broad, clad in stiff black leather garments, soiled and much patched. Little of his face was visible between a wide leather hat and a bristling beard—both of them black—but I could make out a broad, flat nose and evilly glittering eyes.

I clenched my jaw to prevent my teeth from chattering insanely. I was streaming blood. There were claw marks horribly close to my groin. The cause of my injuries was sitting on its haunches near the fire, watching me narrowly with a third yellow, slit-pupil eye, wiping its jowls with one paw. It was furry and black and as large as an adolescent girl. It had eaten my dinner.

"What's your name?"

"Knobil."

He kicked my shin—hard. I yelped and staggered. The animal spun around, snarling.

"Address me as 'master'!"

"Yes, master."

He nodded. "If you give me any trouble, I'll have my friend here bite your knackers off. Makes a man more docile—understand?"

"Yes, master!"

"How many more of you are there around?"

"None, master."

He kicked my other shin—harder. I staggered again and almost fell. The panther crouched threateningly. "The truth!"

Shrill with terror, I insisted that I spoke the truth. I babbled about the angel and the great ones.

He nodded and reached up to the amulet that was the only thing I wore. Checking for valuables, I supposed. "What's in there?"

"Angel tokens, master."

He guffawed. "More pilgrims end in the pit than in Heaven, dross! They won't help you." He snapped the tie and contemptuously hurled my precious amulet away. "Now kneel!"

I lowered myself reluctantly under the panther's steady glare.

"Stay very still. I'm going to have Feather lick those scratches. That stops the bleeding and prevents sickness, but it stings, and if you make any sudden movement, she'll strike. You have been warned!"

He made a sign with his fingers. Snarling, the monster crept forward toward me, low to the ground, keeping its forward eyes on mine. Its muzzle came close to my face and I gagged again at its fetid breath. Then a big pink tongue reached out to lap the blood on my savaged shoulder. I felt only a rough scraping until it reached the wound, and then the sudden pain was excruciating, like salt, or fire. I managed not to flinch too much and I did not scream. I was never lucky enough to faint.

* * *

I reeled up the valley, following the stream, with the panther close behind me and the man behind her. Thorns ripped my bare skin, rocks cut my feet, and I was in constant danger of vomiting from pain and terror, but I believed every one of the man's threats, so I just kept moving, as fast as I was able.

We came at last to a small glen where tents nestled under the trees. Half a dozen black-clad men were lounging around, and two more were bathing in the stream. They were all short and broad, with dark porcupine beards. Their faces were burned red, but the rest of their skin was almost as pale as mine, as I could see from the bathers. Their features were broad, their legs short and bowed, their shoulders broad as mountains. More of the great black cats roused from their slumbers to eye me hungrily.

An older man climbed to his feet. "You got one!"

"The fish are running," my captor said. "This seems to be the first."

The headman looked me up and down approvingly. I was a healthy young male for his slave work force, and much swimming had given me bulk. He rolled hair back from his teeth in a gruesome smile. "Good silk, too!"

The man behind me chuckled. "When he's older, though. You . . . dross . . . over to that tree!"

He handed me a length of coarse rope and told me to sit, to tie one end round my ankle and the other round the tree. He signaled instructions to his cat. It dropped to a crouch, watching me fixedly.

"I know you can untie that," the man said, "but I don't advise it."

He walked away. The panther stayed, and so did I.

Four men went off downstream to wait for more victims. Later two others came in carrying the carcass of a deer slung on a pole. Beside them stalked the panthers that had caught it for them. The men ate the best parts, the panthers the second best, and I got some scraps of offal. Long conditioned to a fish diet, I soon became deathly ill.

Two or three sleeps and meals later, more captives began to arrive, escorted by men and cats. We were roped in a string, ankle to ankle, with the same token tether that held me. The real bonds were the watching cats, the ropes merely an added humiliation.

Obviously the slavers had known of the coming migration, and seafolk were easy victims as soon as they set foot on shore to find water. These newcomers were all gibbering with terror, like frightened children. By that time my gut had begun to adjust to red meat and I had recovered a tiny sliver of self-control, so I tried to reassure them as well as I could. Tacitly they accepted me as leader. I did not realize how greatly that increased my danger.

We were not allowed to stand upright and we were kept naked. This deliberate degradation was intended to break us, as was the frequently imposed agony of having our injuries licked by the panthers, although that brutal torment did speed up the healing.

The seventh and eighth victims were both women. They were stripped and gang raped by the slavers before being brought over to us. We soothed them as best we could, and did not molest them.

Eight was apparently a convenient number to transport. Our ankles were untied; we were roped neck to neck instead, and marched off under guard. Two men and two panthers accompanied us, although one of each would have been sufficient to balk any attempt at escape. We did not know that, yet we were all so cowed already by the systematic brutality that not one of us even tried.

The worst part of the journey was still the lickings. At every stop, the guards made the panthers clean our scrapes and the raw flesh on our feet. The pain was frightful. Once one of the women flinched too abruptly. The cat's instant reflex uncovered her ribs.

Our way led high up into the mountains. The guards carried rations for themselves, but not for us. Only once did they stop on the journey to hunt, and then we got some scraps to eat. We slept eight or nine times, I think, but we were half starved and staggering when we eventually arrived at the mine. Had the distance been very much greater, some of us would not have arrived at all.

The site had originally been a notch in a mountain, for two sides were steep and covered with natural scrub. A high wall of tailings partly closed it off, forming a boxlike hollow.

Along one side stood a row of small cottages with bright-painted doors and cheerful window awnings. To me they were wooden tents, but obviously a pleasant settlement, shaded by stately trees. Grass grew there, and even flowers. A small stream wound through this pleasant hamlet, then crossed over the bare roadway to water the livestock on the other side of the hollow.

There, in barren sunlight, the slaves' pen was a paddock of dry clay outlined by a ramshackle rail fence. There was no shade, and at first glance I thought it was littered with corpses. Then I saw that those were sleeping slaves. Most had animal hides to cover themselves, but some just lay in the open. All were filthy, and all naked. About a quarter of them were women. Two or three were mumbling or chanting in the monotonous tones of the insane, praying to the various deities who had forsaken them.

I was to learn that there were about seventy or eighty adults and children in the tribe, and perhaps a hundred slaves at that time. We were close to High Summer, so rain was rare and very welcome. Sun was the problem, and the lack of shelter and clothing was more of the deliberate brutality I had come to recognize. But recognition did not stop it from being effective. My father had treated his woollies with more respect.

The long torment of the journey was over. We were fed, then permitted to fall on the dirt and sleep.

When I awoke, groggy from the heat, I drank and bathed in the stream. I could see women washing clothes in it by the cottages, and I wondered what other purposes it had served before it reached me. Then I stood awhile, to consider the problem. Now that the first shock was wearing off, I must start thinking of escape. A life of captivity held no appeal. I wanted to return to the sea before all the great ones left for the South Ocean.

The talus behind me could have been climbed, but not quietly, nor unseen. The opposing hillside, behind the huts, was steep and coated with thorny-looking shrubs. I decided that panthers would move through those a great deal faster than I could. The end of the hollow was almost sheer, with an ominous tunnel opening in it. Slaves were going and coming with barrows.

The fourth side looked out across a wide valley at some spectacular mountain scenery, which I was in no mood to appreciate.

I already knew that the track up the hillside had been long and bare. I remembered a corral with some runtish ponies in it, but the panthers could surely run me down long before I could reach that, and run down the ponies also. Obviously my departure was going to need some organizing and assistance.

The compound was not busy; nor was it deserted. Men of the tribe strolled to and fro as if on business, while vague hammerings and jingling noises suggested that there were probably more of them around. At the heels of every adult male stalked one of the big black panthers. A group of children and kittens played loudly together near the stream. By the shacks, women were tending babies or doing womanly things, like spinning. Few of the women had cats.

Whoever these people were, they were ugly in my eyes. Even the younger men had dark beards as bristly as thistle patches, but they were all bald—males lost their hair at adolescence and most of the women went bald later, although I did not notice that then. Men wore black leather and women dresses, whose gaudy patterns merely stressed their wearers' toadlike squatness.

Around me, thirty or forty slaves lay or sat within the paddock, some sleeping, some just staring at nothing. They were all scabby and dirty, more like dry weeds than people. The mad ones were still wailing, or else another group had taken over their religious duties—insanity was never absent from the compound. Then I was astonished to notice a man with hair as fair as my own. I walked over and sat down beside him.

He was older than I was, thin and wiry. His legs and back were a network of fine red and white scars. There was gray in the flaxen tangle of his beard. His tan showed that he had worn no clothes for a long time—my loins and buttocks were burned to blisters where my pagne had formerly provided protection. He turned to look at me with dulled blue eyes.

"Knobil," I said and held out a hand.

He hesitated and then responded. "Orange."

I blinked. "Orange *what*?"

He winced and looked away. "Orange-brown-white."

"Sir . . ."

"Just 'Orange,' please. Even that is a mockery. I should not use it."

"I was a herdman," I said, "and then a pilgrim, and then a seaman. Now I am a slave?"

He nodded. "And that is the end of your story."

"Tell! I don't know who these people are, or why they want us."

"They call themselves 'miners.' Everyone else calls them 'ants.' Don't let them hear you do that, though."

"Ants or miners—I intend to escape."

He shook his head. "I expect somebody will try soon. Wait and see what happens before you try it yourself."

"What happens?"

"They usually tie him up by his thumbs and have one of the panthers shuck him."

"Shuck him?"

"Peel him, in strips. Did you ever watch a cat sharpen its claws?"

I had never even heard of cats, although later I met them. They are very like small versions of the panthers, without the third eye. Cats are said to be useful for catching small vermin, but I never liked them.

Being ripped to death had no appeal, either. "Does no one escape?"

Orange shook his head again. "Panthers are deadly, and impossibly quick. Compared to a panther, you move like a snortoise. They can see body heat, and watch you even when there is no light in the mine. They patrol the tunnels, guard the captives, catch game . . . ants depend on panthers like seafolk depend on great ones."

"Can they talk?"

"No. But they understand very complicated orders. They are very well trained. Don't try it, Knobil . . . not until you're ready to die." He sighed as if he were reaching that point himself.

I was thinking that over when he added, "And don't ever anger the ants or draw attention to yourself. They like to execute someone every now and again. It's a good example. And entertainment. Anything but utter humility is savagely punished. You showed too much purpose in the way you came over to me. Look cowed!"

I grunted, trying not to show my dismay. This man was an

angel? Then I caught his eye. For a moment the glazed, waxy look was missing. It flicked back again like a lid on a basket.

"Notice that there aren't quite enough hides to go around?" he asked softly. "They watch who sleeps under cover and who doesn't. You're allowed to enjoy the women if you want—if you have any strength left after your shift, that is. But if you start getting possessive, then that's noticed, too. Don't go to the same one every time. Any slave who begins to gather status is marked."

That was better! An angel would be an obvious leader, so he was merely being cautious.

"You mean there's no way out except death?" I asked.

He hesitated, glanced at my hair, and then nodded. "That's right."

"What do the angels think about this slavery?"

"Ah!" He sighed. "There is a very remote chance that Heaven will raid the nest and release the slaves . . . this is a small tribe. But there are never enough angels, friend Knobil. Ants get their name because they keep slaves. The life of a mineworker is nasty and usually short, so why send your own sons into the pit when you can send someone else's? Any traveler is fair game. In fact, ants are notorious for all sorts of violence. Sometimes one tribe will attack another and try to take its mine . . . that wouldn't help us, though. There would just be more slaves. No ant army ever ends its march with fewer people than it started with, either."

What, I asked, was an ant army?

For a while he did not reply, then he lay down. Puzzled, I copied him. "We were noticed, Knobil," he mumbled, staring at the sky and barely moving his lips. "Friendships are dangerous. You mustn't come near me now for a while—four or five tours, at least. So listen, and I'll explain.

"You know that every tribe, every people, moves west? That's the law of nature. Herders and ranchers drift around, but overall they move west. Traders come and go, but even a trader ends his life farther west than he began it. Seafolk move north to warm seas or estuaries. They go south to round the capes and headlands—or sometimes across them if they must—but in the end they're moving west like the rest of us. Forests spring up before Noon and wither a month or so west of Dusk, so you could say that the forests move, also, and so do the people who live in them. Even Heaven moves.''

I had known that the herdfolk stayed ahead of the sun . . .

"What happens if you get east of the sun, then?" I asked the sky.

He grunted, as if surprised at my ignorance. "The sun goes away. Cold and dark and snow. Half the world is black and covered with ice, Knobil."

Angels were always talking about this "ice" thing—Brown had. I tried in vain to imagine a sky without a sun.

"The ants are different. Nature didn't spread ores around evenly, like forest or grass. The ants have kept more of the old wisdoms—reading and writing, and even a few arcane things that the saints have forgotten, so they say. The ice of Darkside and the floods of Dawn destroy everything. Nothing made by human hand can last from one cycle to the next, and the world is always born anew. The landscape is changed, the workings buried or stripped away, but the ants keep records that tell them where the nests were in the last cycle. Each tribe has its own list, I suppose. They probably try to steal one another's, which may be why they like to move to a mine site as close to Dawn as they can get, right up in the wetlands, to take possession early."

Orange could have had no idea how little of his lecture I was understanding, but I let him talk.

"And they'll stay at a mine as long as possible . . . unless they know of a better one thawing out, of course. They say that an ant can be born and live and die all in the same place . . . the sun low in the east when he is born, passing high overhead, low in the west when he is a very old man."

To a herdman, accustomed to an unchanging sun, that idea was utter insanity. I wondered if captivity had driven this ex-angel mad.

"So, when a tribe of ants does move," he continued, "it may cross almost the whole length of Dayside. A child could be conceived after its parents left one home, and be walking and talking before they reached their next. That's an ant army—a nest on the move. There can be two or three hundred of them, or more. The opportunities for pillage are not always overlooked . . . slaving, too, if they get the chance."

"Don't the angels care?"

"Yes, they do! No matter what nonsense you've heard, the angels do care about the ants! They try to keep watch. A big army will have chariots hovering around it like sheepdogs, but it may be spread over a huge tract of terrain, and there are never enough angels."

He sighed again. "And sometimes the sheep catch the dogs."

Before I could ask what nonsense I was supposed to have heard, someone shouted a warning. Orange scrambled to his feet, telling me to do the same. Sleepers were hastily kicked awake, and the whole paddock of slaves lined up at attention as a party of ants approached. And then we were divided into gangs and marched off.

And I was shown what my father's hymns and prayers had never succeeded in explaining to me when I was a child—what Hell was.

## 2

That first descent into the pit was worse than anything I had yet endured at the hands of my captors. I was assigned to a gang of five other men and a woman, under the supervision of a weedy, tufty-faced youth. He sent the others off to their labors and looked me over contemptuously. Then he gave me a list of the punishments he could inflict on me if he chose: confinement in total darkness, clawings, mutilations, or lingering death. Him I could have broken in half with my bare hands, but he had his panther at his side; so I cringed and groveled and promised to be a good slave.

At the mouth of the mine we met the other shift coming out. I was told to choose a man of about my size and take his gear. Thus I found myself pulling on a stinking leather smock, stiff with old sweat and dirt, shabby and patched and abrasive. It barely reached my knees. The rest of my equipment consisted of a metal helmet, a pick, a canteen, and a candle. The ants, I noted, also wore iron-toed boots and heavy breeches. I would have settled for the breeches. I was ordered into the tunnel.

We were close to High Summer and there were always fifty or more living beings in those workings, not counting cats, and yet the dusty air was bitterly cold. I had never known cold before in my life. I had seen darkness in the waters below the seafolk's grove, but this darkness had a weight and solidity all its own. The tunnel sloped gently, going on and on, relentlessly deeper, branching often. The faint flicker from my light showed rough wet walls pressing in on either hand. Ahead of me was thick, heavy blackness, into which I must force my unwilling body.

Worst of all, though, as I stumbled and scurried ahead of my sneering guard and his four-pawed enforcer, was the sense of being buried, of the mountain peak squeezing in on me. I had been reared under the limitless sky of the grasslands. This living burial was in itself a torment more terrifying than almost anything I could have imagined. The cold and the smell of rock and the darkness knotted my insides in spasms of fear.

Eventually we took a smaller branch, then another, and came at last to a dead end. The ceiling was so low I had to crouch, and the whole cramped space was visible, even in the faint glimmer of my tiny candle and the ant's lantern. I was puzzled by a steady clinking, for I could not see where it came from, and it echoed mysteriously all around.

"That one." The kid pointed at a row of small holes around the cave at floor level, looking barely larger than miniroo burrows. I hesitated, nauseated by the weight of mountain above me. The boy gestured and the panther sank on its haunches, snarling. Quickly I lay down with my clutter of equipment and began to wriggle in.

And wriggle . . . and wriggle . . . The walls spread out, but the ceiling stayed right above my head. The floor was cold, and wet, and abrasive against my legs. Water dripped continually. I could hear that I was being followed, and I was pathetically grateful for the company.

At last the journey ended, the two of us lying side by side on our bellies, facing a vein of crumbling black rock that was obviously worth much more than I was. If I tried to raise my head to look at it properly, my helmet struck the roof. The tunnel was wide enough that I could have just touched both sides by stretching out my arms, but floor and ceiling sloped sharply to the left. I was hard against one wall, and the kid almost leaning on me. Two battered buckets were there, waiting for us.

"You fill ten buckets." The contemptuous voice was at my ear. "The black stuff. None of the white—that's dross. Like you.

As you fill each one, you shout for another, and the woman will bring it.''

"Yes, master." And the echoes whispered, *master, master.*

"You stop and come out when the candle dies. If you haven't done ten, you'll be encouraged to do better next time.''

"I'll try, master.''

"You'd better, slag. Look back.''

I twisted awkwardly around and saw two eyes, glowing in the faint flicker of the lantern.

"Sliver will be checking on you," my driver said. "He can see you even without light, and you won't hear him coming.''

"I'll work hard, master!''

"Yes, you will. If I don't hear that pick going, I'll send in Sliver." He gestured with one hand. A big padded foot stroked along the back of my bare calf. I squealed and the boy laughed.

"He won't have his claws sheathed next time." He took his lantern and began to scramble away, then thought of a last warning. "Work forward, not sideways. If the cut gets too wide, the roof will fall.''

"I'll remember, master.''

"This one's too wide already." He departed with a clatter and scratch of boots, leaving me in a silence broken only by the clink of my pick and the harsh breathing of a man working as hard as terror could drive him.

How long? I don't know how long I was a slave for the ants.

I survived, and perhaps nothing in my long life is quite so strange as that. Many other seafolk were brought in after me, and obviously the ants had expected the great migration. All they had need do was set a trap by the first fresh water. Seafolk came easy.

Seafolk went easy, also. Those gentle people made very bad slaves. Strangers to violence, they just lay down and died.

The third or fourth batch after mine included Whistler, one of the boys from my own tribe. He brought nightmare news of women giving birth in coracles as they were towed through the madness of the Great Canyon. Several had died most horribly, including Sparkle. I spoke but once with Whistler, for after his second shift he tried to run away. I was lucky to be underground at the time.

His news should have killed me faster than the panthers killed him. I had been very fond of Sparkle—indeed I would have sworn that I had loved her as much as man could love woman, for I had not then learned what true love is. Her death seemed to mark her as just one more victim in the wake of disaster I trailed—my parents, Violet, Pebble, Sparkle. Anyone I ever cared for died, it seemed.

And her death was entirely my fault. Even in the worst parts of the canyon there had been quiet pools where a boat could have lingered. Had I not been so stupid as to let myself be caught by the ants I would have been there, in that canyon hell. A little common sense and Sparkle would have lived. Even young Whistler said that much, and I believe it still.

I was a seaman—I should have lain down and faded away, as so many of them did. Even if I could escape from the ants' nest, where would I go, what would I gain? My tribe was already lost on the vast South Ocean. I had no family there anyway, for not one child was recognized as mine. The ant who caught me had thrown away my angel tokens, but I had long since lost any desire to be an angel. Sparkle's death was as much the fault of Brown-yellow-white as it was mine, and the prisoner Orange was no hero to admire. The angels had failed to save the herdfolk, they had destroyed my idyllic life in the grove—or so I thought—and they apparently could do nothing about these monstrous slave-owning ants. I hated and despised angels. I had no wish to be an angel. I had no wish to live at all.

Some slaves just seemed to dissolve—that was an easy death, and one I prayed for. Some tried to escape or fight back, but I was far too craven to risk what happened to them.

All the other captives went mad—some in one way, some in others. But we all went mad after our fashion. All of us.

"Knobil?" The whisper came as I crouched at the trench. On one side of me a lumbering hairy herdman named Koothik was mumbling prayers, as he did all the time, everywhere. On the other side was Orange, the former angel.

I whispered back under the madman's gabble and the loud drone of insects, keeping my head down. "Sir?"

"I am planning an escape."

"I'm with you."

"It will be very dangerous. Many of us will die."

Here was the answer I had been looking for! "Of course."

"They don't seem to have any weapons but cats. If enough men with shovels go for a panther, some should survive."

"Of course."

"We'll strike in the mine door at a change of shift. Take the bosses hostage."

"Great!" It would be a quick death, and that was all I wanted.

Koothik rose and lumbered away. Orange's whispering grew more urgent. "Try to enlist two followers and two more leaders. Be very careful who you talk to. Report back when ready."

"Will do," I said, without moving my lips.

"Better to die bravely than linger on as a slave."

"Absolutely!"

"Brave man!" the angel whispered, and walked away before anyone noticed our conversation.

Then I realized what he had just said. *Brave* man? Me? That was the only time while I was a slave of the ants that I ever laughed aloud.


The first three men I approached turned me down flat, and I began to grow desperate. There were so few sane enough to trust!

Before I could try a fourth, Orange was betrayed—or else he had been too obvious. As he came trudging out of the mine at the end of shift, he was ordered to halt in the middle of the settlement, near the stream, while the rest of us returned to the paddock. There was no trial, no explanation, no announcement. He was left there in full view, a naked man dribbling sweat onto his shadow, alone, waiting. He soon fell over, and the life of the compound went on around him regardless, as if he had already ceased to exist. A single cat guarded him, and was replaced by another when it grew weary.

I suppose he died mostly from thirst. He could hear and see the stream, but the slightest movement would bring needle claws slashing down. He did do some crawling, at the cost of much skin and blood, but when he neared the water itself the panther took him by the ankle and dragged him back to where he started. We knew he was dead when it began to eat him, and after that there was no more talk of mass breakouts.

I remember when I first realized that I also had gone mad. I was lying under one of the filthy hides, being cooked, trying to go back to sleep. Unfortunately some herdman had lain down alongside me and was croaking psalms to his Heavenly Father. I could hear him and even smell him, but I was too exhausted to move away.

"Shut up!" I muttered, not raising my voice in case I woke myself completely.

He did not hear me, and would not have reacted if he had. I reluctantly cracked one eye open and saw enough of blood-caked furry leg to recognize Koothik. By then he was as mad as a mating bogmoth, uncomprehending, needing constant clawings to make him heed orders. He wailed on, in hoarse monotone.

"Idiot!" I said. "Your god isn't listening. Try another for a change." There were many gods worshipped in the slave compound—gods hidden in rocks and trees, gods of air and water, wood and bone, many gods.

"If your god cared," I said crossly, "then he would not let this happen to you!" Koothik was no older than I was, but twice my size, a shaggy young giant picked up by traders when he was a loner, or perhaps sold to them by his father. "You haven't done anything to deserve this," I told him, still prone under my cover, the earth gritting against my cheek as I spoke. "You should be lounging in a comfortable tent, counting your daughters, tended by adoring women—lots of them." That was the life he had been raised for.

Koothik, of course, neither heard nor replied.

Then I had an inspiration. I raised my head and checked around, but there was no one else within earshot. "I'll tell you something, Koothik," I said. "A big secret."

Koothik's mind was not there to hear, but I told the rest of him. "He can't hear, Koothik! Our Father lives above the grasslands, and he can't hear us from here. But I'm going to go back to the grasslands and tell him what's happening to his children. Then he'll throw thunderbolts and stop it! Then he'll help us!"

Koothik uttered thanks for grass and wool . . .

"It's wrong to treat men like woollies," I explained carefully, lying flat again. "But I have a plan, Koothik! No use praying here, Koothik! I shall go back to the grasslands and pray to the

Father and he will hear me there and then come and rescue us all!''

Now I can detect certain logical weaknesses in that plan, but it seemed very reasonable then, and very comforting. And yet somehow I knew it for the insanity it was.

I turned over, but I was too excited to sleep. I decided I had been foolish to blurt out my plan to Koothik. He might tell the ants, and they would be frightened, and kill me. I decided to tell no one else about my plan.

# 3

Not long after that, I met Hrarrh. Again I was stretched out on the hot clay of the paddock, just drifting off to sleep. This time my cover was pulled away—a not uncommon event. I decided to resist. I was crushingly exhausted after a hard shift in a place called the canyon, where the slaves worked in couples and the supervisor could watch us all the time. The woman running me then was the worst in the mine, worse than almost any of the men. She had paired me with an inadequate adolescent, forcing me to do more than my share. I felt as if I had *earned* that cover, although all a slave could earn by any effort was temporary freedom from pain.

I sat up and jerked the leather back again. Technically this was fighting, and someone would be watching to see who won the exchange. Too many wins would bring a mauling, but I was one of the best workers, so I could hope to get away with minor offenses once in a while.

Adjusting the stinking hide over myself once more, I glared challengingly at the would-be thief lying facedown on the dirt at my side. Then I looked again. He was barely more than a boy, still round with puppy fat, and he had the worst case of sunburn I had ever seen. His back was a marshland of water blisters, and his shoulders were cooked meat. Every part of him was red and peeling. By pulling off the cover, I had hurt him. His eyes were screwed up in pain.

"Maybe you do need this more than I do," I said, feeling guilty. "Let me wet it for you."

I clambered to my feet, limped across to the stream, and soaked the hide. Then I returned and spread it over him.

I flopped down at his side. "You won't mind if I tuck my head under the corner? I'm Knobil."

He scowled at me and said his name. It sounded like a cat snarl, and "Hrarrh" was the closest I could ever come to it. He had only a hint of moustache, but his shoulders were broad, and already his scalp was balding. Sunburn meant pale skin.

"You're an ant!"

He opened his eyes again to glare. "A miner!"

"Beg your pardon! But it looks like you're a slave now." I had not seen him before. He was not of this tribe.

He nodded faintly and closed his eyes again. I put my head under the edge of the cover, for that made sleep a little easier. We spoke no more.

When I awoke, he was sitting with the cover draped over him, trying to shade himself. His burns had bled a lot and I decided that he was dying. A man can lose only so much skin. He was rigid with pain.

"Did they raid your nest?" I was recalling what Orange had said.

He shook his head without bothering to look at me. "Prospecting parties . . . but we killed three of theirs." He bared his teeth in satisfaction.

"And they took away your clothes?"

"Of course." He seemed to find that deliberate cruelty quite reasonable.

When the bosses came to round up their gangs, Hrarrh knew what was expected of him. He lined up with the rest of us, looking surly. He was obviously too badly injured to work, but newcomers were normally given time to heal.

Slaves never learned any of the ants' names. We addressed every one as "master" or "mistress," and referred to them among ourselves by the names of their cats. At that time the slavemaster was a fat, rather tall man with gray in his beard and a face even flatter than most. He walked with a limp and was shadowed always by one of the largest panthers in the settlement, Whisper. Now he curled his bushy moustache at the new boy. "You're excused, cat food!"

Hrarrh fell on his raw knees, touched his face to the man's

boots, and said loudly, ''Master, I humbly beg permission to work in the mine!''

Any backtalk was cause for immediate mutilation, but the leader was obviously nonplussed by this insane request.

''You're dying, dross!''

Still speaking to the man's feet, Hrarrh said, ''Then let me die working at the face, master, I beg you! Please! Please!''

The leader glanced at the gang bosses. They shrugged and grinned.

''I'd have to let Whisper clean you up first,'' he said. That brought wider grins from the ants, and made me shiver. The pain of the rough tongue and corrosive saliva on so much raw flesh would be unendurable torment.

''Thank you, master!'' Hrarrh at once sat up, leaned back on his heels, spread his arms, and lifted his chin. He waited, with eyes closed and teeth clenched.

The big cat glided forward at its master's signal. Hrarrh flinched when the tongue first touched him, then remained motionless while the washing continued. The whole paddock, slaves and masters alike, watched this incredible display of endurance with something like awe, waiting for the screams to start . . . but they did not start. How the boy remained conscious and sane and even silent, I could not imagine. It must have felt like a swim in boiling water. Sweat streamed down his face. He shivered convulsively with the effort, but otherwise his only motion was a steady jerking of his juvenile Adam's apple.

''Now stand and let him do your legs!''

Hrarrh rose very shakily. He kept his eyes closed. He swayed, but he suffered even that additional torture in silence, his features visibly ashen under the burns. When it was finished he sank down with his head on the ground once more and hoarsely said, ''Thank you, master.''

Even the ants were impressed. Clearly the leader had not expected the victim to withstand the torture, for he chuckled admiringly. Then he assigned him to the same gang as myself.

The site called the canyon lay deep in the mine, where the ore vein was almost, but not quite, vertical. It had started, I suppose, as a tunnel and was by then a deep trench, just wide enough for two men to stand shoulder to shoulder. The slightly sloping walls towered over us, up into darkness. They had been cross-braced with props, but we all knew that sooner or later the overhang would collapse. Still, it was more pleasant to work standing up, more companionable to have the whole gang in the same dig, and much less stressful when the panthers could not sneak in behind us unseen. We had a double gang, eight with picks and four with shovels. We paused at intervals to pass the buckets back to a winch hoist, and thus we all had to work at about the same pace.

Hrarrh was last to arrive, and of course the bitch-boss put him in the pair closest to her, at my side. I had expected that. In the gloom his legs were already streaked with black lines of blood, so the coarse smock was abrading his tattered shoulders, but he at once began swinging his pick like a maniac. I wondered whether he was trying to kill himself. Probably the only unin- jured places on his body were his palms, but soon the handle of the pick glistened wetly as he wore the skin from those also. He was only a youth, he was grievously ill, and yet I could barely keep up with his stroke.

In the canyon's teamwork, the slowest pair governed the times for bucket passing. With any reasonable partner, a stronger worker like me need not force himself very hard. We did need good judgment, for if one pair got too far ahead of the others, then the others would be disciplined. So would any man who slacked too obviously. I was sure that this addle-brained kid would soon flag, but he held the pace, our shovel boy was soon shoveling as he never had before, and we filled our first bucket long before the other teams. The sadist boss woman screamed at them for being outworked by a cripple. She confiscated all water canteens except ours.

The same thing happened with the next bucket. This time every man in the team got clawed, except Hrarrh and me.

About halfway through the shift, Hrarrh began to have faint- ing spells. When he came to, he would stagger to his feet and go at it again, but by then the other men had caught the smell of revenge, and the pace quickened. Try as I might, I could not do the work of two. Ours was now the late bucket. Hrarrh was unconscious, so I was the one punished, but even the boss had been impressed. Instead of her cat, she used her iron-toed boots, giving me a few mild kicks on the shins. From her, that was almost praise.

By the end of the shift, Hrarrh had apparently collapsed for good. Candles were flickering out. The boss had a couple of the weaker workers scratched, as always, and then dismissed us, leading the way up the ladder. The others followed, stepping over Hrarrh's motionless form.

We two remained, in the dark. I checked his pulse and he was alive. I carried our picks and canteens up the ladder, and even that was an ordeal at the end of a shift. Then I came back down again. He was still unconscious, still alive. If this kid could work miracles, I decided, then I could. Somehow I got him over my shoulder; somehow I climbed the ladder, all the way wondering if any of the shoddy rungs would collapse under our combined weight. I laid him down rather clumsily when we reached the top, thinking my heart was about to explode.

"Who's that?" he asked.

"Knobil."

"Leave me."

"No."

"They'll skin you."

For a while there was no sound except my gasping. Then I said, "Can you walk?"

"Yes."

"Then hold my coat. I know the way."

It was not the first time I had left the mine in the dark. Once in a while we could steer by the candles of the incoming gangs, but mostly we just walked slowly through the blackness, fumbling at walls to locate branchings. I carried the equipment and Hrarrh kept a hand on me.

We reached daylight and waited for the dazzle to leave our eyes. Then I pulled his smock off for him, feeling it tearing loose from his sores. He was completely coated in blood, both wet and dry, his face haggard as death. The next shift was still milling around, dressing, but sneaking interested glances. Hrarrh straightened his shoulders, reeled over to one of the bosses, and crouched at his feet to beg for another licking. I decided he was mad.

The ant regarded him angrily, probably wondering how to punish a man who was being insubordinate by demanding punishment. If it was mockery, it was unanswerable. "Why?"

"So that I may heal faster and be able to do more work."

"And why would you want to do that?"

"I was born a miner, master. I must be able to outwork the dross."

The ant shrugged. "Then lie down."

That was a wise precaution, for if Hrarrh fainted during the licking, the cat would slash him as he fell. He did not faint—his eyes opened afterward—but another slave had to roll him over so that the panther could clean his back. I carried him to the paddock.

I scrounged a few scraps of food that had not yet been consumed. I managed to rouse him enough to force it into him. No one else was coming near us. No slave ever wanted to attract attention, and the ants were openly watching from their side of the compound.

Hrarrh chewed with determination, forcing lumps down his throat and repeatedly gagging. His eyes were unfocused, and he shivered uncontrollably. He was in deep shock, probably very close to death.

"Why are you doing this?" he asked faintly.

I shrugged. "Just eat."

"You think I can help you escape?"

Certainly I would not mention my plan to an ant, even a captive ant. "If I did, I wouldn't dare be seen with you."

He nodded. "Then why?"

I was not sure of that myself. Probably, as a coward, I admired courage. "Someone helped me once, when I was hurt and alone."

He worked that out while he chewed some more. Then he said: "You're a fool. And so was he."

I was surprised to find him still alive when I awoke. He lined up for the bosses, and then went through the whole incredible process all over again, from licking to final collapse.

But he had not fainted quite so often during the shift, and he was conscious as I carried him up the ladder. That was a bad journey, for I was weakened by overwork and lack of food, and we almost ran out of luck before the top. The other slaves again ignored us when we reached the compound, but they had left enough refuse in the trough for two good meals, and a pair of the dirty leather covers lay nearby, apparently overlooked. Such consideration was unusual and might be lethal if the ants chose to interpret it as a sign of admiration or approval.

Three . . . four . . . By his fifth shift Hrarrh had stopped fainting and was producing almost as much as the slowest of the healthy men, yet he still needed my help on the ladder, and so it was that the two of us again returned to the paddock together. The other slaves were continuing their pretense that we did not exist. The two pariahs sat alone in a sun-baked emptiness to chew their roots and gristle.

Hrarrh had pulled a hide around himself to protect his new skin from the sun, but that skin was in itself vindication of his faith in the healing powers of the panthers' saliva. His puppy fat had already gone, which was an improvement, but the scars on his face did nothing for his looks. His nose seemed to have been applied too hot, so that it had melted and spread, and brow ridges like tree branches made him seem permanently surly. Tufts of wiry hair protruded through the scabs around his big mouth. He was an ugly kid. He was going to be a very typical ant.

I knew I had taken a risk by befriending him. Every moment we remained together increased that risk, so I had to satisfy my curiosity before retribution separated us.

"Now," I said, "tell me why."

He scowled. "Why what?"

"Why did you volunteer to be licked?"

"So I could work."

"But why want to work?"

"Obvious! They have three dead men to avenge."

I was baffled. "So?"

"So they wanted to give me time to heal. Then the bosses would have taken turns with me."

"You hoped to die?"

He looked offended. "No!"

"They can do nothing to you that would hurt worse than that."

"It would go on longer. And be more permanent."

"But they still can!"

He shrugged, and obviously regretted doing so. "You're only a herdman. You don't understand pride."

"Pride? You endured those lickings for *pride*?"

"Partly. But I've shown I've got balls, so maybe now they'll let me keep them." His gaze flickered across the compound toward the cottages. "Most tribes need new blood. Who knows? I'm a miner. Maybe one of the girls'll take a fancy to me when I get some hair on my chest."

I wondered if even a female ant could ever think of Hrarrh as good-looking, but perhaps he was a better judge of that than I was. While I was pondering this, I saw that he was looking hard at me.

"So I've got a chance," he said. "You don't. Why do you stay?"

"What do you suggest I do? Walk out?"

"Step off the top of the ladder."

"I'm a coward."

He scowled. "No slave ever escapes! Never!"

"What about angels, though? Don't they sometimes raid a mine?"

"Angels? You're crazy! Angels don't mess with miners!"

"Are you sure?" I was remembering what Orange had told me.

He spat out something unchewable and stuffed a lump of unidentifiable meat in his mouth. "Certain! Heaven needs what we produce—lead, iron, copper . . . The angels leave the mines alone. If that's what you're waiting for, then you'll wait till the sun sets."

"But . . ." Was this what Orange had called nonsense?

"But nothing! Even if Heaven sent an army of angels, it couldn't approach a mine like this without us . . . them, I mean . . . without them knowing. So all the slaves go down the mine, the ponies come into the paddock, and where's your evidence? What angel is going to venture into the mine to look? What happens to him if he does?"

I did not reply. He was very convincing.

"Or we just fight it out. Cat against gun is a fair match at close quarters. How many angels can Heaven afford to lose?"

"Not many, I suppose."

"Damned few." Then he said in a low voice, "Knobil, I'm grateful. It hurts me to say it, but I am. Now leave me alone! You're going to be punished, and if you keep defying the rules like this, you'll be shucked for sure. I've given you the best advice I can: Die easy!"

"Thanks."

After a moment he added, "One other bit, then—stay away from traders."

"Traders?" I had not seen traders since my youth on the grasslands, but of course the ore we dug must go somewhere.

Hrarrh's scabby face was grim. "Traders sell slaves to us— even a herdman must have discovered that by now. They're one of our main sources. A trader will sell his grandsons if he can see profit."

"So why tell me to stay away from them? I'm already in the worst place I could be."

He hesitated, glancing at my hair. "I'm not sure about that. Just remember my advice. The first bit was the best."

He struggled to his feet and I said: "Hrarrh?"

He paused, scowling down at me. "Yes?"

"Good luck with the beautiful lady miner. And if it works out for you . . . remember me?"

He nodded. "I'm greatly in your debt. I won't forget that, Knobil!" He limped away, clutching the ragged hide around him like a cape.

That was how I met Hrarrh.

# 4

I avoided him on the next shift and he managed on his own. As I came out of the mine, I was stopped by one of the bosses and sent back in with his crew. Double duty, without rest or food, ranked fairly high on the list of punishments—it had been known to kill a man—but it was better than some of the things they might have done to me. It also put me on the opposite tour from Hrarrh, so we could not meet again.

It was bad, but I survived. So did Hrarrh. For a long time thereafter I saw him only in passing, sometimes trading clothes and tools with him at changeover. He was one big walking scar, but his great ant shoulders soon bulged with muscle. The rumor mill said that he ranked with the best workers, yet the bosses were hard on him. No matter how much he produced in a shift, he could rarely escape blooding. But he was spared real mutilation, so his brutal gamble had apparently paid off.

\* \* \*

How long?

I don't know how long I was a slave for the ants. I saw their women progress from wedding to pregnancy to weaning—then to more pregnancies and children growing. I saw Hrarrh develop a huge black beard and his scalp go bald as a fish's belly.

We worked to exhaustion, we ate, we slept, we worked to exhaustion again, in unending, uncounted repetition.

The only recreation was casual copulation. The only excitements were rockfalls and counting the bodies. The only release from the brutal discipline was death. Anyone too sick, too mad, or too badly injured to work died and was fed to the panthers—not necessarily in that order.

Not all work was done underground. Good workers would be rewarded from time to time with a spell on the surface—tending fields, crushing ore, working the sluice and picking the valued dark pellets off the hides that trapped them . . . cutting timber, grinding grain, wheeling barrows. Some of those tasks were as strenuous as mining, but at least they were done in daylight, and we worked our hearts to pulp in the mines to earn them. Then a moment's hesitation to obey an order, or someone else's turn, or just the whim of a surly boss, and the terrible dark returned.

Gangs and shifts changed. Sometimes I found that I was back on the same schedule as Hrarrh. Rarely we would talk—at the food trough or the pits, or in the drowsy times before sleep on the hard ground. We were careful not to be seen together very often, but I think I was the only slave he ever spoke to at all. As a born ant, he regarded slaves as dross and beneath contempt, although he was now one of us himself. Even with me, his manner was always gruff and arrogant.

And yet Hrarrh himself was the second straw of hope that kept me afloat. "I won't forget," he had said. So if he had a chance, then I had one also, however slim.

And Hrarrh's reward arrived eventually, as I learned when I saw him striding across the compound in smart new leathers, leading a half-grown panther off to training. Soon afterward, I watched his wedding. Bald and bearded, he was indistinguishable from any other young male ant, but he owed me a favor. It might be long before he achieved enough seniority in the tribe to do anything about it, but from then on I could believe that I was a little less unfortunate than all my fellows. One ant was in my debt.

There were bad times and worse times, and a very few not-quite-so-bad times. Rarely the ants held a wedding or some other feast that left nobody to supervise. Then the slaves gained a holiday also, to sit idle in the scorching sun and watch the dancing by the cottages under the trees. At those times the women shimmered in gowns of iridescent gossamer, swirling clouds of color. The slaves laughed behind their hands at this futile attempt to beautify such ugliness, but the male ants seemed to like their women that shape.

Half the races of Vernier were represented in the slave pen at one time or another. Herdmen were the most common, though, and the most prized. They were huge and they were docile. Trained to absolute obedience to their human fathers and then betrayed by them, betrayed also by their Heavenly Father, deprived of the unbounded sky of their youth, herdmen went mad very quickly, but they continued to obey. The great haul of seafolk boosted the work force greatly, but thereafter the numbers dwindled as deaths outran recruitment. New slaves were brought in from time to time by the ants' raiding parties, and many were brought by traders, although I never saw a trader in the compound.

I learned much about Vernier from the scattered moments of conversation with men and women of other shades and shapes and size. But I told none of them about my plan. As an oyster locks tight about a pearl, so I closed my ill-used body around my tortured mind, and closed that in turn about the tiny fire of purpose that gave my existence meaning—my plan. I would go to the grasslands and there complain to the Almighty.

Die or go mad—there was no other choice. I made friends and saw them die or go mad like me. I had sex with women who were forbidden to refuse, gaining small relief and no pleasure.

My plan ran round and round in my head when I was awake. Asleep, I was consoled by a recurring dream, where ants became snarks. Every sleep I dreamed it at least once. Leading an army of seamen, riding on great ones, I ravaged the ants' nest. How wonderful were those dreamed great ones! They bounded in and out of the hard clay of the dream compound as if it were water, while I skewered ants by the dozen on a weightless and untiring spear, and panthers by the score. All the ants in my dream, though, had Hrarrh's face, which seemed curious even to me.

Then I would awaken to perform the most arduous or disgusting tasks eagerly and without hesitation. Even small children could give orders to a slave, and throwing rocks at us while we slept was their favorite sport.

I saw shuckings. Once the victim was a woman, and after that even Anubyl did not seem so bad to me.

How long?

I don't know how long I was a slave for the ants, but in my memories it seems to me now that the center of my life is missing, that what should have been the peak of my manhood is marked by a gaping black wound.

# 5

I do not remember leaving the ant's nest, but it was Hrarrh's doing.

Once we had been friends of a sort, two slaves muttering careful asides to each other and watching for watchers. Then we had been slave and ant, seeing each other at a distance, never speaking, living in separate worlds. Suddenly we were slave and slaveboss.

The workers hated a change of supervisor. Even those with a reputation for decency were always hard on a new gang for the first few shifts. Even more we hated the beginners, for they had to prove to the others that they were tough also. Hrarrh was one of those, and it was my misfortune to be assigned to his first shift. Nor did I like the look of his panther. It was fully grown now, but it twitched restlessly, as if poorly trained, or not completely under his control.

Of course nobody spoke. We stood in a line while he looked us over—the usual six men and one woman, all standing like dead trees, eyes downcast. A woman or boy was always included to carry off the buckets and keep tally.

He began with her. "Tell me what each of these cripples did on the last shift." Then he walked along the line with his panther pacing at his heels, and she called out the number of buckets each man had filled. I had done twelve, everyone else the usual ten. He paused for a while in front of me but did not speak. I watched the ground until he moved away.

"For me," he said, "each of you will do two more than last time. If not for me, then for Chuckles, here. I should warn you, though—she's inexperienced and she tends to cut deep. Last man at the face gets two strokes to start with, so run!"

We ran.

Very few men could achieve twelve, no matter what the threat. Fourteen was an impossibility. Fortunately our worksite was not far into the mine. Unfortunately it was a bad one. The vein was thin, the air bad, the roof almost too low for the buckets, and a man could barely raise his head at all. I usually worked there without my helmet. I banged my head often, but it eased the strain on my neck.

Flat on my belly, I flailed my pick against the rock in panic. I scrabbled up the cuttings and crammed them into a bucket, in reckless disregard for the scrapings of my hands against the roof. Could Hrarrh have been serious? Perhaps it was only the others he had hoped to inspire. Surely he could not expect any man to produce fourteen full buckets? Surely my long-ago kindness would carry some weight? He would not be hard on me if I failed . . . would he?

*Fourteen?*

Between the clinkings of my own pick, the faint sounds from the other rooms were an almost continuous barrage, so the others must believe he was serious. But fourteen? I heard a few yells as time wore on, as the men tired and Chuckles was sent in to inspire them.

When I was topping off my thirteenth bucket, my candle died. That was the signal to stop. From the corridor outside drifted sounds of begging and screaming, as Hrarrh carried out his threats against those who had not managed to fill twelve. I continued to work in the dark, waiting to be called out. Perhaps thirteen and a quarter would satisfy him.

Thirteen and a half . . .

Silence outside, and inside only the sound of my pick and strident breathing . . .

Thirteen and three-quarters. Why did he not call? Had he forgotten me? But a faint flicker from his lantern showed that he was still out there.

Fourteen!

It was done. I wriggled wearily to turn around on the gritty rock, struggling with my pick and two buckets of ore. I crawled painfully forward, pushing them, and emerged into the corridor at Hrarrh's feet. I rose to my knees, fighting back the dizziness that always came after lying so long on my belly. Then I just stared at his boots, feeling so exhausted that I did not think I would care very much if he sent me out to be shucked.

For a while neither of us spoke. Instead of sitting or crouching beside him, the panther was pacing restlessly to and fro. Then the familiar voice said, "You are still a fool."

I did not look up. "Why, master?"

"Have you ever heard of a man digging fourteen buckets in one shift?"

"No, master."

"Why would I order you to do the impossible?"

"I don't know, master."

"Put it back."

In horror I tilted my head to look up at him, although that was forbidden. Put it back? All that work and pain? My knees, hands, elbows were raw. In the flickering light there was nothing of his face visible between beard and helmet, except a glitter from his eyes.

He sighed. "No man can do fourteen! But you have—so now they'll expect you to do it every time. For your own sake, slag, put the ore back where you got it. Now!"

I was so exhausted and so enraged that I did another impossible thing: I hesitated to obey an order.

Then—at last—he started to laugh. "Knobil, Knobil! I wanted to talk to you! Alone. How else could I do that? I never dreamed you'd actually manage to fill fourteen buckets, you dumb herdman! The next shift'll be here soon . . . now move!"

I gasped with relief. "Sorry, master . . . at once . . ." And so I pushed the two heavy buckets all the way back to the face and left them there. The next worker was going to have a pleasant surprise.

I crawled back out to the corridor and knelt once again before him, expectant, stirred by a growing excitement. What vital news could he have that he needed to impart to me alone?

"How many did you fill, then?" he asked.

I grinned. "Twelve, master."

"But I told you to do fourteen."

My relief froze before a cold breath of terror. He was only teasing, of course. Wasn't he?

"Master, I am sorry."

"You're going to be more sorry."

"But . . ." I stopped. My tongue was too dry to move.

He tilted my head back so I could see the sadness in his face. "The others are waiting to see, Knobil. They remember how you befriended me, so they are waiting to see what I do. I have to damage you. Surely you can see that? I have to show them. You're two buckets short, slag!"

Two buckets short . . . a terrible failure.

Never had I suffered a major clawing. I had been scratched often enough, of course—my calves were a network of scars. A moment's rest that slipped into an exhausted sleep . . . a pace that flagged near the end of a shift . . . even the unearned spite of a sadistic boss . . . any of those could bring a black terror creeping in unnoticed behind a worker, the sudden flash of pain. But never more than that. I had seen, and heard, other men's backs or legs being shredded like lace, but always I had worked as hard as I was able and been a good slave . . .

Hrarrh was waiting—for what? What was I supposed to say?

"Yes, master."

"Well, lie down! My wife's a very good cook. My dinner's getting cold."

Trembling with both terror and my deathly exhaustion, I turned around and stretched out, nose against the floor. The mine was silent except for distant dripping noises. There was another pause. I wished he would get on with it. I ached everywhere, and only fear was keeping me from falling asleep.

"Those are remarkable calves, Knobil! After so long in the mine! You must have been very good dross!"

"Yes, master."

Then two rock-crusher hands grabbed my ankles and jerked me backward, dragging me half out of my smock. He dropped my feet.

"And there isn't a single mark on your thighs yet! Amazing!"

I shuddered and was silent. The panther had taken up position beside me, but I just stared at the floor, smelling damp rock and my own terror.

Suddenly Hrarrh began to laugh again. "Oh, Knobil! You believed me, didn't you? You think I'd worry about the others? You think I'd claw a man who saved my life—just to please them?"

"You won't, master?"

"Certainly not!"

I relaxed with a gasp of relief and was taken unaware by the searing rip of talons raking my right thigh from knee to buttocks.

"I'm going to," Hrarrh explained, "but not because of them. Just to please me. You're two buckets short—aren't you?"

"Yes, master."

I could not see the signals, of course, but the cat could, and each movement of his hand brought another fiery slash. Then I would spasm, and scrabble my fingers on the rock, and wait for the next one—but I did not cry out.

Hrarrh kept making *Tsk!* noises. "She's still cutting too deep," he said. Somehow I stayed silent, and no panther ever made a sound. There was only pain, and more pain, and greater pain, and Hrarrh's voice, soft and patient and almost bored. "Do try not to jerk like that, Knobil. It makes it very hard for her to judge."

And finally . . . "There, that ought to do it. Well . . . you might as well be symmetrical." Two more . . . "Yes, that looks better. Now we have to clean you up, and I can go home to momma."

Very bad. Now I knew what a major clawing felt like. But now came the licking, and that was always far worse than the scratching itself. I had not known a man could have so much sweat left in him after a full shift in the mine.

"They don't enjoy this, either, you know, Knobil. They dislike the taste of human blood—that's how they learn not to cut so deep. She's really having trouble stopping the bleeding. But she's only a beginner, so we'll just have to be patient with her."

I never was lucky enough to faint. I bit my tongue, and I bruised my face and hands by beating them against the rocky floor, but I did not disgrace myself by losing control of my sphincters, and I did not cry out. Hrarrh himself had endured such pain without a sound. He would despise me if I screamed.

And nothing can last forever. Eventually he was satisfied. Drained, finished, I lay like a rag on the rock at his feet. He had proved to his buddies that he would savage his former friend. I wondered if I would have the strength even to stand up. I waited for the order, and braced myself to make the effort . . .

"Turn over."

"What?"

"Roll over!"

With great difficulty I obeyed, and the cold sandy floor gritted on my cuts. Lying on my back with my smock up around my belly, I felt even more vulnerable than I had before. The lantern flickered gently from a high ledge, making shadows writhe on the rough walls of the little crypt. The panther was pacing again. Seeming to stand very tall, Hrarrh was staring down at me, rubbing his whiskers.

"Two buckets short? Is that enough, do you think?" he asked.

I just grunted, tasting the blood from my bitten tongue, feeling the cold air on my sweat-soaked skin.

"I think that ought to satisfy them . . . don't you?"

I managed to mumble, "Yes, master."

"But it doesn't satisfy me, Knobil."

"Huh?"

"We're going to do more. Yes, it's too bad, but we will have to do more."

"What? Why?"

He sighed. "Once a herdman, always a herdman! They make good slaves, but they're not very smart."

I had no strength to take any more, and I began to weep silently.

"You don't understand pride, do you? I told you that before."

I sobbed and choked and finally found my voice. "Please, master! No more clawing! I'll work a double shift . . . I'll lick your boots . . . I'll do anything, anything at all . . . but, please! No more clawing . . ."

He shook his head in disgust. "That's not good! You'd do any of those things anyway, if I told you to."

He gestured. The panther slunk over rather sulkily and sat opposite him, on my other side. It looked down at me with eyes that momentarily glowed red.

Faint voices and clumping of ants' boots echoed eerily through the mine.

"The next shift is coming!" Hrarrh said. "We must get a move on—my wife will be furious. The right shin to start with, then. And do keep still this time, or you'll lose a kneecap."

He gestured. I felt the talons scrape along the bone. It was the worst yet.

I screamed.

It burst out before I knew it was coming—a howl of terror and torment beyond endurance.

"Ah!" Hrarrh said approvingly. "You did it!"

"What?"

"That's what I wanted! Ever since you helped me, dross, I've wanted to hear you scream. Pride, remember? That was a very good scream—but I think you can do better. So now Chuckles is going to practice clawing, and you're going to practice screaming. You're going to weep, and you're going to beg, but mostly you're going to scream. You're going to scream your lungs out for me, Knobil, my friend."

# 6

When it was over, two slaves carried me back to the paddock.

I did not sleep, and the clay where I lay became soaked with blood. As the bosses arrived for the next shift, I did manage to stand up, but I knew that he had ruined me. Nevermore would I be a top worker. No food, no sleep, loss of blood, too much pain . . . work was out of the question. The only remaining secret was how I would be put to death—quickly or slowly? Certainly he would begin the shift by ordering another licking for me. I wondered if it would be possible to blacken his eye before the panther felled me, and I knew that my quaking limbs were not even capable of throwing a punch.

What I had not expected was the amusement on the faces of the other bosses, the smiles of tolerant reproof directed at Hrarrh. They thought he had gone a little too far, but he would know better next time.

He looked over the gang and tapped me on the chest in passing. "You stay. The rest of you—the target is the same as last time, twelve buckets apiece. Penalties are doubled. Run!'' They ran, and most of them were limping.

He was fooling himself. Any sadist could jack up output for one shift. We had delivered sixty-nine buckets for him, but now the output would drop because of injuries and exhaustion—and one death to come. Apparently that was something that every new boss had to learn for himself. Unfortunately the slaves paid for the lesson.

Gradually the paddock was clearing. Hrarrh had gone after his workers, leaving me standing alone. He had not said I was excused, nor that I could sit down. Bending my legs only increased the agony, so I just stayed where I was and sweated in the glare. The off-duty shift came trailing back, heading for the food trough. With luck I would faint soon.

Eventually he came strolling out of the mine, blinking at the light. He was wearing work clothes and the helmet concealed his bald pate. At the gate he paused to lay down a small bundle he had been carrying under his arm, then he headed for me with Chuckles gliding at his heel, a black threat half the size of a pony.

I was the taller. I kept my chin up and looked him in the eye, and I tried not to sway. He was amused.

''Plotting rebellion, Knobil? Looking for a quick death?''

''That was what you advised, wasn't it? Well, take me to the canyon ladder and I'll do it for you.''

He shook his head and moved closer, glancing around cautiously. ''Put your eyes down. Now listen carefully. You're leaving!''

''Ha!'' Talking back to a boss was an intense pleasure after so much humility. I had forgotten how good it felt to contradict someone.

Hrarrh's eyebrows shot up. ''Great! I was frightened you'd do a fade. You mustn't die on me, Knobil!''

''I should hate to spoil your fun.''

A grin twisted his beard. ''I knew you had guts! You couldn't have saved me otherwise. Now . . . it's dangerous for me to talk to you here, and worse in the mine. You know how it echoes. Can you listen while Chuckles washes your legs? You've got to have them done, or those cuts will go bad. It won't hurt so much as before.''

"What choice do I have?"

He nodded approvingly. "Good man! Anyone watching will think I'm gloating, but you try to listen, because it's important."

The workers from the other shift had completed their meal and were stretching out to sleep. They were staying well away from the dangerous ant and his victim. The panther crouched and touched a rough wet tongue to my ankle. I shuddered and waited for the flames to start. Hrarrh put his hands on his hips and leaned forward, sneering into my face, but his voice was softer than his expression.

"Believe this, Knobil. I did all that just to get you out of here!"

*Pain* starting . . . "Dead."

His eyes flickered warily around again, but apparently no one was watching too closely. I was shivering and streaming sweat as fire began to engulf my leg. But he was right—it was not as bad as before. Nothing could have been.

He was still talking . . .

". . . won't believe me, but I was bluffing. I swear it!"

Just for a moment, relief—No! It was another round in the game. He was going to cure me and then do it all again.

The deep-sunk eyes registered concern. "Warn me if you feel giddy—I'll call Chuckles off. You all right?"

The tongue had reached my thigh now and my own mouth tasted of blood again. I nodded.

"I don't expect you to believe me—but you will. There are traders here."

Traders?

"It's those blue eyes of yours, Knobil, that hair. Traders sell us slaves, but never wetlanders. They buy wetlanders!"

For a moment a flash of hope drowned out the creeping agony in my leg . . . then again disbelief. "Why?"

"I don't know. No one knows for sure. They don't much care how old, or what sort of shape they're in . . . men or women, doesn't matter. But any trader will buy a wetlander. One bolt of silk is the standard price. It's your only chance!"

The black cat had completed my right leg. It sat back on its haunches and moved its mouth as if to get rid of a bad taste. Then it stared hungrily at my navel.

"Ready for the other one, or do you need a break?" Hrarrh's

sudden concern for my well-being was more terrifying than his previous open sadism. He was going to restore me to health and then do it all over again.

He saw the doubt in my eyes and grinned wolfishly. "I'll show you!" He signed to the cat and a paw flashed. I flinched and then peered down at my foot. There was a single, faint red line on it, but the skin was unbroken. I looked up again at Hrarrh in bewilderment.

"You made her cut deep?"

He nodded, still grinning. "She's the best trained pet in the mine. I showed them a thing or two about cats!"

"But . . . but why?"

"To make you bleed lots. You look much, much worse than you really are. You'd have needed a hundred times as many normal scratches to bleed like that. No one's looked close, right?"

Again, hope squirmed very softly as I tried to believe.

"I had to do it this way, Knobil! They think I went mad in there." He glowered. "This is costing me, too—I'm in big trouble for spoiling a good slave. I was only supposed to have a little fun with you, but you trailed blood all the way out to the paddock . . . Even my wife heard you, back in her kitchen."

"That wasn't what you said when you were doing it!"

"But you're not nearly as bad as you look, as long as you don't get fever in the cuts. You sounded real bad and you look real bad. What the traders will do with you, I don't know. But certainly you've got a better chance of escaping from them than you have from us."

At last the torment of the licking ended. Hrarrh glanced around at the hot, bright paddock, littered now with sleeping slaves. Outside, in the main compound, ants were going about their business as usual, but the other shift's barrows had not yet appeared.

"Right." He grinned uneven teeth at me. "Let's go!" Unwanted slaves not publicly executed just vanished inexplicably. Now I was about to do the same, and no one would know where I had gone.

My heart beat insanely as I reeled along behind him. At the gate he retrieved his package and pointed with it . . . pointed away from the mine, toward the road. The road to freedom?

Keeping my legs stiff, quivering as violently as I had during the worst moments of his tortures, I stumbled forward, hearing his boots behind me, knowing that the panther was there also.

At the end of the long ridge of tailings stood a big shed, used to hold supplies. Hrarrh directed me in behind it, out of general view. Grinning again, he unrolled the bundle to reveal shabby old leather trousers and a pair of tattered boots.

"Traders don't like damaged goods," he said. "Try not to bleed any more until they've shaken hands on a price for you."

The traders were real. Two of them stood with three ants, a short way down the road. That must be why I had never seen them before—they were not admitted to the main compound. But they were certainly the same sort of traders I had seen in my youth—smart little men in ornate leather garments, decorated with brightly colored beadwork and pipings and tassels. They had curved-brim hats and neatly trimmed moustaches and pointed beards. Traders!

This was real!

My brain seemed to fade away. I registered only vaguely that a team of horses nearby was being burdened with sacks, that bales were being loaded and unloaded and carried around. This was real . . . I was going to escape! Shaking uncontrollably, I stood with eyes downcast until one of the traders snapped, "Look at me, slave!

"Blue as blue," he admitted. "What's wrong with him, Minemaster? He seems healthy enough."

"Lost his spirit," one of the ants growled. "Used to be a good worker. What's he doing now, Hrarrh?"

"Two short last shift, sir," my benefactor mumbled. Then he whined, "I think I can scratch more sense into him, if you'll give me another chance, sir."

"One more chance and you'd kill him!"

The discussion wandered around, and so did my wits. I was going! Freedom! Or at least another form of slavery. Nothing could be worse than the mine . . . *nothing!*

"As Our Lady Sun is my witness," the trader said. I remembered the words from my childhood, but this time it was I who had just been sold. The two men shook hands and one of them mentioned paper.

Hrarrh coughed deferentially. "Do you wish him hobbled, sir?"

The trader said, "What? Oh, yes, please." He went back to complaining how difficult it was to find paper, because the only good paper came from Heaven, but he did happen to have . . .

Hrarrh gave me a shove and pointed farther down the road, toward the horses. I stumbled off ahead of him. *I was leaving*. My life could start again. Whatever use traders had for wetlanders, whatever value wetlanders had for traders, *nothing* could be worse than the mine. Never again need I crawl down into that cramped dark hell . . .

"Here!" Hrarrh barked behind me, pulling my fluttering mind back to reality. We were almost down to the vegetable fields, standing between the pony corral and the tannery, outside a big shack they called the machine shed. It was issuing loud clanging noises, as always. This was where the smiths worked.

"Master?"

He laughed and suddenly clapped a hard hand on my shoulder. "I'm not your master any longer, Knobil!"

"You're my friend!" I said, trying to suppress sudden tears.

"Yes, I'm your friend. And you were mine also, when I needed one."

"Hrarrh!" My voice cracked. "My friend! Hrarrh . . ."

"Calm down! It's my pleasure, Knobil, truly! Now, there's one last thing to do . . ."

I choked, suddenly wary. "What?"

He grinned at my nervousness. "Traders don't have cats to guard their slaves. They use fetters."

He gestured to his panther to sit by the door, while his strong damp grip on my shoulder eased me into the shed—loud and impossibly hot despite the dim shade. Three or four ants were apparently trying to make as much noise as possible with hammers and rasps, raising dust. A grotesquely thick youth was grinding a plowshare on a treadle just inside the entrance. His shoulders were remarkable even by ant standards, burying his bald head in muscle up to the ears, making his beard protrude straight out from the top of his chest. In any other race he would have been regarded as deformed.

"The traders just bought this," Hrarrh told him. "They want it hobbled."

The smith looked me over without expression, wiping his forehead with a bushy arm. He nodded his head to indicate direction. "Put it on the anvil."

Hrarrh's hand turned me and propelled me gently but relentlessly over to a shiny round-topped anvil.

"Lie down," he said, "and put your ankles up here. Don't look so worried, Knobil! I'm not going to hurt you, promise!"

Still alternating wildly between hope and distrust, I lowered myself gingerly to the floor and lifted my feet, wincing at the pain in my thighs and wondering if the move would tip pools of blood out of my boots.

Hrarrh went round to the other side of the anvil and took a firm grip on my ankles, adjusting my calves across it. "Can you flatten out?" he asked. "Raise your knees?"

I had no choice, for he was levering hard, and also pulling. I curled myself until my shins were level and my buttocks high off the floor. Sharp things dug into my neck and shoulders. I pushed down with my hands to relieve the stress on my abdomen. My thighs stung where the muscles flexed, and if Hrarrh thought he was not hurting my lacerated calves . . .

He looked content then, smiling down at me fondly. I did not like that sleepy smile.

"I didn't tell you, did I, Knobil, that I'm a father now?"

"Congratulations . . ." If he was going to put fetters on me, then why was he not removing my boots?

He nodded in satisfaction. "Minemaster Krarurh's first grandson—after eight granddaughters! I'm a hero, Knobil!"

Suddenly I understood, and was filled with terror. "So he gave you a present?"

Hrarrh nodded. "Certainly. I explained that I had a problem, and he understood at once. He said I could do whatever I wanted to correct the matter."

My heart could hardly sink any more, not in that upside-down position. "And what did you decide?"

He grinned like a cat. "I was going to shuck you . . . but we do that for mere insolence, don't we? I could have let Chuckles eat bits off you, but that's commonplace. An offense like yours calls for something special."

Pride! Long ago he had been too weak to refuse my aid, and I forced it on him. I was a constant reminder of that time of weakness. I insulted him by just being alive.

"And the traders are better?"

The gloating was back, quite openly. His eyes were shiny. He licked his lips. "Much better! Of course I won't be there to see, but . . . a fitting end! Much better."

He turned his head slightly, and I saw that the mountainous youth was standing beside me, impassively clutching a sledge.

"Which one, Hrarrh?" he asked.

"You said you weren't going to hurt me!" I yelled.

Hrarrh sighed happily. "I'm not. He is."

Screaming would not help me now. I howled—almost upside-down, more utterly helpless than ever. "I did you a kindness!"

Hrarrh bared his teeth. "It was a humiliation, slag!"

"Which one?" the smith asked again, raising the hammer overhead.

Hrarrh looked at me, and for a moment I thought he was going to ask me to choose. What I saw in his eyes then taught me what true hatred really was. How had he managed to keep it bottled up for so long? It had driven him mad. Perhaps all ants must be crazy, for they could not treat their slaves as they do if they believed that those slaves were people like themselves.

I have no doubts that Hrarrh was mad. Since adolescence, he had been waiting for this revenge, this chance to wipe out the memory of a kindness that was an insult, a debt owed to an inferior . . . a non-ant.

He heaved my feet back, so that my knees, not my shins, were on the anvil. I yelped with pain and surprise.

"Do them both!" he said.

Later he dragged me outside and draped me over a horse's back like a blanket, and at last I fainted.

I do not remember leaving the ants' nest.

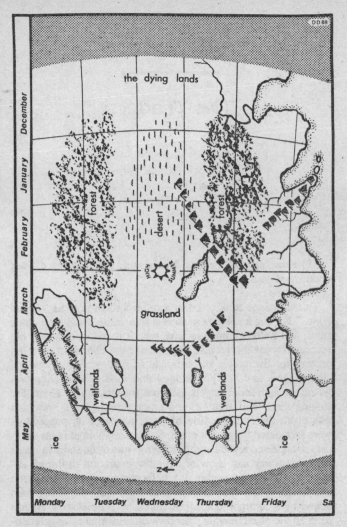

the dying lands

December
January
February
March
April
May

forest

desert

HIGH SUMMER

forest

grassland

wetlands

wetlands

ice

ice

z←

Monday    Tuesday    Wednesday    Thursday    Friday    Sa

DD 88

# 7

---

# The Traders

The trouble with the ants, Kettle said, was that they did not understand pain.

I disagreed.

This exchange took place in a room known only as "Cloud Nine." No one knew where so absurd a name could have come from, and Kettle claimed to have seen it mentioned in very old records. It was the recreation nook for the cherubim, just big enough for five tables and a tangle of mismatched stools and chairs. Dark and stuffy, cramped and loud, Cloud Nine was where the apprentice angels gathered for relaxation. There was singing there, and arguing, and much drinking of a brew that was given the courtesy title of beer, although its progenitors were fermented fungi, not grain. Storms might rage in the darkness outside and icy gales shriek; damp furs often stank in heaps by the doorway and snow might eddy in around ill-fitting, antique casements; but within its smelly squalor there was warmth and laughter and the rambunctious fellowship of young men bound by a common dedication and a purpose shared. Angels scorned the place, having their own establishment—angels usually regarded themselves as beyond consorting with mere cherubim anyway—but sometimes a saint would drop in, and once in a while even one of the archangels, although a presence so august tended to dampen the joviality considerably.

Saint Kettle was a regular visitor. A true scholar, was Kettle. He had studied more of the arcane lore than anyone, even Gabriel, his nominal superior. He was a wonderful teacher and great company. Knowing ten times as much as the curriculum required him to teach, he tried to teach all the rest anyway. He liked nothing better, even after a long session of lecturing, than to join a group of us around a table in a snug and shadowed corner of Cloud Nine and let us ply him with foam-capped steins of ale. Then the conversation would range over all of Vernier and all the wisdom of the ancients, while the gleam of lanterns painted fresh young faces on the circling dark.

Kettle's own round, seaman face would wax ruddier and ruddier; the girdle constricting his voluminous purple gown would strain tighter and tighter; and his laugh would roll louder and louder from the shadows, but he would still be booming out triple-distilled wisdom when all his juvenile listeners were much too befuddled to understand a word of it. I knew how to switch steins unobtrusively in the gloom, although the smart ones eventually learned that beer seemed more potent if they sat next to me.

It was in Cloud Nine that Kettle and I argued about the ants. With Kettle argument was always permissible, and in Cloud Nine he blatantly provoked it.

There were six of us on that occasion, squashed in around the table beside him—Ginger, the Fox, Dusty, and me, plus two young newcomers known as Ham and Beef. None of them were ants. Indeed, I only ever knew two ants in Heaven and both were angels, so I never heard their original names.

By custom, no cherub ever addressed another cherub by his true name, either. Every cherub naturally expected to win his wheels eventually and be known thereafter only by a color scheme, so perhaps that preference for nicknames was not merely a juvenile aping of the angels, but also a sort of hopeful superstition. Moreover, a man's real name was a reminder of his racial origin, and we were always careful not to reveal prejudices about those. All cherubim were equal, at least in theory. Of course in practice the subject was skirted often, in cautious teasing and careful testing. That was education also, for angels need to know the idiosyncrasies of all races, but in Cloud Nine I was neither Knobil nor Golden. Usually they called me the Old Man, which I did not mind, and sometimes Roo, which I did.

On this occasion, Kettle had challenged the racial matter head-on, stamping all over our usual taboo. He had been explaining why peoples differed—why herdfolk men were much larger than their women, but trader women larger than their men, or why seamen like himself had lungs like water butts—

And bellies like beer barrels, Ginger remarked dryly, and was sent for the next round in consequence.

Good times.

There were three reasons for races to differ, Kettle said. First was just culture, and he pointed out that a—say—wetlander raised in a—say—herdfolk tribe would think like a herdman because of his upbringing . . . not that herdmen thought much at all, of course. That was a calculated taunt, so I vowed violence upon him and anyone seen smiling, as I was expected to.

"Second, of course," he said, "is natural selection. Human beings are not as susceptible as other species, because we can control our environment, but obviously a seaman with a big chest is less likely to drown than a skinny one."

Thereupon I raised my stein in a silent and solitary toast to a departed friend. In all the world, and all of Heaven, I had found no better man.

"And selection explains why ants have skulls like marble bowlingnuts, less likely to damage if banged into a tunnel roof . . ."

"Does it explain their big shoulders?" asked Ham, who was well endowed thereabouts himself.

Pleased by this posing of a new problem, Kettle pondered, then wobbled jowls in dissent. "I doubt it can be directly survival of the fittest, no. In a human culture, even a weaker man is rarely forced to starve. He can usually still reproduce. Sexual selection, perhaps—a woman may choose the mate best able to provide, and so pass on to her daughters a preference for husky men. But yet . . . a young man who found mining difficult would be more likely to leave the nest and seek other pursuits, wouldn't he? Emigration of the unfit . . . if it was deliberate, I suppose that would be a uniquely human subcategory?"

Awed into silence, Ham nodded.

"Was that a 'yes' or a 'no'?" I asked.

"Certainly!" Kettle quaffed long and then wiped foam from his lips and chuckled. "Who can say?" Unlike some other saints, he was never reluctant to admit ignorance. He taught us that the best questions have no answers.

"The third reason is founder effect, as the texts call it. There were so few of the firstfolk to start with, and when they divided at the time of the Great Compact and then fragmented and later subfragmented into all the various tribes and peoples and races . . . some of those groups that seem so numerous now must be descended from a mere handful of men and women. And if even one of them had a conspicuous deformity—red hair, say—then it would not be unlikely . . ."

And Ginger, copper-haired man of the deserts, calmly promised violence upon him and anyone seen smiling.

Some raucous forestfolk right behind me were growing loud in one of their tribal rondeaux, accompanied by much complex drumming on the table. We were having to raise our voices to compete.

"Then consider wetlanders," Kettle continued, unperturbed, "since Roo has already undertaken to slay me, and can only do so once. The normal brown or black colors of human hair and skin are due to the presence of a pigment called melanin. Roo's hair and eyes lack it, so he is a blond. His skin will produce it under the influence of sunlight, so bright sunlight would soon darken him from that pretty baby pink shade he is at the moment to about your color, Fox. Conversely, if you were to put Roo in a completely dark—"

He dried up. During all my long stay in Heaven, that was the only time I ever saw Kettle embarrassed. The others noticed, and were puzzled. Our table fell silent, while the others clamored as loudly as before around us.

I was about to reach for my tankard, but my hands had started to shake, so I quickly put them under the table. "That's all right," I assured him, although I knew what nightmares would haunt my next sleep. "Pray continue, holiness."

Much redder even than usual—almost maroon in the dimness—Kettle drank beer while the others exchanged perplexed and wary glances. Then he launched forth again, slightly less loudly. "Now, in areas of low sun and cloudy weather, fair skin is an advantage. There is some evidence that blue eyes see better under misty conditions. We know from a reference in the ancient texts"—here he beamed smugly, to indicate that the reference was some extremely obscure passage he had discovered himself—"that some of the firstfolk had those blond characteristics. Indeed, the firstfolk seem to have included all the shades we have now, from Roo to Beef, there!"

Beef was almost invisible in dim light, but his teeth and eyes flashed now in a grin.

"I thought," the Fox said, "that the Venerable Ones all had skin of the same color, and Our Lady Sun punished—" He was drowned out in boos and groans. Religion was *never* discussed in Heaven.

Kettle chuckled. "Not the firstfolk! But a few generations later the annals mention that almost everyone was by then becoming a sort of middle-brown color, because of inbreeding . . . I don't think we need take that too literally!" He peered around pugnaciously, but no one argued.

"So the redivergence into different races came later still?" Ginger asked.

"Exactly! Environments on Vernier selected for the same adaptions as similar environments had on First World—of course! Hook noses in dry climates, for example. Persistence of the lactase enzyme into adulthood among cattle-herding peoples. That sort of thing. But we have a question, class! Are the wetlanders descended from original blonds—by chance—or have they been selected for blondness by their environment, or did blond humans deliberately choose a climate that suited their blond coloring? Mm?"

After a long pause I said, "Tell us the answer, then."

"I have absolutely no idea," Kettle boomed triumphantly, "and I can think of no way to find out! That's why people are so interesting."

That was also why—Ginger muttered darkly—the most ancient texts told of saints being martyred.

But ants had been mentioned, and ants were always of interest to me, who still nursed secret dreams of vengeance. I had never mentioned them to anyone, but everyone in Heaven must have known of my obsession with ants. Where did ants get their sadism? I asked. Which of the three causes produced that?

Natural selection, Kettle thought. "Survival of the ruthless? A squeamish ant would leave, probably, or be driven out."

"Or founder effect?" I suggested. "Someone must have invented slave owning."

He agreed, rather grudgingly. The conversation began to drift elsewhere, but Kettle suddenly dragged it back with his remark about ants not understanding pain.

I replied that they used it so effectively that they must obviously understand it. Knowing how I had come by the disability that led them to call me Roo, the others fell silent, but Kettle argued. He eventually convinced me that the ants could use their slaves more efficiently if they terrorized them less. Or he almost convinced me, for I knew that I would never have worked so hard for so long under a kinder rule.

"But talk to Blue-red," he added. "Get him to tell you about the ant with half a foot!"

Blue-red was not then in Heaven, so of course we all demanded that Kettle himself tell us about the ant with half a foot, and after another long draft of beer, he did so.

Blue-red-brown had met an ant once. The encounter had been quite amicable, for although the ant had been part of an army on the move, Blue-red had been unable to prove anything against that particular man or his companions. This ant, Blue-red said, had been missing half of his right foot. When younger, he had gone to sleep before a roaring fire—his mine had been approaching Dusk, of course. A burning log had rolled. It had charred his toes before he awoke.

"Are you saying that ants don't feel pain?" I demanded, astonished and suddenly enraged. I could remember Hrarrh having his blisters licked. That had been a true ordeal for him, and the other ants had been impressed by his stoicism.

"They may feel some," Kettle said sympathetically, "but not as much as we . . . others . . . not like we do. I've seen an ant stick a knife through his hand on a bet! It may be a founder effect. It may be an adaptation—a banged elbow in a mine is painful, but not an indication of great danger . . . I don't know, cherub, but I am sure that ants do not feel pain as much as you do."

As I had . . .

"Tell me, holiness," inquired the Fox, who was a trader-slasher cross—a studious and smart little fellow, a born saint but never angel timber. "Can founder effects explain some of the sexual differentiation characteristics?"

Kettle's teacher eyes flickered over the blank expressions on the faces of Beef and Ham. "You mean like herdmen being so much larger than herdwomen? Or like trader males being smarter than their females?"

That raised a small chuckle. Before the Fox could work out a believable retaliation, I unthinkingly said, "But I'm not sure that's true, Kettle. I think trader women are a lot smarter than they like to make out. I knew one who certainly was."

Across the table from me, Beef smirked. "Hot stuff, was she, Old Man?"

My tankard and its contents hit him in the face just as the room made one of its frequent lurches. That lurch distracted the others, and even a cripple can be effective at close quarters. I had overturned the table and Beef also before they could block me and then Beef and I were both on the floor, with me on top and my thumbs on his carotid arteries. Fortunately even that grip takes a moment to kill a man, and I had not thought to do anything more sudden, like crushing his larynx. Ginger and Dusty methodically broke my hold and lifted me off my victim. They pushed me back in my chair and held me there until my fit passed and I stopped screaming. The furniture was righted, the beer replaced, and the rest of Cloud Nine's clientele persuaded to overlook the incident.

Beef was a big kid, but he knew that he had just missed something nasty, and he did not know how to fight a cripple twice his age and half his size. He allowed himself to be restrained. He even apologized, still not understanding his offense. The others were looking to Kettle, wondering why I was not being immediately hurled out of Heaven for such a display of violence. Of course my status in Heaven was not orthodox and Kettle certainly was aware of that. Even more certainly, he was not going to discuss it in Cloud Nine.

With difficulty, I mumbled an apology, still quivering with the urge to maim Beef.

Kettle growled. "Not enough, Roo! You owe him an explanation. There were special circumstances. Tell them."

I muttered mutinously, but eventually I explained how I had journeyed with traders, and found love.

Of course the traders were incensed. Mol Jar, the one who had bought me, insisted that the goods had been damaged after purchase. By then he had discovered my lacerations as well as my smashed knees, but the lacerations had been done beforehand, so he had no hope of recourse for those. Hobbling meant shackling, he insisted.

Hobbling meant breaking a leg, Minemaster Krarurh replied, and any time he had sold a wetlander to a trader, that was how he had delivered it. It was mere inexperience that had led Hrarrh to smash both my knees instead . . . a trifling excess of juvenile zeal. The esteemed trader had been offered free hobbling, not shackling, and had accepted that offer. Had he wanted chains applied, then he should have said so and supplied them, because he did not include chains with the slaves he sold.

The traders demanded their bale of silk back, offering to return the cat food. They threatened to blacklist the mine.

The ants leaned toward ripping the traders to shreds and feeding them to their panthers, while retaining the horses, wagons, and goods. Violence began to seem likely.

Meanwhile I was dangling head-down and feet-down across the back of a horse nearby. Even when the darkness lifted briefly from my mind, the thunder of my pain drowned out the talk. I learned about it later, at third or fourth hand.

Hrarrh eventually became fearful that I would not be accepted as valid merchandise, and persuaded his father in-law to settle the matter by throwing in another ten sacks of ore to compensate for the second knee. He also promised to work his gang overtime to replace it. Grumpily the traders departed with their loads, which included one crippled wetlander, unlikely ever to come out of his coma.

The relative value of ten sacks of phosphate ore and one bale of silk is debatable. It is possible to argue that the traders were being paid to haul me away like trash. And there, I think, is the most despicable of all Hrarrh's villainies—that he was willing to torment his wretched slaves even harder, solely to provide himself with the personal satisfaction of sending me off to the worst fate he could imagine.

I wish I could have heard the settlements made over me. Traders' business affairs are much akin to a school of minnows in a whirlpool, and I never came to understand more than one flicker of them. The men have incredible memories for the details of their dealings, all of which are done verbally. Mol Jar owed one bale of silk and in return could offer ten sacks of phosphate and a dying man. The phosphate had value. He had no use for me himself, because he was heading in the wrong direction, and Kal Gos—who had owned the silk—did not want me either.

The argument between the traders and the ants would have been trivial compared to the bizzare and acrimonious hagglings that took place regularly between the traders themselves, both before they traded with outsiders and even more so afterward. The varied goods from a dozen wagons might be offered, but always one man would be deputized to do the dealing, with another sent along as witness. The respective values of everything sold and everything purchased must then be agreed upon and the profits fairly distributed. The system is contentious, inefficient, and utterly beyond an outsider's comprehension. The traders love it.

As far as I ever could understand, I was exchanged by Mol Jar for one more sack of phosphate, then traded to somebody else for a quantity of assorted fabrics. I ended after a few more exchanges being owned nineteen twenty-sevenths by Jat Lon, five twenty-sevenths by Lon Kiv, and three twenty-sevenths by Misi Nada. Her share was a conditional payment for services, if she could keep me alive. Had I died, then she would have owned no part of me—but that would not have stopped Jat Lon and Lon Kiv from disputing over their respective residual interests in a worthless corpse.

And so I began my life with the traders. Astonishingly, Misi Nada did keep me alive. At first I was barely aware of her—between pain, shock, and loss of blood, I was barely aware of anything. Later my wounds became fevered, and I screamed and babbled insanely while she cradled me in her great arms. She fed me and bathed me, and treated me with herbals and potions collected from all over Vernier, sternly denying me the release I craved.

Slowly the fogs began to clear, and I would catch glimpses of bloated features that seemed like one more figment of delirium—a face baggy and shapeless, with an obvious moustache, with brown skin as coarse as a wood rasp, rimmed by ragged lank brown hair. Always she wore a drab, sack-like garment, long-sleeved and all-enveloping. I had heard in the mine that trader women were big, but I had not realized how huge they could be. I had seen few herdmasters, even, who would have outweighed Misi Nada.

Slowly I came to understand that I was not to be allowed to die. I saw her then as an enemy, imprisoning me in a life that held only worse terrors in store. Hrarrh himself had warned me once to stay away from traders.

"Why?" I whispered, staring up at that globular face hanging high above me, a brown moon against a sky of well-crafted wooden planks. "Why?"

For a long time I was too incoherent to frame my question properly, and Misi was apparently too stupid to understand— trader women were not only huge but also moronic, or so I had been told. Eventually she seemed to grasp what I was trying to ask—why did traders, who sold slaves to the ants, buy wetlanders from them?

Then Misi paused in her endless chewing of *paka* leaves. Her amusement reminded me of the leather sack in which Pebble had brought home live eels. Squirming and pulsing, Misi's face rearranged itself in surges of apparently unrelated motions until it wore a parody of a smile.

"Lucky!" she boomed. "Wetlanders bring good luck."

"No! No!" I wanted to weep. "You can't expect me to believe that!"

She nodded, all her chins flexing. A finger like a sausage stroked along my beard, which she had already trimmed short, in trader fashion. "Hair gold, like Our Lady Sun. Eyes like sky. Dawn child!"

Then she chuckled, which in Misi was a huge subterranean *woofing* sound. She bent over. Breasts like meal sacks crushed down on me briefly as she placed a big wet kiss on my forehead.

I caught a whiff of the turpentine odor of *paka*. "Dawn child!" she repeated.

I had heard of Dawn, of course, a land of surging glaciers and sudden, catastrophic floods. It is a place where few travelers venture, in whose misty, twilight landscape of snow and storms, blond blue-eyed men like me skim their canoes through icy waters. Of all the peoples of Vernier, only the seafolk and the wetlanders live beyond the reach of trader wagons.

"Sun child!" Misi said, straightening up. "Blessed!"

Traders worshipped the sun, and with that explanation I had to be content. There was no way to argue with Misi Nada. Later, when I felt stronger, I tried the same question on Jat Lon.

Trader wagons are long and narrow, balanced high on many pairs of wheels. Most of their length is taken up with the storage area, a blank box entered from side doors. At the front is an open cab for the owners and their families. Among the traders, women usually own the equipment and men the livestock. The men do the trading, mostly, although the goods may belong to either.

Misi's cab was of standard design—square, with three sides taken up by big windows. Those could be closed off with shutters when the weather was bad, and their low sills allowed them to serve also as doors. This box was Misi's home and my sickroom. It was furnished with a collection of cubical chests, and these she shifted around to suit her needs of the moment. Put together they made a bed large enough even for her; spread around they formed benches. With my legs immobilized in splints, I sat or lay on these and watched the world go by.

The wagon was driven by either Misi herself or Pula Misi, who was obviously her daughter. As my wits began to return, I came to realize that Pula was barely more than a child, although she was already taller than I was. Had she wanted, Pula could have been striking, even beautiful, for she had an unconscious grace and the inner glow of youth; but Pula invariably wore shapeless muumuus of sickly green, her hair was a greasy tangle, and her face stayed as blank as a cloud.

Trader wagons move very slowly, but hippos, like woollies, never sleep, and their inexorable crawl will eat up any distance eventually. Usually wagons are linked in pairs, a combination that the traders call a "train." Rich owners may hook up three or even four wagons in that fashion, but any combination will allow the women to spell each other off at driving. Pula also owned a wagon, and hers was towed by Misi's, its living quarters facing the rear.

Other trains came and went, although always we would have three or four in our company. Trader men came calling quite often, the women very seldom. The locals I met not at all, and by far my most frequent companions were Misi and her own family. The oldest was gray-haired Lon Kiv, but I soon decided that the true leader of the group was his son, Jat Lon.

Jat was younger than I, short and lean and fast as a blink. His russet beard was trimmed to a point and his moustache twirled up in horns. He wore tan leather trousers piped in bright colors and emblazoned with swirls of beadwork, and his shirt was intricately embroidered. I never met a man more dapper than Jat Lon, or more sociable. Gems flickered on his fingers and his ears and on the hilt of the rapier hanging from his belt. His hazel eyes flashed with intelligence, gazing intently at me when I spoke, studying my reaction when he did. Misi I had already dismissed as a kindly moron, capable of only a few very limited endeavors, but I could see that Jat Lon missed nothing. His penetrating gaze was only bearable because of the understanding half smile that always accompanied it.

Misi and Pula, Lon and Jat . . . there was a fifth member of the family. Dot Jat was a lop-tooth lad, whose uneven grin already showed much native charm. At times in my delirium I had hallucinated that he was my lost son Merry, but all the babies I had sired on the seawomen would have grown beyond the tooth-dropping stage by then. Obviously Dot Jat was son of Jat Lon, the son of Lon Kiv.

Jat spoke to Misi as one might address a very slow child—firmly, yet not without affection. He called her anything from Momma to Big Pig, depending on his mood. Jat was Pula's brother, I surmised, and Lon must be Misi's husband. Dot's mother seemed to be missing, but certainly Jat was the brains of the family. The older Lon Kiv seemed a much less sinister, an easier-going man. My danger, whatever it was, lurked behind the smile of Jat Lon.

The first time I held a true conversation with Jat, the cab was unusually crowded. He was kneeling on the floor, oiling a saddle. I was reclining on the bed, watching the scrub and the far-off hazy shapes of the Andes, almost lost now over the bend of the world. Another train was visible sometimes in the distance, grinding through the chaparral on a path paralleling our own. Misi, for once, had chosen to sleep in her own cab. Mostly she preferred to go to the rear and the privacy of Pula's wagon, but now she lay at my side like a mislaid mountain, and her monstrous snores echoed back from the hills. Immobile as I was, I could not shake an uneasy belief that a bad lurch would roll her bulk on top of me and crush me to paste. Pula, shapeless in her wind-rippled green tent, was sitting out front on the step, holding the traces and gazing over the hippos' backs in mindless silence.

Little Dot sat sleepily in a corner, doing double-jointed finger exercises. Trader's hands are extraordinarily supple. When two traders trade they wave their fingers at each other all the time, either calculating or pretending to do so. They can count any number up to 59,048 that way, in a simple ternary system. My fingers never learned to move independently of one another, so I never could make the symbols, but I learned to read them well enough—a skill that other traders did not expect in me.

"Jat," I asked, "will you answer a couple of questions?"

Jat flickered his inevitable little smile. "Of course! Not necessarily truthfully, of course."

I was too tense to smile back, as I was meant to. "All right. You bought me. Why?"

"Because I can never resist a bargain."

"Huh?"

He chuckled and sat back on his heels. Then he wiped his hands fastidiously on a rag. "I paid Kan one shirt for you. You looked dead already, but Misi said she thought you could be saved, and that is a very good price for a wetlander."

So far I could believe him. So I asked the big black one—"And what will you do with me now?"

"Oh, you're not mine, Knobil. I gave you to Momma right away. That was why I bought you—as a gift for her."

"Gift?"

"Misi wouldn't have taken all this trouble doctoring you if she didn't care for you, now would she?" Jat's smile was not

Pebble's smile. Pebble's had been happiness and sharing; Jat's was calculated reassurance.

"Or thought I was valuable." I was still very feeble, but my wits were coming back—slowly. "So *why* does she want me? What will she do with me?"

"Free you." His pale brown face was guileless as the sky.

"Why? Why go to all this trouble over a crippled slave?"

"Ex-slave."

"But why?"

"Because we worship the sun," Jat said solemnly. "Wetlanders are her children—blue eyes and golden hair. To free a wetlander slave is a deed of great merit, well rewarded always."

I studied him in baffled doubt. "You believe this?"

Jat peered past me at the sleeping Misi, and then turned his head to look first at Pula, who was seemingly engrossed in guiding the team, and finally at Dot, intent on his finger-wiggling.

"Maybe not quite as much as some do," Jat admitted quietly. "But . . . but there have been cases, Knobil. I only ever met one man who'd done it . . . but the wealth! Four wagons, loaded to the roof. And women . . . !" He sighed avariciously.

I did not believe, but I could think of no alternative explanation. Hrarrh had left me almost dead, and certainly maimed for life. As a working slave I now was worthless. Why indeed should Misi struggle to heal me? Why should these hard-headed merchants waste food and shelter on me? Hrarrh himself had said that traders would buy wetlanders regardless of age or sex or health. I could think of no logical reason except what Jat and Misi were telling me—if a reason based only on religion could be called logical.

In my weakened state I was no match for Jat Lon. At outright lying I never was, I suppose. He saw my doubts, and again his eyes strayed toward Misi's thunderous snores. He smirked.

"Momma was very grateful for the gift! I tell you, Knobil, she's a lot of woman always, and that session was a bone-breaker! I thought I wouldn't survive such gratitude!" He chortled lecherously. "But what a way to die, you know?"

"Huh? You mean she's . . . she's not your mother?"

Jat guffawed, causing Dot to sit up with a jerk.

"Mother? Never! Ask Lon if you want to know about my mother—I don't recall her at all. He may." Jat's bright eyes twinkled. "No, Misi and I are cab partners. That's what 'Momma' means among traders. And she's some partner . . . but don't you dare tell her I said so!"

I struggled to rearrange my understanding of these curious people. "Then Dot's mother . . ."

"A woman called Dako Jeeba. We disagreed over some furs. Sons go with fathers, of course, and we had no daughter. Misi and I get along well—but we won't stay partners till the sun sets, I'm sure."

I nodded and glanced at the motionless green figure out on the step. "And Pula?"

Jat glanced again at Pula's motionless back and then smirked quizzically at his son. "Dot?" he said. "Tell Knobil what's negotiable."

The kid grinned. "Anything's negotiable."

"Good boy!" His father nodded. "I admit I fancied Pula, Knobil. But Lon's a horny old goat, and he outbid me."

Pula? That child—Misi's daughter—and Jat's gray-pate father?

Jat chuckled and rose, holding out a hand to his son. "Come, little twister, let's go and see about a meal. Now you know more about trader ways than most people do, Knobil."

"Pula and Lon are cab partners also?"

"Right. He pays her by the trick. Misi pays me."

Chuckling—I suppose at the expression on my face—he squeezed by Pula and sprang down to the ground, catching Dot as he jumped after. That was neither the first nor the last time that Jat diverted a conversation away from subjects he wished to shun. He had explained some curious customs, but not what use traders had for a crippled wetlander.

Slowly my pain and fever subsided. I progressed to the point where I could attend to my own bodily needs—a highly undignified procedure that involved hanging my rear out a window, but a great triumph for a man with planks on his legs. Dot found the performance hilarious, and would bring other junior members of the trader community to watch. I suspected he made them pay him.

Gradually, too, I became less of an animal and more of a human being again. Even conversation was a skill I had to regain. The traders' life was pleasant by most folks' standards, varied and even luxurious. They ate well and enjoyed material possessions I had forgotten or had never seen. One, for example, was a mirror. I had not viewed my face since I was only half as old, admiring the arrival of my moustache when Violet and I had just escaped from the grasslands. I saw nothing to admire now—pallid skin and deep ravages of suffering. The freakish blue eyes were the same, and yet they looked older than the world itself. I wondered how anyone else could ever bear to look at them.

Whatever dread destiny the traders had in mind for me—and I felt certain that Hrarrh knew exactly what it was, so *dread* was likely an optimistic outlook—I could see no chance of escape until my knees healed. Always there was a driver in the cab with me, either Misi or Pula, and never was I allowed to meet a nontrader.

My obvious strategy was to try to be as pleasant and cooperative as possible—grateful, helpful, and dumb. I asked Jat for things to do, and thereafter I peeled vegetables when it was his turn or Lon's to cook for the caravan. I strung beads for him, sharpened knives, cleaned tack, polished pots, kneaded dough . . . anything to keep my mind off its fears. But there was never enough.

"Misi? Can I help you? Will you teach me to sew?"

The wagon was crawling across a level, empty plain. With nothing but low scrub to eat, the team was making unusual speed—a fair walking pace—but the flat ground presented no challenge to the drivers. One side was shuttered against a wicked dusty wind. Misi was sitting indoors, only rarely needing to interrupt her embroidery to lean out the front window and yank on the hippos' traces. She was a very skilled seamstress, producing the finest needlework imaginable with hands that could have strangled bulls.

After a moment the big onion eyes came up to stare at me. "Men don't sew, Knobil."

"There's no reason why they shouldn't. I can't ride or hunt. Why not sew?"

She thought awhile, then made her strange subterranean chuckle noise. "I don't know why not." She heaved herself to her feet and began to rummage in the chest on which she had been sitting. She eventually produced a bundle of fabrics and brought it across with her bag of equipment, settling massively at my side. The wide bed no longer seemed spacious.

She unwrapped the bundle, spilling a wide selection of fabrics in many colors, some plain and some already embroidered. She selected a beige rag and handed it to me. "For practice."

I fingered it curiously. "What cloth is this?"

"Cotton, Knobil."

"It is so fine! Not like woollie cloth . . . what sort of animal has a fleece so fine?"

"Not an animal." She scowled, as if thinking hurt. "Cotton comes from a plant. It grows in hot swamps . . . there aren't many of those just now. When I was little, cotton was cheaper. Mostly costly now."

A long speech for her! I tried to imagine Misi as little. I wondered how one sheared a plant. "What are all these others, then?"

She began handing them over and naming them. "Linen . . . taffeta . . . burlap . . . felt . . ."

"This shirt that you are sewing. Which is this?"

I had been watching that shirt blossom under her touch. A plain brown garment had sprouted a forest of flowers, arabesques, and insects, in an exploding rainbow of color. It was almost complete. This was the first time I had had the chance to handle it, but I had already noticed the fineness of the material.

Pause. "Silk," she said reluctantly.

"And what does silk come from—animal or plant?"

"Don't know!" That was a very speedy retort by her standards.

"I was told . . . did you trade silk to the ants?"

"Might have done."

"Where does it come from, then?"

She waved a great hand vaguely southward. "From forests."

I fingered the shirt again. "When the ant women dressed up for their feasts, they wore very bright gowns. They seemed to be made of very light material. Would those have been silk?"

Misi nodded. I waited until she said, "Likely."

"It's beautiful."

She began to roll up the bundle, but I took it from her and

started to go through it, comparing. I had found something that interested Misi! For the first time we were having a conversation that was not a wrestling match.

Then I found a tiny rag of something different. It was clear and iridescent, of no color yet of all colors, so fine as to be very near transparent. I held it up in surprise. "What's this?"

Another pause, and a long one. "That's water silk."

"Beautiful! I can almost see through it. What's the difference between water silk and ordinary silk?"

"Color."

"That's all?"

She nodded reluctantly, her chins bulging. But I had learned to wait and at last she said, "Plain silk is brown. Light brown. Or dark brown. Black, the most common."

"You can't bleach it?" A herdwoman's son knew all about bleaching.

Misi shook her head.

"Or dye it?"

"Can dye water silk. Not ordinary silk. Very rare."

I admired the water silk some more. "Expensive, I suppose?"

A nod.

"How many bales of ordinary silk for one water silk?" I knew now how the traders saw the world, in comparative values.

"Fifty, or more."

Her expression suggested that I should be impressed. She was watching me very intently, as if frightened I might damage her precious fragment, or run off with it.

I whistled again, thinking that would be an appropriate reaction.

But I really was not very interested in silk.

Male traders scout, hunt, and cook. The rest of the time, if there is no trading in progress with the locals, they haggle among themselves . . . just to keep their tongues in practice, Jat said. Two of the four hippos belonged to him, two to his father, Lon. Both men also owned horses, and the number of those varied continually, although Jat never parted with his favorite, a high-stepping bay mare. Horses, like all two-eyed creatures, need sleep; they need water and time to graze, so the community's horses were rarely to be found near the wagons. The men took turns at tending them and from time to time the whole herd would go thundering by, heading for fresh grass and water somewhere up ahead.

And the wagons continued their endless crawl. Rocks and rivers, woods and cliffs—our road was never straight for very long, but I had assumed that we were heading mostly westward, because more often than not our shadows lay ahead of us. As a child, I had learned that sunward was east and shadows pointed west. Given the limited range of woollies, that rule was accurate enough for all herdfolk purposes. Now the sun was already farther from the zenith than I had ever seen it.

But then a chance remark by Jat told me I was wrong. We were going east. He proceeded to give me a lesson in basic geography.

We had just finished a wonderful meal, I recall. The scouts had encountered a band of hunters who had slain a grotesquely tusked animal that I had never heard of. Dot called it a "yum-yum," and I could understand why. Jat had bartered a haunch in return for a sack of cubenuts and now, proud of his prowess as both cook and breadwinner, was leaning back complacently, digesting. Dot had curled up on Misi's ample lap and gone to sleep. Pula and Lon were missing.

The terrain was light woodland, and the animals crunched and smashed as they grazed through the thin trunks. The wagon heaved and rocked. Every time it came down hard, Misi would belch. She had eaten more than all of the rest of us together, and her eyes were even more glazed than usual. The reins lay slack in her ample hand.

"East?" I said. "How can you tell which way is east?"

"The curl on the trees," Jat replied, and twirled his moustache triumphantly. "Trees always grow toward the sun."

Any child knew that trees curved near the ground. On the grasslands their uppermost trunks had been near vertical, but here the tops curled over farther. East of the sun the vegetation is older, Jat explained, and farther north or south, trees twist in a spiral. This may be one reason why traders worship the sun— given a glimpse of it and a few trees, a trader can make a very near guess as to where he is on Vernier. The angels have more accurate methods, of course, but the traders get by with trees.

And where were we, then, I inquired.

"The borderlands." He waved a hand. "North of the forest, south of the desert. Trader country, this!"

"Take it from the beginning," I said humbly. So he did.

The world is born anew at Dawn, as Orange had told me once, but a couple of months to the east its childhood excesses of flood and storm come to an end. Plants colonize the jumbled mud and rock and loess as the sun climbs higher in the sky. A fuzzy adolescence sets in, with trees and shrubs maturing into woodland and then nigh-impenetrable forest. In Wednesday, though, the sun climbs too quickly, choking off the tree growth and leaving the lonely grasslands I had known in my youth. High Summer eventually destroys even the grass, so that most of late Wednesday is desert. The hot desert is well named and barren, but the cool desert can be very fertile in spots, and is inhabited.

The great forests are found in late Tuesday and Thursday, flanking the deserts. The borderlands between are highways for traders, with water and forage for their livestock, with a passable terrain and a mainly bearable climate. It was eastward through this country that Misi and Pula were driving their train, the path twisting incessantly, taking ten or twenty steps upon the ground to achieve one upon our path, wending up and down hills, flirting with desert and jungle, skirting rock and swamp. The borderlands are well settled, mainly by farmers of various types, and visits to their settlements added more meanderings to our route.

Finally Jat yawned. "Ask Lon. He's been everywhere from the edge of Dawn all the way to Heaven."

Later I did ask Lon. He told me of the mud that had barred his wagon's way westward into Dawn, and also of the Dying Lands in the east, beyond which Heaven lurks amid the blizzards of Dusk. I did not want to discuss Heaven with the traders, though.

"Where are you heading now?" I asked Jat.

But of course that was a matter that Jat was reluctant to discuss with me. "To and fro," he said, waving a lazy hand. "Borderlands give the best trading."

Neither of us was aware that Vernier was about to spring yet another of its traps, although a fairly harmless one. Angels had been passing the word for some time, and Jat's ignorance showed how reluctant traders are to share information among themselves.

The conversation had died of too much caution. The wagon paused and then lurched. Misi belched. She twisted her thick torso around so she could look at me.

"Where do you want to go, Knobil?" she asked.

Misi had been listening to the talk, had understood every word, and had then asked outright the one question I preferred not to answer, but by then I was so completely convinced of her stupidity that I did not notice when the mask slipped briefly.

"Will I ever walk again?" I countered.

"Yes. Maybe not well, though."

I eyed Jat, whom I still thought of as the brains of the partnership. "When I get these splints off, would you teach me to ride?"

"Of course, Knobil!" If he meant that, he had an exceptionally slow horse in mind for me. "Be glad to."

"Then what, Knobil?" Misi asked. "Where will you ride to—to Heaven?"

"Why should I do that?" I retorted, still not realizing that I was crossing wits with the woman I believed to be a mental snail. "I have no desire at all to go to Heaven!" and there, at least, I was speaking the truth.

"Thought you'd want to tell the angels about the slaves in the mine," Jat remarked blandly.

This was dangerous ground. Whatever they said, these wily traders were harboring me only because they could smell profit—somewhere, somehow—and Hrarrh had not sent me on this journey out of benevolence. Angels would be able to give me advice and possibly rescue. And, yes, they would certainly ask me about slavery.

When I had denounced Anubyl for killing my mother, Violet had ignored my protest. Wiser now, I knew how angels defined violence—they would intervene only if the violence was between cultures. A herdman beating his women was not breaking the rules of his own group, and angels had already far too much to do without trying to change social patterns. But slavery crossed boundaries, and the angels would take action if they could.

Yes, the ants owned slaves—they bought them from traders.

Heaven was powerless against a mine full of ants, but a trader caravan was vulnerable.

So I met that rapier gaze as steadily as I could. "I have a very low opinion of angels, Jat—very low!" Again I was being truthful. "You ever trade in slaves, Jat?"

Amused, he shook his head. "Not so far. It's a mean way to make a living. But if I'm ever crossing the grasslands and a starving loner crawls up to me . . . I suppose I'd feed him. Then he'd owe me, wouldn't he? It would be like having a plump doe drop dead on your campfire. Hard to refuse."

"Let him starve! It would be kinder. But as far as I know, there are no slaves in your train, nor any of the others. If an angel comes by, I won't make trouble. I'm very grateful to all of you. I won't start cuddling up to angels."

The little man nodded in unusual silence. I did have a strong suspicion, though, that one of the other wagons held slaves—I had seen some youths being exercised once, in the far distance. And I knew for certain that one of Misi's storage chests had held a gun, because I had snooped, early in my recuperation. It had not been there the next time I looked, but it would be around somewhere. Angels would certainly want to know about that gun, and where it had come from.

"So?" Misi said. "Not Heaven. Where do you want to go, Knobil?"

I had not been long enough out of the mine for my wits to have healed. I knew I must return to the grasslands and I still vaguely believed that that was because I had business with the Heavenly Father there . . . but I also knew that I no longer believed in any of the myriad gods and goddesses I had heard worshipped in the slave compound. My logic needed more work, but my intent was clear. Back to the scenes of my childhood I must go.

"If I can somehow earn a horse of my own, then I shall head for the grasslands," I said. "Being a seaman on the March Ocean was pleasant. The cold seas of Saturday don't attract me."

"Be a herdman?" Jat snorted in disbelief.

Misi pouted doughy lips. "That's no life! They're animals! You learn to ride and then stay with us! We'll make a trader of you."

She turned her attention back to the hippos as if the matter were now settled. Jat grinned at the passing scenery and said nothing. He was perhaps thinking, as I was, of Knobil and Misi as cab partners. My reaction had perhaps shown on my face.

I promised to consider Misi's suggestion. I was quite sure that Jat had some other end in view for me, but I could do nothing until I got my legs back, except continue my attempts to seduce Misi Nada.

In retrospect, that conversation ought to have warned me that I had grievously underestimated Misi. How stubborn the human brain is, how reluctant to change any of its own opinions! I should have seen the evidence. A moron could not have hauled me out of death's gut as Misi had. A moron could not play apothecary and healer to the whole caravan, as Misi did. A moron would certainly not have been allowed to trade with the slashers.

We were now approaching the most fertile part of Vernier, where the inhabitants follow a form of agriculture called slash-and-burn. The women raise crops, harvest them, and then move west to where the men have already cleared new ground. After the planting and its associated rites, the men gradually slip away again westward to start the next clearing. In Heaven I met several slashers, and at least one had obvious trader blood in him. In theory, though, the male traders stayed away from the women's villages and sent in their own women to bargain. When Misi was chosen for this duty a second time, I at last began to wonder.

Part of my blindness certainly sprang from pride. Ever since Jat had explained the traders' customs to me, I had been trying my wiles on Misi, the skills I had developed so highly in the seafolk's grove. Whenever the two of us were alone, I expressed my desire by word and eye and hand. Misi's reaction was one of complete incomprehension, leaving me baffled. I peevishly concluded that she could understand nothing more subtle than an outright business offer—and I had no trade goods. To admit that there was a mind inside that big head would be to admit that it had outsmarted me.

And when Misi began removing my splints for short periods, my suspicions became hard to ignore. I did not want to exercise my knees, for even the smallest bend produced fearful agony. Misi insisted, standing over me, threatening to use force. Cursing and screaming by turns, I would obey—but only because I believed her threats. And when I was incapable of bearing more, she would gently tie the planks to my legs again and wipe my streaming brow.

But she only did this when we were alone. When Jat asked how I was progressing, she told him straight lies. I was surprised, but I did not contradict her . . . so perhaps I had guessed.

In the end it was the shirt that convinced me. Ever since I had known her, Misi had been working on that shirt. Now bright thread hid every scrap of the underlying silk. It was obviously a man's garment and, I assumed, intended for Jat. But traders gave nothing away, in spite of Jat's tales of freeing slaves to bring good luck.

Taking advantage of some smooth terrain, I had been sleeping. I awoke to the sound of voices. For a moment I thought they were discussing me. When I opened my eyes, however, I saw Jat wearing the new shirt. Another lay discarded at my side, beside his leather coat. He was preening mightily, admiring as much of himself as he could contort into the little mirror. If one's taste ran to such ostentation, then that shirt was the treasure of a lifetime. Even I could see that it was a masterpiece.

The dealing had started. Misi was sitting on one of the chests, set outside on the step, and had now turned around to plant her big feet flat inside the cab. Her meaty hands rested on her knees, and her eyes had shrunk back into sinister caverns of fat.

"Not one more twenty-seventh!" Jat said over his shoulder. "Pick something else, anything else but—oh, hi, Knobil . . . Anything else at all."

Misi's pout became a glare.

"Fourteen sacks of phosphate?" Jat suggested, earning a loud snort. "Well, how about the dapple foal? Kan wants it . . . Well, nine-eighteenths of the copper pots?"

She seemed to like none of his ideas. She shrugged hugely. "The rest of the bronze pelts?"

Jat's attention went to his fingers. "Nineteen thirty-thirds of my twenty-two thirtieths?"

"The molasses and your share of the oats?"

"Thirteen twenty-fourths of the wool and the bag of agates?"

"All the wool and two-thirds of the agates?"

"The bleach, the sickles, and the glass beads?"

They kept this up for some time, while I listened in amazement. I had seen Jat bargaining with Lon, and even with some of the other men—it was their favorite occupation. But I never heard it done faster, with less hesitation or more authority. Offer and counteroffer went leaping around the cab like a herd of roos—speed was part of the technique. Misi apparently knew the details and values of Jat's holdings as well as he did.

Usually such sessions ended with an agreement, a handshake, and a repeat of the terms before a witness and in sunshine. But not this one. "Leave it, then," Misi growled, and swung around once more to attend to the team.

Angrily Jat pulled off the overpriced garment, threw it down, and flounced out like a sulky child. He was still fastening buttons as he cantered away.

Stunned, I stretched out to catch hold of the discarded shirt. I lifted it and had begun to fold it when I saw that Misi had twisted around to glare her grotesque ugly face in my direction.

"Work those knees more, Knobil!"

"Yes, Misi," I said humbly. "I will."

If she had fooled me for so long, which one of us was the smarter?

# 8

## Black-white-red

I had barely had time to adjust to my new vision of Misi when, with no warning at all, there was trouble.

Our train happened to be in the lead. The men had been up ahead on a scouting or hunting expedition. Now they came cantering back with bows strung, with horses steaming and prancing. They were all good horsemen, those trader males, but they were shouting a lot, and I could see that some of their mounts were giving trouble, as if anxiety was infectious. When Jat scrambled onto the platform, I saw his eyes and nostrils dilated, as if he were spooked himself. Then he turned to Misi and began to whisper urgently in her ear.

The country was patchy woodland, rolling in large hills and ridges under dismal low clouds. The rain had stopped, but the air was still full of the feel of it. Odd movements of wind stirred gusts of mist amid the copses, and the twisted white tree trunks hovered like flocks of ghosts on the edges of reality.

Often, as now, I huddled in a blanket for warmth. The sun, when visible, had fallen halfway down the sky, lower than I had ever known it. Shadows stretched out eerily to the east, and I sorely missed the constant cloudless blue of the grasslands.

For several sleeps we had been skirting a large river to the south of us. Jat had spoken of deep jungle beyond it. Faint to the north rose bare spines of rock, higher than anything I had seen since we had left the Andes. Long ago burned off by High Summer, those would now be incapable of growing anything, even when watered. So this might be a natural pass, a narrowing of the borderlands, an obvious place to ambush traders. There was danger—I could smell it.

I could stand on my feet now, but only briefly, and not without pain. Walking was still beyond my powers, and I was happier wearing my splints. Whatever lurked ahead of us, I could not flee it at any greater speed than the snail crawl of the hippos, for I could not even sit a horse yet.

Of course trader women never rode and would never abandon their wagons . . . the men, I suspected, might. If the danger was some predatory animals—or men—then I could expect to take part in a collective defense. I had not shot an arrow since I joined the seafolk, but even a sitting man can use a bow.

Or I might be the danger. Jat straightened up and looked back at me again. He smiled automatically, but for once his jauntiness failed him, and his smile seemed as utterly false as I suspected it always was. He jumped down and hurried over to the other men, who had dismounted and were walking their horses, arguing fiercely.

So the trouble did concern me. I laid away my sewing, untied my splints, and began some leg exercises. Misi was keeping her eyes on the team, and had not looked around.

Angels?

Slave trading was a forbidden violence. If there was an angel waiting up ahead, then the traders had only three choices—turn back, kill the angel, or dispose of the evidence. I was helpless. Dreams of jumping out the window and running for the woods must remain only dreams.

Jat and the other men were standing in a group just ahead, holding their horses' reins and still arguing. Lon Kiv cantered up and dismounted also.

Puffing and bedraggled from sleep, Pula scrambled onto the platform to relieve Misi, who clambered down, painfully awkward, and plodded forward to join the discussion. The talkers stopped to form a circle in a sheltered spot, the train drawing slowly away from them.

All the trader men had gathered, with only the one woman?

That confirmed my guess: Knobil was the problem. I wondered if I dared hang my head out the window to watch, and decided that I would be wiser to pretend unconcern. That was not easy.

I lay back, grunting with pain as I gripped and bent each leg in turn. The amount of movement I could tolerate was pitiful, and even short exercise sessions still left the joints puffed and sore. I felt as helpless as I had when Hrarrh had loosed his horrors on me. I hoped that traders granted quick deaths. A sword thrust would be better than being tossed aside in the bushes and left to die.

The talk lasted a long time. I worked my knees until I thought they would smoke. I even lurched over to sit on the front bench, near to Pula, and tried talking to her, but that was always hopeless. Misi was certainly much smarter than she pretended, but I had not yet discovered whether Pula had a brain at all.

Then Misi returned, wheezing from unaccustomed exertion. She heaved her great bulk up on the platform, evicted her daughter, and took the reins again. Pula dismounted without a word.

"Misi, what's going on?" I was still on the chest beside her—barely—but facing backward. Her feet were out on the platform and mine inside, on the floor.

She chewed her usual wad of *paka* for a while, until she caught her breath. "Nothing."

"Rubbish! Is it angels?"

That earned no detectable reaction.

I did not wait for the ruminated response. "Misi, I won't tell! I'm very, very grateful to you. You saved my life! Trust me!"

Pula had somehow found her way into the middle of the team and was doing something with the harness. Misi yanked on the traces—those are attached to the hippos' ears, which are reportedly their only tender part, and certainly the only place that any attachment could be made on their vast brown smoothness. I once tried to steer a team of hippos. It took all the strength I possessed, and much more patience, for if hippos are smarter than woollies, then the victory is narrowly won. They remember no signal for longer than a man could draw a breath. To make a team stand still for more time than that is impossible.

Misi halted the rear pair. The front two continued to plod ahead, bearing their great yoke. In a moment the rear pair began to move again, but now they were pulling the train by them-

selves. The loose pair advanced more quickly, with Pula following, holding the traces and gradually turning them in a slow arc
to the left.

"Trust you to do what, Knobil?"

"Trust me not to tell the angel that I'm a slave."

Chew . . . chew . . . "You're not a slave, Knobil." Chew . . .
"What angel?"

I considered trying to strangle her, but my hands would not
have girdled her neck. She would have swatted me like a bug,
anyway.

And she was right not to trust me. One glimpse of an angel
and I would start screaming at the top of my lungs, yelling for
rescue.

She began to turn the train to the right. We were going back,
then? But why divide the team? Seething with mingled anger
and worry, I could do nothing but wait and watch. Eventually
we had turned to retrace our path, and I saw that the train itself
had been divided also. Pula was guiding the loose hippos toward
the now-stationary rear wagon. Jat and Lon were throwing open
doors, pulling out goods. Now I could guess what had been
decided during the long debate—the various partnerships had
been dissolved.

Later, when all the rearranging was complete, I found myself
riding with Misi and Pula in the cab of a very short, one-wagon
train, and still heading back to the west. All the others had
vanished eastward, with Jat and Lon driving the other half of
what had once been the joint rig, although I had never seen men
handling a team before. Apparently Misi and Pula had traded
one of their wagons for two of the men's hippos. Certainly other
merchandise had been involved in the transaction, including me.

Among traders, anything was negotiable.

My two huge companions sat on the bench at the front of the
cab. I was stretched out again on the bed, at the back, and almost
ready to weep from frustration. Which woman did I belong to—
or did they each own a part of me? Six clay pots for his right
arm . . . I should be grateful they had not shared me out with a
saw. I was certain now that the traders had heard word of angels
up ahead, and now I was being borne away from them, and
from my only hope of rescue.

The rain had started again. Misi and her daughter seemed to converse during their long silences by means unknown to man, for without warning Pula rose and closed the shutters on the north side. Then she hauled a leather cape from one of the chests, swathed herself in it, and went out on the platform to take over the driving.

Misi came in and shut the front shutters. She stared down at me for a moment in silence, and without expression. I was wearing a blue wool tunic and a pagne, for breeches would not go over my splints, but I also had a blanket pulled over my legs, and now I instinctively tucked it tighter around me, disconcerted by this calculating study.

My nerves were the weaker—I spoke first.

"How much of me do you own now?"

After a moment she made her peculiar *woofing* chuckle. "We're partners now, Knobil."

I was about to ask what sort of partners, and then didn't dare.

Misi stooped to rummage in one of the cubical chests, stretching brown cotton over hips as wide as hippos' backs. Once I would have reached out automatically to pat or pinch. Now that her pretense of idiocy had failed, I had abandoned any pretense of wanting Misi Nada. Incredible as it seems to me now, at that time I felt a powerful physical revulsion when I looked at her—her bloated obesity, her coarse but greasy skin, her lank gray hair. Herdmen preferred their women small, even tiny, and perhaps that was the origin of my distaste, although Sparkle had been built on generous lines.

I had turned away to stare broodingly at the scenery. Then Misi flopped down heavily at my side as the cab rolled. She was holding two pottery beakers.

"Drink to our new partnership!" she boomed in her deep, harsh voice. She curled her moustache in a smile.

I accepted a beaker with poor grace. "I'm no trader, Misi. I can't ride, or hunt . . . or scout, or cook. I can't even walk yet. I certainly couldn't haggle . . ."

"You're a better man than Jat!" she said, and tossed off her drink. Then she looked at me expectantly.

I shrugged and swallowed mine—then gagged at one of the worst tastes I had ever met. Misi leered and pursed her lips so that I might seal our agreement with a kiss. I pretended not to understand. "I'm not a better man than Jat for what you want," I said, hoping that I was wrong about what she wanted.

"He's a coward! Trouble makes every one of his parts run."

"Afraid of angels, is he?"

She heaved her great shoulders in a shrug, took my beaker, and threw it out of the one open window. She tossed her own beaker after it, in what seemed an oddly extravagant gesture. "You're my partner now."

"Business partner? But I have no skills, and no goods . . ."

"I paid Jat. I'll pay you," she said complacently, and slid a giant hand under the blanket to feel my left knee. She frowned, for it was hot.

"I was exercising."

She threw off the cover and began tightening the straps on my splints with quick, deft movements, the normal pretense of stupidity now discarded. Her touch brought goosebumps up on my skin. She noticed and chuckled again. She stroked a finger along my thigh, tracing one of the thin red scars.

My heart was pumping furiously. "Misi, why do traders buy wetlanders? And don't throw manure about luck!"

She smiled mockingly. "Wetlanders are great lovers."

"That's not true! Hrarrh told me you buy men and women, both. And you don't care what sort of shape they're in . . ."

"What sort of shape are you in, Knobil?"

I was sweating. I wiped my forehead. "I'm hot . . . *Misi, what was in that drink you gave me?*"

She nodded thoughtfully and patted my leg. "It comes from the jungle. Makes tall tree grow in forest."

Yes, it certainly did that. A wild shivering seized me, a strange excitement. "Misi . . . when I'm better . . . When my knees have healed, then I'd like—"

"Not till then, Knobil?"

"Well . . . I suppose I could try . . . Yes, now!"

Pulling away from my grasp, she rose and hauled her great tentlike garment over her head, revealing the bulging form that I had only guessed at before. Her belly was as broad as the Andes, and hairier. Her breasts were even more enormous than I had expected, or had imagined a human frame could bear. As I reached for them, she stepped away to slam the shutters on the third window and to dismantle the bench, hauling those chests across to add to the bed and make it wider. Blood roared in my ears, and my whole body throbbed. I heard my tunic rip, although I had not been aware of trying to remove it. Gasping with eagerness, barely able to speak, I stretched out my arms to her in the gloom. "Now, Misi! Now!"

She straightened, putting her fists on her hips. I could not see the expression on her face, but it was there in her voice—mockery, and contempt. "Ready for that kiss, Knobil?"

"Oh, yes! Please, Misi! Please . . ."

# 2

They call it the virgin's web.

Long afterward, in the archives in Heaven, I was shown a treatise written nine or ten cycles ago by a man identified only as Saint Issirariss. With a name like that, he was probably a forest dweller himself, and his account was so detailed that he must have had firsthand experience of the web. I was asked to add some notes of my own to the records.

The greatest jungles of Vernier are not found, as one might have expected, in the hot areas near to High Summer. Farther east the trees are older, the forest thicker, and the undergrowth more dense. Where topography favors heavy rainfall, the true deep forest is a cool twilight of perpetual damp, and it is there that the dark folk live. As Kettle was fond of pointing out, heavy pigmentation is an adaptation to jungle life, and while it is possible that the dark races are descended from original black ancestors, more probably their pigmentation has been increased by natural selection. The seemingly sinister name refers only to their color, for of course the dark people as a whole are neither worse nor better than any other folk. It is among them that a spinster may arise, but any race can produce a villain when the opportunity is present.

The basis of the elixir, Issirariss wrote, is a brew prepared according to a secret recipe, thought to consist of roots, herbs, insect eggs, and spider venom. In that form, he referred to it as nuptial beer, and stated that some of the forest tribes use it in their wedding ceremonies. When the dancing and feasting reach a climax, the young bride and groom share a bowl of the concoction and retire to the marriage chamber, there to find climaxes of their own, no doubt. Nuptial beer is relatively harmless, and socially beneficial, or so Issirariss claimed.

He speculated that the drug known as the virgin's web is prepared from nuptial beer by simple concentration. Long simmering over a slow fire, he thought, might be sufficient. The process cannot be very difficult, because spinsters seem to have no difficulty in obtaining an adequate supply for their evil purposes, and yet the secret is jealously kept.

Only very rarely can any outsider obtain the web. Misi's sample had been handed down from her grandmother, or perhaps from some farther ancestor than that, but it had not lost its power with time. From the effect it had on me, I suspect that it may even have grown more potent.

The human race has a long history of seeking aphrodisiacs, putting faith in many—all, according to Issirariss, either ineffectual or dangerous. The virgin's web is certainly not ineffectual. Moreover, it has several properties peculiar to itself, not found in any other.

It acts on persons of either sex, which is rare. Of course Misi had only pretended to drink, for she would have defeated her purpose had she taken the drug herself. That was fortunate, I suppose, because a Misi roused to the same sort of insane fit as I was would have killed me. It was I who almost killed her.

Poor Misi! She had known by hearsay what effect the web would produce, but she could not have expected the manic strength it induced in me, or the insatiable violence of my reaction, or the long ordeal she would have to endure until the effects wore off. She must have believed that her greater size would let her remain in control, but no one could have resisted my frenzy. In my fruitless striving for release, my frantic quests for variety, my cataclysms of mindless ecstasy, I tossed her around as if she weighed nothing.

Oblivious to pain, I hurt myself also. Early in my madness, I ripped off my splints—we found the broken planks and snapped bindings. My knees were not ready for vigorous exercise. The half-healed bones were cracked, the weakened tendons strained, and any chance that I might walk properly again was lost. Yes, I hurt Misi, but fortunately I inflicted no broken bones or permanent injury on her, only innumerable bruises, and probably much terror.

Dear Misi! In spite of that terror, she never cried out or tried to disable or kill me. At least, I do not think she did; I probably would not have noticed if she had. She endured, and even co-operated—not that she really had any choice.

According to Issirariss, a second peculiarity of the virgin's web is that it will not provoke a general orgy. Once I had fixed on Misi as the victim of my lust, then the cab could have been invaded by an army of the world's most desirable women, and I should have ignored all but her. That, he wrote, is a great danger for a woman who takes the potion, for no normal man can satisfy her need and she will go mad with frustration.

I was not frustrated. Once I started, Misi could not resist me and I was incapable of stopping until the madness wore off. Again and again I struggled to a climax, but the relief was momentary, being succeeded at once by even greater urgency. Driven by my frenzy, I could not have done otherwise than I did, so I feel little guilt, yet I regret most bitterly that I hurt her and frightened her. Eventually the effects waned, or my strength gave out. After uncounted orgasms, my arousal vanished as suddenly as it had come, and I collapsed into deep coma.

And the virgin's web had a third unique property, one I did not appreciate or comprehend until much later.

My unconsciousness probably did not last very long, for I awakened howling at the pain in my knees, which were black and hugely swollen. I was sprawled naked on the floor of the cab, surrounded by shreds of bedding, lit by a cruel sunlight streaming through a broken shutter, sweat-soaked and shivering in spasms of feverish reaction. Misi, equally bare, was trapped below me, battered and bruised and bloody, half stunned still by her long ordeal.

In a few moments, I recalled how I had maltreated her. While I had been experiencing unending deliriums of rapture, she had been hurting. Then I forgot my own troubles. I wept. I stroked her cheek. I struggled to move out of the way so that she could rise, for we were crushed together in a very small space, and I was incapable of rising—and meanwhile I apologized a thousand times.

I told her over and over how sorry I was, and how much I loved her.

Oh, my beloved Misi!

For I did truly love her—beyond measure, beyond expression. I cherish her memory still. No other woman ever has, or ever can, mean to me what Misi Nada did, and still does.

Issirariss called that the imprinting effect.

# 3

My guess had been correct. Heaven had set up a roadblock at a natural narrowing of the borderlands in the east of January, middle of Thursday. The angels were still there when Misi and Pula and I returned, long after my experience with the virgin's web. Now I could walk, after a fashion, keeping my knees straight. We had detoured very far back westward, waiting on my recovery.

That was a strange journey. Misi and Pula had to trade in little settlements for food, and even do the cooking. They were appallingly horrible cooks, both of them, never having cooked before. I was in great pain at first and could do little to help, but the thought of taking over the cooking myself was a big incentive for me to heal.

We were fortunate that no unscrupulous men or hungry animals took advantage of us—two women and a cripple wandering defenseless in the borderlands. Yet I remember that long loop west and then back east again as the happiest time of my life. I was with Misi, and nothing else mattered. I would have joyfully journeyed at her side forever . . . and even eaten her cooking.

Where a great spur of mountain reached close to the wide river, we came within sight of an encampment of four tents and three angel chariots. The landscape was spotted with thickets of white-trunked trees amid glades of the greenest grass I had ever seen. A soft rain was falling.

As our hippos munched their lazy way along the narrow plain, a solitary long-legged angel came stalking through the woods to talk to us. His stripes showed him to be Black-white-red. There must have been others around, staying out of sight.

I was sitting on the bench, just inside the front window, with my feet out on the platform. Misi was at my side, driving.

Black was well named, being as black as anyone I have ever met. Most of the forest races are short, but he was very tall, very lanky. He wore no hat, and his frizzled crown of jet hair shone with diamond sparkles. He strolled alongside the cab, and I was looking down at him, which is why I noticed his hair especially. His nose was broad, but the rest of him was as elongated as a fishing pole. He wore the fringed leathers of an angel, and he carried a long gun.

He was very young. So even the angels looked young to me now?

He studied me carefully, peering up with deep black eyes that seemed to brim with melancholy. "May good fortune attend you, trader," he said formally.

"May Our Lady Sun shed her blessing on you also, sir. I am Nob Bil." I did not introduce Misi.

I was very nervous, and the angel's steady scrutiny was rapidly making me more so. I was also in pain, for although my legs were stretched out before me, I could not keep them completely straight without looking unnatural, and they were howling at the slight bend I had imposed on them. Agony and fear together were soaking me in sweat. I could only hope that the rain was disguising that.

"You are brave to travel alone, trader."

"There are four other trains right behind us, sir."

That statement was true so far as it went, but the others were not associated with us, and might even be unaware that we were now ahead of them. We had followed their convoy eastward and had then outrun it with our single—and almost empty—wagon.

"And your horses are with them, Nob Bil?"

"They are, sir. I have twisted my knee and cannot attend them myself at the moment."

Black frowned glumly at that tale. Misi had coached me well, but I decided to take the offensive in the hope of diverting more questions. "And what brings you gallant angels to these parts? Not danger, I hope?"

The angel's eyes continued to examine me morosely. "We have been passing a warning to traders. Have you heard of it?"

"No, sir."

He sighed. "You traders are as bad as herdmen!"

"I am told that herdmen slaughter one another on sight," I said reprovingly. But I was remembering one of Violet's old jeers—that herdmen smelled different. I was a herdman halfbreed . . . had this angel broken my disguise already?

"True. I only meant that traders do not cooperate at all."

"Give away information, do you mean?" I tried to sound shocked. Despite my pain and the quiverings of my normal cowardice, I was starting to enjoy the game. I wished I dared look at Misi.

"I suppose that sounds immoral to you? Well, here is the problem. You are between jungle and desert, of course, but the west end of the borderlands is cut off now by the Andes and the Great River. That's an impossible barrier for traders. We can guide people and their livestock across the canyon, but not wagons. Or chariots. And the barrier is moving east, obviously."

Jat had long since vanished from my life, but I could recall his geography lessons. "You mean we must head north, across the desert?"

Black nodded, sparkling all the jewel drops on his hair. "We have arranged a truce . . . and we provide escorts," he added before I could say whatever he expected from me.

"How urgent is this?" I asked, worried about my inability to defend my beloved Misi and her daughter, recalling vague yarns about the fierce red-haired men of the desert.

"Not very," the angel confessed. "You have time for a trip or two back to the mountains. Before you bounce grandchildren on your knee, though, you must cross the desert to the north borderlands. You may stay there or come south again across the grasslands as you wish . . . Just don't say you weren't warned! And don't wait too long, or there will be no one left to trade with. We hear there is a spinster at work."

My spine tingled. Black had thrown in that unrelated remark in the hope of eliciting a reaction from me, and I had no idea what sort of reaction. Obviously I was supposed to know what a spinster was, but I didn't. Was it dangerous? In all her lessons, Misi had not thought to mention spinsters, so they must be rare. I could not ask her for help, for she was playing moron again. But Misi was no moron. She had steered the team into a stand of small trees, heavier growth than she would normally have chosen. They slowed us, of course, but the noise of crunching was much louder than usual, making conversation difficult. Moreover, Black was being squeezed between the side of the cab and the sides of the cut we were making, and must constantly step over stumps and fragments of trunk. This made it harder for him to keep his eyes on me. The slash also made the cab bounce and lurch repeatedly, jarring hot irons through my knees.

But if hard work gains rewards, then I ought to pass scrutiny. Misi and Pula had made me a leather jacket and breeches in trader style. They had tried to use an old set of Jat's, but I was much too large for those. My coat was unfastened, to display the fine floral shirt that Jat had coveted—actually it was only the front, for Misi had taken it to pieces to fit my wider chest. The cuffs showed, although the top of the sleeves did not reach my shoulders. I sported the appropriate curved-brim hat; my hair and beard and eyebrows had been dyed, my face and hands darkened also. We had not been able to do anything about my eyes.

I looked like a trader—unusually large for a male, but a trader nonetheless.

Spinster? "Where?" I asked, playing for time.

Black's expression grew even more lugubrious. "If we knew that we wouldn't be here, now would we?"

"I suppose not."

The conversation lagged for a while. The hippos continued to browse their noisy way through the trees, and Black continued to study me. I stared back down at him with all the confidence I could feign. I had promised Misi I would get her safely past the angels, and I was going to do everything in my power to keep my promise.

"You have seen no slaving, then?" Black asked suddenly.

I shook my head, attempting to display disapproval.

"Wetlanders in particular, of course." He watched my reaction very carefully.

"No blonds here, sir. Nor in the other trains."

"You will not mind opening your wagon for me, though, trader?"

Misi had warned me that he would ask, and we had agreed that this was going to be the tricky part, for I could still barely walk.

"I would not mind, sir . . ." I waved at the trees crowding in around us. "But we can't open the doors in this."

"There is a clearing." Black pointed ahead and to the left.

I frowned, as if not wanting to be diverted from my road, but in truth we should have to veer very little to reach the clearing, and to refuse would only prolong the ordeal. I shrugged and turned to Misi, yelling at her and pointing. She played stupid for a while, but the clearing was a large one, and we could not keep up the pretense for long enough to slip by it. Eventually she nodded and began turning the team toward the gap.

Black was till sauntering beside me, and his manner reeked of suspicion.

"Tell me, sir," I inquired jocularly. "Whatever will you do if you open my car and a wetlander jumps out at you?"

He frowned. I had to wait a while for his answer, but he could not hold a silence as long as Misi could. "Save him, of course."

I wanted to ask what would happen if the wetlander did not want to be saved, but I dared not reveal more ignorance. Then we were out of the trees, and the car doors could be opened.

"Pula!" I shouted. "Show the angel what we carry."

Black's eyebrows rose. "You will not do me the courtesy of taking me yourself, Nob Bil?"

"My regrets, angel. My knee . . . Walking is painful for me."

Evidently he was suspicious of my knee story, but Pula jumped from a side window and led him back to look at the stock. Had I been able to accompany him, he might well have asked questions about Misi's trade goods that I should have been unable to answer. Pula, at least, was genuine, and would know about them—if he could get a response from her. The goods were becoming depleted. We had been living off them for some time.

Then Black returned. We were almost across the clearing, heading toward more timber.

"Well, I found no slaves, trader."

"I hardly expected you to, sir."

He indulged himself in more staring, and I became even more tense. Obviously he could tell that something was wrong. Would he let us go?

"You will forgive this inconvenience, though?" he said. "As an honest trader, you must be revolted by the inhuman practice of slaving?"

"Absolutely. I deplore it." I was being truthful there.

"And slaving itself is nothing compared to the barbarous obscenities of a spinster."

I shrugged noncommitally. "If one believes all the tales."

"Oh, they are true! It would be disgusting enough to treat even a dumb animal as a spinster treats her victims. To use human beings so is beyond all understanding."

I remembered Hrarrh's dark hints and shivered. But I had promised Misi that I would save her from the angels. She had professed a great fear of what angels might do if they discovered I was a wetlander. Even though I was no longer a slave, she had said, and even though I were to tell them so myself, they would guess that I had been one originally. Then they would be hard on her, perhaps even burning her goods and cars. I loved Misi. I trusted her, and here was my chance to show her she could trust me. Given a chance for rescue, I was staying with her by choice. So I was proving that I loved her.

"Oh, I agree," I said.

The angel nodded, reluctantly. "Then good fortune, trader."

"And good hunting, Angel."

We had made it! As soon as the angel was out of sight, I threw my arms around Misi and kissed her.

Wary of treachery, I intended to retain my trader disguise until we were well past the angel roadblock, but as soon as I felt that we were reasonably safe, I turned to Misi with determination.

"Now you know you can trust me!" I said. "So I want to know why! *Why* do traders buy wetlanders?"

She had three techniques she used to avoid answering my questions. Sometimes she played moron again, although that was hardly credible now. Sometimes she wept, and that always reduced me to tears myself, for I was tortured by the memories of having manhandled her in my drugged frenzy, and I could not bear the thought of making her suffer any more. Her third evasion, and always the most effective, was merely to join me on the bed. That never failed.

This time I was not on the bed. Misi smiled and patted my shoulder. "Because wetlanders are great lovers."

"That's not the reason!"

"Yes it is—I'll show you!"

She picked me up and carried me inside.

In my long life I had known many women, far more than my fair share; but none could ever rouse me faster or more frequently than Misi, with her enormous hands and her great soft body. In none did I ever find greater joy.

As I was to refuse to admit long afterward to Cherub Beef in Cloud Nine, Misi was very hot stuff.

More important, though . . . I loved her.


Now we were facing unknown country. I could barely walk, and we had no horses. I could neither scout nor hunt, the two main duties of a trader male. Once the caravan behind us was also safely past the roadblock, Misi doubled back to meet it.

The negotiating session was very long, and I was not present. At one point she brought three or four of the men to meet Pula, who was driving, and I began to guess what sort of things were being discussed. They also wanted to talk to me, for they could not believe that we had managed to smuggle a wetlander by the angels. My hair was still dark with dye, but the paleness of my legs convinced them. They all laughed as I described the conversation with Black-white-red. They congratulated me on being a fine trader, and Misi beamed proudly at me.

Eventually a deal was struck, and we joined the caravan. We even acquired a new man, a youngster named Mot Han. He was just reaching adulthood, and his father contributed some wealth to set him up on his own. Horses and hippos were included, and a second wagon. It must have been a very complicated agreement.

The new wagon was hooked up to Misi's, and Mot and Pula set up home in it, for Pula was also a party to the deal—and a very willing one. In almost the only remark she ever volunteered to me, she admitted that Mot was a much more interesting cab partner than old Lon Kiv had been. She expressed great surprise at this discovery, almost excitement. I sometimes think that maybe Pula really was no smarter than she seemed.

Mot was a pleasant enough kid, so small and fresh-faced that I had trouble believing his moustache was real. As for his beard—I had seen better on old cheese. He, in turn, tended to avoid me, and he had an annoying habit of not meeting my eye when we did talk. Nevertheless, the little guy was a wily hunter and a superb cook. Our fare improved greatly.

Part of a community once more, we continued to wend our way east and south. We forded rivers, gradually penetrating deeper into the great jungle. As their forage became denser, the hippos' progress became slower. I was too ignorant to realize that traders normally shunned such terrain.

I could stagger around stiff-legged, and Mot taught me to ride a horse and also how to cook, after a fashion. I regained my old skill with a bow, and tried hunting. My hair grew in and many cuttings made me a blond once more. Being a trader was even more enjoyable than being a seaman, because Misi was there.

The men scouted our path, and of course went trading. They must have made inquiries about the spinster, although I did not know that. They gathered information, and they passed word. It was the lure of the spinster that was pulling our path so far into the heavy jungle. Misi could have obtained such cooperation only by contributing some portion of me to the whole caravan. She would have been able to afford it, for a wetlander delivered to the right quarters represents the most valuable cargo a trader ever sees.

I had no inkling of any of that. When I was sold, I was asleep, dreaming of my love. I awoke to find the cab full of stocky, dark-brown men armed with spears.

# 9

## The Spinster

The newcomers were not as dark as the angel had been, and their black hair was straight, not woolly. They wore only brief pagnes of spotted fur, but bright green and yellow bands of tattoo writhed all over their faces and chests and around their limbs. They were thick and broad, and their rain-wet skins shone like polished walnut. The blades of their spears were even shinier.

They stripped me, for my clothes had not been included in the purchase. They clucked approvingly at my paleness and disapprovingly at my wasted legs. They made me stand, to show I could. They enveloped me in a burnoose of heavy brown stuff that seemed absurdly big—the hem trailing on the floor, the sleeves covering my hands. The hood pulled right over my head to fasten in front, with only a tiny gap for me to see through. I was too bewildered to believe all this was happening.

Then they lifted me down to the ground. Misi was standing nearby, towering over a group of the male traders and more of the short brown men, like a duck training chicks to swim. They were examining a pile of dark-colored bales, in much the same way the newcomers had examined me.

"Misi!" I shouted, and started waddling toward her in the absurd, straight-legged gait that later led the cherubim to call me "Roo." The traders glanced at me and then turned away—except for one. Little Mot Han was staring fixedly, his face strained and pallid, as if he were about to throw up.

I reached Misi and fell against her, my knees screaming pains of protest at my haste. I clutched her, but she did not return my embrace. "Misi, what's happening?" I knew what was happening.

"Dear Knobil!" Misi said. "I want you to go with these men." She bent her head a little, to plant a kiss on my wet forehead.

"Why? Misi, I can't bear to be parted—"

"To please me, Knobil? To make me happy?"

And to make her rich. I glanced bitterly at the heap of wealth. Misi was a trader, and wealth her dream of heaven. I must not judge her by others' standards.

"You go now, Knobil. I want you to go now. Please. You were a great lover, Knobil." She went back to counting.

One of the men gripped my arm to urge me away, then two of them scooped me up to carry me. My feet dropped and I howled in agony. All I could think of then was to scream that my legs must be kept straight. When I managed to make that clear, four of them hoisted me shoulder high and bore me off like a corpse. So I did not get another glimpse of Misi.

She had sold me. Yet I cannot hate her for it. Even now I love her and cannot think badly of her. We must all follow our own paths in this world, and Misi was a trader. I'm sure she really was sorry, for I saw a tear in her eye.

I don't think it was rain.

My pallbearers did not carry me far. Beyond a stand of great trees lay a wide river, and there we came to three canoes drawn up on the bank in the steamy jungle gloom. I was dropped into one, not gently, and before I could even free my hands from my sleeves to make an attempt at scrambling out again, the craft had been launched and was under way, surging over the dark oily waters. A line of six kneeling men labored before me. Six rain-slick backs rippled, six paddles flashed.

I unfastened my hood, and a spear shaft thwacked my ribs so hard they rang like a drum. I yelped and looked around.

A seventh man sat at my back. "Stay covered!" He was bigger than the others with a broad, strong face. Without all the green and yellow tattoos he might have been quite handsome, but his expression was unfriendly. He looked young enough that he might not have realized how hard he had hit me. He also looked capable of hitting much harder.

I fumbled to close my hood, even as I was asking "Why?"

He bared big white teeth in what he probably thought was an approving smile. "Wetlanders must stay out of the sun."

Even if the sun had been shining through the drizzle, most of the river would have been shaded by the great timber that walled its banks. "Why?" I demanded again. "Who says so?"

"Ayasseshas."

"Who's Ayasseshas?"

A curious dreaminess danced in the darkness of his eyes. "She is our queen. Our goddess. She is Ayasseshas."

"A spinster?"

"Of course." He produced a rope, and leaned forward to tie one end around my waist. "Ayasseshas expects us to deliver you, wetlander. Not a man of us would not die for her. You will not escape."

I did not know what might live in those gloomy waters and we were a long way from the banks. I could swim, of course, but not as fast as a canoe traveled, and probably not while wearing a tent. The sort of escape he was talking about was suicide.

And suddenly suicide seemed like a very good idea. The thought of losing Misi was unbearable, and the notion that she had betrayed me was unthinkable. Had my guard not tied that noose on me and fastened the other end to a thwart behind him where I could not reach, then likely I would have tried to kill myself. Hrarrh had warned me once that a trader would sell his grandsons, but I would not believe that Misi had sold me. Despite the evidence, my mind rejected the possibility. There had been some horrible misunderstanding. Or it was a trick, and she was planning to rescue me . . . I slumped over in a heap of misery and stayed like that for a long time.

The three canoes headed upstream, eastward. The current was sluggish, the still waters moving without a ripple, dark with the reflections of the undersides of branches arcing overhead. Paddles flashed in a murderously swift rhythm, but the canoes were large and we made slow progress along that serpentine tree canyon. Later the sun came out, with patches of blue showing high above us. Then came thick clouds of insects to torture the paddlers. I alone was well protected in my voluminous burnoose, although I soon began to feel like a steamed fish.

Eventually I recovered enough from my shock to twist around and talk to my guard. He was quite willing to be friendly, as long as I behaved myself. His name, he told me, was Shisisannis, and he was of the snakefolk. When the other canoes happened to be close, I noticed that two or three of the men were obviously of another race, more like the lanky black angel I had met. Those, Shisisannis said in a contemptuous tone, were swampmen. Swampers were cowardly types who fought with bows, he explained, while real men used spears.

How did snake people gain their name? I asked. He grinned and reached behind him for a bulging sack, weighty enough to test even his brawny shoulders. Already I had begun to regret the question, but he untied the neck and peered inside. Then he shot a powerful walnut hand in and pulled out the head of a snake, a snake so large that his fingers could not close around its neck. I bleated in fear, seeing yellow crystal eyes staring at me and a forked tongue flicker.

"This is Silent Lover," Shisisannis said fondly. "Do not be alarmed. As long as I keep my thumb hard just here, she cannot move."

I believed him, but I was very glad when he closed the bag again. He explained—at length and eagerly—how he hunted with his scaly friend, hanging her on a branch over a game trail. Then he would circle around through the jungle, seeking to drive some unsuspecting victim underneath. His snake would fall on it and crush it. The trick was to get to her before she began to swallow and then to use that secret grip again to immobilize her. He bragged a lot about the things she had caught for him, most of them creatures I had never heard of.

Despite my shock, my fear, and my bereavement, I rather liked Shisisannis. Only much later did I learn that no other race ever trusts the snakefolk. I had no need to trust him, though. I had no choices to make.

We paused briefly to eat. The canoes were beached, but the men ate where they had been kneeling. Then they set off again.

I was impressed. Except for Shisisannis, who was both my guard and the overall leader, every man was working at his utmost. They poured sweat, they were tormented by insects that they could not brush off, and their endurance was astonishing.

I said so.

Shisisannis gleamed his teeth at me again. "Ayasseshas told us to hurry back. Nothing else matters. She is eager to meet you, wetlander." He sighed. "Ah, how I envy you!"

"Why?"

He looked surprised. "You do not know?"

I shook my head, and then decided he might not be able to see that gesture inside my tentlike robe. "No."

"Then I say only that you are to have the most glorious experience that any man can hope for in his lifetime. Few are ever so favored. You are fortunate beyond imagining."

Which was not what the angel had said. Or Hrarrh. But it might just possibly explain Misi. Had she parted with me out of love, so that I could enjoy this promised paradise? Of course that was a ridiculous idea, but it was all I had, and I clung to it.

"You speak from experience?" I asked.

"Indeed I do!" Shisisannis rolled his eyes in rapture.

"Describe it."

"It is beyond words."

I gave up.

A man in one of the other canoes signaled that it was time to stop—he did so by collapsing. His companions tried to keep up for a while, and another of them did the same. Shisisannis called a halt. The paddlers beached their canoes and prepared to make camp, every one of them staggering from total exhaustion. Even in the mine, I had never seen a group of men more weary. Some needed help even to stand. However this Ayasseshas did it, she inspired a devotion that went beyond pain, to the very limits of endurance. Shisisannis had said they would die for her and now I believed him.

Shisisannis himself lifted me ashore, and told me to walk. I set off with my absurd skirt held high, but the ground was tangled with lush undergrowth and I fell repeatedly. Each time I raised myself again, buttocks first, walking my hands backward and keeping my throbbing furnace knees straight. I heard chuckles of amusement, but I persevered until I took a worse than average tumble and Shisisannis's voice behind me said that was far enough. I lay on my belly and panted, groaning at my weakness and humiliation. Eventually I recovered enough to roll over and sit up. I had covered about fifty paces, yet I felt just as exhausted as the paddlers.

Food was passed, but half the men were asleep before it even reached them. Soon they all were, stretched out on crumpled bushes or wet moss. Only Shisisannis remained awake. He sat on his heels, alert and watching, a darker shape of menace in a deep gloom, staring at me without a blink.

Back from the water's edge, the undergrowth was not so thick as it had been on the bank. All around us, giant pillars of trees rose up ten times higher than any I had ever seen on the grasslands, solid as rocks nearby, but fading away with distance into murky wraiths. The close-packed jungle trees grew almost vertical, with little twist. Only rare speckles of blue showed through the canopy roof and the thick tresses of creepers suspended from every twig. The air was cool and damp, reeking of mold and rain, and so laden with water that it was visible, a dark mist hanging in all the vacant spaces. I was grateful for my all-enveloping garment, wondering how my near-naked companions could bear the chill. Bright-hued birds flashed past sometimes, and their calls echoed eerily among the continual faint dripping sounds. It was creepy and oppressive.

"Food?" Shisisannis inquired.

"Not hungry."

He shrugged and continued to stare.

Nor was I sleepy. One thing was certain, however—I was not going to escape. I might be capable of launching one of the canoes, if I could reach them, although they had been pulled well clear of the water, but Shisisannis was not going to take his eyes off me. He could apparently squat there in the undergrowth forever, watching me unwinkingly, with hunters' patience. He was not even bothering to swat at the bugs and flies that walked on him.

I lay back, head on hands, and reviewed my hopeless position, bitter with the rank taste of betrayal and the dread of unknown horrors to come. Oh, Misi . . . how had I failed her? I wallowed in the depths of my ill luck, I soared to heights of self-pity, and I piled up mountains of despair. At last, though, another problem asserted itself, one of the trivial indignities that our bodies use to mock our souls when they seek to transcend mundane affairs. I sat up to meet Shisisannis's unwavering gaze. I explained.

He shrugged and pointed with his chin. "Go that way."

My captors had all stayed between me and the river, and he had told me I should go deeper into the jungle. I was not to be allowed to approach the canoes.

So I rolled over and levered myself vertical again. I raised my long skirt, and I rocked my way cautiously through the tangles, my bare feet sinking into clammy moss and a mush of rotted leaves. Shisisannis would be able to see me and hear me, and without question catch me if he wanted. I found a fallen tree to use as a seat. I attended to my needs.

I stood again and was about to return . . .

Bird calls, and the stirring of the wind, and drippings? The sky had turned gray once more and probably rain was falling on the forest roof, but I could hear something else, a deep humming. It was tantalizingly faint, but as I concentrated it grew more distinct, nearer, and I could tell that it was song, a gleam of silver melody in the green hush. Someone was coming!

I wondered if Shisisannis could hear it yet. I glanced covertly in his direction, and he did not seem to have moved. How much time did I have before he roused his warriors? How far could I travel before he came after me?

Cautiously I planned a path between the nearest obstacles and then rocked my way slowly forward. I could not tell if I was hearing a wordless voice, or an instrument, or both together, but the tones were growing louder, and I was sure the source was approaching. *Rescue!* Music meant hope. It meant people, my fellow man. If spinsters were as horribly evil as the angel had suggested, then surely other human beings would take pity on me. No matter who this musician was, I could hardly be worse off than I was now.

I still did not know whether the sound came from throat or fingers or both, but I was certain the singer was not animal nor bird. And it was beautiful! It soared. It brought tears to my eyes and a lump to my throat. It spoke of love, and longing, and compassion. Strangely, it reminded me strongly of some of the herdfolk songs that my mother had sung to me when I was very small. No one capable of such beauty could be so heartless as to turn down the pleas of a helpless captive.

Faster I drove my crippled legs, reeling dangerously, tripping, staggering, and never heeding the jarring pains. The melody welled up in unbearable glory, close now, and yet I could see no one in the dense gloom. I wanted to call out, and I dared not interrupt that peerless refrain. Never had I heard such music . . .

Two strong hands slammed against the sides of my hood, covering my ears and then holding my head up when I would have fallen with the shock. Shisisannis steadied me, then transferred his grip to my shoulders. I twisted around to stare at the dark contempt lurking amid the green and yellow serpents of his tattoos. The song had gone and I could hear nothing but a faint and distant humming.

"That's close enough, wetlander."

"What? Who? Wh . . ."

He raised eyebrows in mockery. "I said *spinster*, not *spinner*."

"I don't understand!"

The hum had become melody again, faint and far off. He pointed. "Between these trees, see? No, closer."

A man's length before me, outlined only by faint silver spangles of dew . . . a giant web.

"Harp spider, wetlander. There she is, up there. See her?"

Bewildered, I looked where he pointed. I could see nothing but trailing moss and dark clutters of twigs—and then I made out a tangle of furry legs as long as my shins . . . I shuddered and recoiled backward. Shisisannis caught me and steadied me again.

"I'd let you go to her lover's kiss, wetlander, if that was what you really wanted, but Ayasseshas told me to bring you whole and healthy, and her I will obey."

"I'd have been trapped in that web?"

The aria was soaring louder and nearer again, heart-rending in its wistful glory.

"Oh, you'd have broken free. Only small animals get really caught. But her ladyship would have had her fangs in you before you did. You would have not gone far and would not have shaken her off."

"But the song!" I protested, grateful that my hood hid the tears soaking into my beard.

"Cover your ears!"

I did that, and then listened again . . . a faint humming, far off.

"Do that when it gets too strong," Shisisannis said. "Now, come back and enjoy it at a safe distance. She might jump."

With a shudder of revulsion and fear, I wrenched my feet around and rolled away from the harp spider's web. There could be things worse than spinsters, I thought.

## 2

The exhausted rowers were given little more time to rest. Shisisannis kicked a few awake. They scrambled up without a whisper of complaint and began kicking others, while Shisisannis himself draped me over his shoulder and trotted effortlessly back to the canoes. The others came running after, hastily wolfing down food on the way, laughing and joking in their eagerness to be off. I knew enough about physical overload to know how their bodies must ache. I marveled at their zeal, and puzzled over its source. It certainly did not stem from fear, for the ants had never inspired such dedication, and no one could have used more fear than they.

The second leg of the journey was shorter, and also much hotter. Of course climate is normally invariant, its changes too slow for men to notice, and this unnatural unpredictability troubled me. Much later I was to hear the saints talk of weather and the torus of instability, but I never truly understood how those worked. Whatever they were, we were within them, beset by unpredictable alternations of sun and storm that did nothing to calm my jangled nerves.

Sweltering within my gown, peering out from the hood, I could see no difference between one bend of the river and the next, but apparently my captors did. A shout of challenge rang out, and at once they all rose upright, on one knee, in racing stance. The paddles flashed even more furiously, and the canoes themselves seemed to rise from the water and fly. The pace was brutal, inhuman torment. They could not sustain it, I thought, but they kept it up far longer than I would have believed possible, six men with two passengers in our craft, against five men in each of the others. Ours came in second, driving onto a muddy beach that apparently marked the finish line. The paddlers flopped over, lungs rasping, as the third canoe slid in at our side.

The winners attempted a cheer of derision and triumph, but they were too winded to sound convincing, and still I could see no landmark to determine why this spot on the bank was different from any other. The spinster's lair was well concealed.

Laughing but still gasping, my captors scrambled out and pulled the canoes higher. Shisisannis untied me and bellowed: "Ing-aa?"

One of the black, woolly-haired swampmen stepped over from the winning canoe. He was decorated with beads instead of tattoos, but he looked every bit as intimidating as the snakemen, and I had met trees that would have been proud to have had sons so tall.

"You won—you can deliver the goods!" Shisisannis said offhandedly, himself lifting the bag that contained Silent Lover.

The giant flashed teeth in a beam of pleasure. His great hands scooped me out of the canoe as if I were a sachet of petals. He laid me over his shoulder, went up the bank in two huge bounds, and hurtled off through the woods at a long-legged sprint. With supermen like these to serve her, what possible need could the spinster have for a cripple like me?

Head down, I was jiggled and bounced. My knees enjoyed being bent forward no better than being bent backward, and I was only vaguely aware of a narrow muddy track, winding through dense and fetid jungle, dark and damp. Then we emerged into sunlight. More mud squelched beneath those enormous feet, and the pace quickened. The giant came to a sudden stop and just stood. I remained dangling over his shoulder, rising and falling with every rasping breath.

"You going to put me down?" I inquired of his kidneys.

"No," said a voice, rumbling so deep that I felt it as much as heard it.

I gripped his sweaty loins and levered myself up as well as I could, partly to ease the strain on my legs and belly, partly to look around. As far as I could determine through the slit in my hood, we were in the center of a large and very muddy compound. I saw leaf-covered huts shaped like pots, with glimpses of an encircling stockade beyond. The canoes were arriving, being carried in on the paddlers' heads—on the double, of course. There would be no traces of our arrival left outside the settlement, therefore, except footprints on the mud, and the next shower would erase those. Shisisannis was bringing up the rear, running also, and clutching the bag that contained Silent Lover.

There were other men around. I could hear the rhythmic chant of a gang working in unison, an irregular thudding of axes, a distant bleating of livestock. I could even see a dozen or two of the inhabitants. Half of them were dark-skinned men very like my captors, striding around in spotted-fur pagnes and either tattoos or strings of beads, some carrying spears. But the other half were draped from crown to toe in all-enveloping burnooses, as I was. Mostly those muffled figures were just standing, staring in my direction. Some, at least, were too tall to be women, and with a sudden flash of hope, I decided that they must all be wetlanders like me, being kept out of the sun.

Wetlanders came from the far west, so we must be a rare breed so close to Dusk. To collect a dozen or more of us would take considerable time and expense, so whatever the spinster did with wetlanders, she would not put them to a quick death. I felt a little better, then.

Apart from those mysterious shrouded figures, though, I could see no one but men—no women, or children, or old folk. The spinster maintained a private army of young males, a very impressive and virile collection, judging by those I had met so far. I wondered why she needed them, who her foes were. And again I wondered at the source of her power over them.

In the center of the compound, not far from me, stood a massive carving in the likeness of a rearing snake, its cobra hood spread wide and the rest of its body looped around the base, all painted green and yellow, and strangely repellent even to me, who believed in no god. Then I could not keep my head up any longer. I sagged down, feeling sick and giddy.

Our canoes had been stowed alongside a group of others. The men came running across toward my bearer, Shisisannis going to one side of him and the rest lining up on the other. Then they all just stood, in a silence broken only by heavy breathing, waiting for someone, or something, but with none of the comment or muttered complaint I would have expected. I had my wrong end pointing forward and could not see what they were watching. All I could see was feet, but I did notice that they were placed at the edge of a patch of white gravel, markedly different from the juicy mud that covered the rest of the compound, steaming gently in the sunlight.

Then a sigh ran through the waiting platoon. I heard footsteps on the gravel.

"Shisisannis!" said a woman's voice. "My devoted War Band Leader Shisisannis!"

Shisisannis sank to his knees. "My beloved Goddess!"

"You have done as I asked!" Her voice was deep and throaty, and she spoke as if to a lover.

"To please you is all I seek in life, my Queen. Command and I obey. And if I ever fail you, Majesty, in the slightest detail of your desires, may I be put at once to pasture."

I heard a tinkling laugh that I did not like. "You serve me better thus, Shisisannis my joy. He is a true wetlander?"

"And already very pale. But his knees are worse than you were told, my Queen. He can barely walk."

"Other than that he seems fit?"

"Quite healthy, Majesty."

"Knees are helpful . . . but not the most essential items." The men laughed at her joke. "Rise now, War Band Leader. Ah, too long have I neglected you, you most perfect pillar of manhood. I yearn for your strong embrace." In public such words should be spoken only with humor or mockery, but these sounded like real seduction. Remembering Shisisannis's expression when he had talked of this woman, I decided she must be in earnest, unbelievable though that might seem. "This ribbon is one I give only for exceptional service. Wear it as my personal promise of greater reward in store. As soon as my duties allow, I shall send for you, for none is a more dutiful servant or more deserving of whatever favors a valiant warrior may claim from an eager and grateful lover."

Shisisannis rose. "Majesty . . . I . . ." His voice broke. He sounded overwhelmed.

"You have done well to return so soon. You must go now and rest."

I could not believe my ears. She was sending him off to bed?

"Great Queen, the stockade progresses but slowly . . ."

She laughed again. "You will not serve me well by working yourself to death, Shisisannis, as poor Yshinanosis did. Rest first. It is my wish."

Two more feet came forward into my inverted field of view—brown, female feet in golden sandals. They rose on tiptoe, and I took the ensuing silence to mean that Shisisannis was being rewarded with a kiss. My dizziness and nausea were mounting, my attention was wandering, but I could have sworn that his knees trembled.

Then the woman's heels sank down, and she stepped away again, out of my view.

"And Ing-aa! Canoemaster Ing-aa, my great black bull!"

The blood collecting in my head, the constriction of my gut, the sweltering heat of my gown, and the agony in my legs . . . I was failing rapidly. Red waves surged before my eyes and bile in my throat. Yet I could still somehow register that there were unholy things going on. "Black bull?" She was inveigling Ing-aa with the same crude sexual cajolery that she had given Shisisannis—and Shisisannis was right there, at their side. She had two young bulls present, and by any normal standards of male behavior they should already be rolling around on the ground, doing their utmost to maim and impair. Yet Shisisannis chuckled with the others as she made lewd remarks about Ing-aa's size, promising him the same reward she had pledged to Shisisannis. I did not understand.

Then, through my fog of pain and nausea, I heard her say, "But show me this prize you have brought me, lover."

Ing-aa slid me forward so my feet hit the ground. He lifted me easily and twirled me around to face the spinster, then set me down again and let go.

I caught a brief, blurred glimpse of a female figure in a shimmering gown of water silk.

I pitched forward in a dead faint.

Of course my collapse was mostly a reaction to the head-down position and the sudden correction, compounded by overheating, by fear, and by pain. I was unconscious for only a few moments.

"He is coming around, lady." Ing-aa's voice spoke close above me.

I was stretched out on my back, although I had first landed on my nose and forehead. My hood had been pulled from my face and the front of my gown opened. The ground swayed, my ears sang, and I kept my eyes shut.

"That is fortunate." There was no seduction in the woman's voice now.

"Majesty . . . I was thoughtless."

"Very! You knew his value." She was furious, and that was encouraging for me.

I peered narrowly through eyelashes. A huge black shape was kneeling at my side, his fingers on the pulse in my neck. It had to be Ing-aa.

"Majesty! Forgive me!" He sounded heartbroken, or . . .

"Forgive you? Why?"

"My Queen . . ." No, not heartbroken. I had heard that tone in the ants' nest. The fingers on my throat trembled.

"I want no fools in my service." Her voice cut like a butcher's knife. "Go to the pens and make yourself useful there."

"Oh, Great One . . . I beg you . . ." The giant was whining. A drop of water fell on my chest.

The spinster spoke again, less harshly. "Your strength will serve me well, and if you make amends, then later we shall see . . ."

Ing-aa moaned, and rose. I closed my eyes. Feet squelched in the mud and were gone.

Ayasseshas's voice again: "Um-oao, Ah-uhu? Bear him gently. Put him in the shade. I shall see to him shortly, when I have thanked all these brave fellows."

Hands lifted me and rushed me away. I heard gravel, then bare feet on boards, as I felt myself raised up steps. Continuing to feign unconsciousness, I was gently laid down. The footsteps departed.

I seemed to be alone, but I lay still, pondering what I had learned. I had value—that was very hopeful. But what were the *pens* that could so terrify a colossus like Ing-aa? Pens implied livestock, and Shisisannis had mentioned pasture. I could still hear a bleating in the distance, but the only punishment that came to mind was mucking out stalls, and a trivial indignity like that would hardly provoke such obvious dread.

I had been laid on a rug, I thought, and a cautious glance showed a roof of beams and woven leaves far above. Quick looks to each side . . . I was lying in a sort of porch, stretched out on a thick woolen rug over what must be a plank floor. I raised my head and confirmed my assumptions.

There was no one watching. I sat up and felt only a passing dizziness. I heaved myself back a few feet to lean against a wall, then rubbed the scrapes I had acquired in my fall. There was a door at my side, so my guess of a porch had been correct. In the center, two chairs and a table sat on another richly patterned rug. The only real furniture I had ever seen had belonged to the ants, and this was much finer than theirs, gleaming bright. I knew the style of the rugs. They had come from the grasslands, tough woollie yarn in bright colors, although the specific designs were none that my mother and aunts had ever used. My trader experience wondered how much they had cost here, so far from their birthplace.

Beyond the shadowed veranda the sun blazed on the apron of white gravel. At the far edge of this stood Shisisannis and his little band, black men and dark brown, still in their line of inspection. Only Ing-aa had gone. The spinster was working her way along the line, welcoming each man in his turn. At her back stood two more of the tall swampmen bearing swords, a personal bodyguard. As I watched, Ayasseshas rose on tiptoe again to embrace one of her champions. How did one woman so bewitch so many men?

And in the shadows of the huts beyond the snake totem pole, I saw again those strange hooded and gowned figures . . . solitary, motionless, and apparently watching. Who were they, and why so idle?

"What happened to your knees?"

I twisted around in alarm. One of the brown-shrouded people was standing in a dark corner, beside the door. I had overlooked him . . . or possibly her, although it had sounded more male than female. There was no way to tell who or what was inside that garment, and I could see nothing but darkness within the peephole in the hood.

"How do you know about those?" I asked warily.

Just when I had decided that he would not reply, he uttered a curious little gasping sigh and said, "The lady told me she was buying a wetlander, but his knees were damaged."

"How many wetlanders are there here?"

"Just me. And now you."

My heart sank at the news. I had hoped for more company. But conversely, this stranger must be very glad to have me join him.

"I am Quetti." His voice was muffled by the hood, but there was also an odd quality to it that I could not place.

"Knobil."

"That is not a wetlander name."

"My father was a wetlander, I think. My mother was of the herdfolk."

"That explains . . ." He paused again, this time for longer. Then again he sighed. ". . . that explains your size."

"What about my size?"

"You are too big for a wetlander. We are slighter."

I thought of Orange-brown-white, the ants' captive and the only wetlander I had ever met. He had been a slim, small man. "My mother was little, though."

"Herdwomen bear large sons." The curious quality in my unseen companion's voice was a jumpiness, a quaver. "You're as big as Shisisannis!" He sounded annoyed at that.

I had believed myself a dwarf in my youth, but now I knew I was as tall as the men of most races. Swimming, and then slavery, had given me fair bulk, so what he said was perhaps true, but why did it matter?

"Who are those people, the ones dressed like us?"

"Snakemen. Swampers. A couple of treefolk."

"But why are they being kept covered?"

"It is better to be out of doors than shut up in the pens."

"She just sent Ing-aa to the pens. What—"

"I saw. But he will be of little use at pasture. The lady has told me often: Small as I am, to her I am worth fifty like Ing-aa."

"And me also?" I asked cautiously.

"More, I suppose," he agreed grumpily, his tone showing a trace of the jealousy I had expected in Shisisannis and Ing-aa. "There is more of you."

My questions were not bringing me much wisdom. How much time did I have to cross-examine this cryptic Quetti? Could I trust whatever he might tell me? I glanced out at the spinster. She was nearing the end of the row, embracing one of the snake-men. "How does she do that?" I asked. "Can she really reward so many men with her favors?"

Quetti chuckled dryly under his hood. "She rewards mostly with promises. And pretty ribbons. Shisisannis, sometimes . . ." Again a long pause, another sigh. "The rest of us rarely get more than words. Even me! Um-oao and Ah-uhu do better, I think."

So Ayasseshas was largely a tease? That made the men's ensorcelment even more imcomprehensible. Or did it? "I don't understand!"

"You will."

"And no one has ever told me what a spinster wants with wetlanders."

He grunted. "Do you know why they are called spinsters?"

"Not even that."

"Then you—" He choked. "Wait!" I heard a foot tapping, and he seemed to shrink slightly. He was breathing hard.

"What's wrong?" I asked as the silence lengthened. "Are you ill?"

He shook his head but did not speak, and he was curiously hunched. I rolled over on my belly and levered myself upright. I took a couple of rolling steps toward him, but he held up a hand, draped in its too-long sleeve. He made his curious heavy-breathing noise again, and relaxed.

"You're in pain!" I said.

"Of course." He was proud that I had not realized sooner.

I shook my hands free from my sleeves, reached out to unfasten his hood and push it back so I could see what he looked like. He did not resist, but he stared up at me resentfully.

He was barely more than a boy, his moustache downy, his beard too faint to hide the dimple in his chin. A mop of golden waves framed a thin, rather sulky face. His eyes were a pale, pale blue, like the far end of the sky.

I had thought I was light-colored after my long confinement in Misi's cab, but Quetti's skin was white as raw fish, marked with a single tattoo, a red snake as wide as my finger, running from his hairline, down between his eyes, and then curving off across his cheek to vanish under one ear. It stood out starkly on his pallor, uglier even than the tattoos on the dark snakemen.

I offered my hand. He hesitated, then pulled a sleeve back to respond, but he did not return my smile. His fingers were long and delicate—and white—but I felt the remains of fading calluses.

"How did you come here?" I asked.

"I was a pilgrim. I was caught by . . . Uh!"

He hunched his shoulders, screwed up his eyes, and twisted back his lips to show clenched teeth. I saw sweat break out on his face, and this time he could not suppress groans. Not just pain . . . the kid was in agony. His white skin seemed to go even whiter, and I wondered if he was about to faint. My own heart began to pound, but whether out of sympathy for him or from rising terror for myself, I was not sure. Then Quetti released his breath in one of those long gasps I had heard earlier, and opened his eyes.

I reached out to steady him.

"Don't touch me!" His pallor turned to pink under my stare, and he scowled. "That was a bad one!" He was defensive, ashamed of displaying weakness.

"Then . . . sit down," I said, gesturing at one of the chairs.

"I can't. Not just at the moment."

"Why not, for Heaven's sake?"

"Because I have other, more important uses for . . ." He closed his eyes again, but the fit was briefer and less severe. By now I was sweating also.

*What happened to your face?* The wide red band was not a tattoo. It was a raw, weeping sore, as if a long strip of skin had been ripped right off. Where it reached his scalp, the hair had gone also, leaving a narrow canyon only partly concealed by his waves.

He raised his cotton-fluff eyebrows, showing ironic amusement at my ignorance. "A graze."

"God!" What was hidden under that robe? "You've been flogged?"

"Flogged?" He laughed. "I wish I had. So what happened to your knees, herdman?"

"An ant held them on an anvil, and a blacksmith smashed them with a sledgehammer."

"You don't have much luck, do you?"

"It got me out of the ants' nest."

"You should have stayed."

I was about to ask why, when Quetti turned his head. I followed his gaze and saw that the inspection was over. Ayasseshas was approaching across the gravel, with her two bodyguards at her heels. The band that had brought me were running off across the muddy compound, dismissed.

"Those two with her . . ."

"Ah-uhu and Um-oao," Quetti said. "The pride of my lady's herd."

I had thought Ing-aa to be a giant, but these two snakemen could have made three of him. Their black skins shone in the sun, oiled to show the ripple of their muscles, while their high red feather headdresses emphasized their height. Heavy gold chains around their waists supported brief pagnes of shimmering, translucent water silk, and they had gold bands on their arms and legs. Wide-bladed swords flashed at their sides. A woman who collected men could have found no more impressive specimens, nor have displayed them more outrageously.

And the spinster herself . . . I had been avoiding looking at this terror, but as she mounted the steps to the porch, I forced my eyes to their duty. She was a snakewoman, dark skinned and stocky. Her shiny black hair was tightly braided and piled on the top of her head, pinned tight and decorated with yellow butterflies. From neck to golden sandals, her robe of many-hued water silk iridesced and flickered, but it did not mask the snake tattoos in blue and red that writhed over her belly, squirming up from between her thighs in coils and curves, ending in fanged jaws poised to engorge her nipples. More red and blue serpents wriggled upon her neck and face.

She was of about my age, with youth a memory and decay not yet a dread. Her body had started to thicken, but her limbs seemed muscular rather than fat. Her breasts were generous, but they did not droop enough ever to have suckled babies. She had power—not only the inexplicable authority that ruled her army, but pure physical strength also. Spinsterhood is no occupation for weaklings, of course, but I had not yet realized what it entailed, or what price she paid to encoil each one of her slaves.

Her eyes were fixed on mine. I felt tiny shivers all over my

skin, and I backed away as she approached, discovering that my
ability to walk backward was unimpaired. She was only a
woman, I told myself, but I had heard too many hints and had
already seen too much not to fear her. I stopped when I reached
the wall, and I still could not tear loose from the hypnotic stare.

But when she reached Quetti she turned to him, ignoring me
and drawing in breath with a sudden hiss. "My poor boy! How
you are suffering!"

He was not quite as tall as she. "It missed my eye."

"Ah, but you are in pain."

"I will survive."

She took his face between her hands. "I weep for you. I
should not have asked, not until you were older."

"I am a man!"

"But I know you are, Quetti, my special one. You showed
that when we first met—mightily you showed me. I do not doubt
your manhood, and you are proving it again now, even more."

"I promised you . . ." His voice quavered. "I promised you
twelve."

"And you still have so many?"

"Thirteen."

"My beloved!" Her tone was that of a mother, not a lover.
She leaned forward and pressed her lips to his, still holding his
face, but not letting their bodies touch.

Quetti's ashen face flamed red. "And they must be almost
done?"

"Very near. Not long now."

"Thirteen is good, isn't it, lady?"

"It is very good. Much more than I truly expected. Wonderful
for your size. Did you see what happened with that idiot Ing-
aa? No matter how long he endures, or how many crops he
yields, all of it will not be worth a fraction of what you are doing
for me now, Quetti, my dear one."

He nodded and tried to smile, but I saw the signs of agony
build in his face again—livid lips, and sweat. He was trying to
conceal it from Ayasseshas, but she pulled his head down to her
breast to comfort. For a long moment there was silence and no
movement except a wild fluttering from one of the yellow butterflies imprisoned in her hair.

Then the fluttering stopped, and Quetti sighed and straightened up. "I will deliver on my promise, my lady, and I do not mind a little pain if I can please you."

"Oh, you make me very happy, dear Quetti. And when you have delivered on your promise, then we must let you heal, and I shall call on you to partner me often, for your beauty gives me more joy than any. Are you eating properly?"

"It is hard, my lady."

"You must keep up your strength—for now, and for later. I need strong men to satisfy me, my love. Go and try, dearest, for my sake . . . and try also to get some rest."

She kissed him again and then closed his hood over his blushes. Again an anonymous, shrouded figure, he turned away and floated obediently toward the steps.

This had to be why the men in the canoes had driven themselves to exhaustion. They had been proving—to the others and to themselves—that they could endure pain, because their mistress would demand it of them. I did not know what was causing Quetti's torment, or why this monster desired it . . . and I most certainly did not want to find out.

Now she turned to me again and looked me over coyly, with a sudden change from mother-love to seduction. She smiled, but it was a strange smile, keeping her thick and sensuous lips closed over her teeth.

"Welcome, wetlander."

"I am Knobil."

"I know." She reached a hand for the door and glanced at her guards. "Ah-uhu? Wash him and bring him in when he is ready." Then she was gone.

I did not know which was Ah-uhu and which Um-oao, but when one said "Strip!" I stripped. The other had leapt from the porch with a force that had shaken the whole building, sprinting away across the compound. Soon he came running back, bearing a huge steaming bucket in each hand.

These human mountains were as large as some herdmen I had known and they obviously enjoyed favored status in the spinster's retinue. Yet they now proceeded to play body servant to me, sponging me vigorously with hot water and rubbing suds in my hair and beard. One of them even screwed a massive fingertip around inside my ears until I thought my brains would squirt out. They dried me with soft towels, and trimmed the nails on my fingers and toes. They rubbed me all over with scented oil. Not a word was spoken until they were finished. Then one of them reached out to open the door and growled, "Go in!"

"But I have no clothes!" I protested weakly.

He stared down at me with both contempt and disbelief.

I went in to meet the spinster.

# 3

The room was large and bright and high-roofed, constructed from massive timbers. A glimpse through the far windows revealed another wide expanse of mud, more of the pot-shaped huts, and part of the incomplete stockade, so I knew that this palace must stand in the exact center of the compound. Before me were thick rugs and many gaudy, shiny things scattered around. Yet little of it all registered, for my mind was quivering with apprehension at meeting the fearsome spinster, and my eyes soon fixed themselves on her.

She was reclining on an expanse of rugs and cushions in the center of the floor, an island of turquoise, vermilion, and bronze. Beside her, on a very low table, were silver dishes of fruits and breads, bottles and goblets of gold, and plates of brightly colored sweetmeats.

I stopped to stare, and my buttocks received a slap hard enough to make me stagger.

"Go to her!" growled the giant behind me. I began to roll forward unwillingly in my stiff-kneed gait, aware that he had closed the door and taken up station beside it. The other, I assumed, had remained outside.

Ayasseshas was wearing only her butterflies and her tattoos. As I approached, she stretched out languorously, reaching for a gold fruit from the table, while the snakes seemed to slither over her smooth brown curves. She bit into the fleshy globe, juice gleaming on her lips, and she looked up at me with a glance of challenge.

I had spent most of my adult life penned like an animal in the ants' compound, so my own nudity bothered me little. Yet hers did. Many times I had drawn near to a naked woman, and always with eagerness, with every intention of taking from her as much pleasure as my stamina would allow. There was a peculiarly sinister fascination in those ribbons of color on Ayasseshas's body, and she was a luscious, imposing woman, strong and tempting. She could hardly have been more obviously available. She would be a stimulating partner—inventive in cooperation, tantalizing in opposition, and uncomplaining in subjugation. Yet now I came to a halt at her feet, nonplussed, feeling a revulsion that could have been no greater had she been clad in real serpents.

My reluctance seemed to surprise her as much as it did me. "Sit here, Knobil," she said, patting a cushion at her side. "We shall get to know each other . . . intimately." She sent me a smile that again seemed oddly forced. A skilled seductress should be able to smile better than that.

"What do you require of me, woman?"

She frowned, leaned back, and stared up at me appraisingly.

"You cannot venture a guess? Most of my visitors, when in your situation, are already displaying a certain readiness to satisfy my requirements."

"Obviously I am not, although I mean no disrespect."

She sighed. "Well, we can talk. Now sit, or I shall have Umoao assist you."

I let myself fall forward on the pillows, and then rolled over and sat up. She turned to lean on one elbow, facing me. Her scent was strong and musky, yet even her nearness was inducing no desire in me.

She stroked my thigh with a gentle finger. "You are not quite as pale as Quetti yet, but you are very fair, wetlander."

"I was raised as a herdman."

"Indeed? Do herdmen prefer a more subtle approach?"

"To be honest, they wouldn't know subtlety from rape—nor care. The fault is not yours, lady. You are comely."

Ayasseshas sighed again. "Then we must be patient. Tell me your story while we wait, herdman."

She was dangerous, and I was utterly in her power. To anger her further would be great folly, so I obeyed, recounting my history. She watched me carefully as I spoke.

"Poor man! Well, you are safe here." She sat up also, brazenly cross-legged. "Can I offer you refreshment now?"

The sight of food on the table had already made my mouth water, but I was deeply suspicious. "Thank you, no. Mistress, tell me what you want of me."

"Again I say that it is obvious." For the first time she revealed her teeth. They were large and white, but badly placed, protruding in front, and crooked. I realized that the enigmatic quality of her smile was merely an attempt to conceal this flaw in her beauty.

"You did not give the traders so much silk for just one more bed partner, when you have so many already."

"But golden hair excites me." She ran her finger down my chest. "No salutes yet? I do begin to feel slighted, Knobil."

I had flinched at her touch. "I have no wish to insult you, lady. My lack of response is not deliberate."

"But why? Your tastes do not run to Um-oao, surely?"

"Certainly not!"

"Quetti would be a safer choice?"

"Neither of them!"

She laughed, and I discovered that I had just smiled.

"You must have lain with women before?"

I had lain with hundreds, but I merely said, "Yes."

"Is it fear that troubles you? Are you afraid of me?"

"Perhaps. I do not know what horrors you have in store."

She frowned. "No horrors! As you guessed, I paid dearly for you, so I will cherish and guard you. Of course I hope that you will choose to remain in my service, but any small tasks you may agree to perform for me will be entirely voluntary. You are certainly in no danger at the moment . . . unless your callous rejection should rouse my wrath, of course?" She raised a mocking eyebrow and again displayed her dagger teeth.

Ayasseshas was a skilled manipulator of men. She was running through her repertoire, seeking what would work best on me.

"I see that," I admitted. "I am not a brave man, lady, and I do not mean to defy you. I do not think it is fear."

She glanced toward the giant by the door. "Is it Um-oao? I promise you that he is not here to chaperone me. Do as you will with me, Knobil. He will interfere only if he thinks I am in danger of serious injury. He has never restrained an overardent lover yet, although an enthusiastic snakeman treats a woman much as his constrictor treats it prey."

An audience would not deter me. "Not he."

"You love another?"

"I do." Misi had betrayed me, yet I loved her still.

The spinster pouted. "She is more fair than I?"

Misi was ugly. She was obscenely fat and hairy, and I knew that. Yet had she been in Ayasseshas's place, I should have clasped her to me with rapture. "No, lady, she is less fair than you."

"Then you wish to remain faithful to her?"

I considered that possibility, and then shook my head. There was almost no chance in the world that I should ever see my darling again. She would never know nor care if I took other women, and most certainly she would feel no obligation to me.

Ayasseshas shrugged and sighed. The serpents around her breasts writhed. "I am at a loss! Tell me the answer, then."

Hesitantly I said, "Partly it is this—I heard how you spoke to Shisisannis and Ing-aa. You praised each for his virility in the other's hearing . . . and the same with the rest of the men, I expect. You made a mockery of their manhood. Somehow you have unmanned them all, lady, and I fear that you will cast your witchcraft on me if I accept your offer now."

She gave me a glance of exaggerated astonishment. "*Unmanned?* I swear to you that the last time I checked, there was no detectable flaw in Shisisannis's manhood—neither quantity nor quality. Ing-aa always travels the same predictable road, but the distance he can journey on it is astonishing . . . Unmanned? I have not lowered their manhood, Knobil. I wish I could do something to raise yours!"

I suppose I had nothing to lose. I became rash. "It is unnatural for many men to share one woman!"

Ayasseshas hissed softly. "A herdman, you said? How many—"

"That's quite different!"

Her eyes were cold as shining pebbles. "In what way, exactly?"

The question was so absurd that I think I spluttered before I found an answer. "Babies, for one thing. A herdmaster can breed many children at the same time. How many can you carry, lady? Do you bear sons for all your lovers?''

She sighed. ''Knobil, babies are not what I seek from them. Truly, babies are not my purpose! But if you think you can quicken my womb, then you are welcome to try. Most welcome.''

I shook my head and looked away.

''What does deter you? Am I so ugly?''

''No . . . try to understand this, then, lady. I see no great passion in you, either. You offer yourself to me like a plate of meat. It is brutal and demeaning. You think that because a woman is available, a man must be willing. It is no reflection on my manhood that I spurn you, for you strive somehow to use my body—and use it against me, although I know not how.''

''Goodness!'' the spinster muttered. She stretched out in her sensual fashion, reaching for a grape, and again I watched the play of color on her skin. ''You never *use* a woman? You do it only for love? You never seek to find pleasure, only to give it?''

''Share it.''

''Mmm?'' As if pondering, she held the grape for a moment in those meat-red lips, and then sucked it in, with an audible *plop*! ''They say a man never forgets his first time. Who showed you how, Knobil?''

I know that I blushed furiously, but there was challenge in her eyes. ''A woman on the grasslands, when I was traveling with the angel.''

Ayasseshas took another grape and smiled at it. ''Angels do not *use* women?''

Indeed they did, and all those unfortunate herdwomen whom the addle-headed Violet had so callously thrown my way—I had *used* them without scruple, for my own selfish pleasure. I had even reveled in his praise for a job well done, not recognizing how he had been infecting me with his own twisted bitterness.

''And what of the women in the seafolk's grove?'' That must have been a guess, but her aim was deadly. I could not reply, for I had *used* them to advertise my superior virility.

''And in the ants' nest? Did you find love there, Knobil?''

That was the worst of all.

''What you say is true, mistress. Yes, I have *used* women in the past, but since then I have come to know love. I see now

that men and women should come together in a giving of pleasure, or at least a sharing, and not simply a taking. I do not
think you expected pleasure from me, and I seek no debts to
you.''

"How sweet! And who taught you this great truth?''

Sudden caution tempered my rashness. I must not be too
specific about Misi, lest I somehow expose her to the spinster's
envy. "I told you, lady . . . I love another.''

Ayasseshas stretched her arms overhead and yawned, as if
weary. "Well, this has been a fascinating conversation. I am
always willing to listen to talk of love . . . so ethereal a subject
. . . and you are quite the most pompous man I have ever met.
But now, wetlander, you will fornicate with me, and I shall be
satisfied with nothing less than total exhaustion. If you are unable to rise to the occasion, I have means to assist you.'' She
reached for a goblet on the table.

"It makes tall tree grow in forest?''

She smiled, showing those protruding incisors again. "Usually I reserve it to blow on embers—for maximum effect, you
understand—but in your case it will evidently be required to
ignite the tinder. Drink, guest!''

I thought of my wild frenzy when Misi had given me such a
potion, and the memory of how I had treated her shamed me
anew. I could guess that the brew might be dangerous to me,
but I had survived before, and I would have no compunction
about being rough with Ayasseshas, even had her bodyguard not
been standing by the door. What man could resist a chance to
experience again that firestorm of ecstasy, passion magnified
and prolonged beyond endurance, and farther yet? For the first
time, the potential of the situation began to arouse some reaction
in me. Of course that did not escape Ayasseshas's notice.

"And if I refuse to drink?''

She leaned very close. "I will persuade you.'' Her dark eyes
gazed unblinkingly into mine, and I felt a cool hand slither
gently up my thigh.

My heartbeat had begun to rise, yet I returned her steady gaze.
"How?''

"Um-oao will sit on your legs, Ah-uhu will hold your arms,
and I shall pull your testicles down to your knees.''

Some truths are self-evident. For a long, silent moment we

were eye to eye, while her fingers continued their encouragement. "That would be a convincing argument," I said. "Your logic is inescapable."

"It has never failed. Bottoms up, lover!"

I took the goblet and drained it, wincing at the familiar foul taste.

Ayasseshas smiled and released me. She leaned back on her piled cushions and wriggled herself comfortable. "Proceed when ready, man."

"It takes a moment or two," I said. "So while we wait, tell me what a spinster does with a wetlander. I truly do not know, lady."

That surprised her. "Indeed? I thought you were being courageous. You are merely ignorant?"

"I told you—I am a herdman. We are expected to be ignorant."

"You were serious with all that talk of love? Astounding! Well, you know how silk is made?"

My heart was pounding wildly now, and my belly was a furnace. It did not feel quite the same as the time before, though.

"No," I said. My eyelids were prickling.

"Silk," said Ayasseshas, "is . . . How do you know it takes a moment or two?"

"I've had it before."

"No!" She sat up, staring. "You lie!"

I could not speak—my throat was too constricted. A strange throbbing filled my head, and my lips seemed to be swelling and turning outward. I could barely keep my eyes open, so swollen were the lids now. Vaguely I could hear Ayasseshas screaming for her guards, and then I sank down into a thick blackness. I was trying to vomit and I could not even breathe. Other people had invaded the room and were clutching at me. I roused briefly as something hard was forced down my throat, and I knew that death was very near.

# 4

It was not I who died, though; it was the giant Ah-uhu. Much of what happened I learned later from young Quetti. Restless, suffering, unable to settle, he had returned to stand in his favorite place outside Ayasseshas's door, as close to his beloved as he could be without annoying her. Any other would have been chased away by the guards, but a wetlander was precious and had privilege. When Ayasseshas started screaming for aid, when Um-oao went racing off to fetch Othisosish, when many others were flocking freely in and out of the palace, then Quetti drifted inside also to watch.

The long-ago saint, Issirariss, in his treatise on the virgin's web, had noted that it was dangerous. He did not mention that a second dose is guaranteed to be fatal. The body cannot twice withstand such maltreatment, and even a tiny trace of the drug will provoke a reaction quick and deadly. I may be the only man who has ever survived it.

My survival was due entirely to Othisosish, Ayasseshas's resident medicine man. The oldest person in the settlement, he was also the only one not bound to her by the imprinting effect of the virgin's web. She had his loyalty without it, for he was her father. Um-oao was sent for Othisosish. Luckily for me, he found him at once, and brought him and his bag of magics back at a gallop, bearing him bodily like a child.

By that time my face had turned black, Quetti said, but Othisosish rammed a tube down my throat to give me air. Then he applied the venom of the yellow log snake. It is a tiny, deadly killer, whose bite is almost always fatal. The venom can be extracted from the poison glands, and in very small amounts it is a potent physic, but to slaughter the snake and make the extraction takes time. There was no time, so Othisosish used the only other means available to him. No swampman could be worth as much as a wetlander, and Ah-uhu died to serve his beloved. The snake was then applied to my arm for a second bite. Even that may sometimes kill, but I was lucky. My recovery was as miraculously speedy as the onset of the symptoms. I found myself alive, suspended upside down by Um-oao while I vomited out blood and Ayasseshas's love potion all over her precious rugs.

By the time I was capable of speech, some sort of order was returning. Ah-uhu's body had been removed, and men were busily cleaning up the mess. Others stood around, nervously watching Ayasseshas as she strode to and fro, screaming curses.

She had not thought to dress herself, but they would all have watched her anyway. Quetti lurked in a corner, shrouded in his long burnoose, unnoticed or merely ignored.

The spinster stopped her pacing to come and stand over me as I lay sprawled on cushions. My throat was raw, my swollen right arm smoldered, and my heart hammered strangely. I had never felt more ill in my life.

"He will live?" she demanded.

"He will live," Othisosish replied. He was behind me, and I had not seen him, but I was not paying much attention to anything. "He will be as good as new very shortly." He cackled. "Let him rest—he will be little use in bed for a while now."

"He wasn't before, either," the spinster said. "How do you feel, wetlander?"

I croaked wordlessly.

"Tell me about this woman you love, the one less fair than I."

That mention of Misi cut through my nausea and giddiness. I thought how wonderful it would be to have her fold me once more in her great arms, to hug me as she had done before when I was sick. "Trader," I whispered.

Ayasseshas knelt at my side to take my hand. "Describe her."

I was still much too befuddled to work out why the spinster should be interested in Misi, but not so confused that I could not sense danger. "Beautiful, too."

"Old? Young?"

"Just . . . beautiful," I mumbled, being cautious.

"Shisisannis, come here!"

"My Queen?" The burly young snakeman appeared in my foggy field of view, then knelt opposite Ayasseshas on the other side of me. I had heard her send him off to bed like a child, but he had apparently been summoned back.

"Did you see any trader women when you picked up this rubbish?"

Serpents twisted as he grinned. "I saw two. There was an old, fat one in brown and a younger one in a green dress, driving the wagon."

"Which one do you love, Knobil?"

"Young one. Pula."

Ayasseshas smiled grimly. "Go and fetch her in haste, Shisisannis my champion. The wagon will not have gone far, and a blind man could follow that trail.''

"They may have joined up with other wagons, Goddess. There were eight men there.''

"No matter. Bring this Pula to me as fast as you can.''

I sighed with relief. My instincts had been correct.

Shisisannis looked me over as if planning how best to skin me, and then smiled. "There will be a fight, of course. Angels may hear of it . . . I shall slay all the witnesses.''

*"NO!"*

He chuckled. "The fat one is the one you want, Majesty. He cried out to her, and she said he was a great lover.''

"Ah, Shisisannis, my joy!'' Ayasseshas leaned across me to touch her tongue to his cheek. "You are wise as well as courageous, crafty as well as loyal, valiant and virile also. When you return, you shall replace poor Ah-uhu as my guard.''

"Majesty!''

"And since you will have a fight anyway . . . why not have a good one? Take all the canoes, and as many men as they will hold. Return my silk—and anything else of value that catches your eye. You bring the fat woman here at once. The others can follow later, when they are loaded.''

"It will be a joy to me, my Queen. We shall burn the wagons and slaughter the beasts, of course.'' He rubbed a tattoo thoughtfully. "What about the men? Trader men are small, but quite pale.''

Ayasseshas laughed and patted his thigh. The two of them were obviously enjoying planning their massacre, as excited as children. I rattled my fuddled brains in vain, searching for some way to save Misi or distract the spinster.

"Trader men are small,'' the spinster agreed, "but very fast! Of course, if you manage to trap any that look healthy, bring them, but I expect that they will all be off over the hills as soon as they see you. Do not pursue. You could never catch them.''

"As you command, my Goddess, my Queen.''

She clasped his big hand. "Be careful, lover, and hurry back. You will then be with me always.''

"Lady!'' I wailed. "Do not do this, I beg!'' My throat burned with every word. "Spare the traders and I will do whatever you ask of me.''

"Will you indeed?" Ayasseshas shook her head. "You will do what I want, yes, but only if I hold this trader sow as hostage."

"No!" I forced myself to sit up, although my belly squirmed with nausea. "I swear I will obey you, and be loyal, and serve you."

"But you don't know what I require of my followers, do you, Knobil? You said you did not know."

"No, but whatever it is, I will do it, if only you will leave the traders alone."

"Quetti!"

Men backed away uneasily. Shisisannis rose and stepped aside as the brown-shrouded figure floated forward.

"Lady?"

"Show him your babies, Quetti, my dear. Show him the little ones you bear for me. Teach this ignorant herdman how silk is made."

In silence Quetti opened his hood and threw it back to reveal his face. He stared wanly at me, and I thought that the shadow of pain around his pale blue eyes was even darker than before. There was a lump of white jelly adhering to his cheek, an ugly slug shape as big as a man's finger.

Seeing that I still did not understand, he smiled lopsidedly, unfastened his robe, and held it wide. Some of the other twelve silkworms he was pasturing were not visible, but I saw enough of them, and enough of what they were doing to him, to understand at last.

Had my throat permitted, then, I am sure I should have screamed. As it was, I made a terrible scene, blubbering and pleading in a frantic whisper that changed nothing. My weeping continued even after Shisisannis and most of the other men had departed on their mission of death and pillage.

Returning from her farewells at the door, Ayasseshas scowled at me in disgust. "Um-oao?" she said. "Othisosish said he should rest. Take him over to the pens and tether him. He is no use here."

"And have him seeded, Majesty?"

"Why not? Yes! He is pale enough to get started. And hurry back, big bull. I am much in need of loving."

# 10

## Red-yellow-green

A circle of huts, a half-completed stockade, a forest beyond—these defined the compound. As Um-oao jogged across the mud with my limp form draped over his shoulder, I realized that there were no pens in sight, only huts and more huts. The noises I had thought made by livestock were coming from the huts to which I was being taken, and now I knew what made those noises. A human throat can scream only so long before it stops sounding human.

The journey was so short that Um-oao had not bothered to cover me again, and the sun was warm on my bare skin. He reached his objective, pulled aside a drape, and ducked through into hot darkness. Then he expertly flipped me onto my back. I yelled, expecting to crash on the ground, but I landed instead on a tightly stretched sheet of black silk. I bounced and came to rest, whimpering about my knees.

Um-oao grabbed my right ankle and began to tie it. I sat up, and he cuffed me back like a child. In moments he had skillfully trussed me, spread-eagled and quite helpless. Ignoring my questions, he vanished out the door, returning to his mistress. Gloom became darkness as the curtain fell over the opening, and I was alone with the pounding of my heart.

My wrists and ankles had been bound with twine leading to

the corners of the frame, but loosely enough that I could raise my head and peer around. There seemed to be four of these beds—or stalls, or sties, or whatever I wished to call them. I could see, and smell, the stinking wooden bucket under each, and feel the hole in the silk below my buttocks. Then I sensed that I was not alone.

"Who's that?"

"Ing-aa," said a voice from my left, a deep voice.

I tried to see him, but a naked black man on black silk was not very conspicuous in near darkness. And another—I could hear something on the bed across from me. Each breath was a bubbling whimper.

"Who's that?"

"Don't know his name." Ing-aa's tone showed little interest. "They call him 'Old Faithful.' He's been here a long time. Longer than any, I think."

"He can't talk?"

"No one can talk when he's been here a long time, wetlander. We endure until we can endure no more. Then go mad, then die. Old Faithful just hasn't died, that's all. She takes crop after crop off him, and he just won't die."

I shuddered. The heat and stench were making my stomach heave again.

"You must have displeased my lady?" Like Shisisannis, Ing-aa seemed quite willing to be friendly, although either of them would joyfully have eaten me raw, had Ayasseshas suggested it.

"I have used that love potion before. It did not work on me."

"You are to be pitied. It is the memory of that glorious loving that makes all this worthwhile."

"*Worthwhile?* Have you been . . . seeded?"

"Yes."

"Does it hurt?"

"They haven't hatched yet. They only tickle at first, anyway . . . so I'm told."

My bonds cut into me if I pulled at them. They were silk, I supposed; thin but strong. "You've got muscles, swampman. Can't you break loose?"

"I'm not tied."

"What? Then . . . you're just lying there, with . . . with whatever those things are . . . crawling on you?"

"I told you—they haven't hatched yet. I have to lie flat until they're big enough to hang on."

Then light flared bright again, painfully bright, as an elderly man pulled open the drape. White hair gleamed above me as he inspected my bonds.

"I've brought a present for you, wetlander." He wheezed a sort of chuckle and spread a large leaf on my chest. It felt cool and damp, but its coolness was not the cause of the shiver that convulsed me then. I looked over at Ing-aa. In the light from the doorway, I could see that there was a leaf lying on him also.

"Eggs?"

"Silkworm eggs," the old man agreed. "Thirty of them. Try to rear as many as you can and please the lady. The more you carry to the end the longer you get to heal afterward."

I think I would have cursed him and Ayasseshas most roundly then, but another shadow blocked the light for a moment. It dropped its garment, and I recognized Quetti. His pale skin was scrolled with dark lines of raw flesh, as if his slender frame was wrapped in a giant fishnet. He moved to the one vacant bed.

"Help me, please?" His young voice quavered more noticeably than it had earlier. Assisted by the old man, Quetti managed to stretch out on the silk without damage to any of the vile parasites clinging on him.

He raised his head to look across at me. "Us wetlanders have to stick together, Knobil." If that was humor, there was no joy in it; it might be an appeal for comfort. He was holding three fingers over one eye—the sluglike silkworm had almost reached it. An oozing red stripe on his neck and cheek showed where it had grazed his skin on its way there. Another was progressing along his forearm, and there were two in his armpit. I retched and looked away without speaking. I had no sympathy to spare for Quetti.

He lay back with a sigh. "Othisosish? You'll come and tie me soon, when it's gone by?"

"That I will, lad," the old man replied gently. The drape fell back behind him.

For a moment there was dark silence, broken by the mindless

whimpers from the *thing* on the bed across from me and the animal wailings from other huts nearby.

"How can you do that?" I yelled at Quetti. "Just lie there and be eaten alive?"

"They only take the top layer. It grows back. Hardly a scar. Except for things like nipples, of course."

"But it hurts?"

"Oh yes, it hurts. Indeed it hurts. Especially when they get big like this . . . But they'll start spinning soon, and then it'll be all over."

"Until the next time?"

"Until my lady asks me to pasture another crop," he agreed.

I was drenched with sweat from the heat in that foul place, and yet my insides felt cold as death.

"The big ones are the worst?" Ing-aa asked in his deep voice.

There was no reply for a moment, while Quetti battled agony. Then he released one of the gasping sighs I had heard before and said, "No. The little ones. They burrow."

"Burrow?" I wailed.

"Ears . . . and things. I couldn't save this eye if this was a little one. It would get under my fingers. I've been lucky. I haven't lost anything important yet."

"But how can you just lie there and be eaten?"

There was a longer silence then, until he said sadly, "You still don't understand? I love Ayasseshas. We all do."

"But . . ."

"Who is this fat woman that Shisisannis has gone to fetch?"

"Her name is Misi."

"So when Misi gets here, Ayasseshas will untie you. It's best to be untied, and walking around . . . healthier. Force-feeding is a lot of work, and dangerous. The mad ones usually die from choking, while they're being fed. They often manage to rub the babies off against the silk, too. It's better to be up and free . . . and willing. Except for sleep. That's why I asked Othisosish to come back and tie me. I might pull them off in my sleep."

"Sleep? You can sleep?"

"I haven't slept in so long . . . Yes, I think I'll sleep."

His voice choked off in a whimper of pain, but he had said enough. I could see how Ayasseshas would give me a choice: I must nourish her crop of slugs, or she would pasture Misi instead. Misi was huge and would be capable of feeding many silkworms, but her skin was much darker than mine. Only wet-landers made water silk.

And when I went mad, then Misi would be trussed and cropped anyway. Even knowing that, I would not be able to refuse the spinster. I would try . . . but yet I was a coward. I did not think I could endure as Quetti was doing. Oh, Misi! I must not fail you!

"And it's that potion that does it, isn't it?" I said bitterly. "She gives you that and you copulate insanely, and after that you can refuse her nothing?"

"We worship her," Ing-aa said softly. "We will do even this to please her. I only wish I were white like you, wet-lander. The worms I shall feed will make black silk, of very little value, so I must try to endure much and give her many crops. But I am strong. I will bear anything to make her happy. Double-cropping . . . anything! She is my queen, my love."

"Love!" How could these deluded fools serve such a monster? I could guess now that Misi had trapped me in the same way as Ayasseshas ensnared her army. I had not realized earlier that my feelings for Misi had sprung from that diabolic potion. And yet, even knowing it, I loved her just as much. Love, it is said, is blind.

My companions' mindless obedience to the spinster seemed like inexplicable insanity to me. My love for Misi was a holy, joyful, precious thing.

Spread out helpless in the fetid dark, I lay for a long time, sorrowing for Misi, listening to occasional stifled sobs from Quetti and the rising, falling chorus of agony from other huts.

Hrarrh had known, of course. Ants knew more of Vernier than most races did, and his original tribe might even have dwelt within a forest. This was the vengeance he had wanted. Eventually some trader would come, offering water silk. Hrarrh would buy it for his wife, so she could have a bright-dyed gown to cover her squat ugliness. Every time he saw it he would savor his memories of me.

Hrarrh knew how my screams sounded. He could imagine the rest.

He would have his revenge in full.

Yet it was not the thought of Hrarrh that troubled me most. The blackness that choked me then was worse than anything he had done to me, anything I had known in the ants' nest. There, in the spinster's pen, in the darkest moment of my life, I was faced with the terrible knowledge that my whole life was a failure. I had failed the mother I had sworn to avenge, failed to follow through on my promise to become an angel, failed the seawoman I had married, failed to escape from the traders when that had been my intention, and now I had betrayed the woman I loved. Yes, I knew her faults, but no woman is perfect, and men must follow where their hearts lead them. I had betrayed Misi to the spinster. I had been unworthy of my beloved, and that is a man's ultimate failure.

I wept for Misi . . . only for Misi.

My chest had begun to itch.

# 2

My darling Misi . . . At first I had been fooled by her habitual pretense of stupidity. Later, blinded by love, I had overestimated her cunning.

Silk raising goes on all the time. In nature, the silkworms are tiny parasites of a small burrowing animal called a ground pig. Something in human skin delays their cocoon stage and allows them to grow into the monsters I had seen on Quetti. The eggs can be picked up around any ground pig burrow. It is not difficult to tie up a human victim and seed him, so there is always a small supply of silk trickling into the trade routes.

But, as Quetti had told me, it is hard to restrain an unwilling subject so firmly that he cannot scrape the worms off. It is hard to feed him for long against his will. The key to successful silk production is the virgin's web and voluntary pasturing. Male spinsters have been recorded, but they fare poorly, for any spinster is an unpopular neighbor, needing an army for both defense and recruitment. Female warriors are just not as effective as males.

Furthermore, black or dark-brown silk is of low value, and lighter skin is rarely available in the forests. Ants are a passable feedstock, if their dark hair is kept shaved. They, and the wolf-folk of the far north, yield a pale-tan silk, but real profit comes only from pure water silk, and only wetlanders will produce that. Whenever these lighter shades appear, or the overall supply of silk in the markets increases, then the angels know that a spinster has arisen. It happens, so I was told in Heaven, once or twice in every cycle. All other tasks except the most urgent are then set aside, as the angels move to track down this abomination.

When Black-white-red spoke to me at the angels' road-block, he knew immediately that I was not what I claimed to be. He knew that wetlander slaves, being very precious and yet not required to do physical labor, were usually crippled—a broken leg is more effective than shackles, and cheaper. A blue-eyed trader who could not walk did not fool Black at all. He knew also of the virgin's web, although its use had never been recorded outside the high forests. Misi's plot unraveled right away.

So Misi and I were allowed to proceed, and the angels followed, letting the unwitting victim lead them to the spinster. To track a trader train is absurdly easy. To keep watch on one man within it and yet remain undetected calls for much skill and even more luck. Fortunately Misi, being unable to ride a horse and yet determined to view the transfer of wealth, had insisted on taking her train to the actual rendezvous. That was a breach of custom and a serious error. When the angels saw that one train had left the group, they could guess that the exchange was about to be made. When I was carried off in Shisisannis's canoe, they were watching.

They had even thought to bring a canoe of their own with them—small, light, and speedy. Paddlers, unlike rowers, face forward, and Shisisannis had failed to keep close watch behind him on his way upstream, while his men had all been too intent on playing tougher-than-you to look back at all. Thus the angels' little scout craft had escaped detection. The rest of the force had followed more slowly, for sailboats do poorly on a winding river in a fitful wind, but they had all arrived at last near the spinster's lair. By the time they had concealed their chariots and taken some well-earned rest, Shisisannis had departed again, and suddenly the game was easy.

I had been asleep. I awakened with a start of terror. Quetti was still there, tied down. He raised his head, his pale face just visible enough to show the two crop markings that crossed it. He had saved his eye, at the cost of a little skin from his fingers, and the silkworm had vanished into his hair. Ing-aa had gone, his eggs having hatched. Old Faithful gurgled and moaned on the fourth bed.

My chest itched maddeningly. I tried to work out where the tiny horrors had got to. Not far yet . . . none near my groin, anyway . . .

"What was that noise?" Quetti whispered. His throat was likely as sore as mine, for he had screamed a lot in his sleep.

I thought back to what had wakened me. Before I could speak, the same noise roared again, several times.

"Guns!" I yelled. "The angels have come!"

Quetti wailed and began struggling against his bonds, but the silk cord was unbreakable. There were more shots, and voices shouting. "They'll kill her!"

"I hope so! I hope so!"

More shots . . . more shouts . . . running feet slapped mud, some close to the hut. I began to call for help, as loudly as I was able. Quetti cursed and moaned.

Again there was shooting, then a long, maddening silence.

At last I heard voices and decided they were coming closer. And closer . . . So slowly!

The drape was ripped from the doorway, tipping torrents of light into our eyes. A shadow blocked it, but it was not the outline of an angel in fringed buckskins. Quetti yelled with joy, and it was I who wailed in crushing despair, seeing another of the lanky black swampmen in a pagne, blurred against the brightness.

"Well, look who's here!" a deep voice said. "My old friend, Nob Bil! We meet again, trader?"

*"Get me out of here!"*

Chuckling, the newcomer cut one of my bonds, and then caught my hand as I reached for the unbearable itch on my chest. "Don't scratch them. Go out and let the sun do it for you."

He had to help me rise, but in a few moments I was outside, leaning back against the side of the hut and sniggering idiotically as the tiny maggots fell from my chest, slain by sunlight. I was too choked with relief to speak, yet I wanted to sing. I shivered uncontrollably, but I felt like dancing. I gulped deep breaths of the dank forest air and thought it was the finest perfume in the world. I had been given back my life. God bless the angels!

For the first time I had a decent view of Ayasseshas's log-built palace. It seemed enormous to me, and an impressive tribute to her power, but already flames streamed from the windows. Some of the huts had been torched now, also.

In a few moments Black-white dragged out Quetti, who struggled and screamed, trying to run back into the dark. But the slender young wetlander in his weakened state was no match for the tall swampman. Black just lifted him up and held him at arm's length, helplessly suspended.

"She's dead, I tell you!" he kept repeating. For a long time Quetti would not believe him, and continued to kick and squirm and rave, desperate to save the silkworms he had promised to the spinster. I thought that Black should let him finish a task so nearly complete. The silk would have made him wealthy, and surely he had earned it.

At last he accepted that Ayasseshas had been shot. Then he stood submissively. Tears trickled down his silver-fuzz cheeks as the slugs fell from him also, one by one.

Smoke was billowing through the compounds in acrid, eye-stinging clouds. The sun burned hot one moment and was a pallid white disk the next. We were all starting to cough.

I could see a few dead men lying around. Angels more formally clad than Black were stalking around, appearing and disappearing like wraiths in the haze, all bearing guns and obviously alert for trouble as they inspected the huts. Most seemed to be of lighter races than our swampman rescuer.

"I am very glad to see you, sir," I ventured at last. My wits were returning, my parasites had gone, and I had begun to wonder about clothes.

For a moment Black-white's habitual mournful expression

broke into a smile, although his eyes were streaming tears. "I was very glad to see you, wetlander. You led us here." He sighed, poking the sobbing Quetti, who was still as bare as I. "Turn around and toast your other side, lad. We'll have to find some oil or something for you." He started to cough.

Quetti rotated obediently, in silent misery.

"You followed me?" I asked, working it out.

"Right. Two-white and I work a mean paddle. We followed you, and the rest came after."

"You scared me just now, when you came in . . . How *did* you get in, anyway?"

We were interrupted then, but I heard later how the angels had triumphed by sheer audacity. Black and Two-white-lime had donned local costume and walked brazenly into the compound, unchallenged by the few remaining guards. As soon as they had killed Um-oao and captured Ayasseshas herself, the war had been over. Despite his melancholy manner, Black must have been feeling very pleased with himself.

Another angel had come strutting over to us, a small man whose sleeve proclaimed him to be Red-yellow-green. He was perky, cocky, and weatherbeaten, and so reminiscent of Lon Kiv that he could only be of trader stock. He rested the butt of his gun on the ground and pushed back the brim of his hat to reveal a sweaty lock of white hair. He looked us over in silence, wincing at the sight of so much raw flesh on Quetti.

"Any more of you whiteys around?"

Quetti was not speaking, so I said, "No, sir."

He seemed relieved, and glanced at the tall swampman.

"We'd best get these two out of here fast."

Black nodded. "You're not going to wait and waylay the others when they return, Red?"

The little man shook his head. "They're victims, too. Let them be."

Then I remembered where "the others" had gone. I had been so overwhelmed by my own release that I had forgotten the danger to Misi. Choking with the effort of forcing so many words through my aching throat, I told of the raid on the traders.

The little man nodded. "We guessed as much. It was lucky for us, though. And for you, sucker."

"But you must save the traders!"

He glowered. "They're slavers! They all knew about you. Serve them right—let the spinster's men kill them off, or be killed themselves."

"Angels prevent violence!"

"Why should I risk my men to save either side?"

I was stunned with horror, not knowing what to say, but Black remarked softly, "They have children, Red."

Red pulled a face and grunted. He pondered, tugging his lip. "Well, I'll go and try. If I can get there before the battle, I may talk them all out of it."

"Now wait a moment, great one," Black said. "You shot the spinster. If her men learn that, they'll use your guts for bow-strings."

"I'll tell them you did it!"

"Seriously . . ."

"No argument!" Red had to crane his head back when talking with the gangling black man. "You finish up here. I'll head back downstream and see what can be done."

"Damn it, Red! Spinster's men meeting an angel?"

"Ex-spinster's men!" Red's face was turning an appropriate color.

"They may not believe that."

"They will—I'll take these two dupes along as evidence."

Black regarded him very oddly. He glanced at Quetti and me. "Is that wise?"

"Who's in charge here?"

Black's face went stiff. "You are, sir."

"Right! And you move this job along as fast as you can. That smoke may bring trouble, so finish the clean-up here and then scram. We're overdue already, and Michael will bust me to ser-aph if we're not all back soon. I'll catch you up if I can, but don't wait for me. Understood?"

There was no more argument from Black.

"I won't go!" Quetti shouted. "I want to see her." The palace was a thundering inferno by then. I could feel the heat from it.

"She's *dead*!" Red insisted. "I blew her brains out myself. And you'll do as you're told, you ungrateful little idiot." That last remark was not completely fair—Quetti was taller than he was.

Red-yellow-green had made a curious decision, one that was to be much debated and criticized in Heaven. His situation was perilous. He had a dozen angels, counting himself, and five chariots. The aggressive Shisisannis was somewhere in the area with upward of thirty followers. Warlike young men bereft of a beloved leader by act of violence are prone to notions of vengeance.

Within the compound itself—now a choking mass of flame and smoke—were about another thirty of the spinster's victims. Most of these had been rescued from the pens, but as Quetti showed, they were not necessarily grateful. They ranged from mindless husks like Old Faithful to fit and virile fighters like Ing-aa. In time, perhaps, most of them would recover their wits enough to head off in search of the families and tribes from which Ayasseshas had abducted them, and some might even resume a normal life again, but they were not ready to do so yet. The most hopeless cases were being quietly put out of their misery by grim-faced angels, although I was not aware of that at the time. Other angels, equally grim, were disabling the dangerous by breaking their throwing arms—a brutal, but necessary, precaution.

On the face of it, Red abandoned his troops in midcampaign. He should have either ignored the trader problem, or sent someone else to deal with it.

But the facts were less simple than that, and his thinking more complex. As I was to discover, Red's intention was to save not the traders, but his own angels. He wanted to block any pursuit, and he had evidently concluded that the venture was too risky to delegate to anyone else. He took Quetti and myself along as proof that Ayasseshas had been overthrown, and he may well have planned to kill us both if there was any risk of our falling into the wrong hands. Fortunately I was not smart enough to see that.

Soon I found myself once more sitting in the bow of an angel chariot. It was much more heavily laden than Violet's had been, because it had been home to three angels, and angels tend to collect unusual personal things, like spare sets of clothes.

At my side, Quetti was hunched over in silent misery, list-lessly applying grease to his welts. We were both wearing muddy fur pagnes, and mine was bloodstained. I worried that two fair-skinned wetlanders might suffer sunburn, but the sun was too low in the sky to be very dangerous, and most of the river was heavily shaded.

Red sat amidships, steering the chariot as it floated down the oily water. The wind was rarely helpful, and he spent much time adjusting his sails.

Before we departed, he had ostentatiously laid his gun to hand and ascertained that we both knew what it could do. I could see why he might not trust Quetti, who was red-eyed and surly, but his attitude seemed to imply that he did not trust me, either, and I rather resented that.

Nevertheless, I was free at last . . . or so I thought. In-toxicated by the sense of freedom, I floated amid rainbow dreams of being reunited with Misi. Had my throat not still ached so much, I might have burst into song. The only an-chor on my euphoria was anxiety about what Shisisannis was doing. Our pace must be much slower than his had been, and so I fretted a little that we might arrive too late to stop the massacre—but only a little, for Misi at least would be safe. At every bend I twisted around in the hope of seeing a solitary canoe approaching, speeding my love back to the spinster's lair.

Of course that canoe would also have contained Shisisannis himself and five or six young toughs. What would have hap-pened then, I can only guess, but the problem did not arise. No craft appeared, and only the angel's chariot tremored the reflec-tions.

We ate. We slapped at bugs. We sailed on in silence down the treelined, tortuous river. Then the angel roused himself from a period of deep thought to scowl at his passengers.

"What's wrong?" I asked uneasily.

"Just wondering what to do with you two. I have to get you out of the forest. It's not safe for you."

"Why not?"

His expression said that my ignorance was unbelievable. "Because silkworm eggs are easy to come by. Whiteys like you are just too tempting. You . . . Quetti? Where do you want to go?"

Quetti stared at him for a while and then just shrugged.

"Pilgrim, were you?"

"Yes." Quetti turned his head away, looking sulky.

Red nodded. "Usual story, then. It's a test. If you're stupid enough to get caught, then you're not smart enough to be an angel."

Quetti's blue eyes glinted. He muttered something that I thought was "Murderer!" Red would not have heard.

"You could have a fast trip home," the angel said with a sneer. "Down this stream somewhere is the Great River. It's flowing west at the moment, maximum rate. It would be a hair-raising ride, but you could try it in one of the canoes."

"He'd never get through the Andes!" I exclaimed.

Red shrugged but seemed surprised by my knowledge. "No, he wouldn't, the shape he's in. You'll have to come north with me, lad. The goatherders of the late desert are a hospitable lot; we'll find a tribe to take you in until you heal. And you, cripple?"

"I want to be with Misi Nada . . . if she'll have me. Wherever she is, that's where I want to be."

The little man curled his lip in contempt. Then he broke the news. The world fell apart. My mind seemed to die, and for a while his words made no sense at all. He had to repeat the story several times before I could understand.

As soon as Shisisannis had departed—with me as his prisoner and the angel canoe in pursuit—then the rest of the angels had moved in on the trader caravan. The men, predictably, had all fled on horseback. The angels had fined the other women a portion of their goods, which had then been burned, but Misi Nada and Pula Misi had been executed for slaving. Red had carried out the sentence himself, just as he had executed Ayasseshas, because no honorable leader would delegate so despicable a task.

I wept, my heart shattered into a million pieces.

Quetti studied my grief for a while, then remarked cattily, "Now you know how it feels!"

That journey seemed endless. Red had not thought to bring food and dared not stop to catch any. Quetti curled up on the floor and seemed to go into a coma. I hunkered down in a silent agony of bereavement, my mind churning with regret as it strove to come to terms with the disaster. Red just steered, and worked sails, and grew ever more weary.

Certainly I had gone mad in the ants' nest, for no sane man could have survived that ordeal for so long. Now—had anyone cared enough to ask—I would probably have said that my wits had since been restored by Misi's love and care. I can only suppose that they had been driven away again by the shock of losing her, for it was then, huddled in the bow of Red's chariot on that smelly, bug-infested river, that I made my great decision. No blinding flash of light or voice from Heaven announced the moment; it came slowly, imperceptibly . . . relentlessly.

Misi was gone, Sparkle an ancient memory. My children on the Southern Ocean would not even know my name, and I could never find them anyway. Heaven held no appeal. True, the angels' coup against the spinster had won a brief twitch of admiration from me, but Red's brutality had crushed it utterly—murderer!

I had no desire to become an angel. So where could I go? What could I do?

No blinding flash . . . no carefully crafted logic . . . but when Quetti's shout aroused me from my long reverie, I knew my purpose; I had made my decision. It is a sad commentary on a man's character that, rescued from a horrible death and given back his life, he can think of no better use for that life than the pursuit of revenge. But revenge was my choice, and I even thought I could see how to gain it.

Of course I had just been rescued from the spinster, so she and her methods were much on my mind.

And I was crazy again. That helped a lot.

So I chose my destiny. Of course it would need superhuman luck and a lot more courage than I was ever likely to find, but I was in no mood then to consider those problems. I vowed that I would try, and let nothing stand in my way, not even Heaven itself.

# 2

I had been dreaming my mad dreams for a long time.

Quetti was sufficiently recovered to be sitting up and taking notice. He had yelled to draw Red's attention to the canoes, cunningly buried under piles of brush. Red was still at the tiller, eyes blood-rimmed, cheeks haggard under a silver stubble.

"Grasslands!" I said. "I have to go back to the grasslands!"

"Then you can damned well walk!" the angel snarled. "Get that grapnel ready."

I have often wondered what thoughts went through Shisisannis's head when he discovered the smoldering ashes of Misi's train, which had also been her funeral pyre.

He must have known that he was seeing the work of avenging angels, for only they would have burned valuable trade goods. He must have guessed that he would not now be able to carry out his orders. Perhaps he feared that Ayasseshas in her fury would send him to the pens, for he did not take the news back to her right away. Instead, he left his canoes and led his whole troop off overland. Possibly he was clinging to the faint hope that the woman he had been sent to abduct was still alive and with the other traders, although he must have known how extremely slight that chance was. More likely he thought he was pursuing the angels. He had not seen them on the river, so he may have believed that he could run them down ashore before they found the spinster's lair.

He probably caught up with the caravan. He may have had a battle. I bear the snakeman no grudge. I hope that eventually he found happiness again, but I do not know what happened to him.

What happened to me was that I arrived with a bone-weary

Red-yellow-green and his other wetlander captive at a scrubby sand spit where the spinster's canoes had been stowed. They were well camouflaged, and it was Quetti who saw them. There were no guards to challenge us as the angel grounded his chariot in the shallows. I tossed a grapnel into the shrubbery, he lowered sail. Then we all paused to stretch aching muscles and rub sore eyes.

Red scratched his chin and looked thoughtfully at his passengers . . . companions, but not friends. He had won his gamble. He had evaded Shisisannis and could now destroy the enemy's canoes, saving his own men from pursuit. But he was not such a fool as to trust Quetti or me any further than necessary. Shisisannis and his men were obviously absent, so we were not needed as evidence of the spinster's death. Now what could Red do with us? He would have to sleep sometime. He had placed himself in a very dangerous situation. Black had foreseen this, and had warned him.

Were he unscrupulous enough, Red-yellow might choose to dispose of us before either of us was tempted to dispose of him. He could shoot us, or just abandon us in the forest, but he would be breaking his angel vows.

Of course I did not see all this then. "Now what happens?" I asked bitterly. "You go after Shisisannis?"

The angel shook his head and bared his teeth in a humorless smile. "I never planned to. You stay here, cripple. You jump, boy!"

Quetti had hardly spoken since we began our voyage, his thoughts unreadable under his sullen pallor. He stared hard at the angel before rising and clambering out of the chariot, into knee-deep water.

I watched as he waded ashore and Red followed, carrying his gun and an ax. I watched, also, as Quetti was set to work smashing holes in upturned canoes. The angel went ahead of him, pulling away the shrubs that had been piled over them, but also staying on guard, keeping his gun at the ready and a watchful eye on both Quetti and the forest. No one emerged screaming from the trees to halt the vandalism.

To disable a fragile structure like a canoe is not difficult, and in short order the damage was done. It could be repaired, of course, but not soon enough for Shisisannis to lead his men in pursuit of the angels. Red had achieved his objective, and now he came splashing back to the chariot with the ax. Quetti had been sent to retrieve the grapnel.

"Mission accomplished!" Red remarked with satisfaction. He tossed the ax in—at the stern, out of my reach—and began to climb in after it.

Quetti yelled from the edge of the trees and waved. He was a long way from the grapnel.

Red scowled. "Now what?" But he splashed back to the bank and went to see what Quetti had discovered. He took his gun with him, so he may have been suspicious, or perhaps he just did not want to leave it near me.

When the angel reached him, Quetti pointed at something on the ground. Red bent over to peer. Quetti, displaying more strength than I would have expected, lifted a bulky sack and raised it high.

I took a deep breath . . . I have never been able to decide whether or not there was time for me to use it. Maybe there was. Maybe not. Had I called, then I might have distracted Red and given Quetti a better chance. Or I might have warned Red in time for him to avoid a very clumsy attack, one that should never have succeeded. I didn't call. So was that another of my killings? I do not know. Does one more or less matter? A man is either a killer or he isn't, and I am.

Quetti tipped the bag over the angel's head as he straightened up. Constrictors fall on their prey, and apparently they react in the same way when dropped. Red made no sound. Either a coil went around his neck at once, or else Silent Lover squeezed all the breath out of him before he could speak. The man in the bag fell down in the undergrowth. Quetti stood there and watched until the bushes stopped thrashing.

Then he came trailing wearily back down to the water's edge. He waded out to the chariot, and stopped, standing knee-deep. He stared up at me, and I looked down at him, and for a long moment neither of us spoke.

The expression on his sallow face was reminding me of my childhood. Many times I had seen one or other of my numerous brothers be more naughty than he had intended, and try not to show how scared he felt. Quetti's young face looked just like that—defiant and unrepentant, but wary of what might be said next.

I reached down a hand to shake.

"Well done," I said.

Quetti took it, blinking pale lashes in surprise.

"I'm heading back to the grasslands," I said. "Can I offer you a ride somewhere?"

He stared at me in bewilderment for a dozen heartbeats. Then he began to weep, tears pouring down his hideously grazed cheeks, sobs racking his bony frame. That was what he needed. I hauled him into the chariot and then I held him for a while, until he regained some control and shamedly pushed me away.

I could leave him then, leave him to work out his grief and guilt, while I went to get the grapnel.

Silent Lover had already departed in search of more edible prey. I could not bury Red-yellow, but I dragged his body to the water and sent it on its way. I retrieved his gun.

I was humming as I lurched back to the chariot.

Whatever you do, never expect gratitude.

# 11

## The Angels

"Let's be sure I've got this right," said Black-white-red. "He opened a sack and stuck his head in it, and there was a python there. It wanted to loop around his neck . . . so he let it?" He drummed long black fingers on the table.

"More or less," I said.

"How much more? How much less?" His head was against the bloody glow of the window, his eyes almost invisible, and only the silhouette of his woolly hair was distinctive. He was coldly furious—with some justification, I suppose.

I sighed. "No more, no less. Yes, it sounds crazy when you put it in those words. But he was exhausted, remember. Neither of us was watching . . . maybe he tripped and fell in on top of it. Accidents happen."

"Accidents can be made to happen!"

I faked a little anger. "You're accusing us of murder! What possible motive could either of us have had to harm him?"

"You'd both been imprinted, and he had killed your women."

"If we slew him, why would we have come here, to Heaven?"

Black-white growled low in his long throat and drummed his fingers faster. At my side, Quetti sat in silence, right shin balanced on his left knee, impassively studying a thumbnail. Of course we had murdered Red-yellow, but if neither of us confessed, there was nothing the angels could do about it, certainly not after so long a time . . . Or was there?

Sensing the anger around me, I was suddenly uncertain.

The room was small to hold six men, and was rapidly becoming stuffy. The walls and the low ceiling were curiously irregular, made of variegated slabs of snortoiseshell that creaked whenever the building moved. It was very dim, so that features were hard to make out, for the only lighting came from a foggy casement directly behind Black and the two men flanking him.

Beyond that rattling window lay the nightmare landscape of Dusk—scabby hills tangled with dead trees and monstrous bloated fungi in bilious yellows and mauves, all lit by a baleful red twilight along the horizon. The clearings were buried deep in snow, drifted by icy winds that ran wailing under a dark sky. The snortoise browsed with monotonous crunchings, and in the distance many others issued their weird roaring bellows. This was Heaven, but it was much closer to what I should have expected of Hell.

Since our meeting in the spinster's lair, Black-white had gained promotion. In place of angel buckskins he wore a heavy green robe. The others addressed him as Uriel or Archangel.

On his right sat a leather-clad angel, a fairish man with tawny hair and yellow eyes. His stripes identified him as Two-green-red.

The man on Uriel's left was older, portly, and swathed in a purple robe. He had a tonsure of snow-white curls and a friendly sort of face, and of course he was Saint Kettle, of whom I have spoken earlier. He was there to represent his superior, Archangel Gabriel. Gabriel had a cold—colds are common in Heaven.

There was a sixth man present also, sitting in silence in the corner behind Quetti and me, so we could not see him without turning. Uriel kept shooting him glances, but so far he had not spoken at all.

The snortoise roared deafeningly beyond the window and took a mighty lurch forward, rocking the building.

Kettle coughed.

"Yes, Saint?" Uriel asked.

"I'm curious to know how they escaped from the forest." Kettle shuffled through his notes on the table—I had been wondering what sort of game he was playing, having never seen writing done before. "Even with the spinster dead, wetlanders are precious goods in those parts, but these two evaded recapture. They somehow managed to sail that chariot, by land and river, out of the forest, and that is no mean feat in itself. They must have gained hospitality from the inhabitants, or else lived off the land."

He paused, thinking. "No—they must have done both, so they're good hunters and damned good diplomats, too! They made their way north across the cold desert, then east through the dying lands to Heaven—but without any formal navigation, I assume. They evaded predators, two-eyed and three-eyed. All in all," he added, rubbing a plump chin or two, "those are astonishing accomplishments for a couple of beginners, and one of them a cripple!"

Black . . . Uriel . . . nodded rather reluctantly. "I agree— but it's taken them long enough. Heavens, I've been up to Sunday since then and over to February. How long is it?"

How long was what? I wondered.

"About *three years*," Kettle said.

I wondered what that meant, growing angry at such gibberish being talked over my head. If they were discussing time, then it had been long enough for Quetti to grow from fuzzy boy to a hard-faced young man with a heavy growth of golden stubble. That stubble—and my own—had been annoying Uriel since he had first set eyes on us.

"Long enough that they must have talked themselves into every pretty girl's bed from Friday to Tuesday," he said crossly. "Shaving—masquerading as angels!" He fired one of his angry glances at the sixth man in the corner.

"No!" Quetti looked hurt. "Not just the pretty ones!"

Uriel growled again, obviously a habit of his. I could have told him that Quetti had never needed the angel disguise—he had an astonishing ability to make girls want to mother him. That wasn't true of me, though, so I stayed silent, hoping someone would change the subject.

It was Two-green who spoke into the silence. "I doubt that they could have done otherwise, Uriel. Who else drives a chariot but angels? They had to pretend to be angels or else abandon the chariot . . . and one of them can't walk."

"Can so!" I said. ". . . but not that far, I guess."

Uriel dismissed me with a shrug and looked to Quetti. "How did you manage?"

Quetti scratched his chin loudly with a knuckle. "I didn't."

Then he flashed me a sly grin out of the corner of his eye, and I saw what was coming. I cursed under my breath and glared back warningly. Quetti and I had been good companions on our long trek together, but never close. If fires burned within Quetti, he kept them well banked; no man could ever warm himself on Quetti's friendship. He was self-contained and taciturn—usually. But now, I could tell, he was winding up to make a speech, and he had promised me that he wouldn't. Admittedly I had twisted his arm very hard to get that promise. I had almost dislocated his shoulder.

Quetti turned his grin on Uriel. "It was Knobil, all Knobil. I collapsed—I was a useless heap, crazy. He worked out how to sail the chariot. He brewed up some sort of dye out of tree bark and colored us both brown, just in case. He did it all."

"That's not true!" I said quickly.

Idiot! Once he had recovered his health, Quetti had also recovered his ambition to become an angel—for his only real alternative was to head home with "Failure" written on his heart.

My case was different. I had my revenge planned in detail now, and all I needed from Heaven was a ride back to the grasslands. I hoped that I had earned that favor by returning the lost chariot. Once we had arrived north of the desert, I could have dropped Quetti off to walk and turned my course westward, but that would have been unkind, so I had agreed to sail to Heaven. Besides, the chariot was in bad disrepair by then. In the event, we had been intercepted by an astonished angel, White-gray-orange, and brought in under guard, as murder suspects.

"It is true!" Quetti said. "He repaired the wheels more than once . . . and ropes, and sails. He made traps and caught game—he's a devil of a fine cook, too! He worked out where we were and which way we should go. I went right out of my mind and—"

"He's out of his mind now!" I howled. "Don't believe all this." Yes, Quetti had been sick for a while in the forest—hardly surprising after what he had been through. I had warned him not to mention that, but he was not to be stopped . . .

"Knobil knew how the gun worked—he held off three men

in a canoe with it once. He was bringing down birds on the wing by the time we ran out of those tube things you put in it.''

The snortoise roared, drowning out both my protests and Quetti's tales, but he didn't even pause for breath.

''. . . fished me out one-handed and brained the brute with an oar at the same time. And after that he kept me tied up until I got my head back. He fed me like a baby! He treated my wounds with herbs . . . he found out how—''

"Oh, stop it!" I yelled. "This is nonsense! Quetti caught a fever—'' What the angels thought of me was of no importance. I would not care if they believed I had been helpless dead weight on our journey. He was the one who wanted to stay in Heaven, and by talking like this he was steadily ruining his own chances—but he was determined to spare me not a single blush.

''. . . grabbed its head in a way that paralyzed it, and I ran for the ax. So we ate snake until . . .''

I had never suspected that his cool, sane exterior hid this outrageous juvenile hero worship. I wanted to scream.

''. . . in trade for the snake's skin, and used it to haul the chariot through the swamp. He knows all about horses, and later he sold it off to some sandmen . . . I tell you, Knobil could talk an anteater out of his sandals!''

"Quetti!" I yelled. "You needn't go into all this!" It was intolerable.

''. . . treemen and hawkers and beekeepers . . . mends clothes—''

"I do birdsong imitations, too!"

''. . . best shot with a bow I have ever—''

"You sound like Jat Lon selling a horse!"

''. . . catch fish without—''

"I also sing and dance!" I shouted. "Now will you shut up?"

"He's the finest, bravest man I've ever met!" With that final outrageous untruth, Quetti stopped and sat back to leer at me.

Silence followed, broken by another roar from the snortoise.

"One of you is obviously lying," Uriel remarked acidly. "And I know that Knobil is expert at that, at least."

Everyone else laughed. I choked between several angry retorts and eventually used none of them.

"Where did you learn all this?" Kettle asked me.

I shrugged grumpily. "I'd seen Violet-indigo-red drive a chariot on land, and Red-yellow do it in water. I'd watched Violet use a gun. Brown-yellow-white taught me a little about maps, so I could use Red's. Black, here, told me about the geography himself, and I had a few trader tricks. Quetti knew that Heaven was somewhere in Dusk, north of the deserts. The rest . . . well, I've been a herdman, a seaman, a miner, an all-purpose slave, a trader . . . I just picked it up here and there.''

The three men opposite me all looked up as the watcher in the corner chuckled wryly. He spoke for the first time. "I always told you gentlemen that wetlanders make the best angels.''

Two of the three laughed enthusiastically, and I twisted around to stare at this cryptic onlooker. He was a small, slight man, well muffled in a white gown. He was sitting at an angle to the light and had pulled his hood forward to conceal his face, although I was sure he had been watching us earlier.

"Quetti's a wetlander," I said. "I'm a herdman.''

"I can tell." He was old, his voice thin as a lark's ankle. He did not turn toward me.

"The purpose of this meeting"—Uriel's voice had fallen into a lower, sadder range yet and I was uneasily aware that the proceedings were not the forgone formality I had been expecting—"is to investigate the death of Red-yellow-green. Obviously we should have questioned these two vagabonds separately. Does anyone believe their nonsensical tale about a snake? Kettle?''

"Certainly!" the plump man said. "I vote for acquittal.''

"What?" Outraged, Uriel turned to the angel on his other side. "Two-green? I can rely on you, surely?''

Two-green avoided his eye, glancing unhappily at the cryptic onlooker in white. Getting crosswise between two archangels is a Heavenly nightmare, but in this case one of the two was Michael, and that made his decision easy. "I lean toward acquittal also, Uriel," he said miserably.

Kettle beamed. "Then I shall record the death as due to snake attack?''

Uriel uttered a growl that was almost a roar. "Michael! Red was a friend of yours! He was murdered!''

"It's your inquiry. But I think you're outvoted.''

Uriel sprang up, tall and black against the window, and also furious. "Do it, then, Saint! And may your ink freeze!" He leaned big fists on the table and stared down menacingly at Quetti and me. "We can discuss your future at a later time—"

"Let's do that now," said the quiet voice behind my shoulder. The man in the white gown rose and walked around to the far side of the table. The angel jumped off his chair, and ended without one as Michael took the middle spot and Uriel angrily settled where Two-green had been, leaving him to lean back against the wall, fold his arms, and glower. The face of the little man in white—Michael, of course—was now against the light and no more visible than it had been earlier.

He looked up at Uriel. "Well? There are two pilgrims here. Have you no questions to ask the candidates?"

I was about to interject that I was no pilgrim. I might even have been rash enough to spit out a few of my opinions of angels in general as hypocritical, lecherous posers and of Heaven itself as callous and ineffectual—but I needed transportation back to the grasslands, so I would probably have managed to restrain myself. As it was, I caught sight of Michael's hands on the table, and my thoughts suddenly began to jump in all other directions, like a pack of roos.

Uriel was furious, his fists so tightly clenched that pale spots showed on the big black knuckles. "Very well, Holiness—although I've had no chance to interview them in private, as is the custom."

"It is hardly the custom for pilgrims to arrive in their own chariot." Michael was making no effort to soothe the tall man; indeed he seemed to be trying to provoke him.

Five archangels rule Heaven. Gabriel tends the records and the ancient lore. Uriel trains the cherubim. Raphael builds and maintains the chariots and all the other equipment the angels need. Sariel attends to the housekeeping of Heaven itself—the feeding and housing of many people, the welfare of the dog teams and the snortoises. Michael gives orders to angels.

The hierarchy is clearly defined. At the bottom are the seraphim, who do manual labor for Sariel and Raphael—mostly youngsters of the twilight ghoulfolk, who work off their adolescence in Heaven and then head home with a farewell gift of Heaven's unique manufactures, such as nails and steel blades and certain medicines. With those, they can buy first-class wives.

Above the seraphim come the cherubim, future angels, followed by the learned saints who report to Gabriel—at least in theory they do; some saints have been lost in obscure research for so long that they have forgotten their own names, let alone his.

Above the saints come the angels, and the five archangels.

All archangels are former angels, accustomed to obeying Michael, and Michael appoints other archangels whenever there is a vacancy. In Heaven's long history, there have been few instances of a Michael who could not get his own way in the Council of Five.

There was no question that pilgrims seeking admission as cherubim must be approved by Uriel first. The former Black-white-red was new to the post. He had not interviewed many candidates before Quetti and I arrived, but it was certainly his privilege to do so. His anger at Michael's intervention was understandable, even if Michael's own motives were not. And my own mind was already reeling at what it was beginning to suspect.

"How do you feel about the spinster now, pilgrim?" Uriel asked.

"I worship her memory," Quetti said very quietly. "Could she be restored to life, I would gladly pasture silkworms for her until nothing remained but my bones. Not for anyone else by choice, though."

Uriel shuddered. "You claimed you had a token . . . ?"

I was still staring at the shrouded figure of Michael, and especially at those small, pale hands—wetlander hands. His face was a pale blur within cowled shadow.

"I had one," Quetti said. "But I left the spinster's web with nothing, not even a whole skin—as you know. Knobil had three!"

"Three?" Two archangels, one saint, and one angel all echoed the word in astonishment, or perhaps disbelief.

"Three! But he lost them in an ants' nest."

"Very convenient," said Uriel.

Michael intervened sharply. "Tokens are not important! They are not necessary for admission and they do not guarantee it. Tokens help recruiting, but they are mostly of value to us as a means of learning where the donors were—the marks on the back tell us that. If an angel is lost, we like to know how far he got . . . That's all. What counts is not the token, but the man who brings it.''

"Nevertheless," Uriel insisted, "I am going to ask. Tell us about yours, Pilgrim Quetti."

"I was quite small," Quetti said cheerfully. "Paddling along in my kayak. I chanced upon an angel about to be eaten by a pack of ice frogs. He seemed to appreciate my help."

"His name?" Uriel queried suspiciously.

"Orange-lime-orange."

"I have his report here, Archangels." Kettle was fumbling with his papers. "He has just returned from the Thursday venture, so we can call him as a witness if you wish. He described the incident as 'terrifying' and an 'extremely narrow escape.' ''

Quetti returned Uriel's glare with a smirk. "You gotta know where to hit 'em, that's all."

Uriel grunted, as if impressed in spite of himself. "Michael, this man is obviously a survivor. I recommend that we accept Candidate Quetti."

"Agreed. Welcome, Cherub."

"Thank you, sir."

"As I said," Michael continued, "I believe that wetlanders make the finest angels of all. We are loners by nature, yet our background has taught us to cooperate. We are not frightened by open spaces. Is this not so?" He chuckled an old man's dry, cynical chuckle. "And we also have a streak of ruthlessness that can be very convenient at times—true?"

"Er . . . yes, sir," Quetti said, turning red.

I thumped him on the shoulder. "Congratulations!"

"The other candidate," Uriel said—

"I am not a candidate, Archangel."

Quetti spun around on his chair. "Knobil—"

Uriel sighed. "Then I am saved the duty of refusing you. You are about twice the age we require, and a cripple. And a herd-man!" He hesitated. "But I admit I would like to hear how a man collects three angel tokens in one lifetime."

I saw Michael's hands clench.

"Violet-indigo-red gave me one . . ." For a moment I re-called my old, old dream of marching triumphantly into Heaven, and Violet coming forth to welcome me and declare me a cherub. Nothing remained of that dream, nothing at all.

"Why?"

"He saw me running from a tyrant . . . perhaps it was a reward for intelligence? He was a little crazy. The second I got from Brown-yellow-white, because I rode a great one up the Great River. But hundreds did the same right after. The third was only a promise, not an actual token. From Orange-brown-white—"

Quetti shot me a startled glance but said nothing. Michael's fingers unfolded slowly.

"Orange-brown-white?" Saint Kettle sat up eagerly. "Where? Roughly how long ago? Why only a promise?"

"A promise because he had no tokens to give me. He had nothing left but his skin—and not as much of that as feels good. He promised me a token if we escaped. It was humor; not very funny humor, but then we had very little to laugh about."

The audience exchanged glances, and Uriel leaned across the table as if he wanted to bite me. "Orange was a slave? You are saying that those ants had the audacity to enslave an *angel*?"

"Is that worse than enslaving a herdman?"

"Well, if . . . No, I suppose not." He obviously thought it was, though. "We shall need a detailed report. He's dead now?"

"Very." I outlined how Orange had died soon after I was captured, long, long ago. It had been about then that I had lost all hope that Heaven would ever—or could ever—do anything about the ants, but suddenly I had realized that in this case they might at least try, inspired by my tale of the captive angel. My mouth began to water at the thought of Hrarrh dying at my feet, slowly and painfully.

Uriel looked over Michael's head at Kettle. "Is there a mine recorded near the Gates of the Andes?"

The fat man nodded. "I believe so. I'd have to check, but it seems to me it is one of the poor ones, not exploited in every cycle."

The snortoise took another giant lurch forward. The room rocked and creaked. Then came the bellow.

When silence returned, Michael was already speaking, or thinking aloud. ". . . a Friday Freeze due, but latest word is that the seafolk are already on the move . . . I could free up more men there, at least until the ice actually closes . . . The Thursday party's back . . . Have we the equipment, though?

That's the problem!'' He rose, and the others followed, the angel straightening off the wall.

I was astonished by the little man's authority, the way he could make larger men than he behave like herdwomen around their master. How did he do that? I saw that there might yet be things I could learn in Heaven—things that would assist me in my planned revenge. Even if nothing came of this proposed attack on the ants' nest, I might want to stay around for a while and observe.

Michael was not done yet. "Kettle—tell Gabriel I want a full report on that location. Two-green, you get one from Raphael on ordnance . . . and check it yourself. Uriel, you'll administer the oath to Cherub Quetti? I want to hear more details from Knobil.''

The others scuttled like beetles. I stayed safely in my chair, not yet trusting my balance on so uncertain a flooring.

As the door closed behind the others, the tiny man in the bulky white robe came around the table and turned to face me. By coincidence, the clouds were clearing on the skyline, and a smoky yellow light began to brighten the casement. Michael threw back his hood, and for a while the two of us just stared at each other.

His hair was silver, yet thick for his age. He was not as pale as Quetti had become in the spinster's lair, but still unusually light, his skin roughened by long weathering. And his eyes were brilliant flecks of sky.

Then he smiled. "The promise from Orange made four,'' he said, stepping close. "There was a third token.''

I just nodded, gazing stupidly up at him. Could I really remember? He was certainly much smaller than I would have imagined.

He held out two hands, as if expecting me to take them. "I never dreamed! They told me two wetlanders. When I heard your dialect, I knew you were never from Dawn . . . Then I realized that I had heard your name before . . . Knobil! After all this time!'' He blinked rapidly.

"I remember you.''

"You do? I find that hard to believe. You were very small.''

"But you frightened me. I was not accustomed to seeing my mother used so.''

The offered hands were withdrawn. Michael studied me now with a hard, blue stare. Then he hooked a chair to him and sat down, his feet between my outstretched legs. I am sure that my own gaze was no softer then his.

"It was an accident," he said. "I'd been sent to tell the wetlanders that it was safe to move south again. I was told to go by the grasslands and estimate the herdfolk population. On my way home, by mere chance, I arrived at a camp I had visited on the way out."

"And you broke the rules by tumbling the same woman again."

He pursed his ancient lips, thin lips, turning them white. "I really wanted to play with you, but you wouldn't come near me. Do you know why the angels have that rule?"

He reminded me a little of Jat Lon—a smarter man than I, seeking to mold me to his own purposes; certainly very devious. I wanted a favor, a ride to the grasslands, and now I knew who made decisions in Heaven.

"I don't think I care. Nothing could justify the demeaning manner in which angels use women."

"Indeed? So Uriel was wrong when he surmised that two imposters had been accepting that sort of hospitality?"

I dropped my gaze to the hummocky, whorled floor of scuffed snortoiseshell. "Mostly I left that part to Quetti," I muttered.

"But not always, surely? Some resolutions are harder to keep than others . . . You must certainly have been invited."

I nodded in bitter silence.

"And you had to stay in character for an angel."

"Damn you! Yes, I did what they asked! And yes, I enjoyed it."

"But yet you feel guilty? How curious!" Michael considered me for a moment in silence. "Few would. Well, so I bent the Compact—I gave your mother a token for you. I doubted that she would even remember it when the time came, and I certainly had no real expectation that it would ever reach Heaven. Even hope died a long time ago."

"I did not exactly come by the fastest route."

"Obviously! I want to hear your story, all your story—son!" He laughed. "How strange to say that word! I am very grateful that you did not talk of the token."

"You're not supposed to make angelbrats, are you?" I was recalling Violet then.

"Not supposed to *recognize* angelbrats!" Michael said. "The more we make the better. But they'll guess soon enough. I don't usually condone my lads dying in mysterious circumstances. I saved your life just now, you know?"

"No."

"I did. Uriel was going to take you both out and shoot you."

I started to protest and he waved a pale, thin hand, like a dead child's. "Don't be any stupider than you must. You and the other one killed Red—it's quite obvious. I twisted Uriel's neck to get that acquittal. They'll gossip. They'll guess. We have records. I was the only wetlander angel on the grasslands two months ago. Longer, maybe? Anyway, there are records, so they'll know. I can offer you hospitality, *son*, but no more than that. The Great Compact . . . but let's leave it to the saints. You can't be an angel, obviously."

The only reason I had not asked to be a cherub, as Quetti had, was that I did not want to be a cherub. Yet now I felt an irrational spasm of annoyance. So I would have been refused? Did he think that my disability disqualified me? I had already proved that I could do anything any angel could—in chariot or elsewhere. Still, the last thing I wanted was to be an angel.

I had been staring absently at the dusty, sun-gilded casement. I turned a wary eye on the shrewd little spidery man before me—hunched in his white robe, gently rubbing his tiny hands as he watched my thoughts roll. If I antagonized this long-lost father of mine, I would not be able to collect on the debts he owed me.

"You look tired, and I expect you are hungry," Michael said. "We'll have to put you in with the cherubim, for we have no guest rooms. The food is plain, but plentiful." He stopped, frowning. "But I forgot—you won't be able to manage the ladders."

"I can—I did! I may be slow on them, but I can manage."

"You came up. Going down may be harder. If you fall, you'll snap your pelvis for certain."

"I'll manage."

Michael was not accustomed to argument. Anger flared in his wan cheeks. "Ice can build up on those rungs at any time, with no warning. Cherubim fall all the time, and angels, too. Broken legs are one thing, but a broken back—''

''I'll manage,'' I said flatly.

He scowled testily. ''It's your pelvis! But I don't suppose you'll be here long . . . When you've rested, we'll talk again. You're going to have many eager audiences during your stay, Knobil. And you will be very useful to one of my little campaigns . . .'' He rose then. Chairs are difficult for me, but I eventually restored myself to vertical without having to ask for help.

''Angels cross the grasslands a lot,'' Michael was saying while I struggled, ''as you might guess. I've been trying to persuade them to hand out tokens there. They do it everywhere else! All those loners—such a waste! I could use them here. They'd certainly have enough heft to make good wood-chopping seraphim, even if their brains are too woolly for angels.''

I stared down at him in silence.

Despite his pale skin, he did not blush. He chuckled instead. ''Ah! You see? Even I do it!'' He reached up and squeezed my shoulder. ''Accept my apologies, Knobil. Please? Then go and show my lads that herdmen are human, too.''

I trusted him even less when he tried to be charming.

# 2

Michael lived and worked in a building borne by a snortoise named Throne, which happened to be one of the smallest and therefore a fortunate choice for my first attempt at descending a ladder. While I was still wrestling with my borrowed furs in the porch, peering out at twilight fading before a gathering snowstorm and wondering how I could find a bed, I heard a chorus of barking and shouting. Three dogsleds came into view, racing through the trees. Four young men scrambled up the steps and burst in upon me, armed with ropes and pulleys.

Two-green-red had sent them, they announced breathlessly, to lower a cripple down to ground level.

I rejected that offer with a few corrosive expressions I had learned in the ants' nest, which earned their instant approval. Then I went outside, lay down on the platform, and prepared to break my back on the ladder or on the jagged tree stumps below it. I didn't, and by the time the cherubim were tucking me in on a dogsled, they were already addressing me as Old Man. They had been too considerate to offer sympathy, but they had granted me patience, which was all I wanted. They must have spread the word later, I suppose, and it must have become an immediate tradition, for thereafter the cherubim always behaved that way toward me.

We set off then on a hair-raising twilight ride through fungus jungle and dead trees, through looming rocks and flying snow. Snortoises bellowed unseen all around; dogs yowled and young men yelled insults. I just sat with my eyes closed and a fixed smile on my face until we arrived at the cherubim feeding trough, invariably referred to by the name of its snortoise, Cloud Nine.

There I found Quetti already penned in a corner, being plied with beer and questions by a dozen or so cherubim and a few angels. Forced out of his usual reticence, he seemed mainly to be telling more lies about me. As soon as I had taken the edge off my hunger and thirst, therefore, I began to relate some of Quetti's own exploits. His prowess with women was noteworthy, as I have said, but now I raised it to the status of legend, making the younger cherubim in the audience wide-eyed and their more discerning elders purse-lipped. Quetti's less salacious tales were soon finding few listeners and no believers.

In a hundred cycles Heaven has seen almost anything possible, but imposter angels were new. The audience varied, as men came and went, and the two of us were kept there talking until we were both ready to fall off our chairs. I felt as if I had recounted my whole life story three times before we were at last released and escorted over to Nightmare, the snortoise that bore the cherubim's dormitory.

Heavenly beer is not especially potent. Quetti and I had learned during our long trek to accept hospitality with moderation, so I am certain we had both been discreet when describing the death of Red-yellow-green. Yet before that long meeting ended, the cherubim, with deadly intuition, were addressing Quetti as *Snake*. He accepted the name with placid amusement, as if it were a compliment, and Snake he remained until he became an angel.

I was the Old Man. Some time later, while learning to use snowshoes, I earned a second name. Snowshoes are tricky even for a man with real knees. Although I eventually became proficient on them, my early attempts caused me to lose my temper thoroughly. One of the spectators, a young swampman named Tiny, grew intolerably raucous over my tangled efforts to walk.

"Faster than the wind," he exclaimed, "it moves over the grasslands in mighty bounds!"

I swung at him, missed, and fell headlong. Thereafter I was still the Old Man, but I was also known as Roo.

Then there was Kettle. Right after a long first sleep and a hearty second meal, Quetti and I were taken in hand by the saints. I think Quetti was given his first reading lesson, but Gabriel was howling for information on the ants' nest, so I was cross-examined about it by a team of six. They came at me in relays, hurling questions until my head spun. It seemed to take half a lifetime.

That was in the scriptorium, an unusually large and bright room, well fitted with windows and drippy skylights, but always so crowded with chests and desks that there was barely room to move. There the saints fought an unending battle to copy out ancient records before the damp of Dusk rotted them all away. The air reeked of mold, and there were insects. Young men with good eyesight struggled alongside old men with experience, striving to decipher crumbling paper or sodden leather. The most valuable texts have been transcribed to gold-plated shell slabs, but there is a limit to the weight the snortoises can transport.

Weight has always been Heaven's problem, as Kettle explained to me soon after the questioning had ended.

He took me off to his own cell, a nook of highly irregular shape, even more cluttered. Bundles of old manuscript were mixed in with discarded garments, and there was barely room to stand, let alone sit. The bed itself was heaped with books and a lap-top desk and brass instruments for observing the stars. I was never to see it any other way, and I eventually concluded that Saint Kettle, if he slept at all, must sleep standing up. He cleared a place for me on the end of the bed and squeezed his portly form onto one corner of a chest. And beamed at me.

"Where do you want to start?" he asked.

"Where do I want to start what?"

He looked surprised and waved a hand at the chaos. "Learning."

"Is a herdman capable of learning?"

"That depends on what sort of herdman!" Chuckling, he bent over to scrabble in a heap on the floor, rising red-faced with a relatively neat and respectable ledger. He found the page he wanted and held the book out to me. I took it, surprised at its weight, and stared in incomprehension at the thousands of tiny, close-packed squiggles and at one large and unsightly ink blot.

"What does this mean?" I asked crossly. I had only a very hazy idea of writing, even then. "What use is this? Someone has been very careless."

"Yes, that happens." Kettle sighed. "It's quite impossible to read what was written underneath. That page tells of an expedition sent out a long time ago . . . before you were born, certainly. Four chariots went across the grasslands to Dawn, to the wetlands. Purple-white-blue, Green-red-orange, Indigo-two-black . . . and now the fourth name can't be made out at all! Not that it really matters, of course."

He was prying, wanting to see my reaction—and I in turn was studying his baggy brown face. He was still smiling, and I did not detect a threat, which must be one possibility. "You ought to report that blot to Michael."

Kettle shook his head, swinging jowls. "Michael needn't worry about such details. Nobody else need, either, in my opinion."

"Who's the enemy?"

His eyes twinkled. "Gabriel and Raphael. They don't like some innovations he's trying to make." He explained about the five archangels and their unending rivalries.

"So why antagonize Uriel?"

"Uriel's one of Michael's—this present Michael's—own appointees, and he's starting to waver, so 'tis said. The meetings are private, of course, but the story is that he sided with the others in the last vote."

"So why antagonize him?" I asked again.

Kettle chuckled. "Michael doesn't need to bribe. He rewards or punishes. You watch him—he's a master."

Yes, I thought, I might well learn a thing or two by watching Michael.

I dropped my eyes to the book, to tales of things that had happened before I was born, to the deeds of men who might be dead by now. The tiny script seemed to dance before my eyes like midges. I thought of Misi's delicate embroidery. I had never managed to match her at it . . . but I had learned to sew after a fashion. I thought of the heaped documents I had been shown, full of the voices of the long dead, full of wonderful things. I shivered at the thought of being able to hear those voices and see those things.

But reading would be no use to me back on the grasslands.

I closed the book. "Tell me about the Great Compact."

Kettle looked disappointed. "The Compact? Then I must speak first of the firstfolk . . . and therefore of time. How much do you know of time?"

The answer, we soon discovered, was "not much," so Kettle set to work to teach me about time, and that took much time in itself.

At rare moments, when there are large hills to the west and the sky is clear, the inhabitants of Heaven can glimpse the stars, the Other Worlds, shining in the sky. There are millions of them, and they are terrifyingly beautiful. Which one is First World, and how the firstfolk drove their great chariots through between all those shining worlds, even the saints do not know. But the Other Worlds turn about Vernier in a predictable path. Were a man to observe the sky when he lay with a woman and she then made a baby, he would see the same pattern repeated when she was delivered of the child. The saints call this amount of time a *turn*.

At our first meeting, I had heard Kettle refer to another measure of time, one that the firstfolk used, the *year*. The *year* is about one and one-third turns. Heaven keeps its records in *years*, but—as everyone admits—it is a very impractical unit and is preserved only because it is sanctified by age and custom.

More convenient is the month, which is almost sixteen *years*, or twenty-two turns. I was two and a bit months old, Kettle informed me smugly. He expected me to ask how he knew, but he'd already told me that, so I didn't. Almost a month had passed since the seafolk's great migration—and much of that month I had spent in the ants' nest. One month makes a baby an adult.

A man can hope to live for four months, and a very few make five . . . and so on. Time is handiest in months.

Twelve months make a cycle, when High Summer returns to the same place. A cycle is three men's lives end to end, seven or eight generations.

The firstfolk came to Vernier almost a hundred cycles ago.

"Copies!" Kettle would exclaim sometimes, when he became annoyed with the old texts. "Copies of copies of copies! Reports of rumors of commentaries on critiques of analyses! Bah!" Sometimes he used an even stronger word than "Bah!"

Despite the efforts of generations of scribes, and of the many high-loaded snortoises who bear Heaven's library, there are lamentable gaps in the old learning; much has been lost. What, for example, were the *goods* whose loss the firstfolk lamented? Kettle thought they must have been like the sorts of things that Heaven guards so carefully—the smithy, the pottery, the toolmakers' shop—and most likely the legend that many *goods* were lost means that they were swallowed up by nightside. Other saints disagreed. *Goods*, they maintained, had been related in some way to gods, and their loss was somehow tied in to the way the gods had scattered all across Vernier. Every group has its own god, they pointed out, and some have several, all lost to Heaven. Kettle made very rude sounds at this idea. The various gods had come much later, he insisted.

And why, if the firstfolk could move themselves and their *goods* through between the Other Worlds, could they not also keep those *goods* moving when they came to Vernier? Kettle had a theory that . . . but then, every saint had theories.

In that first lesson, he did little more than confuse me on the subject of time, but at least I heard the words of the Great Compact. In Heaven, everyone is required to know it by heart. Long ago, Kettle said, all of Vernier did. Then he began to quote, almost chanting:

*We, the people of Vernier, in order to preserve the wisdom of our ancestors from the dark of ignorance, our goods from the dark of night, our liberties from the dark of tyranny, our minds from the dark of superstition, and our children from the darknesses of inequality and intolerance, violence and oppression, do hereby enter into Compact together, for ourselves and our descendants forever.*

He paused, looking reverent, which was not easy with a face so much better suited to registering mirth.

"That's it?"

"That's just the beginning. It goes on to describe 'the college,' which means Heaven, and 'the instructors,' which we now call angels—"

"Why? Why change the names?"

"I have no idea!" The solemnity slipped slightly, and his eyes twinkled. "There is an old tradition that it started as a joke. A heaven is a place where a god lives, and the Great Compact bans all gods from Heaven. Let me tell you the rest of it . . ."

And so he did. But then and later, he left many questions unanswered and hints unexplained, and in time he had me begging for reading lessons so that I could find out for myself, which was what he had intended from the start. Probably I wanted to show that herdmen and reading were not incompatible . . . and Quetti was learning, too, of course.

After that first session with Kettle, though, I returned to Cloud Nine with my head full of wonders and my belly empty. I discovered a near riot in progress because the seraph cook had been removed to attend to more urgent business. The cherubim were solving the problem with beer and loud indignation. Feeling too hungry for such behavior, I headed for the kitchen and set to work on my specialty, an all-inclusive stew.

My news of an angel slave had rocked Heaven as if all the snortoises had taken up dancing. Michael was planning a force of forty men, which meant at least fourteen chariots, and no such effort had been mounted since the mission to the herdfolk, back in my childhood. Everyone became involved. I was to see learned saints wielding paintbrushes and archangels sewing sails. The seraphim were run to exhaustion.

Technically I was only a guest, but I did not escape. Angels were too busy now to instruct, while senior cherubim were frantic to win their wheels before the war party departed. Quetti's stories must have found gullible ears—a blushing cherub asked if I would give him some tips in archery. Then it was marksmanship, although I had not shot a gun since I ran out of ammunition in the crocodile swamp. Then horses. Soon I was as insanely overworked as everyone else—and mostly I was training angels, which I found ironic. In exchange, I demanded lessons in dogsledding and snowshoeing, so I could make my own way around Heaven and not need help all the time.

Then Sariel invited me along to meet some traders and I found myself haggling on Heaven's behalf. The traders did not appreciate my intervention. Sariel was horrified at the difference it made.

But I am getting ahead of my story . . . About the second or third time I was playing cook in Cloud Nine, Michael sent a seraph to fetch me. He only wanted to chat, but Michael's whim was Heaven's law.

I refused the seraph's dogsled and set off on my own snowshod feet. The sky was black, with a murderous cold wind coming in from nightside, and I was red-faced and breathless by the time I arrived at Throne. Michael made me welcome, apologizing for having taken so long to call me back. He led me into a small and very cozy office, where lantern flames danced happily and logs crackled in a tubby iron stove.

The chairs looked soft and difficult. I chose to settle on the floor with my back against a wall. Michael fetched some shabby old cushions for me, and then proceeded to warm dulcified wine on the stove and roast beefnuts. He was being charming again, and that put me on guard.

But I seemed to have misjudged him. He was amused and excited at having a real live son turn up in Heaven—to console him in his old age, he said with a laugh that came close to a cackle. We must get to know each other. Tell me about your childhood. Have some more wine. Have you heard the story . . .

He was bright and inexhaustible, witty and irascible by turns. I was weary after a long series of lessons given and taken. I sat there and we talked until my neck sagged and my eyes glazed. Finally he relented.

"You're weary!" he said—as if that had not been obvious for a long time. "I was hoping the weather would clear. Well, I can summon a dogsled . . . unless you'd care to stay here?"

I looked up at him blearily. "Would that be wise?"

He sulked for a moment. "No, I suppose not. There would be more gossip." Then a flash of humor—"You make me feel like a maiden guarding her reputation!" And a pout—"Such pettiness!"

"Can they throw you out?"

The blue eyes narrowed. "Certainly not! Oh, it's been done a few times—Michaels who became too old, or went mad, or became corrupt . . . I've done nothing to provoke that. But they can stop me experimenting with new things that need to be done—like trying to enlist herdmen. No angel wants to be the first, in case it doesn't work out." He paused, thinking. "If we suffer serious losses against the ants, then they might pull me down, I suppose."

He sighed in exasperation and rose from his chair. "Well, I have enjoyed our chat. We'll have time for lots more, I'm sure."

Relieved, I levered myself away from the wall on my seat. "You're coming . . . You're coming along to lead the mission in person?"

"Eh? No, I'm not going! Who would I blame if it failed? I'm not going, and neither are you!"

I had been about to do my roll-over and double-up maneuver. "I'm not going? But I'm the one—"

"A war party is no place for a cripple." He folded his arms and was suddenly *big*. Partly it was a trick of the giant shadow dancing on the wall behind him. Partly it was his bulky white gown, and of course I was sitting on the floor looking up—but the little man did look big, suddenly. I saw that I was not going to accompany the angels' attack on Hrarrh's nest.

"Damn! I can shoot as well as—"

"So I've heard. Uriel admits you're a better all-rounder then most of the cherubim; and many of the angels, he says. So's your young friend, and I suppose you trained him."

"Well, then—"

"He can't be an angel until he can read and write. He needs some book learning, but in fieldwork he's ready. Don't tell him, though." Michael had not moved. Only his shadow writhed and swayed.

"And me?"

That surprised him, and suddenly he showed caution. "You said you were not a pilgrim. Not a candidate, you said."

"I wasn't. But I want to go on this war party, and—"

"No." He sank down on his chair again, which happened to put his face in shadow. "Don't you understand, Knobil? Hasn't Kettle explained?"

"Explained what?"

"Why you can't be cherub or angel as long as I'm here in Heaven. You shouldn't be here at all."

"Because you're my father."

"Yes. But that's not the scandal. Angels make bastards all the time. We encourage it! It spreads the genes around . . . I mean it reduces the inbreeding, and that's a bad problem in many areas. Groups don't mix much, but seamen angels visit the deserts and treefolk angels the wetlands . . . The more angelbrats the better! But we never know who they are. And . . . hasn't Kettle explained the Great Compact?"

"Some. We've both been busy."

"Of course." Now he became kindly and gracious. "I could leave, of course. You'd make a good angel, and if you weren't a cripple, I might even do that, so that you could be one. But that is an important factor, Knobil. You can't deny that being a cripple makes a difference? And I think I'll be a good Michael, given more time. As for going home . . . I don't know what my arthritis would say to the wetlands now."

I felt suddenly sorry for the little man, and angry at myself because of it. "This is why there are no women in Heaven?"

"Talk to the seraphim if you get desperate. There are usually some trader wagons just over the hill."

Anything's negotiable.

"That wasn't what I meant!"

He chuckled, then sat back to stare at nothing. "No. And yes. No women in Heaven—that's what the Compact says. And no sons. No known sons. Because knowledge is power, and power leads to tyranny and oppression. You know how men feel about sons—son."

"I know how herdmen feel about them. They kill them."

He turned his blue-blue eyes on me without revealing anything. "I forgot again, didn't I? Apart from herdmen, then? Most men favor their children over others. They will pass on their goods when they die. And their power, if they can."

I had seen enough of traders' customs and met enough village herdmen to be able to nod in agreement.

"So that's the Compact! That's why angels expect to be trusted with power—they have less temptation to abuse it. That's another reason we get to tumble the women—we can't have any of our own." We both sat in silence for a while.

Then he murmured, "Do you feel more or less guilty now?"

I rolled over and jackknifed myself upright. Then at least I could look down on him. "I thank you for the hospitality."

Michael might not have heard me. He was gazing dreamily at the misshapen wall opposite. "I often wonder about the first-folk and those mysterious *goods* of theirs . . . How many trader wagons would it take to move Heaven, Knobil?"

"I don't know a number big enough."

"Ironic, isn't it, that the answer was something as simple as snow? Those poor firstfolk, seeing all their precious *goods* destined to be destroyed by the dark . . . and then they discovered the snortoises. Nothing else can move a load like a snortoise can."

I hesitated and was about to head for the door, but apparently he was still musing.

"So they saved their knowledge, their library. Ironic again—this is the worst place on Vernier to live, except nightside itself. Do you see the problem?"

"Er . . . no."

Michael was a curiously changeable character, but this dreamy introspection was both new and surprising. Then Throne uttered an enormous bellow, and I hastily lurched across the room to lean both hands against a wall while the building rocked.

Michael did not seem to have noticed. "Some people staying to guard the snortoises and the books and things, others spreading out all across Vernier . . . finding all sorts of ingenious ways of earning a living . . . I suppose at first they all sent their youngsters back here to be educated. Gradually the distances would get greater . . . So the girls wouldn't come any more, because girls would be precious. Boys . . . well, it's always nice to get the boys out of the compound when they get to a certain age—the rowdy ones. Send them off to learn, you know? Like the ghoulfolk still do?"

"Yes?" I straightened up cautiously.

"More restful." Then Michael's eyes flicked round to regard me, and he smiled his thin-cheeked, old man's smile. I wondered if he'd been playing a part deliberately. "Then fewer and fewer boys—just the adventuresome ones—and they would be sent back to advise and teach . . . That must have been how it all came about, I think—the start of Heaven and the angels. But maybe I'm wrong. It was a long time ago."

# 3

Eventually the army was ready and departed—forty-two men and nineteen chariots. I stayed behind in Heaven, and so did Michael. The commander was Three-brown, a heavy-jawed, long-armed slasher. He did not impress me. I thought better of his deputy, who had the typical yellow eyes and tousled hair of a wolfman. When I cheekily said so to Michael, he explained that wolfmen rarely made good leaders, because they were always too eager to please, but they were infinitely loyal subordinates and dogged fighters.

An exhausted peace settled over Heaven. It lasted about one sleep, then all the duties that been neglected had to be caught up. Only a few aging angels remained, but the cherubim were still anxious for promotion, and thus I found myself instructing in everything from chariot driving to herb lore—the little I had picked up from Misi.

There was nobody heading out, to the grasslands or anywhere else, and without transportation I must needs remain in Heaven. Of course I could have stolen a couple of ponies and just vanished into a snowstorm, but that would have required a stouter heart than mine, for I knew I should find Loneliness waiting out there for me. Moreover, Michael could have sent angels to bring me back. Instead, I cravenly accepted the situation and settled down in Heaven for the time being.

Some of the blame belonged to Kettle, who managed at last to open my eyes to knowledge. I discovered that herdmen, or at least herdmen half-breeds, were not too stupid to learn to read. My penmanship was better than most—thanks to Misi's embroidery lessons, I suppose. Somehow I found myself absorbing all the history and geography and sociology and biology and the myriad other things that cherubim must learn.

I had no real duties and no status. I taught cherubim. I exchanged lessons with angels—trader signals in return for navigation, for example. I copied archives for the saints, and listened to their lectures. I played seraph at times, for I thereby learned skills I thought might be useful to me later. I sharpened knives, shoed horses, blended gunpowder, threw pots.

I visited often with Michael, drinking his sickly wine, arguing and swapping stories. We shared jokes, skirted sensitive spots—quarreling, arguing, probing, testing, stalking around each other like suspicious dogs.

Heaven was a seductive trap for a man who had a mission and a purpose elsewhere. It was safety after danger, and fellowship after loneliness. I had friends . . . even, I suppose, family.

I had sung in my childhood, and with the seafolk. I had sung when I was with my darling Misi, and even sung sometimes on my long trek with Quetti—usually lounging by a campfire, with a pretty girl or two. And in Cloud Nine I sang along with the cherubim.


The war party returned, tails down, having found the mine long deserted. The tribe had formed itself into an ant army and vanished into the forest, undoubtedly heading for some better lode that their ancestral wisdom had told them was due to emerge from the wetlands. Before leaving they had killed off many, or perhaps all, of their slaves. They may have taken the better ones with them or sold them to traders, although traders usually shun slaves in large numbers. Had Hrarrh sold me off to save me from enjoying a quick death?

The angels had failed me again, and I was not surprised.

Heaven settled back into its age-old routine. Now angels were heading out on missions all the time, even if only on routine patrols of neglected niches. It was time for me to go. Heaven was a snare. I was procrastinating, thinking of a million excuses to put off my departure. I had learned much and there was much more I could learn still, but if I tried to learn everything then I would die first. I could feel my courage ebbing away. I began to tell myself that I was dreaming impossible dreams, that I had been mad when I first thought up my plan and now was sane again. Nothing argues more convincingly than cowardice.

I did ask. In one of our long chats, Michael started riding his hobbyhorse about herdfolk yet again—how he wanted to save the poor loners. This piece of hypocrisy always infuriated me. He wanted to use herdmen, but he secretly despised them. In his eyes they were merely muscular brutes. I suffered in silence for a while and then forced out the words. "It's time for me to leave."

He straightened in his chair, bristling. "To go where?"

"Home," I said simply.

He looked surprised, then pleased. "Well, you'd never get into a kayak, but that shouldn't matter. Did you know I had four brothers? The wetlands must be teeming with your cousins, if you could ever find them—"

"Home to the grasslands."

"What?" He threw back his head and cackled.

I glared in silence. I no longer need sit on the floor when visiting Michael. He had ordered a special chair made—solid, high enough to be easy for me, with a footrest. It was infuriatingly comfortable.

"Rot!" he said. "Decay and putrefaction! Why would a civilized being like you want to go back to live among those animals?"

"They're my people. I don't belong here, nor in the wetlands. I want to go home. Everyone does in the end."

That was not quite true. Some angels, like Michael, elected to live out their life span in Heaven, but most headed off eventually in search of wife and hearth and children. Michael, having considered the matter, was now openly suspicious. "No, you're no childkiller. Why? You've got something else in mind!"

His insight stunned me—but of course that was the key to his success at manipulating people. "No, I don't! Will you let me go?"

"Not until I know why!" We were both shouting.

"I've told you!"

"No, you haven't!"

"Animals, are they?" I swung my feet down. "But the women perform satisfactorily?" I heaved myself upright.

Michael switched moods, a common trick of his. He stayed in his pillowed chair and beamed up at me jocularly. "Now what vast confusion is churning inside that blond head of yours, son?"

"Just that word—'son!' You took my mother like a loan of a blanket!"

"You ought to be glad I did, surely?"

"You made me a yellow-haired freak!"

He sniggered. "Your complaint is paradoxical. You display an unthinking lack of gratitude. Your mother was very grateful."

I screamed at him.

"Seriously!" he said blandly. "She told me she'd never realized it was supposed to be a pleasure."

"Liar! Filthy liar!"

"No. And when I returned and found you . . ." He paused, eyeing me oddly. I was shaking with wild fury. "Lithion? That was her name, wasn't it—Lithion?"

"Yes." I took a lurching step toward the door.

"What happened to her? Did she have many more children after you? How many others?"

"Damn you to dark hell! I don't want to talk about her!" I stepped for the door again, just as the snortoise lurched. Caught off-balance, I staggered, missed a grab at a chair, and pitched to the floor. That was not the first nor the last spill I took in Heaven, but it was one of the worst. Throne must have felt my skull hit his shell.

The strange lights faded from my eyes; the building settled. I was lying on my back, listening to the rumbles of the world's mightiest digestion. I struggled to sit up and discovered Michael kneeling at my side, assisting me.

"Easy!" he said. "You took a bad knock. Easy, son!"

"Don't call me that!" I flailed vainly.

"But you are my son! Mine and Lithion's."

"No!" I had tried to shout and only groaned. My head was spinning, but I knew I must go, and go at once. "I won't talk about her. I killed her. Help me up—now!"

"Easy!" He tightened his grip, with more strength than I would have believed he possessed in his withered little frame. To stand up I must first lie down, and he was supporting me. I floundered like a child. My frustration made me start to weep.

"Tell me," he whispered, hugging me tight. "Tell what happened."

I blurted out the story of Anubyl—or some of it, anyway. I

don't know how much I told, because I wasn't listening to what I said. At the end of it, I buried my face in the collar of Michael's coarse white gown and sobbed like a baby. He clutched me firmly until at last I snuffled away into shamed silence.

"Better now?"

"Mmmph." I felt like an imbecile. "Banged my head . . . better go lie down for a while."

"Listen first," he said. "You were only a boy—and a very small boy by their standards, right?"

I tried to protest, and was stopped by a surge of nausea.

"He was twice your size. He had a club, and a sword, too. Would the others have helped you if you'd called on them?"

I grunted. Michael knew the answer as well as I did.

"*There was nothing you could do!* If you'd as much as breathed a word, a single word, he would have cut you down. And then probably her also, for not teaching her son manners. You know that, Knobil!"

"Let me up."

"Knobil . . . he's dead! Long dead! Less than a third of the herdfolk got by the Ocean, and he'd be an old man by now. No herdmaster ever lives to be an old man. He's long dead, Knobil."

"Gotta go to bed." I began struggling again, and still he held me.

"There's nothing you can do about him now, Knobil. Even if he were alive, there's no way to track down one man on the grasslands."

"*Let me up!*"

"It wasn't your fault, Knobil—what happened to Lithion."

"Shut up!" I screamed, knocking his hands away. "Don't talk about her! She was my mother! My mother, you understand? And to you she was just a couple of sweaty romps, that's all! You used her like a spittoon, to catch some unwanted secretions!" I broke loose and rolled over on my belly, preparing to rise.

"I offered to buy her. And you, too."

I stopped, then raised myself on my elbows. "You did what?"

"I told her I could love her. I told her I would try to buy the two of you, and we could go to the wetlands together."

"Mad!" I whispered, appalled. "If my father had heard . . ."

"I'm your father, not that hairy bull who owned her! We both knew that. So do you." His voice softened. "Oh, Knobil! There we were, lying in each other's arms. You were sitting in the corner, sucking your thumb and scowling at me in very much the same way you're scowling at me now . . ."

"Idiocy! She wouldn't have left the others."

He nodded sadly. "That was a problem—she wouldn't leave her other children. And I suspect she didn't trust me not to kill them if I took them, as well. She even said that . . . what was his name, the herdmaster?"

"I don't know." I wrestled myself up on my feet at last, although I still felt limp and sick. "I never knew his name."

"Well, she said he'd likely kill you if I even hinted that you were mine and not his. He hadn't thought of it, she said, and the women had never dared suggest it to him."

"Hadn't thought of it?" I echoed, dusting myself off and trying to look dignified. "Hadn't thought of it? Of course he'd thought of it! He knew perfectly well. He used to call me . . ." I choked over a sudden flash of long-lost memory, of being cuddled and tickled by that huge, shaggy man with the dread dark eyes, both of us slickly wet in the hot, dim tent—him cooing and chuckling, me I suppose giggling . . . I must have been very small. It could not have been long after the second visit by Green-two-blue. "He called me his dasher. His little pink dasher who ran into his tent! I wasn't as brown as the others, you see."

Michael rose also, struggling up from his knees. "Indeed? How touching! I'm not sure it proves much."

I lurched toward the door. I was far too deeply enraged to want more conversation with this lecherous, filthy-minded old angel.

"She was very dear to me," he said. "I never made an offer to any of the others like that."

"Ha! And of course there were hundreds of others!"

"Yes, there were. But you're no shy virgin yourself, are you?"

I hauled open the door without a word. My head was still ringing.

Now he was shouting. "She wanted to come with me. She said so. It was just that she was frightened of . . . ah, her owner. That was the only reason. And why would your mother have lied to me?"

I stopped, halfway through. "Well, perhaps . . . just for argument . . . you might consider the possibility that she loved him?" . . . *him*, my father, whatever his name had been. I turned, gripping the jamb fiercely. "He was three times the man you ever were, midget. She may not have found you so great a lover as you believed. Maybe she was being polite to the runt she had to serve so demeaningly? She may have expected to be beaten if she displeased you. She may just possibly have resented having to bear your child. It hurts them, you know."

As I rolled off down the corridor, I heard Michael shouting, "Come back here! Knobil! It wasn't your fault!"

He often babbled nonsense about guilt, did Michael. He was obsessed by guilt. From then on, I just refused to listen.

Time slipped by unseen. Heaven continued its unending journey, following the setting sun. Angels departed on their missions, singly or in groups. They returned, or they vanished into the unknown. Older men said their farewells and departed. Pilgrims arrived and became cherubim. Cherubim became angels . . . or not, as the case might be.

Promotion was an ordeal. A senior cherub could usually be recognized by a distinctive jumpiness as his time of decision approached. Uriel kept track of every man's progress, and reported to Michael. Any cherub who was an obvious misfit would be weeded out early in training, but there were few of those, for the wilds of Vernier are an exacting test. Incompetent pilgrims do not arrive.

No one ever told a cherub he was ready for his wheels. The decision was his alone, the final test of his judgment. If he waited too long he was assumed to be lacking in nerve or in ambition, and eventually he would be summoned to Michael's presence to be offered a lesser position, as saint or seraph. The only alternative then was a knapsack of food and a good pair of boots.

That was humiliation, and few waited for the dreaded call. Instead, a cherub would request an audience and go to ask for his wheels. He might be offered one of the lesser posts instead. Rarely, he would be told to return later and try again. But if he had judged himself correctly he would emerge from the ordeal with shining face and three colored ribbons, heading for Cloud Nine and a celebration that usually waxed near to riot.

Snake-who-had-been-Quetti was a determined young man. Older than most recruits when we arrived, he made up for that with a very fast progress. He told no one that he was going to visit Michael, and the first we knew of it was when he walked in with three blue stripes already sewn on his sleeve. Three of one color was a very unusual honor, perhaps given in his case to show that he bore no stain of suspicion over Red-yellow's death. Cloud Nine was almost demolished by that party, and my hangover afterward was hardly less bearable than the torments of slavery.

So Snake became Three-blue, and almost at once departed for late Friday to warn some seafolk in danger of being trapped by advancing ice. We had not been close friends, but his absence was a warning that my time might be running out, if I was ever to make anything of my life.

I was not a cherub nor a seraph nor a saint, but I played all those roles at times. My relationship to Michael must have been well known, but it was never mentioned. He seemed to make no secret of it, and came more and more to use me as a confidant.

Thus I learned about his petty political struggles and how he handled them. Those became easier as Uriel's loyalty steadied. Later Raphael headed home to the tundra and his successor was more cooperative. I thought the changes Michael was trying to make were all very trivial, but after nearly a thousand generations, Heaven is grimly resistant to any change at all.

Time slipped by and I did not leave. I might be there yet, had I not fallen off a ladder.

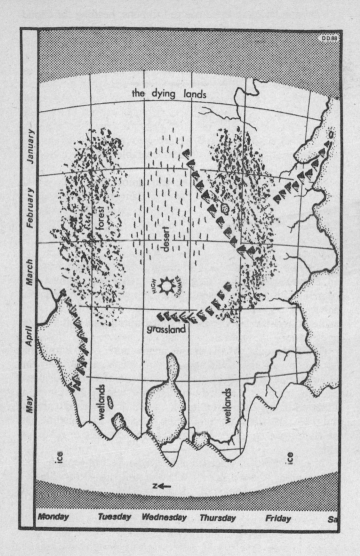

# 12

## Three-red

When I was told that Three-blue had returned from yet another mission, I was disgusted to realize that it must have been his fifth, while I was just frittering my life away in Heaven, achieving nothing. I found him in the scriptorium, in bright sunlight and the usual clutter, with Gabriel and half a dozen worried-looking saints.

Quetti was one of the senior angels now. His dimple had become a cleft and scalp showed through the golden hair, but otherwise he was little changed. His grin of welcome was broad enough, but brief. I envied him his tan. Sunshine was one thing I missed badly. In Heaven the sky is not only often cloudy and dull, but actually dark about half the time, an unnatural and unwholesome condition that always reminded me of mine tunnels.

"Roo?" Kettle's voice boomed across the big room as soon as I entered. "Now I know we have a problem—Roo's here!"

"Always glad to help out," I agreed. They knew why I always turned up when there was a problem.

Quetti had been dispatched far to the northwest, to where the Alps were emerging from Dawn's ice sheets. As the sun crosses March in every cycle, meltwater builds up north of the range in a gigantic lake. The tundra drainage freezes off at just about the time the icecap clears the western end of the barrier. The result is the Great Flood, a catastrophe in the wetlands. It had been the height of the lake that Quetti had been sent to inspect.

But angels' field reports never quite agree with those from previous cycles, because the geography is always changing. The saints' job was to turn Three-blue's notes into maps and maps into predictions.

Kettle was leaning over the big table again, growling. "This is impossible! Blind wetlander! Michael should have sent a seaman!"

"Three-blue's a match for any seaman," I said, winking at Quetti.

Kettle just muttered, attending to the task at hand.

Somewhat later—at about the time my stomach's rumblings became louder than the snortoise's—we had reached a consensus. Not only was the lake too high, but the ice was receding too fast. Moreover, the Great Flood had been coming earlier every cycle, and no one had noticed that trend. We made notes all over the current reports to warn the saints in the next cycle . . . but that didn't solve our problem. The timing looked very bad.

At length Quetti left the learned men to their disputations and took me aside. He perched one hip on the edge of a desk, blithely upsetting carefully stacked papers. "I'll get this one?"

"You want it?"

He nodded, so I nodded. "Likely, then."

He smiled briefly. "How's the equipment situation?"

"Same as usual," I said. "Drivers'll be your headache. Four ant armies on the move just now."

Quetti made a lewd remark about ants and the impossibility of angels ever keeping them honest. "Who's around?"

I listed the angels presently in Heaven, starting with seamen and wetlanders; and he nodded or pouted as I went along, rarely having to ask for details on one he didn't know. I left out a few who were too old or sick, and I included Two-gray, whose broken leg was almost healed, and White-red-white, whom Quetti disliked.

By the end, his face was grim indeed. "Seven? Only seven of us?"

"You want rough-water sailors, them's yer choice."

He muttered an oath, his blue eyes staring bleakly past me at unseen horrors. I felt very, very glad that I was not in his place. Seven men could never warn all the wetlanders in time. They would get caught by the flood, and more than likely that meant Scroll of Honor. Another disaster Heaven had failed to prevent!

Blots, the scriptorium's snortoise, had started slithering down a long slope. Saints muttered angrily as their light failed.

Quetti turned that cold glare on me and cocked an eyebrow. "Fancy a little fieldwork for a change?"

I suppressed a shiver. "Oh, I'd love to help you out, but Michael just can't bring himself to give me my wheels."

My feeble attempt at humor was ignored. "I'm serious. This is going to be a bad one, Old Man."

"You're crazy!" I said hastily. "I'm no rough-water sailor."

"I'll cook breakfast while you're learning."

I told him firmly: If he wanted angels just so he could drown them, then we had a plentiful supply better qualified than I.

"Seamen or wetlanders," he said. "But you're both! I know how fast you pick up things. Well, do this one for me—seven men and seven chariots for the mission. Double drivers to get there faster. Three per cart coming back, naturally. How many to start?"

Was this some sort of trick? "Twenty-eight men and fourteen chariots of course."

His smile was almost lost in the gloom. "See? I tried to do those sort of sums all the way back from April, and I never came up with the same answer twice."

Gabriel had adjourned the meeting. Daylight had gone, and candles were not allowed in the scriptorium. A saint nipped out to raise the flag over the door, an appeal for dogsleds. Quetti and I told the others to go ahead, being happy to sit and talk angel talk. With cherubim I talked cherub talk, and seraph talk with seraphim. I had no group of my own.

We two were the last. We went out to the porch and began pulling on damp-smelling furs. Judging by the racket outside, Blots had found a thick grove of dead trees buried in the snow of the valley bottom. He was likely to remain there for a considerable time, until complete darkness and falling temperature triggered his primitive reflexes. Then he would go looking for the sunset again.

Without warning, Quetti said, "Roo? Why won't you ask for your wheels? There's so much to be done, and so few of us to do it!"

"Ah! Three-blue, you are treading close to one of Heaven's great mysteries, one of Cloud Nine's favorite philosophical debates! Is it even worth doing everything you can, when it amounts to so little compared to what's needed? I've noticed that eager young cherubim never doubt—'Of course!' they say. But the rheumy old saints and retired angels . . . they usually shake their heads. Men even older than me, each one of them looking back on a whole lifetime of achievement and seeing that it doesn't really amount to anything at all. None of us is going to change the course of history, Quetti, so why—"

"Stop evading the question."

I hauled at legging laces, doubled over and unable to speak.

"Knobil, you'd make a great angel," Quetti said.

I unbent slightly. "You know why Michael couldn't give me my wheels, even if I asked for them. Everyone knows, so you must."

"That is plain idiocy!" Quetti said hotly. "You came to Heaven by pure accident. The Compact wasn't designed to prevent accidents, it was designed to stop men setting up dynasties. Heavens, Roo, you're not going to set yourself up as a king!"

I went back to my lacing without commenting.

"Have you asked him?" Quetti persisted.

I did not have to answer that either, because a dogsled came yelping and jingling over the snow, following Blots's wide track. Quetti held the door for me to go first, and I stepped out on the platform, reaching for the rail at the top of the ladder. Far to the east, the sky was black and twinkling with stars, the Other Worlds. Rail and platform both were slick with black ice. Without warning or understanding, I was airborne.

Blots was one of the largest of the snortoises, a small mountain of unimaginable age. For scores of human lifetimes he had hauled his great bulk along, lubricated by snow, munching deadwood and fungus, heedless of anything else except the direction of sunset. His roars were mere belching, not communication. He had no enemies and if he had offspring they were of no more interest to him than the scriptorium he bore on his back. In all my time in Heaven I only once saw a snortoise mating, a procedure that demolished the paper mill and tilted the bakery almost vertical.

On the way down I had time to reflect that, although this was far from being my first fall in Heaven, I had never fallen from the very top of a ladder before, and never had time to wonder what I was going to land on. Dead trees tend to break off in very nasty spikes. I wondered also about the resulting damage—broken hips seemed about the minimum for starters. The ladder was at the snortoise's rear of course, because the flippers can crush a man quite easily, and the snow there would be rock hard after Blots had slid on it. Anything I hit would probably smash me to pieces.

But no. With the sort of perfect timing a man could not repeat in three lifetimes, Blots saved me. What Heaven usually regarded as a rare but highly unpleasant threat proved to be my salvation, and I came down into an explosion of snortoiseshit.

Quetti and the seraph sled-boy dug me out, cleaned me up so I could breathe, and then rushed me over to Nightmare, which happened to be close. I woke up lying on my own bed, in the largest and most comfortable cubicle in the whole dormitory building, one I had appropriated long ago.

"Just lie still," Quetti said. "The kid's gone for a medic."

What kid? Why did my ankle hurt? Then I began to remember, and also discover a whole world of additional bruises. Oddly enough, although I had been stunned, my head did not ache at all.

"I think I survived," I said. "What is that appalling stink?"

"You stepped in something," Quetti said. He was sitting close by my bunk and even the flickering lamplight showed the concern on his face. I felt rather touched.

"I'm okay, really." I reached out to clap him on the shoulder, and caught a glimpse of my arm and suddenly understood my miraculously soft landing. "Oh, hell! I won't be okay when the cherubim come back here! The place'll never be habitable again."

"The important thing is that you're alive!" Quetti said. "It had to happen eventually, I suppose. Those gymnastics of yours give us all the willies. Your luck had to run out eventually."

"I'd say my luck did all right."

He nodded and swallowed and did not speak for a moment.

I counted bruises and scrapes, moving limbs gingerly. Nothing too serious.

"Knobil!"

"Mmm?" I opened my eyes.

"You're drowsy! Stay awake till the medic comes." Quetti looked even more concerned than before.

"Minor concussion," I said. "Talk to me."

"You talk to me. Tell me why you stay around here? A man with no knees shouldn't be running up and down ladders all day long."

"No wings." I did feel sleepy, now that he'd mentioned it.

"You're getting older, Knobil. How much longer can you manage those ladders?"

I wanted to drift away . . . without the stench if possible. With if necessary. "Got no choice."

"Be an angel! You'd be much safer in a chariot than climbing ladders here in Heaven."

I shook my head, fighting to keep my eyes open, watching golden lamplight play over the crooked snortoiseshell ceiling.

Quetti's voice rose, as if he were angry. "You mean Michael won't let you? You've asked?"

"Don't want to be an angel. No good angel. Want to go home to the grasslands."

"Oh, of course!" Quetti said skeptically. "Nothing like the roo-eat-roo life of the grasslands. And I suppose Michael won't even give you leave to do that?"

I shook my head, my eyelids drooping in spite of all I could do.

"What?" He sounded startled. "Seriously? You're a prisoner?"

"Can't walk."

"Then why not just bum a ride with someone and go?"

"Michael," I mumbled. "Revenge."

That—if I have remembered the conversation correctly—was where the misunderstanding arose. I meant that I was certain Michael had guessed my secret dream and would feel bound by his angel vows to hunt me down and stop me at all costs.

But Quetti said furiously that he was the best damn angel Heaven had, and Michael wouldn't dare take any revenge on him, by Heaven, and the senile old bogmoth would likely be dead before he came back the next time anyway, and I could ship out quietly with him, Quetti, anytime I wanted.

At that point sheer terror should have snapped me wide awake—the realization that I could escape from Heaven at last and go attend to my sinister purposes . . . but all I can remember saying is "Thank you."

## 2

The medics kept me flat on my back until my ankle healed and I grew bored. Then I told them to go eat a snortoise, and got up. But the long rest had given me time to think. As my dizziness passed, I began to see what had happened, but I was not seriously worried. Quetti would need time to prepare his departure, and during that time I would find some opportunity to tell him I had changed my mind. Ladders or not, Heaven was a much safer place than the grasslands, so there was no chance that a coward like me would ever find the courage to accept Quetti's offer of escape.

Besides, I told myself sternly, to accept his help would be to abuse his friendship quite shamelessly. Like Michael, he had sworn to suppress violence. Like Michael, he would have to try to stop me if I moved to put my mad plans into effect.

I almost told him so. He had come to visit and was ready to leave when I started to fumble out the words: "Three-blue, you know how the herdfolk live. If I go back to the grasslands to become a herdmaster, then I shall have to kill someone."

Quetti laughed. "Of course! But you're a demon with a bow, Roo. I remember! You'll own half the woollies on Vernier in no time." Still chuckling, he stalked away. Obviously he had not believed me. He probably didn't think I was man enough to kill in cold blood . . . and there I tended to agree with him, so why did it matter?

And yet . . . Even though I never expected to find the courage to go, as soon as I was mobile again, I found myself laying in a supply of arrows. Surreptitiously I made myself a pagne. I already possessed one of the best bows in Heaven. Everyone else was much too busy helping Quetti to notice what I was up to.

Only seven angels had rough-water sailing skill, and two refused the mission when they heard the odds. A couple of cherubim volunteered in their place. They were brothers, and fisherfolk, a scanty people who scrape out a narrow living on the rocky shores of the Ocean with the aid of trained birds. These two swore that they could handle sailboats in any weather. Uriel and I ran them through an abbreviated landside training and Michael gave them their stripes. Seven it would be. They seemed very young to be so eager to die.

I was shoeing a horse when Quetti appeared in shiny new buckskins. He pushed back his hat brim and said, "Ready?"

My heart leapt into my throat, but my voice said, "Sure!" before I could stop it.

Somewhere inside me, another voice said, "Now you've done it!"

I looked around for a seraph to finish the shoe I was working on. The smithy was deserted . . . which was odd. "Just a moment," I said, and tidied up. Then I scribbled a note, threw the pony some hay, and lurched down the ramp to join Quetti.

For once, Heaven was enjoying fine weather. The sun stood clear of the horizon, snow was melting and dribbling from skeleton branches. Open ground was slushy and the sky was actually blue.

"I have to go by Nightmare and pick up a couple of things," I said as I settled on the sled.

And this time it was Quetti who said, "Sure." He was driving the sled himself, and I should have been suspicious right there. Still as innocent as a raw egg, I collected my bow and arrows, my tiny bundle of possessions. We went racing off again over the snow, with the bellows of snortoises rising among the trees on all sides.

Leaving Heaven? I still did not believe I could be such an idiot. And I would vanish with no farewells, and be long gone before Michael realized. Strange, I thought, how all my departures had been like that. My family on the grasslands, the seafolk—even my fellow slaves in the mine . . . each time I had just disappeared without a word of good-bye.

"It wasn't easy!" Quetti yelled in my ear.

Enjoying the exhilaration of my last dogsled ride, I didn't pay much attention at first. "What wasn't?" I shouted over my shoulder.

"Gabriel said you're worth any six saints he's got."

"He's an idiot, and always was," I remarked absently.

"Sariel said you're the only man in Heaven who can get a fair deal from the traders."

Then I twisted around on the sled and stared up in horror at Quetti, standing behind me cracking his whip in high spirits. He was flushed by the wind, and grinning. He had told Sariel?

"And Uriel—Uriel insists that Heaven's training angels in half the time it used to take, and all because of you. A cripple twice their age outperforming them at everything they try . . . drives the cherubim to gibbering frenzy, he says."

"Quetti! You didn't . . ."

"And Raphael says much the same about the seraphim."

"*Quetti! You didn't—*"

But he had. Open-mouthed with horror, I was swept into a wide and sunny clearing. In the center, in splendid isolation, stood a bright red chariot that I had never seen before, while the entire population of Heaven seemed to be assembled around the perimeter. Angels, cherubim, seraphim—I had never seen such a gathering. Quetti drove the dogs at a fiendish pace all around, whirling his whip overhead and howling, while a ghastly, unbearable cheer arose from the crowd. I wanted to melt away like the icicles.

The dogs came to a panting halt alongside a patch of bare mud—and there stood the five archangels, each one distinguishable by the color of his furs.

Quetti stepped down and held out a hand, grinning like a crocodile. I let him haul me to my feet. I was speechless, tongue-tied. What sort of joke was he playing?

He waved a hand at the archangels. "They all agreed nobody ever deserved his wheels more than you do."

"Michael?" I whispered.

Quetti chuckled. "Together they can overrule him."

So he meant *four* archangels, not the one who was already tottering in my direction, unsteady on the muddy footing. He was tiny, even in his bulky white furs, and I could not remember when I had last seen him out of doors. He was carrying a buckskin jacket. There were ribbons on its sleeve.

"But . . . You've ruined him!" I said, aghast. "Shamed him! They'll turn on him now!"

Quetti discarded the grin and dropped his voice. "About time! He's too old, Roo—past it! You've been propping him up too long."

Me, propping . . . ? Then Quetti tactfully strode off, heading for the other four. I watched the handshakes and smiles of satisfaction. Uriel, Sariel, Gabriel, Raphael—they had voted me an angel and now they would depose Michael for violating the Compact. Here was one conspiracy I had not been able to warn him of in time.

Then Michael came to a halt in front of me, and the cheering and chattering died away as everyone waited for speeches. But he spoke too softly for any ears but mine, and the real message was the reproach and hurt in the watery blue-blue eyes.

"You never told me you wanted to be an angel! You could have asked, couldn't you? At least you might have asked!"

"I don't want that! Quetti misunderstood something I said."

He blinked in surprise, then his familiar smile returned. He chuckled with relief. "Then how do we get out of this mess, son?"

Why should he ask me? He was the wizard, wasn't he? But I had not realized how he had aged. Maybe Quetti was right. Maybe I had been propping him up—advising, informing, troubleshooting. I was the loner, the all-rounder, the man nobody questioned.

"I just wanted to go," I said unhappily. "To slip away unseen."

He recoiled as if I had struck him. "Leave me?"

"Go home to the grasslands."

He shook his head angrily. "And who do I get to do my reading for me? Huh? Tell me that! Who can I trust when I want to talk out a problem?" He glared.

I had no answer for him. The audience had gone very quiet—seeing that something was wrong, not understanding.

Michael's eyes narrowed. I could read him now—I saw the sly calculations underway. "You never did tell me why you wanted to go back there, son . . . ?"

"It's my homeland."

He shook his head. "I think there's more to it than that! I don't remember you ever taking the oath, Knobil, do I?"

I should have known he'd have a few tricks left. "No, I never did."

Scanty yellow teeth showed in a leer. "And they won't let you be a angel unless you do! Probably not even let you leave! What happens if I tell them that you haven't taken the oath, huh?"

Knowledge is dangerous—every man swore the oath against violence when he was admitted to Heaven, even a pimply new seraph. I had never been formally admitted, so I never had—and Michael alone had remembered. He had guessed that I still yearned for revenge, and he must be close to guessing how I planned to achieve it. The angel oath would make it impossible.

He saw my hesitation, and triumph flickered in those bright blue eyes, the eyes of my earliest memories.

But there were no gods in Heaven. The oath was sworn "by my soul, by my honor, by my worth and self-respect." I, of all men, should have no trouble with that. "I'll swear," I said with a shrug. Perhaps I was bluffing—I'm not sure.

"Leave me?" he said. Tears welled up. "I saved you from Uriel when you first arrived, remember? Leave your own father? They'll haul me down now, son. The wolves will tear me down. I need you!"

I glanced over at Quetti and the other four archangels—obviously concerned now, and impatient. The sunlight was fading, the onlookers becoming restless, shuffling feet. With Michael deposed, the other four would elect Uriel in his stead. He was the obvious choice.

"Go back and live among those stinking savages?" Michael said.

It is amazing how easily a man can convince himself of something he really wants to believe. Uriel would be a much better leader than this decrepit old ruin, I decided. And perhaps Quetti was right . . . I had been propping him up, meddling in Heaven's affairs and thereby only increasing its usual inefficiency.

"Give me the damned jacket!" I said, and grabbed it.

The awful cheering broke out again at once, louder than ever. If Michael tried to tell them that I'd never taken the oath, then no one noticed, for he was swept aside in the rush of people surging forward to congratulate me. That was a horrible ordeal, but better than watching the old man's distress.

Add that to my list of crimes, then. I betrayed my mother and, when I got the chance, my father also.

# 3

The hardest parts of any journey were always the beginning and end, because Dusk is full of deadfall. Three-blue told me the best route out, but he insisted I drive. When we stopped for our first camp he let me do all the work, and I began to suspect more knavery. Yet to lounge by a campfire with Quetti was a reminder of long ago, of our trek together and of a certain lost innocence. We slipped back into calling each other by our real names, and we reminisced until our eyelids drooped.

Not long into the second leg of our journey we came to a long slope with little snow. I spilled wind from the sails and we glided to a halt. "Time for the wheels," I said cautiously.

Quetti was picking his teeth with a porcuroo needle. "Go ahead."

"You are a traditional, first-class, iron-shod bastard!"

"Your chariot, Three-red."

"Slug!"

He smirked.

"Creep!"

He yawned and reached for a book he had brought along, strictly against regulations.

"What exactly are you trying to prove?" I asked.

He closed the book and blinked his pale-blue eyes at me. "You should be an angel. You're the best. Heaven needs you! But you have a strange inability to appreciate your own accompl—"

"You got that sludge from Michael!"

Quetti grinned. "Long, long ago! In fact, I think it was when he gave me my wheels. He thinks—"

"I know what he thinks! I've heard it a hundred times. Michael, you see, could not tolerate the thought that the only son he can ever know was a dumb herdman, a cripple, a coward, and a total failure! So he invented that absurd—"

"Failure?" Quetti lowered his downy eyebrows. "*Coward?* Spell that! Careless of me not to have noticed!"

"Coward!" I insisted.

"And a failure? You think—"

"Yes!" I could shout louder than he could—afterward I was to wonder what lived in those woods, and what it thought of this argument. At the time I was too mad to think of anything. "You're an angel. You're on your sixth mission, and it will probably kill you. What have I ever done—"

"You saved my life!" Quetti bellowed. He was turning red.

"Then show a little gratitude and shut up!" I said.

And I scrambled down to change skis to wheels.

Quetti smirked again, and went back to his book.

Very soon after we discovered bog, the hard way. That meant winching, a detestable, back-breaking torment. Quetti read his book. I did what was necessary to haul us out of the bog. Muddy, sweaty, and weary, I then settled again in my seat and glared hard at my companion. He gazed back at me with the same bland, wistful innocence that always made girls want to drag him into bed.

"Explain," I said through clenched teeth, "in small words, just what you are trying to prove?"

"That you are capable of being as good an angel as anyone."

"I know that."

He blinked in surprise. What Quetti would never understand was that it is not the amount of good in a man that matters—for we all have some of that—but the quantity of evil. I have always had more than my share of that.

"I don't want to be an angel." I ripped the three red stripes one by one from my sleeve and dropped them overboard. "I never swore the angel's oath. I never will. I asked you for a ride back to the grasslands, and that's all I want now."

Quetti flushed angrily. "My people are going to die, Knobil!"

"Mine are dying already."

He stared at me blankly, and then all the color ran out of his face. Feeling better, I reached for ropes and brake, and the chariot creaked off down the slope, sails filling. The noise made conversation impossible, and Quetti just sat and stared at me with a very puzzled, very worried expression.

When I needed to rest, though, he took the tiller without a word, and thereafter we had little time for talk. Sailing double shifts, rarely stopping even to visit with the locals, we made double time. Scarlet hull and scarlet sails—a bloody chariot bore death swiftly to the grasslands.

Angel chariots travel alone—to cover more country and to ease the burden on the locals' hospitality. The shortest route from Heaven to Dawn lay along the borderlands south of the Tuesday Forest, and Quetti had sent some of his troop that way, but to detour northward over Monday's moors was faster. Northward we went, through country new to me. Blustery cold winds chevied us along. Herds of long-legged wildlife fled away before us over cushioned tundra, darkly green and brightly salted with flowers.

We made good time, yet Vernier is very big. One thing I had not brought from Heaven was a razor. Quetti disapproved of an angel with whiskers, but if mine surprised the ranchers we met, then they were too polite to question. By the time we came to March and began to swing southward, I had a beard I could run my fingers through—perhaps not yet down to herdman standards, but a splendid silver and gold jungle nevertheless.

For the first time I had a chance to practice angel navigation. With chart, compass, theodolite, barometer, and a rough idea of the date, an angel can locate himself well enough to come within sight of any mountain he chooses—nothing smaller makes a reliable landmark. Violet had not needed navigation to find an ocean, so I had been ignorant of it, which was one reason Quetti and I had taken so long to reach Heaven. Now we knew, but our road was easy. We headed west until we were north of the sun, then west-southwest. Soon we were crackling and slapping our way through the immature growth of the early jungle.

Sleep by sleep, the sun rose higher and the heat grew more insufferable. Juvenile woodland faded imperceptibly into endless vistas of waving grasses, and our wheels were green with sap. Quetti became growly and ill-tempered, especially when I made up little songs about the smell of boiled wetlander. He was drowning in sweat, and I in nostalgia—the scent of grass alone brought tears to my eyes. Cotton trees appeared around the ponds in the hollows, and the green-gold hills rolled away forever under an indigo sky. I was coming home. My heart sang like a choir of flute bats.

When we saw the Urals to the east, faint pale smudges on the horizon, Quetti sighed and said they were beautiful—true wetlanders are all nutty about ice. I merely snorted and swung our course more westward. These ranges had been another hazard for the herdfolk, with the flocks emerging larger and less numerous than they went in. Massacre in the passes was a regular affair in every cycle, but Heaven ignored that violence as an internal herdfolk affair.

These were not the grasslands I had seen with Violet, a hellscape of starving woollies and terrified people crammed like cactus into a tiny corner of their normal range. Kettle had estimated that two-thirds of the herdfolk had perished in the disaster, and a single generation could hardly have restored their numbers. Quetti and I could go three or four sleeps without seeing a single herd. Woollies leave a grazed track streaked with dung that a blind snortoise could follow, and yet we saw very few even of those. The landscape was much vaster than I had remembered, and much emptier, and my sense of foreboding grew deadlier.

I was aware of my weakness. If I brooded too long on danger, my resolve would fail. Suddenly I made my decision. I had halted on a hilltop to check our position. When I laid down the almanac, I knew that we were well into the best grazing. A fine little lake sparkled below us, large enough to attract a herdmaster, yet small enough for my sinister intent. The cotton tree grove was confined to one end of it, leaving the rest without cover, an ideal ambush.

I began pushing off my boots.

Quetti was sitting on the bedrolls in the bow. He shoved his hat brim higher and looked at me quizzically.

"This is it," I said. I opened a chest and took out my pagne.

He watched for a moment and then said, "You're still determined to go through with this madness? Ritual suicide?"

"I'm a herdman. This is my destiny."

"Shouldn't you at least wait until we find a suitable herd?"

I frowned, grunting with effort as I removed my pants. "Ambush the sucker from the chariot, maybe? Seems to me you ought to have oath problems with that idea, angel!"

"Oh, Knobil!" His voice went so quiet I could barely hear it over the wind. "Do you really think I'd care about that?"

I dropped my bag of food over the side. I eyed the bedding longingly, and decided it would be cheating to take it. Loners sleep on bare ground. I clawed myself up the mast until I was upright.

Quetti rose also and picked his way closer, saying "Knobil?" again, more threateningly.

"Yes, Quetti?"

"You're trying to prove yourself again! I won't argue that you're not capable of being a herdmaster, because I'm sure you are. But why go about it this way? No herdman is going to ride up to a water hole like this with his eyes closed, just so you can skewer him! You know how grass holds tracks! He'll see them, and then what'll you be?"

"A winner!" I said. "You don't know how those big lunks think, lad. He'll also see your wheel marks and assume that angels made the tracks. If he doesn't, then I just have to show myself—"

"And he'll be off like a scared roo!"

"The hell he will! He won't know I'm a cripple, will he? He'll try to kill me, to stop me trailing him back to his herd . . Don't you see? And I have a secret weapon—this bow of mine has twice the range of any bow made in the grasslands. I doubt that any herdman could even draw it. They're big, but no one's ever taught them the knack. My arrows are better, too. So . . . my shoulders against his legs? That's a fair match . . ."

"You're crazy!"

"Then I'll make a good herdman."

"You'll starve to death first!"

Quetti did have a point there. I glanced around at the bare ridges, barren of anything but grass, rippling in the scorching heat . . . not a sign of animal life, not a cloud. Yet to use the chariot to find a herd and then lay my ambush in its path would certainly be cheating. I could not kill a man without giving him *some* sort of chance. But how long would I have to wait?

"Someone'll drop in," I said. "There may be roos . . ."

"They'll eat you before you eat them!"

I shrugged and held out a hand. "Bye, friend. Thanks for the ride . . . Keep an eye on that front axle."

Quetti narrowed his eyes, ignoring my hand. "Let's try it this way, then. Angels trade sometimes . . . I'll buy a few woollies and a couple of girls for you."

That arrangement would not suit my purpose at all, but how

could I explain this to Quetti? He had had the sense not to ask any more questions, but he must know that I was up to worse things than just killing one herdman. This farewell was being much harder than I had hoped. "And what will those girls see, old buddy? A crippled dwarf, a yellow-haired freak! It's not me I have to prove myself to—it's them! The only way I can impress herdwomen is to ride up on their owner's horse with . . . with his head under my arm."

I still remember the spasm of nausea I felt as I said that.

Quetti noticed. "And of course you'd need herders, too, wouldn't you?"

"Of course."

He blinked and shook his head sadly at me. I could almost believe I saw tears form in those ice-blue eyes. Not like Quetti!

"I'll scout around . . ."

I'd had enough—we'd both start weeping like toddlers in a moment. "Stay out of it!" I snapped. "Even if all you do is divert a herd in this direction, you'll still be breaking your angel oath. This is my life, wetlander. Let me live it out."

I clambered out of the chariot, awkward as a landed fish. I slung my bow over one shoulder, my quiver on the other, and I hefted a bag of jerky.

By then Quetti had moved to the driver's seat and was leaning on the gunwale. "All right! I promise I won't send any herds this way. But I'll come back in . . ."

"I'll put an arrow in you. I mean it!"

He muttered something I missed. Then he shrugged. In silence we shook hands and smiled at each other uncomfortably. We had run out of words, and some things do not fit into words very well anyway.

Braced against the thrust of the wind, I stood barefoot in the grass and watched his sails dwindle away along a ridge until they were wiped out by the rippling heat. Then I spun around and rolled off down to the trees.

By the time I reached them, Loneliness was chuckling in my ear.

# 3

I was disappointed to discover that there were no miniroos around, but of course barriers of ocean and mountain would have thinned out the wildlife as much as the people who shared the same habitat. Probably there would be few roo packs, either, although that was a knife with two edges. I made a fishing rod and caught nothing—few grassland lakes contain fish. Birds passed overhead once in a while, but only angels have guns.

So my existence was limited by the contents of my grub sack. That made life simple. I stowed the bag carefully in a tree, in case something with three eyes came by while I slept. If something with two eyes came at those times, then I would never awaken, so there was no complication there, either.

Herdmasters scout water holes. If one arrived before I died, then he would almost certainly approach close enough to let his horse drink. He would likely ride all the way around, checking for skulking loners, like me. I could hide in the undergrowth, and my arrows would reach any part of the shore. I was ten times as good with a bow as any herdman. If my shot was true, I would fell him. If his horse did not bolt, I could ride back to his herd and claim it. If I could find it. Life was very, very simple now.

I explored the terrain until my feet were sore. I made myself a comfortable place to sit. I sat. I wished I did not already feel hungry. And I wished that Loneliness would stop laughing.

A shot wakened me. The all-red chariot stood on the skyline. I heaved myself to my feet and reached for my bow. Quetti was already starting down the slope, hatless so that the sun blazed on his golden hair. Obviously he had believed my threats, and the shot had been to avoid catching me unaware and provoking a reflex attack. Good angels are cautious types.

I had eaten once and slept twice. That was not long enough for him to be seriously worried about me. Nor had there been time for me to have changed my mind, so there was something new. I laid down the bow and waddled out of the trees to meet him.

He came to a halt before he was within knife range and warily raised a hand in the sign of peace.

"Approach, friend!" I said. God in Heaven! It was good to see a human face again.

He came closer and stopped again, his faint mocking smile playing over his lips. He needed a shave, and his eyes were a sleepless red. "Doing all right?"

"Fine."

He chuckled disbelievingly. "Remember when we first met, Knobil? You told me what'd happened to your knees—and there you were in a spinster's den?"

"So?"

"I said you didn't have much luck."

Again I said, "So?" What was amusing him? If he was playing a game, I could not see what it might be.

He paused to yawn—mostly for effect, I supposed. "Your luck's just changed." He gestured a thumb over his shoulder. "I stopped to check out the sweeties at the first camp I came to."

"And?"

"The herdmaster's name is Gandrak." He grinned to let the suspense build . . . "He's dying."

"What? Why?"

"Fell off his horse. I think he's twisted his gut, or something. Nothing I can help with, Knobil, and he's very close to death. His women are in a panic." The pale eyes were wide and guileless.

"This is on the level? You're not setting this up?"

Quetti shook his head.

"A herdmaster should win his herd by killing a man . . ."

"No. They need you, herdman. There's no other herds around, not that I can find. Three women and their kids . . . they can't ride horses and scout water holes . . . they'll die if you won't come. They need a man, Knobil!"

Holy Father, but it was tempting! I dropped my eyes and scratched my beard, pretending to think the matter over.

Either Quetti was lying and had been biding his time behind some nearby ridge, or he had worked a miracle of tracking and navigation to find his way back to this one water hole.

Angels did not believe in miracles, but a herdman could . . .

"Six horses!" Quetti remarked innocently. "The usual garbage, mostly, but there's one half-decent mare."

I know I reacted to that, for a slight grin teased at the corners of his eyes. I looked away quickly. I did not want to know how much he had guessed about my dream.

"And at least three of the herders were looking down at me. You'll have to clean those out real soon."

*He knew!* Was he going to block me? I looked up and met perhaps the widest grin I had ever seen on his face.

"It's on the level, Knobil. You want to say a prayer of thanks now, or something?"

"Maybe I should," I said. "You first, and the Father next."

He shook his head gently. "Looks like the Father wants you to succeed! But if you're plotting what I think you are, you're going to need a lot more divine help—a lot more! Better thank him first."

I thumped Quetti's shoulder and turned hastily away. "I'll get my bow," I said.

# 4

Again I stood in the grass and watched the scarlet chariot sail away over the ridges, creaking and bouncing; but this time I caught a faint snatch of song from Quetti, and we waved our good-byes. He had refused my offer of hospitality. Neither of us wanted to endure another farewell.

Again I lurched down a hillside in my awkward gait, feeling absurdly naked in my pagne and hat. This time I had no sack of meat, and faint thoughts of roast dasher wandered already around my salivary glands.

I headed for the brilliant tents and the anxious crowd awaiting. Smoke streamed from the fire, and two last small herders were racing in from the distant woollies, passing a fresh grave.

I thought of Anubyl, and his arrival at my father's camp, and I remembered my awful terror then. Pushing my hat back on my head, I donned a cheerful expression. Then I remembered what a monstrosity I must seem to them, and hastily changed it to studied competence.

I reached the first tent, and there stood a wide-eyed child.

Holding a baby.

Great Heaven! I had forgotten how young . . .

"Don't kneel," I said hastily. "I can't, so why should you? I am Knobil."

"I am Jasinala, sir."

"And who is this sweet little lass?"

Jasinala shivered with terror. "It is a boy, sir."

"He's a fine young fellow," I said hastily. "Er . . . you'll do better next time."

"Oh, I shall try, sir!" She seemed hardly able to believe my benevolence. Real herdmasters disapproved of women who bore sons. Pretty little thing, I thought. I smiled again to reassure her, and rolled over to the next.

Tolomith, she said. She seemed very little older than Jasinala, but she had three small children clutching at her. I eyed the youngest and made a guess. "You are bearing?"

She nodded unhappily. "I think so, sir. But I can—"

"No! Keep it! I wish you safe labor, Tolomith." I was no impatient, sex-mad Anubyl. Alongside all these children I felt like a grandfather.

And unless something terrible had happened to all my seafolk offspring I certainly must be a grandfather by now, many times over!

But Tolomith was beautiful.

Then the third . . .

"I am Allinoth, sir."

"I am Knobil."

She was about my age, grizzled and plump. There were ten children clustered around her, but no babes, no toddler. Her two oldest boys flanked her like trees. She must be a survivor of the great disaster, while Jasinala and Tolomith would be the next generation. The herdfolk were only just reestablishing their culture.

I saw bewilderment chase the fear from Allinoth's face and realized that I was grinning widely at her. I was thinking how this camp would have seemed to me when I was traveling with Violet, and how disgusted I would have been then had he chosen Allinoth's tent for us to share. Likely I would adjust to having child wives in time, but at the moment this mature mother of ten seemed a much more interesting companion for me than those two unfortunate girls. Yet why should I think of them as

unfortunate? They probably thought themselves very lucky not
to have been sold to the traders.

Allinoth's oldest daughter was holding her chin up defiantly.
She had her hands behind her, and I decided she was pulling
her robe tight so I would notice the bulges.

"And you?"

"Haniana, sir."

"You're very beautiful."

She blushed and smirked sideways at her mother. Well, I
would certainly make her wait a lot longer than she expected.

Then I could look at Allinoth's sons. As Quetti had said, three
were near to adolescence. The two largest were obviously twins,
alike as two arrows and as skinny. They flinched at my attention,
but their cold and sullen gaze was telling me that a crippled
midget did not meet their standards of manhood. They were
both holding their arms very close to their sides.

"Your names?"

"Karrox, sir."

"Kithinor, sir."

"Can either of you use a bow?"

They shook their heads in terrified denial.

"Then, when I have enjoyed some of your mother's cooking,
and perhaps had a little rest . . . I shall start your lessons. Look
over there!" I pointed across the lake, to where one far tree
stood apart from all the others, in solitary defiance. They turned
to stare uncomprehendingly. I took my time, for it was a very
long shot, even for me. Then my arrow streaked over the water
. . . *thunk*!

"Like that!"

Their eyes flicked back to mine, brimming with instant respect. I wondered if the future of Vernier had been changed by
that one deft bowshot.

"Karrox, organize the herders. Kithinor, dig out my arrow—
carefully! Then you can both cut a good stout, straight branch
apiece. About this long, this thick. I'll show you how to shape
it. Of course you won't be as good as me for quite a long while.
But we'll work on it together. And riding lessons, too!"

One flew off like a startled bird, the other began berating the
youngsters. I turned back to their mother, who was glowing at
me as if she had been promised Paradise.

"I have not tasted roast dasher since I was little older than them," I said. "Have you any dasher meat?"

She beamed, nodding. "It is not quite fresh, sir, but certainly not tainted yet."

I smiled an uneasy acceptance.

"And afterward, sir? We should make up a tent for Haniana?"

I was about to say that as senior, she was entitled to entertain me first. But Haniana smirked again and pulled her shift ever tighter, and I remembered Rilana, my sister, and her ambitions at that age. No real herdman would have hesitated an instant— and I was already far from being the ideal herdman. I resigned myself to staying in character for the role I was playing.

"Of course," I said.

Allinoth sighed with relief. "And . . . sir? You did mean what you told my boys? You will not send them out yet?"

"I meant it. I have big plans for them."

Twins! Truly the Heavenly Father was smiling on my madcap venture. I inspected the horses, then went over to the hearth and played with a couple of toddlers until the food was ready. Afterward Haniana got what she wanted. She seemed to enjoy the process a lot. To be honest, so did I.

Oh, my beloved Haniana!

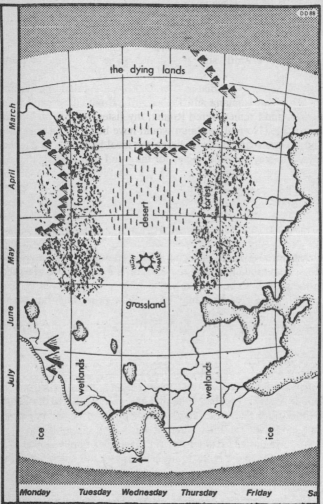

# 13

## God the Father

And so I have told you what you wanted to know—of Heaven and the angels, of my early life, and of how I returned to the grasslands in middle age. Surely you will not also have me tell of my greater shame, of the killing time and the crimes I committed when I was old?

You will? Ah, you youngsters are callous . . .

### 2

Always I had known that what I planned must shed much blood. Always I had hated the thought. I would like to think that a little more than pure cowardice kept me procrastinating so long in Heaven, and if so, then it was hatred of bloodshed.

And even after I had taken over Gandrak's family—even as I worked to bend the twins to my purpose—I still clung to a faint delusive hope that perhaps the herdmasters would be willing to negotiate.

*Ha!* The first one certainly wasn't. His name was Trathrak, and he came out at full gallop, with arrows flying like hail. I was riding slowly toward his camp, through billowing grass high as a man's belt, heading downwind so my voice would carry. I was unarmed, and I held up my hands to show I came in peace. Michael, had he been there, would have screamed that I was being a suicidal fool. He would have accused me of insane delusions of inadequacy that required me to prove myself now because I had gained my herd without killing for it. Sometimes too much insight can blind a man, and he would have been completely wrong in this case, of course—I went unarmed only because I wanted to talk.

Ironically, I should have died had I carried a weapon.

I did not know Trathrak's name then. I knew only that he had many more woollies than I, with four tents showing, and he had been unfortunate enough to steer his herd near to mine just when my plan demanded its first victim. I soon knew that he was big and quite young, and I quickly came to understand also that he emphatically did not want to talk. He wanted to stamp my corpse into a floor mat. I turned tail and fled before the blizzard. As a lifelong coward, I was good at fleeing.

He gained on me—partly because I let him do so, partly because I was being careful to retrace my exact trail. I had headed straight for the sun on my way in, and therefore my shadow should guide me out, but that is not as easy as it sounds in long grass at full gallop. Trathrak drew closer, his arrows zipping by me much too near. Then, just as I decided that I must have strayed from my path and was about to die, Karrox rose up on one side of him and Kithinor on the other.

It was their first battle, and they were still only boys—they could have been excused a miss or two. They did not miss. With icy deliberation, they each put an angel's steel-tipped arrow into Trathrak's ribs.

Aware of an insanely pounding heart, I chased after his mount and caught it. The clammy caress of the wind on my face steadied my nausea as I rode sadly back to where my two young assassins stood in the whispering grass, gazing down proudly at the corpse.

When I slid from my saddle, I almost fell. I felt ill. I have caused many deaths in my life—as you have heard—but this was the first time I had ever planned a deliberate killing and carried it out, and I shivered at a sense of loss. I stared down in shock and disgust at that young giant's body, wanting to shout at him to rise and stop pretending.

Yet I think I mourned less for him than for myself, and for all the others who must follow him if his death was not to be without all meaning. For his sake, now, I must go on. For my own, I must believe that the bloody path I had chosen would lead to a righteous outcome.

The twins would be expecting me to say a prayer for the dead, and I couldn't force out the words. I wiped my forehead and took a deep breath . . . I even managed to fake a grin as I raised my head. I was prepared to send Kithinor to fetch their horses, safely hidden beyond a hill. What I saw on Kithinor's face frightened me much more than anything Trathrak had done. I glanced around at Karrox, and of course his expression was a mirror image of his brother's—sinister gleam in tunnel-black eyes, faint smile twisting the dark fuzz around his mouth.

Finding twins of their age had seemed like a real stroke of luck to me, for twins tend to cooperate more than other brothers—even herdfolk male twins do. As I had come to know Kithinor and Karrox, as I had trained them to shoot and to ride, I had confirmed that yes, they did have cooperative tendencies. And now they had a perfect chance to use them. We had two herds now. They did not need me any more.

I smiled broadly, falsely. "Your arrow hit him in the heart, Karrox! It was the better shot, so you get first choice of the women."

Karrox raised his eyebrows into the dark tangle of his hair and adjusted his grip on the bow. The arrow was pointing down, not at me—not yet—but he couldn't miss at that range. Not if he closed his eyes and turned around three times, he couldn't miss.

"You have both done well!" I said heartily. I pivoted to face Kithinor. He had unstrung his bow and drawn his knife instead. The youths were far taller than me now. They could run, too. "Better luck next time!" I added, less certainly.

Kithinor said, "Huh?" very slowly, and gazed inquiringly past me, at his twin.

"Well, we're certainly not going to stop now, are we?" I said, ignoring the mountain of ice in my belly. "Three herds are better than two . . . more woollies, more women. And four will be even better than three!"

I could hear dice rolling in their shaggy heads. Kithinor frowned down at me as if he were inspecting a rug, or a tent, or something else inanimate and of doubtful value. I am certain that I would have died had I held a weapon in my hand, had there been as much as a knife at my belt or a bow at my saddle. It was the code of the grasslands, the herdmen's way of thought. They did not need me anymore, but equally I might not need them, so obviously they must strike first, before I did.

But I had no weapons except fingernails, and I was a feeble cripple . . . Kithinor's unsubtle features twisted in indecision for a moment and then returned to indifference. He glanced again at his brother and nodded. Obviously they had decided that at worst there was no hurry. "I'll do better'n him next time," he agreed.

Thus the killing began.

I paid off my young henchmen in women, but I took none for myself. I was collecting boys instead.

I combined the two herds into one and angled south until we came across more tracks.

Three herds, then four . . . The twins cooperated because I was making them rich. With so many women to husband, they soon had no time for plotting, anyway—I had to shout at them to make them even keep up their archery practice. They began to turn dangerous again after the sixth or seventh battle, but by then I had outwitted them. With a dozen young bowmen at my call, and two or three close by me always as bodyguard, I could play them all off against each other, ruling as I had seen Ayasseshas do, and Michael.

So I survived, and the killing went on. On all the plains only four or five herdmasters agreed to talk, and not one ever settled down as my subordinate. Even if I sent a troop of twelve mounted bowmen against him, a herdmaster's instinct to fight was still irresistible. Unable to conceive of cooperation, they would inevitably fall into the ambush trap I had used against Trathrak.

Of course few herdmen had ever survived to middle age, but my systematic bloodbath washed a generation from the grasslands. All herdmen are young now, except me.

Eventually some trader told Heaven what I was doing. But I was undeniably a herdman by birth and so my actions did not class as violence between groups, no matter what drastic changes I had made in the local rules. Renegade angels are not unknown in the records—men have often used their Heavenly training to seize undeserved power. Their influence has always vanished when they died, and Heaven could take a long view. In my case, after a hot debate of which I did not learn until much later, the angels decided not to interfere. It was too late anyway, even then.

The younger I caught the boys, the better I could mold them. Karrox and Kithinor had been adolescent and too old to change much, and so were the few starving loners we had found and rescued. Eventually the twins reverted to type and rebelled, together with some others of my earliest recruits. Thinking like traditional herdmen, they could not see that boy babies and girl babies were produced in equal numbers and therefore the only alternative to ritual murder was monogamy—or if they did see that, then they preferred the traditional solution.

I was running out of women by then, and setting limits on the number a man could own. I did not try to take any of the twins' women away from them; I just stopped giving them more. So they organized the Great Revolt, and even there they were using the cooperative habits I had taught them. They lost anyway. Sadly I made examples of them, and shared out their women among more loyal supporters. The ants had taught me the value of terror, and so had the spinster. But her sons' end killed poor Allinoth, and for a while I was so sickened that I seriously considered giving up. It was dear Haniana who stiffened my backbone then and gave me the courage to continue. She can never replace Misi, but without her support I should not have achieved half of what I have done.

Studying the grassland life with saint-trained eyes, I saw that woollies, like snortoises, try to hold position with respect to the sun. Although they are controlled more by temperature than light, they do seek to keep their snouts in shadow; thus they automatically head west. Obviously, therefore, a woollie's natural pace must move it at roughly the same rate as the sun moves. When I understood that, I withdrew all the herders and watched to see what happened. Soon I had one enormous herd, not quite continuous but almost so, stretching in a north–south line across the width of the grasslands. This arrangement needed very little herding, and another of its benefits was that no one could then get lost. Cropped grass lay east of the herd, long grass west of it. People moved north and south along the herd as necessary.

Death by death my power grew. After the Great Revolt, my subjects gave me little more trouble. My boys had become my young men, and they roved the grasslands in my name. I rewarded them with women and ribbons and fancy titles.

Long before the last of the independent herdmasters had been tracked down, I was already starting to move against the two other groups that dwelt within my domain.

Gandrak's horses had been oversized trash, and Trathrak's no better. I knew how traders joked about their worst beasts being "fit only for a herdman." So horseflesh was one of my first problems, one I solved by imposing a fine of three horses for every slave discovered in a caravan. I chose which three. The traders screamed about violence between groups and threatened to report me to the angels. I told them to go ahead, please.

My scheme ought not to have worked, of course. Had the traders simply spread the word to ignore loners and avoid transporting slaves across the grasslands, then that would have been the end of it. But I knew how traders hated to lose an advantage or do favors for one another. By the time the news got around, there were no more wandering loners anyway, and my cavalry could run down anything on the plains.

I allowed no one else to deal with the traders, and I drove up the price of yarn until I could afford some simple luxuries to reward loyalty.

Herdmen, I discovered, were not born stupid—it was their wasted, barren culture that made them so. Under my guidance, the next generation grew up smarter. I founded singing schools and provided suitable songs of instruction. I created a corps of couriers, because a strong runner can travel long distances faster than a horse can in that climate. It also gave the youngsters more to do.

Even from the first, the women were inclined to obey me without question, out of habit, and they raised their children to do so, too. When they saw that their sons were not dying at puberty, when I halved the birth rate with a decree that babies must be breastfed—then I had their souls forever. Now meek little herdwomen will denounce their own menfolk to me if they as much as suspect a disloyal thought. I hate that! It is only Haniana's unflagging support that gives me the strength to do what I then must.

Eventually I was able to stop using women as rewards, but all marriages still required my approval, and I made sure that the woman was content. In an astonishingly short time, young maidens were expressing opinions on all sorts of subjects, and young herdmen were displaying interest in bathing, combing, and paring.

As Michael had long ago predicted, I never found any sign of Anubyl, nor of my family. They must all have perished in the great dying beside the March Ocean.

I was ready by then to realize my dream of revenge on the ants—and yet I had already come to realize that it would be a hollow satisfaction. I had once thought I would destroy Heaven if it tried to block me. Now I saw that it could not block me— and I needed it, an ironic situation indeed. Thus, as soon as I felt I had the power required, I issued a decree banning angels from the grasslands. Heaven and I must deal eventually, and I knew how long Heaven took to decide anything. My impertinence was sure to gain its attention. Besides, my troops enjoyed the sport of chasing chariots even more than roo hunting.

Mineral deposits can occur anywhere on Vernier, but they are more common in Wednesday than in any other day, because Wednesday is bigger. Many mines pass through the grasslands.

As a slave in the ants' nest, I had dreamed of escaping and returning with an avenging army, riding on great ones. That was because the seamen had taught me to hunt that way, and it was the only form of cooperation between men that I then knew.

The spinster taught me much more. She had used an army to kidnap recruits to build her army. Admittedly she had enslaved her victims in a way I never could, but thereafter she had rewarded mostly with ribbons and titles and fine words.

The traders and the ants, the tribes of jungle and desert, and finally the angels—I had learned from all of them. Gradually I had refined my original muddled dream into a workable plan. Heaven can never throw enough men against the ants. My eager young warriors are armed only with bows and spears, not guns, but their shadows darken the hills. They worship me and will die for me.

Traders would always part with information, for a price. I located the nests. I learned the size of each tribe and its slave workforce and the name of its minemaster . . . and one of those was Krarurh. It might not be the same one—a son, perhaps, or even that very grandson whose birth had resulted in my being given to Hrarrh—but I knew which nest I must attend to first.

That was a very bloody business, for my troops were inexperienced and the cats spooked the horses. Fortunately the mine was an open trench, rather than an underground complex of tunnels. Thus, it was not easily defended, and the ants were no more accustomed to battle than my herdmen were. Many slaves died in the carnage, but so did all the cats, and every adult male ant, and many of their women, also. One body I identified with joy as that of the smith who had mashed my knees. Of Hrarrh there was no sign. He was either already dead or merely absent.

A man can't have everything, I suppose.

And yet I almost hope he is still alive, for I probably had taken his family. All the women and children were distributed among my men, along with the rest of the booty. I had my revenge.

All news reaches Heaven eventually, and this time the debate was fiercer. I was already very unpopular with the angels, and I expect the archangels considered using force against me. In the end they wisely decided to negotiate, as I had known they must.

An exhausted young runner swayed on his feet before me as he gasped out his news: Chariots had reached the grasslands and a party of three angels sought audience. In my delight, I promoted the lad to Warrior Junior Grade on the spot, and also all the previous bearers who had relayed that message on its long trip in from the borders to my palace. None of those couriers had even been born when I left Heaven and now, at last, Heaven was coming to me.

I sent back orders that the angels were to be brought in on horseback, without their chariots—and without their guns.

## 3

Nothing in my long life has ever amused me more than the expressions on those angels' faces as they were led into my palace. As always it stood on high ground to catch the breeze, but that particular hill chanced to be especially high. The walls were open on three sides to show vistas of gold-green grassland rolling away forever into hazy distance. Clustered around the stabbing blue of nearby lakes, the myriad bright tents that always accompany the palace sparkled like spilled jewels. I do not know why my presence requires at least a thousand supporters in attendance at all times, but it does, and when the angels arrived there were probably nearer three thousand—but that was not by chance.

Everywhere there was color. Herdfolk love color, and now we could afford the best dyes on Vernier. Overhead the sun glowed through the brilliant fabrics of the roof, which the wind ran in long billows, stirring color in their welcome, soft-hued shade. The thick rugs underfoot were alive with color, and the downy cushions on the chairs also. Color glittered back from polished wood, from silver goblets and shiny silver plates of sugared fruits from Thursday. As the guests sank open-mouthed into their seats, maidens in scintillating dresses were offering them refreshments.

There was brilliance even in the pagnes and headdresses of my bodyguard, the twenty-five young giants who stood around like trees enclosing a forest glade. Tall and rigid as the poles that supported the roof, each held a spear that could have skewered a horse. Ayasseshas would have approved of my audience chamber.

The angels seemed small to me, and old. Yet even the oldest, who was also their leader, must be young enough to be my son, or even grandson by herdfolk ways. Indigo-two-green he was now, but I thought I could remember him as a cherub—it had been so long since I left Heaven that I could not be sure. His stoop might be from fatigue, of course. He was a hook-nose desertman, and in his youth his hair had been red. Now it was mostly white.

And so was his beard! My orders had been followed more strictly than I had intended. The visitors had been snatched

from their chariots with nothing but the clothes they wore—
buckskins now unbearably filthy and sweat-stained. Not
merely guns, but razors also had been left behind at the
borders of the grasslands, and herdmen had no razors to
lend. All three men were thickly whiskered. They would
certainly have been rushed along at the fastest pace they
could endure, and the length of those beards brought home
to me the huge extent of my domain. Sometimes even I
forget how much land I rule.

Exhausted and travel-soiled, those angels were angry.
They knew that I had deliberately flaunted my power to
humiliate them. They were impressed as well as frightened,
and they hated me for it. They must have been thinking that
the Great Compact had failed at last. Never had a despot
risen to such power before.

Their arduous trek along the herdline had brought them
through half the population of the grasslands. They had seen
a teeming, civilized people, a prosperous nation where they
had expected only scattered bands of savages. At every rest
stop—while eating, then falling into exhausted sleep in the
little tent settlements—they would certainly have heard the
singing. Some of my psalms would have shocked them
greatly, perhaps as much as their glimpses of the first real
army ever raised on Vernier. And if many of the troops they
had seen ride by in the distance had happened to be the
same troops going around in circles . . . well, I had been
trained by one of the sharpest traders who ever chewed a
*paka* leaf.

Sitting stiffly upright on their chairs, my guests glared at
me. I probably did not meet their expectations. My long
white hair and long white beard would seem bizarre to them.
So would my golden robe . . . not to mention my ugly bare
feet resting on the embroidered footstool before the throne.

I have had long practice in overawing herdmen—time to develop a certain *presence*. Ayasseshas would say I had just grown
more pompous, I suppose . . . but it works. The angels were
impressed.

I let them gaze awhile. The wind thumped the roof, and a
steady clinking floated up from the smithy halfway down the

hill. Much nearer, the *thunk!* of arrows told of archery practice in progress.

"Tell me news of Heaven," I said when the angels' eyes began to wander. "Who is Michael now?"

Indigo thrust a hand in his pocket. Instantly twenty-five spears were aimed at his heart. He froze. I gestured, and the twenty-five spears returned to vertical, butts thumping the rug simultaneously.

The angels all turned very red.

"You do not trust angels, Herdmaster?"

"Sir, I trust you implicitly," I said with total falsehood. "My lads here are a little nervous. Just don't move suddenly, and I think everything will be all right . . . and be careful how you address me. 'Herdmaster' is a relatively junior rank in my army."

"How do you wish to be addressed, then?" Indigo inquired, his eyelids lowered in fury.

"My people call me . . . but you wouldn't like that, I suppose. Choose one of my earlier names, for I have had many—Knobil and Golden, herdbrat and dross, Nob Bil and Old Man and Roo . . . and I suppose I was indeed Herdmaster briefly—before my apotheosis. Please yourselves." I smiled graciously.

"Knobil, then!" Gritting his teeth and moving slowly, Indigo drew a paper from his pocket. "The Holy Michael sent this message."

A sword-girt youngster twice his size took the letter and brought it over to me, kneeling as he offered it. There was no name on the outside. I broke the seal, and found four words within. I had read nothing for so long that at first they were only squiggles, and blurred squiggles at that. I held the message out at arm's length and forced old eyes and brain to work.

Shaky handwriting: *Remember Silent Lover. Quetti.*

I leaned back on my throne and thought about that. So my friend had survived the Great Flood, and I was glad. He had reached the top, obviously, which was not surprising. He didn't trust his messengers, which was. He was warning me of treachery, and perhaps even admitting that he might have to betray me himself.

Heaven must be divided as never before. Had Quetti seen the same opportunity for treachery that I had, or was he worried only about my life, which was a trivial thing? He must be old now, I realized, and I was much older.

"I shall not attempt to pen a reply," I announced. "Please inform His Holiness that I thank him for his greetings, and I wish him the long life and contentment he so well deserves."

Indigo nodded his head warily. All three angels were as taut as bowstrings.

"Now, what can I do for you gentlemen?" I asked cheerfully.

"You have used violence against a tribe of miners," Indigo said bluntly.

"I massacred them," I admitted. "It was bloody."

"How many men did you lose?" Obviously subtlety was not Indigo's greatest talent, and I wondered if Quetti had chosen him for that reason.

"Only fifty-two," I said, and enjoyed the reaction. To lose fifty-two men would cripple Heaven completely.

"Only?"

"I have thousands—but I grudge every one, I assure you. I was angry even to lose the slaves we were trying to rescue."

"Violence is a breach of the Great Compact!"

"Not always," I said mildly. "Section Six extends the right of self-defense to include vengeance when there are no angels within call. I once suffered grievously from those ants."

The three angels exchanged glances. Perhaps they had known which tribe I had struck and had anticipated that defense. My history was on file in Heaven, and they should have known not to expect an ignorant savage herdman.

"There are other restrictions," Indigo said frigidly. "And the reason that there were no angels within call was that you were keeping them away . . . But even if Heaven could overlook that attack as having been provoked, there have been three other mines since."

"Five, now. It has taken you long enough to get here." I nibbled a date with my few remaining teeth. "But the other mines submitted to me voluntarily and released their slaves. No blood at all was shed. No violence."

"You threatened them with hundreds of armed men!"

"Thousands."

"Are you saying that you were bluffing?"

I shrugged and dropped the pit into a convenient silver bowl. "Hypothetical question."

"One of those mines was outside the normal range of your group."

I nodded. "Two now. And there are many others still within my grasp. I am planning to strike at all of them."

The angels recoiled like startled cats. Heaven had never been openly defied like this before. "You are telling us that we can't stop you?" demanded one of the others, a thick-chested seaman, Two-blue-white. Indigo glared briefly at him.

"More or less," I said. "If Heaven kept the ants under control, then the problem would not arise. Slavery I will not tolerate! Do you defend it?"

"Of course not!" That was Two-blue again.

I let the conversation lapse for a moment. I was unused to such excitement, but I must push on quickly while the angels' weariness gave me a small advantage—so said the trader in me. I had made Haniana promise to stay away, but she would promise anything. If she thought I was overtaxing my strength, she would come scuttling in like a mother platypod defending her larvae. Where would my grandeur be then?

The canopy thumped gently, and the blacksmiths clinked. Most nerve-scraping of all, though, was the monotonous thud of arrows drifting up from the butts. It apparently vexed Indigo.

"Why are you doing this?" he shouted. "Those weapons have steel blades! This drink is cool, so you must have introduced pottery, and a smithy is—"

"Other peoples enjoy such things," I protested mildly.

"But you broke your angel oath—"

"I swore no oath!" My tone was sharp enough that some of the guards twitched ominously. "I obtained all these things from the traders."

The angel scowled and then muttered, "My apologies."

"Accepted. And talking of trade, would you care to make me an offer on fifty-nine guns?"

"*Guns?* Where did you get guns?''

I waved a blue-veined hand vaguely. "We find them when looking for slaves . . . in mines, and trader trains, and so forth.''

The angels were aghast. "Fifty-nine?'' Indigo muttered. Heaven was perpetually short of guns.

"That's whole ones. Three baskets of parts, too.''

"So your hordes will ride beyond your group borders, will they?'' Even in the cooling breeze of the palace, Indigo's forehead shone with sweat. Fatigue and anger and fear all fought for possession of his face. "You will destroy the Great Compact and build an empire? And it will all collapse when you die.''

"Maybe not,'' I said. "There will be no equal to take my place, of course, but my teachings will live on. You did hear my people singing, didn't you?''

Three heads nodded, even as three mouths sneered.

"You are a poet . . . ah, Knobil.''

"I always had a knack . . . it came in handy. Psalms were the only way I could find to spread my laws. So I will live on in their hearts. Herdfolk have always sung. Now they sing my laws, is all. I cannot be replaced, but there will always be a king of the grasslands, I think, as the psalms decree.'' I could no longer hide my amusement at their expressions. "I came from Heaven, of course. When I . . . return . . . then a mortal will rule in my name.''

"A thousand mortals will rule!'' Indigo said.

"No.'' I stared out at the distant skyline. Of course I will never know, but I have thought of this often, and I have convinced myself—most of the time—that it will work as I have planned. "No, I think not. With everyone living along the herdline, one narrow strip . . . just one man, the strongest. You cannot *steal* woollies, cannot drive them off. They are so slow! One long herd—one king. That will be the way of the grasslands from now on.''

"You are insane!''

Indigo was being very brave and also very stupid to tell me so in my own throne room—a typical sandman. He flinched as I frowned at him.

"Didn't we meet once?''

He nodded, looking surly. "I became a cherub just before you left."

"I remember! Twist, they called you! I gave you archery lessons!" For a moment we smiled at each other in mutual nostalgia. Then I pulled myself back to the important business of frightening these emissaries. Frightened men do not bargain well. "Of course I know that angels are the only folk on Vernier who recognize no gods, and I can see that it must hurt to have to treat with one! But I never wanted to be a god, Twist. It just happened."

Suddenly the third man spoke up. He was Yellow-green-gray, the youngest, and therefore likely the smartest. He had the shaggy look of a wolfman, intent and narrow-faced. "But why?" he said in a soft voice, staring at me with steady golden eyes. "Why would you, you who had accepted Heaven's care, you who could have been an angel . . . Michael swears you would be wearing the white instead of him, had you stayed . . . why did you build this monstrous armed force?"

"It began because I wanted vengeance," I said, and concentrated on the bowl of fruit near my hand, wishing to hide the sadness that his youthful outrage roused in me, "but then it just took off on its own . . . I saw the great dying, you know. I saw the angels try. I saw them fail. They failed because the herdfolk would not cooperate. I wanted to teach my people cooperation."

"Nothing wrong with cooperation—"

"And this was the only way I could find to do it."

I looked over at Yellow, and his face was slightly blurred to me. "Cooperation was all I wanted," I said sadly. "I knew if the herdfolk cooperated, then they could cut off the ants' supply of slaves . . . gain this . . ." I waved at the walls of my palace and the tent city beyond.

A note of hope crept into the youngster's voice: "Then now you will disband your army?"

"No . . . No, I can't. Fighting seems to be the only thing that I can make them cooperate for—does not the Great Compact warn us that violence is a disease that breeds and spreads? I knew the danger, Angel, but I saw greater evils than that. First we fought the herdmasters, and united the people. Then we chased traders—and angels, for practice.

Now ants—at last! But if I disband my troops they will surely start fighting each other, and it will all collapse, and everything, all my life's . . .'' I stopped and took a deep breath. I was tiring faster than they were. I ought to wait until another time. They were weary, but I was twice their age. Three times as old as Yellow.

Haniana would be spying on me from behind the drapes.

After a moment, Yellow spoke again, the others apparently leaving it to him for the moment. "If you attack any more nests, then Heaven must act against you. All the rest of Vernier will expect it."

I rubbed my eyes and straightened up on my throne. Could he be serious? "Heaven can't stop me, sonny! My army is preparing to leave very soon, to inspect another mine, and there will be seventeen hundred mounted men, each with a spare mount, plus twelve hundred foot—and they can travel very nearly as fast."

The angels stiffened in shock and exchanged glances.

"Will you tell us where?" Yellow inquired quietly. He must have believed me to be even more senile than I felt—but I did not mind telling him.

"There is an iron mine down in Tuesday, east of here. Do you know it?"

"I know of it." His tone was cautious.

"The ants keep slaves—so the traders tell me."

The three angels all frowned—then Yellow's golden eyes began to twinkle. "The traders load up with the mine's produce, then report slaves to you and so provoke you to attack and thereby drive up prices?"

"Absolutely right," I agreed. "I suggested it to them . . . but if there are no slaves there, then there will be no violence started by me."

The three men glanced at each other and again left the conversation to young Yellow. "If you proceed, then Heaven will lose all credibility unless it moves against you."

"It would be a gnat moving against a woollie," I said. "Do you have power to negotiate?"

"Some," Indigo muttered.

I waved a hand in dismissal. "You are wasting my time. Go!"

The guard with the sword began to come forward.

"We have plenty of authority!" Yellow said sharply, earning a hard glare from his seniors. "Plenipotentiary authority if unanimous."

Ah! I waved back the guard and smiled benevolently at my guests. Good for Quetti! "Then I must make you an offer, I think, since Heaven has nothing to offer me." A lie, of course. The angels went tenser than ever, fists clenched, eyes slitted. They were the worst traders I had ever met. Thank you, Quetti!

"Do you defend these slave-owning ants in Tuesday?" I threw the question at the wolfman cub, who obviously had twice the brains of the other two put together.

"Of course not!" He flushed angrily.

"But you deny me the right to clean them out?"

"Yes. They are outside—"

"Then the answer is simple! You must clean them out before I do!"

"We would if we had the power!" he shouted.

"I'll give you the power," I said. "Three thousand men."

My visitors almost jumped from their chairs, and again a warning ripple ran through the watching guards.

Indigo took over as spokesman. "You are serious? On what terms?"

"That they be used for that purpose and only for that purpose. That the Supreme High War Leader may withdraw if he feels that your orders are unwise and will cost too many lives . . . the Great Compact permits this."

"Yes . . . yes, it does." He glanced in disbelief at his two companions, then back at me. "You will place your army at Heaven's disposal, to support the Compact? All your warriors?"

"Gladly. Heaven knows, I have no other use for them."

They laughed aloud, believing I was joking. Certainly Heaven needed the power. That had been obvious all my life. Long ago Kettle had shown me numbers—there were no more angels then than there were twenty cycles ago, while the rest of the population has surely been increasing as mankind grows more skilled at winning a living from Vernier. Heaven was undermanned, but now I held the center and almost all the world was within reach of my warriors.

"And what do you want in return, Almighty Father?" Indigo asked.

"Call me Knobil."

He glanced uneasily at the circle of guards. "Knobil, then."

"Two things—a promise that Heaven will use my army and not let it rot, because there is much to be done and warriors lose their edge easily."

Three heads nodded in quick agreement. Even Indigo could see what angels might achieve with an army behind them.

"Secondly, I want herdmen in Heaven . . . herdman angels."

"What? That's all? Why?"

"Ask Michael to explain when you get back," I said wearily. Quetti had guessed. Quetti would not betray me, but others might, not yet, perhaps, but in the far future. Silence itself can kill—that was what his message meant.

The angels exchanged suspicious glances.

I sighed wearily. Heavens, but I was tired! Every time I blinked my eyelids grated. "Herdmen have never been angels, until me. Yes, some herdmen angels will return to the grasslands and make a play for the throne—I'm sure that politics will be a bloody occupation among my people in future. Yes, a Heaven-trained king may be dangerous, but ex-angels are supposed to be civilized! Train them well, that's all."

"And in return," young Yellow said eagerly, "the king of the grasslands will lead his army against Heaven's enemies whenever the archangels call?"

Indigo objected: "He can't promise—"

"I can put it in a psalm," I said. "I have it ready."

"And all you want from us is a guarantee that Heaven will accept herdman pilgrims?" They itched with suspicion. Apparently I must spell it out for them after all.

"That's all. Just a fair chance, like any other youngsters. I think you'll find they do pretty well."

The angels glanced around the cordon of giants. Yellow uttered a juvenile snigger. "We'll need bigger chariots!"

"Why?" Indigo demanded again. "Heaven would accept them now."

"Would it?" I asked bitterly. *Remember Silent Lover!* "Would it really? And will it always?"

"The March Ocean?" Yellow was the fastest.

"Yes." The throne room blurred for me without warning. The far views of grassy hills and steel-sharp lakes . . . the unbounded sky and the sprinkled jewels of the tents . . . I saw only a watery white blaze.

"I was there," I said, and the memories were suddenly at my throat, choking me. "I saw the great dying. Two-thirds of my people starved, because they would not cooperate. Children. Beautiful women. Strong men. Now I have taught them cooperation . . . and I do not think they will forget . . ." My voice choked off into silence, into the sound of the wind and the faint thud of arrows and somewhere children singing my praises.

"But they need the warning," Yellow said softly, completing the thought. "With herdman angels in Heaven, Heaven cannot forget to send the warning!"

I nodded, infinitely relieved that it was all out at last, and suddenly feeling older than the grasslands themselves. "I want . . ." I said. "I just want things to be different next time. No great dying, next time the sun comes to the west of January."

# 4

So there you are, lads. That's the true story. Despite what your mothers taught you, I am not a god. I am even less of a man. I was always a coward. I slaughtered hundreds, yet I never fought a fair battle, and I never bloodied my own hands.

No matter what you may have heard, I was never an angel, or even a cherub, only a hanger-on. A great killer, but never a hero. I was lucky, of course.

A contemptible man, really . . . a failure. I failed my mother and betrayed my promise to Violet. I killed Pebble, my first friend, and Sparkle, whom I thought I loved. If I'd been there . . . And above all I failed my adored Misi by not deceiving the angels properly and by telling the spinster about her . . . I betrayed my real father. I abused Quetti's friendship.

I am not a god! The angels will question you hard about this if . . . when you get to Heaven. Remember that—Knobil is not a god!

I shall prove it soon, I think. Meanwhile I can sit in the shade and snooze; waiting for my next meal of juicy roast dasher; remembering what might have been, dreaming what never was . . .

You are the first. You must set an example, every one of you. Heaven will judge the herdfolk by you. You are all big—try also to be great. Travel in groups if you will, but when the road divides, then make your own choices. Remember always that every man must find Heaven for himself.

## ABOUT THE AUTHOR

Dave Duncan was born in Scotland in 1933 and educated at Dundee High School and the University of St. Andrews. He moved to Canada in 1955 and has lived in Calgary ever since. He is married and has three grown-up children.

Unlike most writers, he did not experiment beforehand with a wide variety of careers. Apart from a brief entrepreneurial digression into founding—and then quickly selling—a computerized data-sorting business, he spent thirty years as a petroleum geologist. His recreational interests, however, have included at one time or another astronomy, acting, statistics, history, painting, hiking, model ship building, photography, parakeet breeding, carpentry, tropical plants, classical music, computer programming, chess, genealogy, and stock market speculation.

An attempt to add writing to this list backfired—he met with enough encouragement that he took up writing full time. Now his hobby is geology.

# DAVE DUNCAN
## Fantasy Novels:
# The Seventh Sword